On
Little
Wings

On Little Wings

a novel by

Regina Sirois

VIKING

An Imprint of Penguin Group (USA) Inc.

VIKING
Published by the Penguin Group
Penguin Group (USA) Inc.
375 Hudson Street
New York, New York 10014, U.S.A.

USA / Canada / UK / Ireland / Australia / New Zealand / India / South Africa / China
Penguin Books Ltd, Registered Offices: 80 Strand, London WC2R 0RL, England

For more information about the Penguin Group visit www.penguin.com

First published in the United States of America by CreateSpace
Independent Publishing Platform, 2012
This revised edition published in the United States of America by Viking,
an imprint of Penguin Group (USA) Inc., 2013

LIBRARY OF CONGRESS CATALOGING-IN-PUBLICATION DATA
Sirois, Regina.
On little wings / by Regina Sirois.
pages cm
Summary: Sixteen-year-old Jennifer travels to Smithport, Maine,
to learn about the family her mother has kept a secret.
ISBN 978-0-670-78606-0 (hardcover)
[1. Secrets—Fiction. 2. Families—Fiction. 3. Maine—Fiction.] I. Title.
PZ7.S62184On 2013
[Fic]—dc23
2012033130

Printed in the USA

1 3 5 7 9 10 8 6 4 2

Designed by Eileen Savage
Set in Granjon

ALWAYS LEARNING   PEARSON

I WRITE THIS STORY FOR AUDREE,
WHO LOOKS LIKE A KANSAS WHEAT FIELD
ON A SUMMER DAY,

AND FOR MY PRECIOUS JULIETTE,
WHOSE TENDERNESS IS HER STRENGTH.

YOU ARE MY TRUEST FRIENDS, MY DEEPEST JOYS,
AND THE BEST WOMEN I'VE EVER KNOWN.

YOU ARE EACH MY FAVORITE.

ALWAYS.

On Little Wings

Prologue

NOT EVERY OCEAN is wet. The first time I stared at a wheat field and saw the golden stalks roll like a tide pushed by the wind, I knew I'd learned a secret; there is ocean in Nebraska. And the day I stumbled into the vast, uncharted waters of my mother's past, I learned that some seas are not visible at all. That doesn't mean they can't hit you, wash over you, drown you with one crushing wave after another.

I might have bypassed that sea altogether had I not pulled down a moldy paperback from my mother's bookshelf while working on a school assignment. I almost didn't see the dog-eared photograph stuffed deep in the crack of the back cover. Almost didn't look twice at the unknown face. Until I did. Again and again. Because the face wasn't unknown. Not entirely.

I peeled the photo from the pages, sucking in my breath when some of the melted colors stayed behind, casualties of too many humid summers. Even with the picture's corner torn off, I could see enough. A girl in a pink leotard held her toe shoes in one hand and leaned against a huge brown Buick. She gave the camera a distracted smile, her eyes looking into some beyond invisible to me. I covered her dark blonde hair with my fingers and studied the face. I could see pieces of my mother, like she'd been painted in watercolors, blurred and inaccurate. And then there were the pieces of me. She had the same freckles, same golden olive skin I'd looked at in the mirror for sixteen years. I stared at the empty living room, unaware that a wave of truth was building behind me, hanging over my head. I didn't know that when it crashed, we would all go under.

CHAPTER 1

"NINETEEN HOUSES," I exhaled, which brought my tally of spoken words in the last half hour to three. The only thing I uttered to my parents before leaving was "Cleo's." It told them where I was going, and frankly, they deserved nothing else.

I possess an impressive arsenal of tricks to stop tears before they start. My favorite is blinking while saying the Pledge of Allegiance, but I like to imagine goats eating random things around me, as well. For this special occasion I used pointless facts. I looked hard at my surroundings and repeated silently what I saw, like it could save me. *That is a bed of red pansies. . . . There is a chip in that brick on their house. . . . The Larsons' car has rust on its muffler . . . That window is losing its trim to wood rot. . . .* In noticing every mundane detail, I attempted to forget the biggest one—everyone had lied to me for my entire life.

I let my mind drift outside my fevered head and watched myself walk down the quiet street. The girl I saw looked so peaceful, so normal. I continued my silent narration: *That blonde girl is whispering to herself. She forgot to put her shoes on. There is a hole in the knee of her jeans. She has tiny freckles on her nose. She just saw her parents yell at each other for the first time in her life. She is trying not to cry. She has an aunt. . . .*

She has an aunt.

I have an aunt.

I squeezed the photograph in my fingers until the paper threatened to buckle under the pressure, but avoided looking at it. It contained too many facts that I couldn't say out loud. Not yet. But one clawed more insistently than all the others. *I have the same freckles. I have the same freckles. I have the same freckles.* All my life my mother told me that I had thirty-seven perfect sugar-sprinkle freckles running across my nose. (I tried to count them once. I stopped at forty-three because I knew by then that she just made up the number. I didn't mind.) My mother never told me who else had perfect freckles. There is nothing particularly unusual about looking like your aunt. I imagine it happens all the time. But it is indescribably jarring when you are sixteen and your aunt doesn't exist one second and then is living, breathing flesh the next.

I should have known the photograph was dangerous as soon as I saw the faded colors. I learned that lesson in eighth grade when my dad showed me a colored photograph over one hundred years old. He held up his copy of *National Geographic* and a Russian peasant in a red-and-gold skirt looked sullenly at me from under her purple head scarf. It is easy to look at people in old black-and-white photos; easy to pity them. Easy to dismiss them. But when they challenge you with blue eyes and red cheeks and you can see blood in their skin, it's a strange phenomenon. You become *responsible* for them. It's your job to keep looking and wondering and hurting for them. You are forced to think of her first kiss, her last breath. And then you have to admit that she is dead, which seems horribly rude. I slid the picture of my smiling aunt Sarah into the dark safety of my back pocket and tried to guide my thoughts back to safer waters.

That leaf has been eaten by a bug and is turning brown. . . . Mr. Turner's kids left his hose out again. . . . Sixteen years of being told that my parents were both only children. I caught myself as my hands started to tremble in anger and forced my thoughts back to the visible facts. *Cleo's house is only one block away now. . . . Cleo has green eyes the exact shade of a crocodile in the sun. . . . Cleo will know what to do. . . .*

My best friend, Cleo, and I knew the route between our homes the way most people know their birthmarks and scars. Nineteen houses, two cul-de-sacs, eleven privacy fences, three trellises, five swing sets, one swimming pool, seven dogs, one BEWARE OF DOG sign, only one concrete statue of a dancing frog using a mushroom

5

for an umbrella (thank goodness), and one wooden wheelbarrow overflowing with pink flowers. Everything familiar, predictable, and suddenly, thoroughly meaningless.

I wondered for a moment what Cleo would say. All I knew for certain (as certain as anyone *can* be with Cleo) was the way my story would make her blank face twitch until her reluctant mouth finally rounded into a satisfying, silent "O." I paused my thoughts on her stunned face and smiled at the dimple that dug into only one of her cheeks. That dimple always softened her ferocious beauty into something comical.

Thinking about Cleo's face is not uncommon in our town. She is one of our regional points of pride. A natural resource. But Cleo refuses to notice. It is her unbreakable rule not to notice. And when you begin life as ugly as Cleo, I think you get to make some of your own rules. (And yes, I know it's wrong to call a child ugly, but you weren't there.)

Since Fortune eventually favored her, I don't mind saying that Cleo might have been the ugliest child nature ever allowed—if not in the history of the world, at least in the living memory of Eastern Nebraska. In Constance, most people can tell you where they were when they first saw Cleo.

For me it was age five. Sitting at the puzzle table. She entered the Children's Garden Preschool clutching her mother's hand, standing a head shorter than any of us. Her protruding stomach and bowed legs gave her an undeniably ape-like appearance. Two enthusiastic claps and the teacher announced, "Boys, girls, this is Gerry. She will be joining our class. Let's all say hello!"

Her mouth hung open due to a severe overbite, which made me think she was what all of our mothers called "special." Thick, plastic glasses magnified her lazy eye, which wandered at random before coming to rest staring ponderously at her own nose. The same James Barry who now sits behind us in third period and would happily give up food for a week to have Cleo look at him in disdain wrinkled his nose and eyed me with an expression that said: "Do you see what I see?"

Oblivious to all of us, Cleo stomped to the art table. When her stare caught me out of the crowd, I met it. I was trying to tell which eye she was seeing out of because the lazy one was wandering toward the ever-reproducing snails in the fish bowl, but she mistook my thoughtful gaze as an invitation. Her hand whipped to the table, grabbed a paintbrush, and thrust it toward me. At a loss for what else to do, I took it. Cleo claimed me with that paintbrush like pilgrims staking a flag in the New World.

How ugly Geraldine turned into beautiful Cleo bewilders the people of Constance as much as the question "How did she get that ugly in the first place?" Most people look at her today and think that Cleo is short for Cleopatra, in homage to her shining dark hair, satin skin, and large eyes. I am the only other soul on earth who knows the truth. Her name was gifted to her in the first grade by a cartoon fish. One Saturday morning we were watching *Pinocchio*.

I was gazing catatonically at the screen, but Gerry was shaping her life. When the movie ended, I tried to get her attention by snapping my fingers (a newly acquired skill) and saying her name, but her only reply was "My name is Cleo."

"Like the fish?!"

People took her new name with good graces, figuring someone so ugly needed extra concession. And then, ever so gradually, somewhere around fourth grade, Cleo turned dead average. Her lank hair decided that it was a dark, ashy brown that shone with a strange, silvery luster. Braces in sixth grade eradicated her overbite, lining up her white teeth in a pearly row. By seventh grade, eye surgery eliminated the hideous glasses that dominated her face and left behind two huge green eyes framed in inky lashes. No one at Countryside Elementary seemed to notice. We had grown so accustomed to the ugliness that our eyes kept seeing it long after it disappeared. The boys in Meadow Heights Junior High, however, sat up and took notice. Our ugly little Cleo was ugly no longer.

As I rounded the corner past the dancing frog statue (we named him Gilfred), Cleo's beige home came into view. Something stopped me from going forward and it wasn't just my ignorance of how to replay the disturbing scene at my house. I felt contaminated by the memory, inadvertently rubbing my arms as if the lie had turned to dirt and stuck to me. I pulled my aunt

Sarah's photo out of my pocket, my hands growing shakier with each breath. *If I say it out loud, this will all be real.*

Sarah's smile didn't break in the late evening sun, but her squinting eyes looked more thoughtful. *I am real, Jennifer,* she answered. I turned my head, frightened to hold her stare. The colors made me too responsible for her.

Cleo's front door is burgundy. I am not going to cry. I pledge allegiance . . .

⁊⁊⁊

The door to Cleo's house sprang open, interrupting my thoughts, and Cleo hopped onto the front porch. "Come to beg for help?" she asked. The words shocked me so much that I flinched. She registered my confusion and quickly mirrored it. "Hanshaw . . . the assignment," she prodded. "Are you stuck?"

Understanding flooded me with relief. She was referring to the three-page assignment for World Literature that Mrs. Hanshaw had sprung on us four hours earlier. An assignment that four hours ago had seemed like an actual problem.

"No. Yes. Yes and no." I took a steadying breath, still not approaching her open door. "We need to walk. Or at least be alone."

"Be right back," she promised, then disappeared inside. I could always count on Cleo for instant action. Her steely mind snapped at decisions with blinding speed. Within moments she was beside me holding out an extra pair of brown, plastic flip-flops.

I looked down at my feet. "I forgot I was barefoot."

"Did something happen?" she asked, taking me in from my toes to my face.

"Yeah." Even that small admission crashed through me, dropping from my lips through the middle of my chest and landing with a sick thud in my stomach. I couldn't find the words yet. Cleo started walking while pulling her shining hair into a rubber band.

"Do you want to go to the graveyard?"

"Yes." I couldn't imagine telling this story on the sidewalk, or flopped across her bed. I needed somewhere gentle, wild, solitary. A place where the wind would eavesdrop and then carry the difficult words far away.

"Are you okay?" she asked softly.

"Sort of." I pressed my lips together, trying to master the muscles that wanted to open my mouth in a childish wail. Cleo glanced at me in curious sympathy and then set her eyes forward, leading the way past our streets to the wheat field.

Technically, going to the Cowling Family Cemetery is trespassing since it is in the middle of a farmer's private wheat field, but no one ever stopped us. Years ago, after we'd first discovered it while playing with binoculars, the farmer caught us sitting among the headstones as he passed by on his tractor. From his high perch in the saddle seat, he eyed us angrily; his fierce glare terrified us, but after he'd searched our frightened faces, his expression smoothed and his mouth straightened to a calm line. "Be careful," he growled over the noise of the motor before he touched the brim of his shapeless canvas hat and moved on. We took that as permission.

During the later part of the growing season the small plot is obliterated by the tall wheat, and all we can see from our houses are two scrubby oak trees that stand guard over the graves. I don't know if the farmer got sick of us trying to pick our way through his precious field, but three years ago he cut a smooth, narrow path from the edge of the street straight to the graveyard. Maybe he figured even the dead need a visitor from time to time.

We ambled along that path through the dry wheat while I tried to think of what to say to Cleo. Halfway through the field, as I picked my way through the stalks, I slid Sarah's photo from my pocket. "Here," I said.

Cleo turned her head and looked confused as she took the picture. "What is it?" she asked. I didn't answer and she stopped walking to study it. Her eyebrows contracted and a thoughtful line burrowed into her forehead. She looked up at me, and then at the picture, squinting in concentration. "I don't think you're adopted," she announced with an air of finality.

"What?" I screeched.

"Well, she looks a lot like you. You must be related, but if you're worried you're adopted, I don't think you are."

"I never thought I was *adopted*," I said, unable to stop an incredulous scowl. I took the picture back and brushed past her, taking the lead. "It's my aunt."

"I thought you didn't have any relatives." She took the news so calmly, so characteristically Cleo.

"Precisely," I snapped too harshly. "I didn't think so either. Until tonight." I spun around, pleading with my eyes, unsure of what I was begging for. "They lied to me, Cleo. All this time. Never a word. Never a hint. They both said they were only children."

"Who's sister is she? Your mom or your dad's?" I knew what she was doing as soon as she asked. She was looking for a place to lay the blame. Not in a mean way. Cleo isn't mean. Just efficient. She wants to know who's at fault so a problem doesn't get weighed down with "nuance" or "complications." She likes black and white.

"My mother's sister. Her *big* sister apparently." It all came out in one sagging, heavy breath. Then my throat tightened and my lips pressed together in indignation. "Do you know what I would give for a big sister? Any idea? And do you know what I *wouldn't* do with a big sister?" Cleo's round eyes waited in green curiosity. "I wouldn't pretend she didn't exist!"

"I know you wouldn't. So start at the beginning. How did this happen?"

I recounted the first part of the evening easily. I told her about working on Hanshaw's assignment, how I was thumbing through our family's books in the living room when I pulled down the copy of *The Old Man and the Sea*. I pantomimed opening the battered paperback and flipping to the spot where the photo was stuck tightly between the last page and the back cover.

"I didn't think anything at first. Just a picture, right? But then I looked closer." I stopped and stared at the photo in my hand. "It's the color. The color of her hair. And the freckles."

Cleo reclined her head against Maeve Cowling's headstone, listening intently. "So what did you do? How did you find out it was your aunt?"

"So I just started the biggest fight in the history of my family," I said bitterly. "I took the picture to my parents and asked, 'Who's this?' That's it. Just, 'Who's this?' "

"And?"

"And World War III. My mom said she didn't know, at the same time that my dad said, 'Your aunt.' " I pulled in a deep breath of evening air, letting it whistle cold across my front teeth as I remembered my mother's shocked face. Shock. Betrayal. Anger. Above all, anger. No, that wasn't quite right. There was something else. Something I couldn't name. Even after she yelled my dad's name, even after she crashed her hands down on her thighs like a conductor bringing a symphony to an indisputable stop, there was still something leaking around the edges of her anger, dripping into her fiery eyes. I wanted to tell Cleo everything, but the words stuck like burrs to my throat. "It was bad, Cleo. Worse than I've ever seen them. They never fight. They never yell."

"They were yelling?" Her usually composed eyes betrayed concern.

"Screaming, really. At least at the end. First I started asking questions. Mostly just, why? Why not tell me? Why lie? Why pretend she didn't exist? I got mad because the answers were ridiculous. Mother was saying that she wouldn't talk about it. That the conversation was over and she wanted me to forget all about it. Okay, that's where *I* started the yelling," I admitted. My indignation flared all over again. I pulled a lock of my hair over my shoulder and studied the color next to the wheat. It was identical. The same strips of brown and gold and white woven into one color that no one ever named. That eased the pain somehow and I kept talking, keeping my eyes on the swaying stalks.

"My dad was trying to calm her down and told her that it was time to tell me and stop lying. Then he said that my aunt Sarah hadn't done anything wrong." I shook my head until the memory of my mother's white face fractured into a nondescript swirl of color. "She just whispered, 'Didn't do anything wrong?' like it was the worst thing anyone ever said to her. And then she screamed." I stopped there. The first slow tears had found me. No more tricks. No more evasions. They burned like acid across my dry eyes. I could finally place the other emotion on my mother's face. It seemed as plain as day now. Fear.

"Like, just screamed? Like tribal, guttural screams?" Cleo asked.

"No," I whispered. The terrible image was marching through my head. My dad's voice trying to soothe her. *There's a difference between not telling and lying, Claire. You can talk about this now. Let Jennifer know. Sarah really didn't do anything wrong.*

For one horrible moment his words had hung in the air like a grenade with the pin pulled out. And then it was over. The past, red and raw and shattered, exploded around us.

"Didn't do anything wrong?" my mother whispered in confusion. *"Nothing wrong?"* Her voice had twisted the words into a dire accusation. Tortured the syllables into a confession. Something snapped in her, like a smoldering fire combusting. *"Maybe you forgot that she killed my mother!"* Her sarcastic yell pitched and broke into a shriek.

"No!" he said loudly, looking over his shoulder at me. *"No."* A softer, more frantic pleading edged into his voice. *"No, don't say that."* He pulled her close and held her in something between a hug and a wrestling hold as she tried to pull away. *"Claire, Claire, it's okay."*

I looked up at Cleo, her eyes so still that they looked like green pools of water. I'd whispered the entire thing. Every detail that fit into words. It sounded so much more civilized when I whispered it, when I turned down the volume of the fear and disgust. But horrible things whispered are still horrible.

Cleo took a fast breath and pressed her fingers against her open mouth. A tear made a clear track down my chin and left a dark gray stain on top of William Cowling's weathered tombstone where I sat with my knees pulled tight to my chest. The pulse of cricket song radiated through the air and we listened, lost in the chorus. "Did she really kill her mother?" Cleo sounded like she didn't want me to answer.

"No," I sighed, grateful that the truth wasn't that graphic. "My dad said she didn't. He said that she wasn't there when my grandmother had a stroke. Just lies!"

Cleo threw some more questions at me, but I didn't have anything else to tell her. "Mother just collapsed in his arms and cried after that. We didn't say anything else. We all just sat there. In shock."

"So your aunt is still alive?" Cleo asked.

"Apparently."

"Can we find her?"

I met her unflinching eyes, thankful for the "we." "I've been wondering the same thing. I don't see why not. Her name would be Sarah Dyer. Dyer's my mom's maiden name. Unless she's married...." A picture jumped from the dark recesses of my mind of a smiling family, children, a girl my age. Never had I considered that I might have an uncle, cousins, a family.

"So if we find her, then what?" she asked.

Then what indeed? "I don't know. Nothing? Maybe call her? Write to her?"

"Then let's find her. You should call her."

My teeth started chattering like they always do when I am frightened, and I pulled my arms around myself. "I can't. What would I say? What if she hates my mother as much as my mother hates her? What if she hates me because I'm my mom's daughter?" A strong shiver grabbed the back of my stomach and jerked it into my spine.

Cleo stared at my hand holding the photograph. "I don't think so. I think we find her number and you call and say . . ." She paused for an agonizing length of time while her mind went grabbing . . . . "Say: 'This is your niece, Jennifer.'" The obvious line fell flat.

"Hi," I muttered, "I'm your niece, Jennifer. Sorry I haven't been in touch lately. Hope you don't hate me."

"Or," she said, ignoring my sarcasm, "I'm your niece, Jennifer. I'm so glad I finally found you." I repeated the phrase slowly in my mind. It sounded meaningful when Cleo said it, but she wasn't the one who needed to say it.

We couldn't stay at the graveyard much longer. The day was dimming and a dark walk through the field always felt ominous. "Let's go to your house and see what we find," I said.

"Excellent." Cleo's face flushed with something akin to victory.

"Cleo." I spoke like a parent telling their child that they are going to look at toys but not buy any. "I don't know if I can do this. I said I'll see. Even if we find her, I don't know what I'll do." She nodded soberly, and I wiped a wet spot on William's tombstone, smearing it into a dark streak, before standing up. What I said was mostly true. I didn't know exactly what I would do, but I knew if I found her, I would have to do something. I replaced the tight flip-flops that I had removed while we sat and stood, bracing myself against the worn, granite resting place of C. A. Weller.

CHAPTER 2

BACK AT THE Douglas house we made it past Stephen and Brett, Cleo's younger brothers, and took the laptop into her room, since the boys had commandeered the living room for their noisy video games. Cleo sat me at the desk in front of the computer and knelt down beside me on the floor.

"Are you ready?" she asked.

Most of me answered in the negative: my moist palms, my shivering stomach, the faint, indefinable feeling that I was doing something wrong. I propped Sarah's picture up against the corner of the screen and studied it, hoping for . . . I don't know what. Cleo didn't interrupt or even move. She peered at the picture with a thoughtful frown and a fervent glint in her eyes. I'm convinced her expression propelled me onward. If Cleo wanted to know her—

Cleo the Standoffish, Cleo the Suspicious, Cleo, the wisest judge of character I knew—then I could hardly argue.

Having no better ideas we opened up the main search page and started with the only information we had: Sarah Dyer. I clicked the keys slowly, watching the black letters appear against the glowing screen, looking so official. I paused, studying the name for the first time in my life, feeling the length and weight of it, memorizing the sight of it. And then, sensing Cleo's impatience, I hit ENTER.

The results flew up too quickly. I didn't have a chance to collect my thoughts before the screen filled with Sarah Dyers. "Which one?" I breathed quietly. Cleo gently pushed my hands off the keyboard as her fingers took my place, clicking.

"Here's a bakery in New Hampshire owned by Sarah Dyer. That's not far from Maine. A bakery sounds like something an aunt would do. Here's an artist from Texas. That's a nice painting." She prattled on as the screen flashed from Web site to Web site.

I could barely stand to look, so I stared at the screen itself, not paying attention to individual words. We scanned through the images, quickly discarding anyone under forty, over fifty, and easily picking off the rest because they didn't look anything like the picture at the corner of the screen. After several tense minutes of picking through the results and constantly reminding each other that Dyer might not be her last name anymore, Cleo closed the browser. For a moment I thought she was quitting and I felt nothing but relief and the need to take a shuddering breath. Then she opened a fresh page.

"Start over. Phone book. We need to try the phone book." That jolted me out of my nervous haze. It seemed ridiculously simple. Why didn't I think of the phone book? I nodded at her, a fever rushing under my skin. Cleo clicked in the name and selected "Maine, U.S.A." It took only a blink before eleven Sarah Dyers in Maine filled the screen. Almost all of the Sarahs were spelled without an H and I realized that I didn't know how Sarah spelled her name, but I somehow assumed she would have the H.

"Do you know the town?" Cleo asked as my eyes scanned the directory. New Gloucester, Belgrade, Glenburn, Brunswick, Smithport. *Smithport.* I stared at the listing. I knew that word, though I couldn't remember Mother actually mentioning the name of her town. *Sarah Dyer, 12 Haven Ln, Smithport, Maine*, followed by a phone number. I interlaced my fingers and pressed my locked hands against my mouth.

"I think that might be her," I whispered.

"Which one?" Cleo asked, pushing her face closer to the screen.

"Listing number five. Smithport. I think that's where Mother grew up."

Cleo's face flushed an odd blue color in the light of the screen. "Found you."

I turned to Cleo, my expression paralyzed. "I don't think I can do it."

Her face looked almost as nervous as mine. "I didn't think we would find her so fast," she admitted.

"We still don't know if we did. I might be remembering wrong."

"Jennifer!" Mrs. Douglas called up the stairs, fighting the high, twangy noise of lasers from the video game. I jumped, my stomach careening up to my throat at the sound of her voice, and Cleo slammed down the lid of the laptop, as if we'd been caught doing something shameful. Mrs. Douglas shouted, "Stephen, turn it down!" and then, "Jennifer!" again.

"Coming," Cleo answered for me, and we rushed from the room, stopping on the landing where we could see her upturned face below us.

"Jennifer, your dad is here," she told me. My eyes traveled a few feet past her to the open front door where he stood apologetically on the entrance mat. I nodded mutely and went downstairs. Dad's smile had more to do with politeness than happiness, and he fidgeted, fighting for some casual words in front of our friends.

Mrs. Douglas gave us a calculating look and jumped in. "I'll be right back. I'm just in the middle of something in the kitchen," she said with forced cheerfulness, and disappeared.

Dad waited until I was close enough to hear his low words. "Are you okay?"

He asked so kindly that I reined in the sarcastic voice that yearned to answer. "I guess." We both shifted our weight, and he didn't seem to know what to say, so I continued, "Are you two all right? Is she still mad?"

He blew loudly between his lips, but spoke softly, "She's mad, but we're fine. You probably want to talk . . ."

It's odd how much I wanted answers, and how little I wanted to talk. "I do . . . but later. Could I stay here tonight?" I asked him as I looked up to Cleo for permission. She nodded fervently and I turned back to Dad.

He pulled a hand out from behind his back, holding a plastic baggie with my toothbrush inside. "I figured Cleo would have everything else," he said quietly. My mother couldn't stay mad at him. No one could.

After a brief look at Cleo I took his hand and led him outside, letting the glass door close behind us. The fact that he knew I wouldn't want to come home made me feel a certain pact between us, like we were on the same team. Though I cannot say what we were playing, or fighting, for.

A storm hung in the air, refusing to fall, but blacking out large patches of the sky. We stood in the weak glow of the porch light, and I swatted a bug back from my face. "Do you know her, Dad—Sarah?" I spoke in an undertone.

"No. I don't."

"So how do you know she didn't"—I paused, unable to say "kill"—"do what Mother said?"

"Oh." His face looked a little stunned. "She didn't mean that literally. You are not related to any murderers. Your mother thinks that some things Sarah did kept your grandmother from recovering from her stroke." Then he added hastily, "I don't think that's medically possible."

"What things?" I asked, turning my eyes away from the erratic white path a moth was cutting through the air.

"Jennifer, I don't know how much to tell you. I think your mother should have a chance to speak for herself, now that you know."

"Fine. But you don't know her at all? You don't know where she lives?"

"I spoke to her once on the phone, years ago. But that didn't go over well with your mother, either." He slumped heavily on one leg, his other lanky leg resting casually. My dad has horrible posture and a remarkable face, long and thin and slightly majestic.

"You talked? What is she like?" I asked gently, hoping to gather the truth softly so it would not fall too fast and crush me.

"She seemed very nice to me. Just like your mom."

"Then why won't Mom talk to her?"

Dad stared at me as if telling me to refer to his last answer. He didn't want to say more than necessary. "Where does she live?" I persisted, thinking of that black address against the white screen.

Dad scanned my face critically. "Why?"

I knew he knew why. Honesty seemed the only thing left. "I want to call her."

He looked down and swore very softly. "It didn't go well with your mother when I did it, and I think it will be worse for her if you try. She'll feel abandoned."

My set face didn't change. "I want to talk to her."

He pushed a hand through his feathery, black hair where it receded on the side of his forehead. I wondered, not for the first time, how my level-headed father felt about being stuck between two emotional women. It seemed to be taking its toll tonight. "She was still in Smithport," he conceded almost angrily. *So I did remember the name correctly.* "I guess I can't stop you, but I'm starting to regret that I started this mess. It's getting beyond me." His dark eyes and heavy black eyebrows sagged with worry.

I reached out and put my hand on his wrist. "I won't make it worse. I'll be careful." He didn't seem reassured so I changed topics. "Would she like me?" I asked.

His lips straightened, and then lifted. The sorrow left his mouth and seeped deeper into his eyes. "You have no idea."

That is the exact moment I knew she really existed. I suddenly pictured her for an exquisite moment, smiling, sitting on a porch railing and holding her dark, golden arms out to me.

Then a June bug zipped uncomfortably close to my face and I ducked, losing the image. I couldn't get it back. When I tried to imagine her again, she was sitting on a couch with a bowl of popcorn, pajama-clad and lonely, glancing at her phone, wishing I would call. Only my imagination got it all wrong because she looked just like my mother. When I tried to replace her with the face from the photo she was suddenly a teenager again, sitting on the hood of a brown Buick, wondering why I was calling her my aunt.

Dad pulled me gently to his side and held me there a moment while he looked up at the sky. "I need to get back to your mother."

"Is she still crying?"

"She's not talking," he answered with hesitation. "We'll have to wait it out. Give her a little space."

A person needing space could not be in a better place than Constance, Nebraska. We could almost see the curve of the Earth as our plains dropped into the horizon. I peered past the houses into the night sky, thinking of the strange roads and scenery between the bent Harrison Street sign at the corner and 12 Haven Lane, Smithport, Maine. And then I thought of the phone lines, climbing up the impossible cliffsides, curving around the lakes, traversing thousands of snaking miles and ending innocently as a jack in the wall. The wall upstairs. I shivered and squeezed my dad a little harder.

CHAPTER 3

"WHY DON'T YOU get out some clean sheets for the trundle bed," Mrs. Douglas said to Cleo when I came back inside. To her credit, she didn't ask a single question, despite the motherly curiosity that blazed in her eyes. I climbed the stairs behind Cleo, waiting until we were back in her room and stretching her childhood purple sheets over her spare bed to speak.

"Does your mom know?" I asked her.

"No. I just told her your mom was upset over a relative. She didn't pry." The word *pry* came out as a grunt because Cleo could not force the last corner of the old, shrunken sheet over the mattress.

"Give it to me," I told her as she let go in frustration. I pulled, smoothly looping it around the thick mattress. Cleo didn't look surprised, just mildly entertained. She gives respect where respect is due, and most people find my physique impressive.

Looking at my mother and dad, one could never explain my athletic build. Mother is thin, but not at all sporty, and my dad is a beanpole. Nevertheless, my gym teacher always pulls down the twenty-foot rope for me whenever any particular boy needs a lesson in humility.

Cleo threw an afghan over the sheets and asked, "What are you going to do?"

"I don't know. My dad made it sound like she would want to know me. Then he told me not to call her. I have no idea."

"Does he know her?" She pulled off her jeans and hopped onto the bed, kneeling in her blue boy shorts and T-shirt looking like the next fresh-faced ad campaign for Hanes. I smiled when I thought of what most boys at school would do to trade places with me. Probably gnaw off their feet with their own teeth. I helped myself to her dresser drawers, pulled out some pajamas and lobbed a pair of sweatpants at Cleo's head. While I dressed, I told her everything my dad said.

"Let's go look for some food and wait for inspiration to strike," she said when I finished. I told her I just wanted to think and asked her to bring me back an orange if they had any. Peeling oranges always helps me think. Or maybe they help me stop thinking because I am concentrating on the feel of the peel tearing jaggedly away from the fruit. She left and I looked at the red numbers on the clock radio glowing 8:44. Too early to sleep, but my body felt too heavy to move anymore. I closed my eyes, feeling my spine flatten into the mattress.

I couldn't just call her. Not without thinking of a way to introduce myself. I tried a few different phrases in my mind, but I could not dismiss my overriding emotion of burning disbelief. It's a horrible realization to find you've been left out of your own life.

Cleo returned and tossed me a scrawny-looking orange. "Lucky day—one left." She nibbled on a piece of bread with a slice of Swiss cheese, her favorite snack, and reminded me that we had barely started Hanshaw's assignment. "I could work on it while you think . . . or call . . ." she prodded.

"I can't *tonight*. It's almost ten o'clock there. And *if* it's her, I have nothing to say."

"Nothing to say?" she asked incredulously. "I think you have sixteen years' worth of things to say. She might not even know you exist. I think that is something she wouldn't mind getting a late night phone call for." Cleo's rationale seeped into me. She made it seem logical to pick up the phone and have a pleasant conversation. No worries.

I shook my head, letting my hesitation settle back into place like a weight in the back of my skull. "Not enough privacy here. The boys will interrupt." Stephen devoted himself to me several years ago, which means he often trails us around the house.

"I swear on my life they won't," Cleo promised. "I will go

downstairs for as long as you want and bar any and all interruptions!" Then her voice quieted. "After you say hello. I just have to hear you say hello and then I will leave." She saw my resolve weakening in the silence and added one last thought. "It will probably be the best phone call she's ever gotten."

I looked at Cleo, but it was Sarah's face I saw. I knew I had to do it. Without warning, my eyes pricked with tears. Hopeful tears. I had one instant of almost obscene courage. I reached out my hand. "Give me the phone."

"Really?" she asked breathlessly.

I shook my hand meaningfully at her, afraid if I spoke again it would shatter my fragile resolve. Cleo didn't waste the opportunity. She snatched her silver cell phone off the desk and pushed it into my palm, a lead weight in my hand. Then she opened the laptop, jerking the mouse to wake the screen.

Ten numbers. Next year I would be in advanced trig. I'd mastered a graphing calculator. I could hit ten numbers. I watched my finger press the first button, heard the unassuming chime, saw the digit blink from the green screen. Like a timer. Running out of time. My breaths filled the room, blocking every noise but the tinny sound of the key tone. I never heard Cleo's steps, but I felt her hovering in front of me. My finger kept dialing, each number intensifying the shock running through my body.

One left. I tore my eyes from the phone and looked at Cleo. Her face reflected everything I felt—apprehension, tension, doubt—only her eyes shimmered with the added gleam of excitement. It was much easier to watch than do. I hit the last number.

Silence. Nothing. Until I realized I had forgotten to hit TALK. Before I could consider the consequences I pressed the green button and fought my sudden compulsion to throw the phone. I panicked and looked to Cleo again, wondering how I came to be holding the phone with the faint sound of a ring coming through the earpiece in my hand.

Cleo held her breath, her eyes growing impossibly bigger with strain. She signaled something with her hand when she heard the soft second ring. She made a strangled cry and, finding me helpless, grabbed my hand and put it to my ear. "You have to talk," she whispered desperately.

"Hello?" a woman's voice answered.

My mouth opened. I swear I pushed the air up my throat, but it lodged at my Adam's apple. I just started to make a sound when she said "hello" again, more doubtfully.

"Hi" is the first thing I managed. I jumped up and started taking senseless steps, the frantic tingling in my body demanding movement. "Hi." My thoughts were coming. Lagging, but coming. "Is this Sarah Dyer?"

"Speaking. Who is this?" she asked suspiciously. She didn't sound like my mother, but her voice encouraged me. She sounded smart. And gentle.

"I am . . ." Quick change of tactics. "Are you Claire Dyer's sister?"

I asked. An almost inaudible intake of breath and then silence. Cleo was still there, glued irrevocably to her spot, her expression horrified and hopeful at the same.

"Who is this, again?" she asked, as fear spilled into her voice.

"My name is Jennifer. Claire is my mother." My voice was shaking now. I would begin to cry in earnest any minute. But the funny thing is that the tears replaced the fear. With the hardest words already spoken, crying seemed to be the only way my body could remove the adrenalin racing through my system.

"Jennifer," she breathed. It wasn't a question at all. I knew as soon as she spoke that she had known about me. "Jennifer?" she said louder, wonder breaking her voice.

"Hi, Sarah." I saw Cleo's eyes glisten when I looked up, and she quietly backed from the room, closing the door behind her. I was alone with my aunt.

"Jennifer . . ." I sensed her searching for words, trying to find her first question. I knew how she felt. Her voice took on a new intensity. "Is Claire okay?"

"Yes," I hurriedly answered, "we're all fine. I just . . . I found out about you tonight."

"Oh." She said it so tenderly, it was almost musical. "I didn't think you would know. Did Claire tell you?"

"No. Not exactly . . . Not at all," I amended. Then I went straight into the story of her picture—she made a beautifully happy sound when I told her I looked like her—and she interrupted frequently to ask small questions: How was my father? Was I really sixteen? What grade was I in? When I filled her in all the way to the current phone call, I felt an overwhelming sense of power. Like the story had been told by other people up until that point and now I was stepping in and taking over, picking the words and the scenes. It was the first time the story of Sarah and Claire Dyer, as incomplete as it was to me, belonged to my life.

"Jennifer, I am so glad you called," she said when I stopped talking. "That was so brave and I am so grateful. I . . . I just don't know what to say first. I could talk to you all night."

I glowed. The relief radiated off my skin. "I'm glad, too." The dark mystery pushed far to the corner of my conscious and all I wanted to know were the happy things. What she was like. What she liked doing. When I could see her.

I asked her if she was married, if I had any cousins, and her painful hesitation made me regret my question. She told me no, never married, but she had a family of friends in Smithport she would love to introduce me to.

"You would really love them. They're characters, some of them. Do you like reading . . . literature?" she asked.

"Oh, of course. I absolutely love it."

"Good, good," she said absently. "I was hoping you would." She waited, a question hanging in the quiet air between us. "I'll be done with work in a few more weeks. If you ever wanted to . . . if your mother would let you . . ." she said timidly, and I knew she was trying to invite me to Smithport.

I suppressed my excitement and asked, "What do you do?" She didn't understand my question at first, and I had to clarify and ask her what her job was.

"Oh, I'm a teacher, so I'll be out for the summer on June sixth."

"What grade, what subject?" I asked.

"All grades, all subjects. I teach gifted students from kinder-garten to high school. The district has only one teacher for the gifted, so I rotate with all our students."

We talked for several minutes about her students, but Sarah's answers were distracted. She quickly returned to her more pressing question: "Do you think Claire—your mother—would let us meet? Would you even want to?"

"Of course I do," I assured her. "Now more than ever. But I don't know what my mother would say." *Liar.* I had a very good idea what she would say. "But we are really close. Just let me work on it and see what I can do." There was a good-bye hovering, and I knew our conversation must end soon. The clocked gleamed 9:30. Almost an hour talking.

"Jennifer," Sarah asked seriously, almost cautiously, "I just want to know . . . how is Claire? What is she like?"

"She's good, Sarah, really good. She works as the library director for our school district and she's happy. Until tonight I never guessed that anything was wrong. She and my dad are . . ." I couldn't find a word that didn't sound like gushing, "they're good. She's a great mom."

"Thank God for that," she said and then sighed. I didn't know if she was talking about everything I said or just the last part. "I wish I could . . ." She didn't finish. Too much to say. We were both struggling to straighten our contorted feelings into tidy words. "I should probably let you go, but I want to talk *soon*."

"I know. Me, too." I drew in a breath and tried to express what was throbbing in the middle of my chest. "Sarah, I'll find a way to get there. I'm so glad I found you."

"Amen to that," she answered very softly before telling me good night. I wished her good night in a dwindling voice and closed the phone, feeling it snap in my hand. My chin jerked up at the sound, and I felt dizzy when I realized I was in Cleo's room. It felt like I was coming back to myself from very far away. As far as the ocean.

CHAPTER 4

CLEO FOUND ME several minutes later, sitting on her bed, rolling the unpeeled orange through my hands. She hesitated a moment in the doorway and then stepped in, clicking the lock behind her. I tried to find an opening line, but when I lifted my face away from my hands, I couldn't do anything but explode into a grin.

Her face broke into a smile that nearly blinded me. "Seriously?" she gasped. "Good?" She carelessly flung a small stack of paper she was holding on the pillow and sat beside me, grabbing my hand tightly.

"Seriously good," I answered with satisfaction.

"I *told* you so!" She slapped my arm in triumph.

"You told me so," I admitted. She demanded I repeat every word, which took longer than the conversation itself due to our constant interruptions and commentary. Cleo thoroughly abused her "I told you so" privileges for the rest of the night—*I told you she'd want you to call. I told you she'd like you. I told you you'd have enough to talk about*—and I took it with good grace because I could not deny any of it.

Near midnight we were lying in our beds, whispering quietly, to avoid keeping the rest of the family awake, when Cleo asked, "Are you going?"

I paused to let the question sink in. "I don't know . . . if I can," I said, dropping each word and listening to it fall on the night.

"If she lets you, will you go?" I knew she meant my mother.

"She won't," I replied woodenly. "There's no way. If you saw her tonight . . ." My mother's tirade seemed so long ago. I couldn't believe that it happened just that evening. "If you saw her you wouldn't even ask."

"So then . . . nothing?" Irritation weaved through Cleo's words. She didn't like quitters.

"No," I answered too defensively.

"So then . . . what?" Cleo's question dripped with unmet expectation.

"I don't know, Cleo," I said in exasperation. "Did you think I would have a perfect plan already? Do you think I always know the perfect thing to do next? Like you?" I added, not taming the spite in my voice.

She let one too many beats of silence fill the room before she answered calmly, "No, I didn't think you would know everything. And I don't think I know everything." The flawless poise in her voice made me ashamed, and vaguely livid.

I continued my criticism, fully knowing I was in the wrong. "What about 'I told you so, I told you so'? Why don't you tell me now? What do I do with an aunt I need to meet and a mother who hates the aunt? Maybe you should have come up with a plan while I was having a heart attack trying to talk to her. I've been kind of busy tonight."

Cleo reached out in the shadows to her nightstand and clicked on her small reading lamp, filling the room with the white glare. She picked up the stack of papers she had discarded earlier and handed them to me without a trace of irritation. "I was busy, too. I got half of it done." In my hand were notes of several different paragraphs and page numbers written in Cleo's straight, uniform script. Hanshaw's assignment. "You still have to write out the quotes and explanations, but at least I found them all." Only a hint of haughtiness leaked into her voice at the end.

I apologized, silently cursing my temper. When she turned the light back off I stared up into the darkness, watching the charcoal shadows shift through the room. "I honestly don't know, Cleo," I whispered. "I don't know what to say to her. I don't want to hurt my mom, but I am going to Smithport. It's strange, but I feel it. My bones vibrate from the inside out whenever I think about it. Does that make any sense?"

Cleo doesn't like the supernatural, or the illogical, so it didn't surprise me that she waited to respond. In the late night our answers were beginning to lag from fatigue. "I could help you get a ticket," she offered in her planning voice. It is a businesslike tone, unflinching and thoughtful. "If we buy the ticket, it will be harder to say no."

I yawned. "I thought you wanted to get me to my aunt, not get me killed!"

Cleo made a sound between a sigh and a laugh and we lay still, my mind replaying the conversation, Cleo's mind undoubtedly full of strategy and tactics. Sleep pulled me under first. The last sound I heard was Cleo's quiet murmurs that meant she was formulating a plan, as the first staccato raindrops hit the window.

Cleo woke the next day determined to get to work. The hard, fast instructions she threw at me all morning kept buzzing through my ears. *You can't be stubborn with her, Jennifer. She's kept a grudge for twenty years, so she is more stubborn than you are. Try giving her an impossible option before the real option. Tell her to come with you and make up with her sister.* It went on relentlessly through breakfast and the walk home. I wanted to grab her head and tip her brain into my skull because everything she said sounded brilliant. I just knew I couldn't say it like that. Cleo is harmless, but if she ever uses the power of her mind for evil, then God have mercy on all our souls.

Adding to my nervousness, my dad feigned total ignorance of the entire ordeal. From the moment I entered the door he talked solidly about the unseasonably wet weather, the need to restain the deck, and his menu plans for dinner. I'd never heard him speak so much in my life. It must have been a great sacrifice for him. Well into his filibuster, I stepped up to my mother as she peeled carrots at the kitchen sink. I ignored Dad's frantic look of worry and his sudden interest in the batteries of our smoke detector. I folded my arms around my mother's waist and pressed my cheek against her back. Unlike some mothers and daughters, we weren't made to fight. We rarely ever tried, and the few times we'd attempted it, it never worked out. We just liked each other too much. When I pulled back, I could see her familiar smile playing across her mouth. She resumed her work with swift, fluid strokes. Dad inhaled visibly and, looking like a man who just diffused a bomb, sunk into the sofa with a copy of *Popular Mechanics* and a sheen of sweat shimmering on his forehead.

Taking his lead, I finished my homework and spent the day quietly. When my mother ran to the store, I snuck onto the computer to look up flights to Smithport. It looked like I would fly into Bangor Airport. From there Sarah and I would have an hour-and-a-half-long drive around several lakes and miles of rugged shoreline until we reached her town. I never imagined Maine before, but if I had, I would not have envisioned so many lakes, or such a broken, winding coast. A ticket would cost hundreds of dollars. Not a problem; my personal hoard of birthday, Christmas, and paycheck money more than sufficed.

The funds, I possessed. The transportation, I could arrange. I could make my way across half of the continent, if I could just find a way through my mother's stubborn anger. I cannot say why I felt so compelled to go in spite of her pain. I felt the pull of her sorrow, only it wasn't coming from Claire Newsom in Nebraska. It was a sigh of suffering coming from Claire Dyer of Smithport. I couldn't comfort her until I found her.

In less than a week I had a plan. A badly organized, make-it-up-as-you-go-along plan pieced together with bits of Cleo's advice and snatches of my own intuition. And like all plans, the day came when it had to be tested, for better or worse. The evening of May twenty-fourth my dad fired up the grill for our dinner and I figured he might as well roast me in it. By the time he laid a platter of meat and grilled vegetables on the table, I had never been less able to eat. I stared at the food and willed my parents not to notice me for a few more minutes. No such luck.

"Are you okay, babe?" my mother asked.

I felt nauseated, but I jerked a fast nod and started filling my plate with food I knew I would never touch. My mother stared at me for so long that before I knew what I was doing, I plunged into the abyss. "I want to meet Aunt Sarah."

My dad dropped the serving fork with a musical crash against the metal platter. My mother's expression didn't change but for a fractional widening of her eyes. She was frozen. Silence. Except for a dull thumping sound that filled the quiet like a metronome.

Only after my parents both looked down at my feet did I realize that the toe of my shoe was rapping nervously against the leg of the table. I pressed my foot firmly against the floor. Now the quiet was absolute. And unbearable.

My mother's head fell down, concealing her face. "I thought we finished this business last week. What do you want me to say, Jennifer?" Her words were so heartbreakingly soft that I almost relented. But I was fighting for three now. For Sarah's sake and my own, and my mother's, I had to answer.

"Yes," I answered, choking on the word. "I want you to say, 'Yes, you can go.' "

"Go?" my mother's head rose in alarm. "What do you mean *go*? Go where?"

My thoughts had been so full of Smithport that her confusion startled me and I stammered, "Well, to meet her. I want to go meet her . . . in Smithport."

My mother's voice came out much quieter than I expected, but it reverberated with a steely coldness. "Like hell you will."

I shivered. Never had she spoken with such icy contempt, let alone to me. Dad must have seen some of my inner turmoil reflected in my face because he took a breath and spoke. "Claire . . ."

"Don't." She held up a firm hand to the room at large, as if she were holding back an army of invisible foes. "Just don't. Jennifer doesn't know her. I don't even know where she lives now. This is over. Completely over. End of discussion."

"I know where she lives," I whispered.

So many painful expressions passed over my mother's face in mere seconds. "What do you mean?" her voice dragged with dread.

Too cowardly to tell her the worst of the truth, I edited. "I found her address on the internet. She still lives in Smithport."

Relief flared briefly in my mother's eyes. "And what makes you think you can just go to Smithport and see her? We don't know anything about her. You don't know if she wants to see you. You have no idea what you're asking me, Jennifer," her voice turning pleading at the end.

After my next words, I knew that everything would collapse. Violently. Horribly. I felt like a little girl about to run into a burning building. "I called her last week. We talked." I closed my eyes and then looked down so I wouldn't have to see my mother's eyes gleaming with betrayal. "And she misses you, Mother!" I leaned forward and dared an appealing look at her face. She didn't look like she recognized me. "She was so happy to hear from me. She's a teacher and she's out for the summer and she wants to meet. You could come. We could go together. Maybe you could . . ." My words slowed and then lingered to a stop when she stood abruptly, refusing to look at me. She narrowly missed hitting the corner of the table as she stumbled from the room.

"Then go," she whispered bitterly as she left.

A deadly chill seized my blood and for an appalling moment I wondered if she had disowned me. Then comprehension flickered.

It was nothing that dramatic. She had pushed me away resentfully. But lying in my lap, dropped there almost accidentally, was her unwilling permission. I'm certain she didn't realize she gave it, but I lifted it and claimed it for myself.

My father looked from our untouched plates to my face. He, too, looked like he didn't know me.

CHAPTER 5

I BOUGHT THE TICKET.

After my mother's first wave of shock receded, she fired every weapon at her disposal: guilt, rage, cunning, love, and finally, fear. The guilt stabbed deepest, but the fear seared like the pain after a burn. It throbbed through my brain with little relief. *You have no idea what kind of person she is*, she'd say as I ate breakfast. *She doesn't care about family, Jennifer. She wasn't there for any of us.* Driving to school. Buying shoes. *What if it is a bad situation? What if you want to come home and you're stuck there until your return flight? Did you ever stop to think I had a reason for keeping you away from that cursed place?* Waiting in line at Walmart. Cleaning the bathroom sink. I was never safe from her unexpected assaults. She dropped her acidic fears into my mind at regular intervals, leaving them to eat through my resolve.

She waited for me to relent. She waited in vain. When I timidly mentioned that Sarah had invited me to come whenever I wanted, for as long as I wanted, Mother rounded on Dad, "You need to go with her. Do not leave them alone! So help me if anything happens to her . . . You need to know days, times, flights, phone numbers, who she is with, where she goes . . ." She ticked off the list almost violently on her fingers.

He cleared his throat. "I can't, Claire. The Sunfire job is behind schedule as is, and losing money already. I'll be working nights and weekends this month. I can't go anywhere." His job as a film editor in Omaha often made him fight tough deadlines. "But I think she should still go," he confirmed. "She'll be fine."

"Just by herself? To a stranger? What is everyone *thinking?*"

"Sarah's a teacher. She's family," he answered calmly, ignoring her questions. "I'll talk to her first. I'll make sure Jennifer's okay."

"You've done enough damage," she hissed.

"Mother!" For a moment she glared me down and then seemed to remember who I was. As her expression softened, so did my voice. "Please stop. Dad never wanted to hurt you. I don't want to hurt you. I am asking you to let me know the only other relative I have in the world. Maybe I'll hate her," I said quickly, holding up a hand when she opened her mouth to interrupt. "But I'll always wonder until I know. I feel like I'm supposed to do this. I *want* to do this. I want to go. I don't want to resent you forever."

She opened her mouth in protest and shock. "And I won't if you just let me go find out for myself what she's like." I pointed to my dad, "But not if it makes you hate us. If it makes you hate us, I will stay here and talk to her on the phone and go meet her when I'm out of the house for college."

Her stunned face processed the fact that she could not stop the reunion indefinitely. "I'm not ready for this, Jennifer."

I stepped up to her cautiously, dropping my anger so I could approach her while she was vulnerable, and touched her hair. "I think I'm ready for both of us. I will come home and tell you every-thing. And nothing anyone could ever say would ever change *us*." Warm tears fell from her eyes and dropped past my raised hand onto her shirt. She pushed her eyes with the back of her hand, leav-ing gray, uneven tracks of mascara under her lashes.

"I'm mad because she doesn't deserve to know you. You're mine." My mother couldn't disguise the bitterness in her voice, but her last words came out tenderly.

"I'm yours," I agreed with a small smile.

I put my arms out, watching her study me until she cupped the back of my neck and pulled me gently to her. As she spoke I felt her hot breath against my hair. "Tell your father everything. And buy a flexible return ticket so you can come home as soon as you want to. I don't want you stuck there. And try not to mention it to me because I can't stand to think about—" She broke off. There were probably too many things she couldn't stand to think about.

"I can go? And you won't be mad at me? Or Dad?" I threw in the last part, knowing that he had started all of this for my sake.

"I'll try," she answered honestly.

"Will you be okay?"

"When you're back home, I'll be okay."

"Then let's get this over with so we don't have to torture ourselves any longer." My mother drew back and nodded despite the worry in her eyes. We were on the same team again.

Careful not to rub it in, I went to Cleo's house to call Sarah and arrange the details. I would fly the day after school ended and, though I didn't admit it to my mother, I planned to stay for two weeks. I'm certain she expected me to be gone a few days, shake hands, make introductions, and get home to Nebraska, but every time I spoke to Sarah on the phone the words came easier and my desire to be with her grew.

On the night before my morning plane departure, I eased my mother's bedroom door open and slipped into her room. The light from her bedside lamp made an uneven, yellow circle of light across her blanket and left half of her face in shadow. She was reading with a look of deep concentration, almost certainly trying to distract herself from the thoughts broiling in her brain.

"Mama?" I only call her that when I am feeling particularly small and needy. Now that I had won the fight and my departure was imminent, I felt more generous about her feelings.

"Uh-huh?"

I crawled up beside her and leaned my head against the head-board. "Good book?"

"It's fine." She pulled off her black reading glasses, which freed her dark hair to swing against her face.

"I'm going to miss you tomorrow." Other than short vacations with Cleo's family and slumber parties, I had never been away from my mother. I'd never had anywhere to go. She stared at the paisley pattern of her blanket and didn't answer. "I just wondered if you want me to tell her"—I tried not to use Sarah's name around her— "anything for you?"

Her chin quivered, but she managed to keep an impassive face. I don't know how we sense the difference between someone thinking and someone refusing to answer, but I knew she was thinking— hard. She blew a deep breath between her lips and moved her gaze to her hands resting on her book. "No. If I ever need to say anything, I can say it."

I put my head on her shoulder. "You never have yet," I pointed out.

"That should tell you something. I've just been wondering . . ." Her words came slowly. "I'm wondering how much to tell you before you go, and this is my last chance and I still don't know what to say." I held my breath and waited, but she only sighed. At last she continued, faster and louder than before. "She might tell you why she did what she did and it doesn't seem fair that you will know and I won't." Her voice hardened. "The difference is that you might care why and I never did. Sometimes 'why' doesn't really matter."

I swallowed timidly, "But maybe if you knew, it would help you feel better."

She barked out a soft, mirthless laugh. "I don't think so." Her eyes traveled up the wall and she slumped back into her pillows. "Just think of how long five days are, Jennifer. How many things you can feel in five days. How much one person can stand to lose. If you ask her anything for me, you can ask her how long she thinks five days are. Unless she has a different definition of five days than I do, I don't think I have anything else to say."

"Five days? What was five days?" I surveyed her face, her eyes closed against the memory, her black lashes resting on the purple shadows under her eyes.

"It doesn't really matter anymore, does it?" The way she ended the question I felt more like she was asking herself. "If you leave the past alone, it will leave you alone," she murmured before clearing her throat and speaking up. "Call us every day. Every single day."

"I promise." I kissed her head above her ear, feeling her soft hair in my face.

"I love you, Jennifer. I'm sorry"—she opened her arms like she was trying to hold up the universe—"for the whole mess." I shook my head and hoped she knew that her permission was all the apology I needed for now. I climbed off the bed and reached the door when her voice piped up quietly, "I'm sorry I'm not going to the airport tomorrow. I just can't. There's something about watching you go . . ." She shuddered instead of finishing.

"That's okay. I understand."

Her mouth pulled up humorlessly at one corner. "I hope you never do." I didn't know how to answer that, so I just ducked my head and told her I loved her one more time before closing the door. I bit down on my lip as I shuffled down the dark hall, wondering what was stronger—my reasons for going or her reasons for staying.

"I put your bag by the front door. All set to go." My dad's head rose up from his laptop when I passed the office. He had forgotten to turn the lights on (again), and his face glowed blue in the dark room. "You all right?" he asked. "Nervous?"

"I guess so," I said as I slipped up to his desk. "When I talk to Sarah, she sounds great. When I talk to Mom, I think I'm going to hate her."

My dad grinned. "I think you two will get along fine. I think she's a good person. They both are." He slid his rolling chair away from his keyboard and looked at me.

I fingered the paperweight on top of his stack of magazines. "Do you think I'm doing the right thing?"

My dad smiled. He usually resorts to a bad joke when he doesn't know the answer. I waited for the buildup, but he just said, "Can I answer that when you get back?"

"Why?"

"Because I have no idea. I don't think *you're* doing anything wrong, but I'm not sure I was right to tell you."

"I'm glad you did. *She* should have. I don't understand why she didn't trust me. I would have understood."

His eyebrows arched in doubt. "If she doesn't understand it, how could you? She was trying to protect you from an ugly time in her life."

"Lying is ugly. Hiding is ugly!" I insisted.

He sighed and tapped a pen against his desk. "Well, forgiving is divine, so let's start there."

It's impossible to argue with calm people. I exhaled in frustration. "Dad?"

"Yeah, babe?"

"I'm mad at her, but I'm not going *because* I'm mad. Will you make sure she knows I'm not doing this to hurt her?"

He sighed with sympathy. "She knows. But yeah, I'll watch out for her. The fact that you can be frustrated and love her at the same time is good. Really good." He opened his arms and I bent over and squeezed him tight.

"I'll miss you," he said.

"You, too. I love you."

"Tell Sarah hi for me." He smiled at me. "And tell her that I'm looking forward to meeting her."

That made two of us.

CHAPTER 6

CLEO PICKED ME UP the next day and helped me load my suitcase and carry-on duffle into the backseat of her old Corolla. I kept my eyes on the living room window, where my mother stood with a worried frown and a last wave.

"Feels weird," I told Cleo as we left the neighborhood and headed for the highway.

"How was your mom today? Did she make you feel bad?" Cleo turned down the radio.

"She was okay. She acted nervous, but not mad. She didn't say much." I squeezed my hands together in my lap. The fields outside seemed to float on the horizon as the car gathered speed.

"She's not the only one," Cleo said after a long silence.

"Huh? Oh . . . sorry. I'm nervous."

"Still want to do this?" Her eyes darted doubtfully to my face.

"What? Yes, of course!" I looked at her a moment before my expression fell. "Why? Do you think I shouldn't?"

"No," she said, with exasperation. "You have to go." The breeze from the air conditioner shifted a few loose strands of hair away from her face. "I am just wildly jealous," she confessed. "I wish I could be there." Her lips pursed in frustration. "It will be wonderful, I'm sure. And I have to miss it."

"But I'll tell you everything. Every detail. I don't want you to be sad."

"I'm not *sad*," she countered. "I'm just wishing. There's a difference." Despite her denial, she sounded wistful. I let my gaze travel up to her brooding face.

"You're going to miss me," I said.

She rolled her eyes. "Don't look so surprised, Sherlock. I'll be bored to death without you, and you'll be on a grand adventure. Of course I'll miss you."

"I just didn't think about it till now," I admitted. Cleo gave an insulted huff and I scrambled to clarify. "I mean we've done all of this together. Some part of me thought that I'd get there and you would still be nineteen houses away when I wanted to talk."

"Nineteen hundred miles, maybe . . ."

"Don't be mad."

"I'm not," she said. "Just . . ."

"Jealous." I finished for her.

"Jealous," she repeated with a radiant smile.

❦

When we pulled up to the airport, Cleo narrowed her eyes in concentration. She eased into the drop-off lane, cut the engine. "Remember," she commanded while she shook her finger at me, "text me as soon as you land. Don't forget anything so you can tell me everything. Take lots of pictures. Tell Sarah all about me because next time you go, I'm going with you." Her smile flashed teasingly on that point, but quickly grew serious again. "If you get stuck in a riptide, swim parallel to the shore." I gave her a you've-got-to-be-kidding-look, but she plowed on. "And no boys. If you come home in love with some small-town, summer beach fling, I will disown you. It will be like a bad scene in *Grease*, but without the songs. So just don't."

"I would never tarnish my good name like that," I said in mock astonishment. Cleo and I make it a point to avoid the dramas of high school romance. We decided long ago that we should each save our first broken heart for a boy who can quote something better than SpongeBob and is capable of growing a goatee. "And it goes for you, too. No playing footsies with Barry while I'm gone." Cleo gave me a snarl that could freeze water and I sobered. "I will tell you everything. I've got all my pictures to show Sarah, and she'll be sick of hearing about you." I unbuckled my seat belt, feeling the lightheartedness leave as I went to step out the door. Gravity seemed too strong all of a sudden, making my limbs heavy as I pulled myself out of the car. I looked at Cleo, the first signs of panic showing in my face.

"Go." She pointed to the doors. "Leave me to my boring, normal life and go." I must have looked positively helpless, because she got out of the car, took my arm, and began pushing me toward the automatic doors. I shook free of her grip and turned to give her a tight hug. She pried free first and gave me another gentle shove.

"If you miss your plane then we'll have to do this all over again and it will be very anticlimactic. I love you. Go." She kept command of her voice, but her green eyes glinted with emotion.

I nodded, trying to gather my courage. "I love you, too. I'll call you later." I entered the airport, dodging a steady stream of travelers to look back through the glass doors. Cleo pulled back into traffic and I watched the closest thing I ever had to a sister drive away.

～⊙～⊙～

Going to the ticket counter and through security by myself felt too mature and foreign. I tried to keep a calm, bored face, as if I knew what I was doing, but my pulse was fluttering hard and fast inside my chest. I made my connection in Detroit, but not before I spent two hours sitting in a plastic airport chair, picking at a dry "soft" pretzel.

Boarding the second small plane wreaked havoc on my heart

rate. Those steps had an air of finality to them because I knew that when the airplane door closed, I had only two options left: 1. Arrive in Maine and meet Sarah or 2. Die in a plane crash. I couldn't say which one sounded scarier as I nestled into my vinyl seat beside a middle-aged woman. She gave me a polite smile and a nod and returned to her thick book.

I'm sure I tried to smile back, but it must have been a sickly looking thing. *Hi,* I thought to my seatmate, *my name is Jennifer. I might puke all over you during this flight, but don't worry, I'm not airsick. I'm just having a nervous breakdown. Just hand me an oxygen mask and ignore the hysterics.* I curled my lip and gave the voice in my head a small snort. The woman looked up inquisitively, and I managed a weak smile to go with my blush. *Let's save the lunacy for when we're alone,* I admonished myself as I grabbed the *Sky Mall* magazine.

As the plane lurched into the air, I pushed my elbows into the seat, bracing myself, not for the flight but for the truth. I felt it waiting for me, patiently biding its time while I made the final leg of my journey. The Earth fell away from the plane, and I saw only glimpses of the patchwork world of fields and trees from my aisle seat until we bounded into the white nothingness of the clouds. I watched the wing tip fluctuate hypnotically in the wind until the drink cart came clanking up the aisle.

When the flight attendant finished handing the woman next to me a Diet Coke, she asked me what I wanted. I stared at her for a split second, bewildered how she could look so happy about drink preferences. I whispered "Sprite," and started drinking before the burning bubbles stopped jumping from the glass. I breathed hard, suppressing a cough, and my seat companion took the moment to study me more carefully.

"Are you alone?" she asked.

I nodded my head too enthusiastically.

"Coming or going?" she asked.

"Going," I said as casually as I could manage. "Do you live in Maine?" I asked out of courtesy.

"No, no. I am going for a girls' weekend out. No kids, no husbands. Just a spa on the coast with my girlfriend."

"Sounds great," I said, not really caring. "Me, too," I added, surprising myself. "I'm going for a girls' vacation, too. With my aunt." I smiled, feeling my fear push ever so slightly to the side. *My aunt* felt good to say offhandedly, as if I said all the time.

"What town?" she asked.

"Smithport," I said as I took another sip.

"Hmm, I've never heard of it," she said, deepening the wide wrinkles around her mouth as she thought. She looked like a spa would do her good.

You're not the only one, I thought wryly. An hour after our short-lived conversation, the plane began its descent. I craned my neck to see the ground as we sunk beneath the solid clouds. More trees than I expected. The fuzzy texture of forest seldom gave way to the smooth carpet of open land. When the pilot made a wide turn, our window tilted to the ground and I could see a river twisting languidly through the landscape.

The plane jostled momentarily and then steadied. The flight attendant said something, but my ears were thundering with my own blood. Hugging myself tightly, I willed my stomach to stay where it belonged. *I'm here. I'm here. I'm here.*

With a jolt the plane wheels grabbed the asphalt and the engines shrieked in protest as we hurtled toward our terminal. I'm sure the people around me thought the landing terrified me from the way my white fingers clutched the armrest. My seatmate smiled at me sympathetically, but I couldn't reciprocate. Our plane stopped. Dying in a fiery crash was no longer an option. "Oh crap," I breathed almost soundlessly as the seat belt light blinked off with a loud chime.

CHAPTER 7

AFTER A QUICK text to Cleo telling her I landed, I gripped my
blue duffel bag, twisting it mercilessly in one hand, and shuffled
forward in the halting line. In my other hand I clung to the photograph of Sarah like a talisman. Our plane was so small we exited
onto a portable, metal staircase and ducked under the nearly palpa-
ble noise of the tarmac into the airport. Nothing looked exceptionally different from Nebraska in those first hazy glances. An open
field around the runway and trees in the distance. My brain took in
the surroundings sluggishly, too tied up in my internal struggle to
devote attention to details. The tide of passengers pushed through
a glass hallway and emptied me into the bright, open gallery of
the airport. I didn't have to scan the crowd more than a few seconds. Apart from the throng, flushed and leaning onto her toes
with impatience, stood a pretty woman with caramel-colored hair.

She had my mother's short, trim frame, but lighter eyes and higher cheekbones.

She was different from the ballerina in the picture, but still lovely. Her skin had the same strange, olive tint as mine, perpetually tan without being brown. Her intriguing, slanted eyes flashed recognition and her hands jumped to her chest. She hopped once on her feet and then closed the distance between us with fast steps. When her arms grabbed me hungrily, I dropped my bag and hugged her back, aware of, but unconcerned by, the people watching curiously.

"Jennifer . . ." she breathed like a prayer against my face. I loved the smell of her—a mix of sea salt and dryer sheets. I surprised myself by how tightly I gripped her. I've always been affectionate, but never one for big public shows. At that moment my brain didn't spare a thought for the crowd.

"Hi, Sarah," I said without releasing her. At last she drew back, keeping a strong grip on my arms.

"Come here," she said walking backward, steering us to an empty seating area away from the mingling people. "Let me look at you. I can't believe it." Her eyes traveled over my features and warmed with delight after studying me. "Those are the same tiny freckles I used to have. I couldn't see them in the pictures you emailed. Mine faded, but they looked just like that, like tiny sugar grains."

"Thirty-seven," I answered without thinking. Then realizing

that answer required explanation, I said, "My mother always told me I had thirty-seven perfect freckles across my nose. I've counted them before and there were more than that, but we still . . ." I stopped talking when a stunned look came into her eyes. *What did I say?*

"Thirty-seven," she repeated, her hazel eyes bright and moist.

"What's wrong?" I asked in confusion.

"Nothing," she affirmed with a smile. "My mother always told me I had thirty-seven freckles. I had completely forgotten. I guess Claire remembered."

Hearing her name made me ache for my mother. Maybe somewhere beneath her anger she kept happy memories of her sister. I wanted her there, gripping Sarah's wrist in excitement the way Sarah gripped mine.

I swallowed my sadness and held up the picture. "This is how I found you. I found this in a book." She took the battered photograph reverently and skimmed her finger over her face and then the damaged part where the page had melted to the ink of the photo.

"I wasn't much older than you here. This is my senior recital. I was seventeen." She looked up and said, "My mother took this picture. I still remember her telling me to smile." And then, though she had already asked me many times before on the phone, she could not restrain the question, "How is Claire?" The longing in her voice hurt my chest.

"She's fine. This morning she was calm when I left. I think it's sinking in."

"I miss her," she admitted.

"I know." I wished I could say *She misses you, too.*

I think she saw the conversation wading into gloomy waters and she shook her head, brightening her smile. "I didn't know what to do with myself today. I can't remember the last time I felt this nervous! I didn't know what to wear. I didn't know what to bring. I thought about flowers, but that felt awkward. So what is the appropriate gift for meeting your grown niece? Do you have any idea?"

I laughed and waved my hand in dismissal. "I don't need anything."

"I can't tell you how relieved I am after seeing you. This would have felt like a long visit if you stepped off the plane wearing a dog collar with spikes."

I laughed again, her warm, easy voice putting my fears at ease. "I only wear my collar on weekends," I replied.

"No, but really," she said seriously, "you are beautiful. I can't look at you enough."

"I think I look like my aunt," I told her.

"With several improvements," she said as she stood up to direct me to the baggage claim. "My hair was never that light. And your skin! What do you remind me of? The sand? The sunset? Maybe the last light of day on the ocean, when everything is glowing."

"Wheat," I told her as I set my duffel by my feet in front

of the rotating carousel that was just starting to spit out battered bags. "My mother says that I look like a Kansas wheat field on a summer day."

She fixed her eyes on me intently, thoughts spinning behind them. "I've never seen a Kansas wheat field, but I can imagine that is true." Then, "Why Kansas? Why not a Nebraskan wheat field?"

"I think because she saw the Kansas fields first," I answered as I spotted my suitcase high on the belt, entangled with a golf bag. I grappled it to the floor. "This is everything," I said, pointing to my luggage. Sarah led the way to the parking lot while I talked. "She tells me all the time that she wishes she named me 'Kansas.' She went to college in Kansas and thought it was beautiful. She told me a story about it growing up." I paused there, trying to assess if I was babbling.

"Can I hear it?" she asked, unable to suppress the fascination in her voice.

"It probably sounds silly. But yes." I had to stop while a loud, smoky bus crossed in front of us. Despite the Bangor airport being small, the traffic kept a steady pace and we concentrated on crossing at the right places in-between hurrying travelers and cars. Sarah's black SUV chirped loudly and blinked its lights as we approached and I loaded the luggage.

"So the story?" she asked when we were all arranged inside.

"Right. I guess it isn't so much a *story* story—just something she told me. She said that she looked at the fields all the time and

64

when she got pregnant with me the fields soaked right from her eyes into me, and that is why I look like them." I hoped she didn't think I sounded vain and shook my head to show her I didn't necessarily agree.

"My mother says that if she could have seen a picture of what I would look like, she would have named me Kansas. But I was born with dark, curly hair so she didn't exactly think I looked like a wheat field back then." The truth is that my mother threatened to change my name to Kansas often when I was a child. I think a part of her hoped I'd prefer Kansas and adopt a new name like Cleo did. Unfortunately for my mother, I was perfectly content being called Jennifer. And even as a child I recognized, without being able to put the complex idea into words, that Cleo cornered the market on name changes in our town and copying her would only look affected.

"So how did you get the name Jennifer, then?" Every question rang with excitement.

"Nothing special. Before I was born, a pretty waitress brought some chocolate cake to their table. They read her name tag and voilà—here I am."

"Here you are," she repeated with satisfaction. "I want to know everything. You'll go hoarse from talking, but first, do you need food? We're more than an hour from home, so we should probably stop if you're hungry." My stomach was painfully empty now that it was no longer full of fear. I nodded and told her that sounded great.

"Would you like to stop at a crab shack? Or a lobster house? Whatever you want. We are celebrating. We could grab some cod sandwiches at the next town."

"Oh," I stalled uncomfortably. "It doesn't matter. But I'm not really . . . I don't, um, like . . . seafood that much," I apologized.

Sarah's eyebrows inched up. "Really? Not any seafood?"

"Fish is okay. I can do fish . . . sometimes." I was stretching. My seafood tolerance usually ended at fish sticks with ketchup.

"No shrimp? Crab? Lobster? Mussels? Clams?" I tried to hide my shudder at the word *mussels*. I once saw a woman eat them and thought I'd be ill just from the sight.

"I'm sorry," I answered, praying she didn't hold it against me.

Sarah's eyes narrowed in suspicion, still unable to believe me. "What about Claire? Doesn't she ever cook seafood?"

"Not really. My dad's allergic to shellfish." I cringed, waiting for her reaction. Her eyebrows contracted and she chewed softly on her bottom lip. "But we can go wherever you want. I'll find something I like."

"No!" she exclaimed, grabbing my knee and smiling. "No, you don't have to eat anything you don't like. I was just thinking. I made lobster spaghetti for your first dinner tonight, and that isn't going to work, is it? I should have asked you first." She smiled kindly, and I felt my face melt with the heat of embarrassment. They put lobster in *spaghetti*?

"I'm so sorry. I'm not trying to be rude," I told her.

"Of course not!" she cried. She pushed one hand toward the windshield and extended her fingers. "Stop. Don't worry about it for a second. I'm sorry if I made you feel bad. I'm just surprised. More at Claire than at you." She looked at me quickly. Looked *through* me is a better description—as if she were trying to see past me to my mother. "Do you know what your grandfather did for a living?" The teacher in Sarah became very plain in her querying, expectant face, and I felt like I just entered an oral test.

"Um, a factory, right? Didn't he can fish?" I squirmed closer to the door as Sarah's jaw dropped, dumbfounded.

"Claire!" Sarah scolded the empty space in front of her. Tears crept to the bottom of my eyes. I didn't want to look stupid in front of Sarah, or more important, disappoint her already. "Jennifer," she said firmly, throwing a piercing look straight at me, "your grandfather was a *waterman*." The last word reverberated with authority, as if nothing could be better. "He worked on the seas all his life. Anything the sea would grow, he harvested. He eventually managed to buy his own boat and employed three men. Four families, including our own, all fed and clothed by what my father could coax out of the ocean." She held up four fingers, looking at them like the number surprised her even now. She stared at things I could not see before her eyes refocused on the highway. "There were bad years. He worked in the canning factory across the harbor to make ends meet. That's true. But he was not a factory worker. He was a waterman." Sarah's eyes blazed with the luminosity of pride.

I felt like an idiot: I had no idea what a waterman actually did. I didn't know boats. Didn't know tides or stars or engines or whatever they used these days. "I am so surprised that Claire never told you that. I guess I won't know where to begin until I know where she left off. What do you know?"

Wild horses couldn't make me tell the truth and say "nothing," so I stalled. "About what?"

"All of this," Sarah said, letting go of the steering wheel and throwing her hands into the air like she meant to encompass the entire world. "Our family, our home, your history, your heritage . . ."

"I know Grandma was a teacher. I know she met your dad when she took a job in Smithport." I let my words out slowly, monitoring them carefully. I didn't want to hurt Sarah more by reminding her that my mother had never even hinted at her existence.

"That's something," Sarah conceded with relief. "Have you ever seen the ocean?"

"Yes," I answered, thankful I could give her one answer that pleased her. "We went to San Diego when I was ten. My dad has a cousin there that he really likes."

Sarah wrinkled her nose in distaste. "I mean *our* ocean. The Northern Atlantic." The way she said it, one would think that all other oceans were second-class citizens in the kingdom of Poseidon.

"No, never," I answered reluctantly.

"Well," she said with a strange thrill in her voice. "You will soon. I think you will love her." The highway careened through hills covered in dense trees, taking us away from the airport until signs of humanity grew sparser. A few farmhouses peeked out from intermittent clearings, showing advanced age in their sagging roofs and bowed walls. "Shelter Cove is just off the beach. Though it probably isn't like any beach you've ever seen. Our bay is *wild*."

A tiny shiver ran down my arms in anticipation. "What is Shelter Cove?" I asked, picturing a park or a marina.

"Home," she answered. "Shelter Cove is the name of my home."

"You named it?"

"Heavens, no. Herman Miller named it Shelter Cove when he built it in nineteen hundred and one. It has been in our family for a hundred and twelve years. All the homes have names around here."

"I can't imagine naming my house in Nebraska. It's a nice house, but just a house." I pictured my two-story stucco sitting pleasantly on our small, ordinary yard with a plaque that read FRED in gilded letters.

"Well, houses here earn it. When something stands up to the sea's temper for that long, it garners a certain respect. Our homes deserve names because they fight the elements with us, beside us." She pointed to a two-story home covered in gray wooden shingles. A clothesline bravely flapped unmentionables for all to see, including men's long, white underwear I thought ceased to exist fifty years ago.

"Does Shelter Cove look like that?" I asked, pointing to it. "Covered in roof shingles? Are they all like that?"

Sarah laughed. "It's called shake shingle. Surely you've seen it?"

"I've never seen a house quite like that," I said. In truth, I found them unsightly. The thick, uneven shingles ran from the roof's peak to the ground, stopping only to shaggily outline the windows and door.

"No, Shelter Cove is clapboard. Whitewashed. Beautiful." She spoke of it tenderly. "Are you ready to see it?" I pictured a clean, white home overlooking the topaz ocean, and the hunger in my stomach turned into a longing. I needed to touch the water more than I needed food.

"Let's go home," I answered wholeheartedly.

CHAPTER 8

SARAH IGNORED MY claim that I could wait for dinner to eat and stopped at a small . . . I wanted to say restaurant, but that conjures the wrong image entirely. Shack is the nearest description I can find. It was a long, metal trailer with a tacky plastic sign almost too small to see from the road that read PHISH AND CHIPS. We had to park and walk up to a hole in the wall, where a woman with a taciturn face appeared to take our order. The establishment was seedy at best, and I earnestly doubted the safety and cleanliness of the food, but in all fairness, my hamburger was excellent. Similar establishments littered our drive home, their names growing successively more creative until one entrepreneur gave up and simply advertised: "Same old, same old—But I fry it better!" I almost wished we had waited and stopped there, if for no other reason than to reward his honesty.

It is a tribute to the scenery that it could distract my attention away from Sarah. The trees grew recklessly close to the shoulderless road, almost stroking the car as it careened by. Meandering in an organic path, the small highway followed the lay of the land until it seemed as natural as the thin rivers that snaked in and out of view along the way. I couldn't refrain from pointing out what must have been clichés to Sarah: the murky marshes ringed with cattails, the plaques on homes bearing impressive dates like 1790, the smooth forest floor covered in orange pine needles.

The hour passed like minutes until the road, twisting ever more drunkenly as we went, stumbled to a halt at a stop sign. "Almost there," Sarah announced. "These are the first inland homes in the town, but Main Street is farther down. And Shelter Cove is a mile past that, on the bay." She paused the car at the empty intersection to let me soak in the sight.

There wasn't much I wanted to soak in, quite truthfully. The tiny, decrepit houses leaned wearily. Several lay in a tattered row, with no garages or sidewalks, and only a few weedy flowers for adornment. The towering trees blocked out the sun, casting the already dismal sight in deeper gloom. "They get prettier," Sarah promised. "The hired hands without boats of their own used to eke out a living here from pocket change and fish scraps. These were built in the Depression. This is Langston Street, but for the last seventy years no one has called it anything but Shanty Street. Let me show you the real town."

The car creaked gently as it rolled slowly down the street littered with loose rocks. True to Sarah's promise, the homes began growing, both in size and cleanliness as we moved toward the town. A tiny sidewalk appeared, followed by old-fashioned streetlights. Soon garages and porches and trellises burdened with fat flowers came into sight. And then, with no transition between residential homes and businesses, a hardware store with a large burgundy awning stretched along the street, its goods spilling onto the sidewalk. Several more homes followed, two-story with delicate stained glass in their narrow upper windows, each painted at least four different colors.

"It looks like a postcard," I said, gawking at the detailed, geometric carvings at the top of a porch post.

"That might look like a postcard, but *that* looks like a poem." Sarah pointed out her window as the car followed a wide turn. We broke free of a stand of trees and the docks of Smithport bustled into view. I pushed the button to roll down my window and with the first sweep of wind burst the mingled smell of fish and salt and sea spray. Large rusted boats docked beside larger, rustier ones, with a mess of cranes, nets, cages, and crates littering the scene. One syllable shouts burst into the air like shots fired all around me. "Oy," "Off," "Down," "Ho!" *They really said Ho!* Not to mention some other one syllable words that aren't repeated in polite company. "They're getting ready for dinner," Sarah explained. "In the summer, they take their catches across the harbor to the tourist towns and sell directly to the public. Put on quite a show, too."

Above the disorganized docks, three wooden buildings crowded together on a stony rock ledge where two restaurants with small patios shouldered aggressively against a general store, each pushing for a view of the water. I could see the waves bobbing and dying far on the horizon, but the current rolled in gently here, sheltered by the distant, rocky arms of land fending off the determined ocean.

"Is this where my grandfather worked?" I asked as I watched the men in thick yellow overalls loading their boats as they called directions. It wasn't difficult to imagine the scene fifty years ago. All I had to do was switch out the cars for older models and put the women in dresses.

"Often. But usually he took his catch to the canning facility in Anchorton. They canned sardines. It closed ten years ago, but it did well in its time." Sarah pulled over and parked so I could look longer. An annoyed car zipped past us with a rude squeal. "They think we're tourists, coming to look at the fishermen," Sarah said with a laugh, nodding to the disappearing car. "That's why they got mad."

"They don't like tourists?" I asked in surprise.

"Not . . . really." Sarah let the words out grudgingly.

"Why?"

Sarah deliberated, opened her mouth and closed it again thoughtfully before delivering a prudent answer. "Smithport is an old place. It is fiercely proud of its history and it tends to be just a bit . . . exclusive. Newcomers aren't exactly embraced."

My pride rankled at her words. "So they don't want me here?" I challenged.

"Oh, no!" she said with a relieved laugh. "There are a lot of people curious to see Claire's daughter. You are a true Smither, without a doubt. Even if you didn't know it."

"A what?" I asked.

"Oh, a Smither. It's what we call each other. So," Sarah said happily, as if all my worries had been put to rest, "do you want to see Shelter Cove now?"

I nodded, my eyes still riveted to the men on the docks. They moved with a sharp focus, never still, never distracted. I wanted to stay longer, walk down the crooked planks for a better look, but Sarah reversed the car back into the street.

The houses farther down the road lacked the grandeur of the structures on Main Street, but did not have the shabby, run-down feel of Shanty Street. Here they nestled into the trees, contented and natural. No neighborhoods existed in Smithport, only clusters. A few homes huddled together, followed by the untamed wilderness, followed by another group of buildings. Sarah turned down a gravel road with trees nearly touching their tops high above the car. Haven Lane. Turning one last time, the car coasted into a short driveway and sat idling before Sarah turned the key and killed the engine.

"This is it," she said. A square yard pushed the trees away from the house, but could not tame the sand and rocks. Grass grew intermittently between the sandy bare patches and clustered stones. In the middle of the struggle between lawn and wilderness stood a bright, orderly home. A brass plaque reading SHELTER COVE EST. 1901 hung beside a faded, red door. The thin, white paint did not completely obscure the sheen of weathered wood, but every imperfection felt carefully calculated to add to the charm. Two colorful floats, just like the ones littering the boats on the docks, swung from the porch railing while red flowers spilled from the window boxes.

Sarah didn't speak while I took it in. I felt the past push against the car window, its hands thrust to the thin glass, waiting to clasp me the moment I exited. I would meet ghosts here. Not the kind that haunt and wail, but the ones that make you remember. The very air seemed to be a memory. I could never explain it, but I felt it in the tiny bumps of raised flesh on my arms.

"It is so beautiful," I said at last. The words *Beauty is truth, truth beauty* leaped into my mind. I stepped outside, trying to remember who said it. Emerson? That didn't sound right. Not Shelley. Regardless, I had never agreed with it before. I can't say

I agreed with it in that moment, either, but it pierced my mind, cutting away all other thoughts. *Beauty is truth, truth beauty.* I met Sarah's curious eyes over the hood of the car, watching her watch me. Somewhere in all this beauty, I would meet the truth.

CHAPTER 9

I FOLLOWED SARAH to the front door, my suitcase bouncing over the gravel driveway and clumping against the wooden porch steps. Before we reached the door handle, there was a rustling from the yard and I turned to see a medium-sized dog burst from the forest and race across the yard.

"Don't be scared," Sarah said, "that's just Charlie, my mutt." The dog reached us in seconds and began a frantic dance on his back paws as his tongue waved indiscriminately, looking for exposed skin. "Charlie, sit! Sit down!" Sarah yelled, pushing his bottom rudely to the porch planks, where he commenced wagging his entire body back and forth in glee. "Sorry about that."

Charlie's short white hair was only interrupted by a large, black patch that encircled half of his head, including one dark eye and a floppy ear. "He's friendly," I said, wondering if petting him would calm him or just increase the hysterics.

"He's crazy," Sarah said, affection tinting the insult. She looked at him sternly, "You behave. Be still." Charlie's head tilted intently each time she spoke. When Sarah was sure he wasn't going to jump back up, she turned to me. "Now, let's try this again."

She pushed the front door and stepped back as it swung open. The first thing I saw was a kaleidoscope of deep but faded colors from the Oriental rug laid over the honey-colored wood floors. Then the walls, lined in black shelves crammed with books of every size, color, and condition. The shelves stopped only for the large stone fireplace and the windows on either side of it. Marooned in the middle of the room were a slouchy, white sofa and chair. A single, twisted piece of driftwood sat atop a large book on the wooden coffee table. A fat ginger cat rose from his spot on the chair and gave a weak hiss.

"That's Chester, our resident grouch. He only loves us when he wants to," Sarah said. My jaw dropped open as I stared across the room to the most astonishing feature—a mural only God could paint. The windows framed a rim of stubborn trees at the edge of the yard that thinned to brush, then to glossy gray and black boulders and at last to patches of thin, high grass and sand the color of tin. It seemed impossible that that such a sight could be summarized in three tiny letters. *B-a-y.*

I had the sudden impulse to *touch* everything: the planks of the floor, the thick banister at the foot of the staircase, the velvety smooth piece of driftwood, even the panes of glass in the window. I felt like a blind person in a gallery of sculptures. My fingers folded into claws as I restrained them. I didn't speak, my eyes too hungry to share my brain with my mouth. Framed photos cluttered the entire wall of the stairway. I wanted to run to them, but I forced my feet to walk at an acceptable pace. "Who are they?" I asked as I stood before the multitude of strange faces.

"It would take all night to name all of them," Sarah said, casting her eyes up to the last of the pictures at the top of the steep staircase and back down again. "Besides, I don't know all of them. My mom put most of these up. This is her—your grandmother, Hazel." She pointed to a large photograph of a young woman with yellow hair, green eyes, and painted pink cheeks. Her face looked more like my mother, but her coloring resembled Sarah's. "I was my father's girl," Sarah said, reading my thoughts. "This is your grandfather." She pointed to another picture, blurrier, taken outside, of a man with a boat behind him. His floppy cap threw his eyes into shadow but did not hide his high cheekbones that looked just like Sarah's. I ran my finger over my own cheekbone, disappointed that it fell lower than theirs.

My eyes kept drinking in the faces until one hit me like a wave in the face. "That's you," I breathed softly, meaning *you* in the plural. Two little girls in bathing suits and cut-off jeans laughed up at the camera while they draped their arms around each other. Their long, wet hair dripped in tangled strands in the sunlight as they stood on a rocky beach. "You and my mother." My mother's silly grin squeezed her eyes nearly shut.

"Your mom was a goof," Sarah said as she smiled at the memory more than the picture. "We can put your things in your room." Sarah took the handle of my suitcase and grappled up the steep, narrow staircase with the heavy luggage while I followed with my smaller bag. She led me to a door just at the top of the stairs. "This was my room, growing up. I use my parents' room downstairs now, but I think this is still my favorite," she said as she turned the brass knob.

Inside, a black iron bed covered in an exquisite quilt made of the tiniest, most colorful blocks I ever saw stood against one wall. A small sheepskin rug lay beside the bed and through the window I could see the entire cove glinting in the afternoon. An antique desk with an outdated globe squeezed against the wall across from the bed and a tiny closet door, looking like it had to suck in its breath to fit, crammed itself into the far corner. "This is amazing!" I cried as I rushed to the window. I spun around and reached out for the quilt. "This is . . . amazing," I repeated.

"Your grandmother made that. It took her over a year. She loved that quilt."

I gently fingered the chaotic, clashing pieces of cloth, forced together and somehow made beautiful, orderly. "I think it is the prettiest quilt I ever saw. It looks perfect in here." I scanned the room again, catching new sights with each glance, like the framed maps on the wall and the brass reading lamp on the wooden nightstand.

"It's not big," Sarah admitted. "Claire and I once wanted to share a room but my father couldn't fit her bed in here." She gestured to the opposite wall, to illustrate the size. "We kept bugging him about it until he finally agreed to try. I remember him taking the frame of her bed apart and when he reassembled it in here . . ." Sarah's shoulders shook lightly and she giggled. "When it was back together . . ." This time the giggles deepened into a laugh. "He got the last screw in somehow and there was less than a foot between the bed frames." She held her hands apart by only a few inches.

She sat down on the bed and slipped off her sandals before digging her feet into the thick rug. "Claire didn't want to admit defeat so she kept on swearing that there was plenty of room and she could get through just fine. She was only seven. She did this sideways shuffle-walk on her tiptoes between the beds . . ." She shook her head to brush away the funniest part of the memory to continue. "So she gets to the middle of the beds and turns around to show my mother that it isn't bad at all and," Sarah's voice built and exploded in hilarity, "she got stuck!"

"Stuck?" I exclaimed.

"Her little hips wedged tight!" Sarah's laughter rang out. "I don't know how! She just turned around really fast and looked up with a panicked face. She managed to turn sideways again and get free, but she bruised both her legs and Mother made Dad take the bed back to Claire's room. We never got to share. It became one of those family legends."

As our laughter dwindled it left a faint trail of sadness behind it, like the white clouds that follow airplanes through the sky. We both knew, very quietly and in the back of our minds, that Mother should have passed that story down to me years ago.

Sarah showed me the rest of the house. My mother's old room was next door, its sloping ceiling making it even smaller than Sarah's. A blue tiled bathroom at the end of the hall completed the upstairs tour. Sarah's current room downstairs was decorated entirely in shades of off white and light beige and looked like something out of *Better Homes and Gardens*. French doors opened from her room onto a brick patio overlooking the waves. Sarah had converted the dining room into an office, which, oddly enough, was entirely devoid of books. "I can't get work done if I'm tempted to read," she clarified. In the kitchen new stainless steel appliances stood out against the antique cabinets and the original brick backsplash.

"I've done a lot of work," she explained when she caught me staring at the gas stove that looked like it belonged in a restaurant. "I know it's silly with only me, but I like to cook. My neighbor has four children, and she lets me feed them my experiments."

The smell of garlic and tomatoes wafting from the Crock-Pot

filled the house and stood as a testament to her skill. It would have made my mouth water even more if not for the slightly fishy undertone tainting the scent. Truly, lobster in spaghetti? It seemed an irresponsible thing to do to perfectly good Italian food. "We can eat in about an hour, after we're hungry again," Sarah offered. "I won't put lobster sauce on yours."

"Do I have time to go see the water first?" I asked meekly.

The question delighted Sarah. "You bet. I'll set the table and get everything ready while you go explore. You can go alone. Take your time. I won't interrupt," she promised. "Just go out that door," she said, pointing to a door at the back of the kitchen, "and walk until you get wet." I smiled back at her, thankful that she understood.

Once in the yard the garlic and tomato smell disappeared instantly, but the fishy undertone did not. It seemed to seep up from the earth here, the way the smell of warm dirt seeped into the air in Nebraska. But outside, bathed in the tilting slant of sun and washed in the cool, salty breeze, the smell didn't rankle—it belonged.

The underbrush at the edge of the yard grew thorny and thick, divided only where a small path led to the beach. Sarah was right—as soon as I saw it I knew it wasn't like any other beach. It was an untamed mix of elements. What should have been sand looked like a seashell battlefield, the devastated remains shattered and scattered across the dark shore. *Definitely not a barefoot beach,* I thought as I traversed the wild wreckage of nature.

After meeting Sarah, Smithport, and Shelter Cove, there seemed to be only one introduction left to make. I picked my way carefully over the sand until my toes, peeking out from my sandals, kissed the cold, moving water. I lowered myself to the ground, not minding the chilly wetness soaking through the seat of my shorts. Sarah would understand if I came back wet. I threw a self-conscious glance over my shoulder and, reassured in my absolute solitude, I whispered to the water, "I'm Jennifer."

I closed my eyes to hear her answer. The gentle hiss of the water pervaded the air. A bird called from the forest, but other than my voice and the short conversations singing through the trees, the ocean hummed her lullaby by herself. The sounds felt so tangible that I kept my eyes closed and let the sunlight make shimmering patterns on the inside of my eyelids. When I finally opened them again the beauty of everything seemed doubled. I peered at the sight, surprised to find it still there.

"I am really here," I whispered. "This is *mine*." My chest swelled with possessiveness for the little cove. I sat with my chin tipped up, my ears straining to memorize the foreign sounds, until a fast movement in the sand caught my eye. My body reacted before my mind, jumping up and away before I realized it was a crab. I raised my foot nearest the white, spiderlike creature and took another hop backward. It never changed its trajectory and, still running, rose on its back feet and clicked its fat pinchers at me. I let out a scream as I stumbled and fell into the water, sitting down hard against the brutally sharp bottom. And despite the pain and the cold (the water seemed to flow directly from Iceland), I kept—forgive the pun—crab walking, to put more space between the offensive creature and myself.

If that crab didn't look just like a tarantula wearing armor I wouldn't have lost my balance, but nothing terrifies me like a spider. Or to be more precise, nothing terrifies me like the way a spider *moves*. While scrambling in the cold water I collected not a seashell or sand dollar, but the most humiliating moment of my life. I never knew until I turned around how much I hated that crab.

Bursting my assumption of privacy, a boy, taller than me, but roughly my age, appeared. I saw his shoes first, grass-stained and ratty, jogging toward me. When I raised my head the rest of him came into view as he halted in front of me, slightly breathless, his hand extended to help me up. The shock of his sudden materialization made me scramble unsteadily to my feet. Instead of taking his hand I leaned away from him, scrutinizing. He looked like an average scruffy boy. His hair was dark blond, streaked liberally with light browns, just like mine, and stuck up in spikes over his perspiring forehead. He wore a gray T-shirt with sweat marks under the arms and cargo shorts with one pocket half torn off. A thin white scar ran a reckless line from his top lip to his nose. And then, there was the remarkable: I tried not to stare at his dark blue eyes. I will never describe them as they should be described, but they tightened at the corners, giving him a perpetual, thoughtful squint and an aura of intelligence.

"That's just a crab," he said, looking where the creature now squatted, still and docile on the sand. "Are you okay?" He said it like he worried more about my mental health than physical. He lowered his hand, seeing that I refused to take it.

"Where did you come from?" My eyes traveled the entire cove, wondering how I had missed a person in plain sight. Angry at the way his eyes studied my dripping clothes I murmured grumpily, "This is private property."

That made his squinting eyes wrinkle at the corners, and his mouth twitched up. "You're bleeding," he said bluntly, nodding toward my leg.

It didn't burn until he said that. "Shoot," I sighed as I smeared a small red trickle across my ankle with the side of my hand. The boy took a few steps and with the skill of a snake charmer grabbed the crab by the claw and flung it into the waves before it could pinch. "He won't bug you anymore," he promised.

I pulled my T-shirt away from my body, aware of the way it stuck to my skin, and tried to sound nonchalant. "It didn't bug me. It just surprised me. I was thinking about something else and I slipped." He pulled a serious face and nodded while the amusement flashed through his eyes. My face flamed. "I have to go." I didn't like turning around and leaving him on my beach, but to avoid any more humiliation I picked my way as quickly as possible over the uneven ground. With each step the heat in my cheeks increased and poured down into my chest. I felt his stare as I stumbled, my waterlogged bottom dripping, and my self-consciousness made me angry. When I reached the strip of sharp, but stable sand, I spun around and called back to him with my last vestige of dignity, "This is my aunt's backyard. You should ask her before you come back here." He looked completely unconcerned by my rebuff and stared back without word or apology. I whipped around and continued to Shelter Cove. *Rude,* I spat furiously inside my head. *Rude, rude, rude.* When I opened the door to the kitchen, my fuming face and wet clothes made Sarah jump away from the stove in alarm.

"Are you okay?" she asked. "Did you fall?"

I tried to temper my response, rein in my frustration. "I saw a crab and I slipped."

"A crab made you slip?" she asked, perplexed, her slotted spoon suspended in mid-air.

Why was that so hard to believe? Do people in Maine not slip? "It just ran at me and when I tried to get out of the way I fell. I'll just go clean up," I muttered. A small throb made me look at the heel of my hand and I saw minuscule pools of blood in the skinned flesh to match my ankle. Sarah saw it at the same time and grabbed some Band-Aids from a drawer. "There was some kid at the beach. He came out of nowhere," I confessed as she handed them to me.

"Kid?" she asked in a surprised voice. Then a small light dawned on her face as I sunk into a kitchen chair. "Do you mean a boy? About your age?"

"Yes," I answered, annoyed at the memory. How stupid had I looked? I tried to replay the scene from his eyes and my stomach fell painfully. Pretty stupid.

"Did he introduce himself?" she asked, a puzzled look on her face.

"No. He snuck up on me. I told him that it's not a public beach," I pressed the Band-Aid over my leg, watching the blood ooze through the tan fabric, turning it pink.

"Wash that first," Sarah murmured, but then her smile twitched up in amusement at my story, exactly like the boy's. Remembering his small grin provoked me. "What?" I asked, too passionately. "What is so funny about that?"

"Nothing," Sarah said quickly. "Well . . . it's sort of . . . that's Nathan. He lives on the cove, too. You can't see his house from here, but he's just down the road. He's one of my students I told you about when you first called." Sarah's eyes scanned my face, mixed with pity and humor. "I got confused at first because I've never thought of him as a kid."

My stomach, which had been falling a moment ago, landed with a horrible thud that made my heart skip a beat. Pretty stupid, indeed.

CHAPTER 10

SARAH WAITED UNTIL the end of dinner to mention the boy again. She set down her spoon and drummed her fingers on the table. "There is a sort of game that we play here. Well, no. Not game. Habit? Ritual? I don't know what to call it, but it's something we do every night."

"We?" I asked, very aware of the quiet emptiness of the rest of the house.

"Nathan and I," she said.

"Oh." Nathan. I hope she meant every night when I'm not visiting.

"You see, Nathan is a special . . . person. I'm sure he didn't mean to sneak up on you. He's not like that. I'm sorry you met him that way." Sarah propped her chin in her hand. "He is the smartest person I ever knew. But he is hindered in other areas."

I nodded, inviting her to continue, my interest in his flaws surpassing my interest in his intelligence.

"Technically, he isn't my student anymore because he doesn't attend public school now, but he is the closest thing to family I have." She looked down bashfully. "Had," she corrected. "But Nathan is like a son to me. I found him when he was three. They sent me out to assess him because his preschool teacher suspected he was mentally handicapped." Sarah shook her head in disbelief. "I might not have ever known him as anything but a neighbor, but the special education teacher that worked with handicapped students was on long-term leave. I had the degree, so they sent me."

"Why?"

"A few reasons. He didn't talk much. Almost never. Nathan was born with a cleft lip and a cleft palate. The surgery to correct it went wrong, and he needed two more surgeries before they got it all fixed. Then he had his tonsils out when he was three. So people assumed his speech delay was due to his medical conditions. But when they finished fixing his mouth and throat, he just stayed silent. He could talk, but he didn't."

That explained the odd scar. "So what was wrong?" I asked, watching her face soften as she spoke about him.

"We'll never know. He wouldn't interact with people. But I did a few tests on him and quickly saw that he was not delayed. I suspected something along the lines of autism, but I couldn't be sure because he wouldn't speak to me. He didn't fit the typical symptoms. At any rate, he got my attention. I kept going back to work with him. His mother was young, poor, living with a deckhand who was always gone on the boats. She didn't know what to do with him." Sarah stood up, clearing our plates as she talked. I followed suit, taking the leftovers to the counter. "And then one day I caught him. I brought some books to his house that had interesting pictures. I had an animal book, a book about space, some others. I laid them out on the floor and realized I had left my notepad in the car so I ran out to get it. When I came back he was poring over the book about space." She smiled, just begging me to ask why that was significant. I took her bait.

"And he really likes space? Physics genius?"

"No," she said triumphantly, "he was looking at a page . . . with no *pictures*. He was *reading*!" No mother could beam more proudly than she did. Sarah stacked the dishes in the sink and asked, "Do you want to eat dessert outside tonight?"

I agreed quickly, and she returned to her story while she cut two large pieces of chocolate cake and carried them out to the porch. Thank goodness they don't put lobster in *that*.

"After a month he would whisper a few words to me. It is a very long story, but to make it short, he finally let me in. He started talking to me, and his depth of understanding unsettled me, even after all my schooling for gifted children."

Outside, the fresh sea breeze moved gently, caressing my face. I ate slowly, picturing the things Sarah said.

"The strange thing is that Nathan wouldn't use his own words. He quoted. Not exact quotes. He mingled them with his own thoughts until I could barely tell his own words from the words of others. He filled his conversations with snatches of things he read. He borrowed descriptions, metaphors, even dialogue." Sarah stopped talking to take another bite and I filled in the quiet.

"How old was he? When he started quoting?"

"Not old. I didn't pick up on it until he was almost five. But the more he read, the more apparent it became. A preschooler talking about 'life being a damned muddle' is hard to ignore. That was Fitzgerald, by the way," she said as an aside. "Do you know how hard it was to figure out who he was quoting without the internet?" she asked. "Nowadays I just type the words into Google. Fifteen years ago I had to research. Half the things I suspected of being quotes I never found."

"Does he still do it?" I asked as I reluctantly reached my last bite.

"No, not really. If he starts to quote now he catches himself. It is my theory, and I am confident that I am correct"—she cocked her head as if challenging naysayers—"that he had to borrow words until his vocabulary and fluency caught up to his thoughts. He just didn't have the skill to express himself the way he wanted to. Needed to. So he stood on the shoulders of giants." Sarah set her plate on the wide porch rail and leaned back in her chair, closing her eyes to soak up the low, flat rays of the setting sun. I could see the remnants of her dancing days in her leisurely, rhythmic movements. When she brought her hands up to sweep her hair off her cheek, even that action was poised, just slow enough to make her fingers look like they floated effortlessly through the air.

"So the game," she said brightly, remembering her original topic. "I wanted him to see the difference between what he read and his own thought, so I gave him a daily assignment to find his favorite words and read them to me. It evolved into our nightly readings."

Sarah explained their non-game as the motion lights over the garage blinked on, chasing back the falling darkness, and catching Charlie in the act of hunting down a frog. "There are no rules. We each pick a line or passage out of something we read that day—be it cereal box or Shakespeare—and recite it to each other. Nothing long. Sometimes three words. Sometimes a paragraph."

I asked her if that was all—it didn't seem like much of an activity—and she said the only other thing was a brief discussion. Sometimes about the words. Sometimes about life in general. "So, how do you choose? What sort of things do you read?" I asked.

"Anything. There are no qualifiers. If it stands out for any reason, if you find it worth a second thought, you can read it. Funny, serious, nonsensical. Doesn't matter." She leaned forward, her face open in invitation, "Would you join us? Tomorrow? We're skipping tonight because I wanted to spend it just with you."

The memory of sputtering in the sea on my bottom assaulted

me. Could I really look at him again? If he came every night, could I avoid it? "Why night?" I asked, my errant thoughts stalling. Sarah tilted her head in confusion and I clarified. "Why do you only meet at night?"

She closed her eyes and inhaled. "All the reasons. Work is over, school is over, there's nothing else to do. Maine nights can get pretty cold and long. I can't tell you how often the cable goes out. And our guard is down. Ever notice how you feel more self-conscious in the daytime? Everything is so logical in the daytime. So literal. But at night"—she opened her hand to the sky like she was releasing the stars into the firmament—"you just believe more. You think more. You say more."

I followed an invisible path from her fingertips to the darkening sky and saw the faint, glimmer of daylight dying. "I'll do it," I said quietly, as the sea's song called the stars out of the blackness. I wouldn't have agreed to spend time with the boy an hour ago when the humiliation was fresh, when my clothes were dripping—when the sun was beaming. But here, in the dark, I let my guard down. I believed more. I thought more. I closed my eyes and listened to the ghosts of words in the air.

CHAPTER 11

ALL THROUGH THAT night, voices weaved in and out of my dreams, replaying the spent day: My dad's eager questions when I called home after dessert mixed with Cleo's laughter when I told her about my ordeal with the child prodigy. The clipped shouts of the boaters jumped in between Sarah's soft narratives, and even the nameless photographs on the stair hallway flashed like an album flipping its pages. I woke cocooned in my grandmother's quilt as a wet, gray fog curled against the windowpanes.

The house was eerily silent. I tiptoed downstairs in case Sarah was still asleep but her room was empty. The beach seemed the only possible place to look, so I zipped up my sweatshirt and picked my way through the cold grass. The fog stuck to the water, growing thicker as I neared the noisy waves. At last I made out Sarah's hazy shape perched on a boulder by the water's edge. She called out good morning in a surprised voice and I waved, concentrating on my steps. No falling in the ocean today.

"Did I wake you?" she asked apologetically. "I couldn't sleep so I came to sit for a while."

"No, I never heard you. I just couldn't find you so I decided to look here." I took a chilly seat on a smaller rock beside hers.

"I'm glad you did. You'll want to see this."

I asked her, "*See what?*" and she pointed up to the brightest part of the gray sky.

"The sun will burn off all this fog as soon as it gets going and we'll have a beautiful day. Crystal clear. I thought we'd go into town, maybe even take the ferry over to Monteg Island, see some of the tourist towns." We discussed plans enthusiastically for a few moments before we both lapsed back into quiet, looking over the ocean. Stakes of blinding light sliced through the clouds and hit the rippling water. "There it goes . . ." Sarah said, and sure enough, the cloying mist spread like a great bird extending its wings, lifted off the sea, and disappeared. It took no more than ten minutes. "You never get used to her," Sarah commented in awe. "She flattens our houses, sinks our ships, wears out our men, and still, we wake up just to look at her."

I gazed at Sarah, more mesmerized by her words than the ocean. A question mounted in my chest, overflowed to my lips.

"Then why did my mother leave?" Gulls cried raucously and fell through the sky as I watched the locks of Sarah's rumpled morning hair flutter against her shoulders.

"She couldn't forgive us. Couldn't forgive me. We all failed her. It took me a long time to see that." Sarah turned back to me, a plaintive look in her eyes. "I can't tell you the entire story, Jennifer, because I don't know it all. I was gone for a lot of it. I've waited twenty years to hear what really happened. But I can tell you what I know."

I looked squarely into her eyes and then down at my toes which pulled up, to avoid the spray. "Do other people know? Am I the only one who has no clue about my own mother?" That question was indefinably important to me.

Sarah inhaled thoughtfully and pushed her lips together. "Lots of people have a piece. You might be the first one, oddly enough, in the right situation to put the puzzle together." She looked harder at me like there was a riddle to solve in my face. "Imagine that. The one who didn't even know there was a puzzle," she murmured before she scooped up her shoes from the floor of broken seashells and slid down from her rock. "But you should at least have a good breakfast in you before we delve into the dysfunction of our family, agreed?" She smiled brightly.

"Fair enough," I agreed and stood, brushing off the seat of my pajamas.

"Good! Lobster and eggs?" She laughed before I could answer.

"Truly, the best of Maine is wasted on you, Jennifer," she called as she sprinted lithely over the slick terrain like a child. I stumbled less gracefully and caught up to her when she paused at the top of the beach. "I might be able to tell you why she left, but I can't tell you how." Her inscrutable expression swirled with emotion as she looked at me.

We walked back to the house and Sarah made an egg soufflé while I showered and dressed. While Sarah dressed I perused her bookshelves, wondering how to pick a line for the reading that night, when two sharp thumps resounded on the porch steps.

"Sarah?" A girl's voice called loudly. "Sarah!" This time louder with impatience.

The water was still running in Sarah's room so I crossed the living room and opened the front door. A little girl, no more than five, with curly red hair frowned at me. Before I could say a word she blurted, "Are you Jennifer?"

"Yes," I answered, studying her strange eyes. They looked Asian in shape, but they were a wild mix of yellow and green. And who ever heard of an Asian redhead? With *curly* hair? "But I don't know who you are."

"I'm Darcy," she said, clearly annoyed at my ignorance. She rolled her eyes when I continued to look perplexed and said slowly, as if I spoke another language, "Darcy *Cass*." She stepped past me, nudging me aside to search the room. "Where's Sarah?"

"In the shower. Did she know you were coming? Are you here

alone?" I stuck my head back out the front door and scanned the street and yard looking for an adult. Nobody.

She flopped onto the couch, her short legs sticking straight out in front of her. "I always come," Darcy said. She looked at me curiously and I returned the stare. "Nathan said you weren't pretty," she said flatly.

Her words had the force of a physical blow, but I managed to hide the shaking in my voice. "You know Nathan?"

"He's my brother." She said the entire sentence in the exact voice that a person would say "Duh!" I didn't like this kid any more than I liked her brother.

"But *I* think you're pretty," she said, giving me her first smile, complete with two dimples that reminded me of Cleo.

Okay, a little better. "Thank you." The shower turned off and I sighed with relief. Now Sarah could deal with the little one. Then realizing this might be my last minute alone with the girl, I spun around and said quietly, "Your brother said I wasn't pretty?" She nodded with glee. "Why would he just say that?"

Darcy bobbed her legs up and down against the cushions and said, "Because Claude kept asking about you and kept asking if you were pretty and he said, 'Knock it off. Shut up. No.' And he said that you were scared of crabs." Her words rushed out without pause and my face went red.

"I'm *not* afraid of crabs," I whispered vehemently. "Who's Claude?"

"My biggest sister." Darcy smiled, enjoying the question game.

"Your big sister asked about me?" None of this made sense yet.

"No. My *biggest* sister. Hester is my big sister, and Claude is my *biggest* sister."

"How many of you are there?" I asked. *Are you all this rude?*

"Four," we said simultaneously, because I suddenly remembered Sarah saying she cooked for her friend with four children. That made Darcy giggle, and I couldn't resist smiling back. Manners completely aside, I'd rarely seen a more adorable child, and that was saying a lot considering that I had a job as a swim teacher for preschoolers.

Before Darcy could say anything else, Sarah appeared in her robe. "I thought I heard you, Darcy," she said as Darcy sprang up to hug her. "Are you being good?" Sarah asked in a doubtful tone.

Hardly.

"Yep," Darcy said, smacking her lips loudly.

"That's good, and I would love to play, but Jennifer and I are going out now. You can visit until I'm dressed, but that's all today."

Sarah gave me a sympathetic look and hurried back to her room. Darcy turned her pout on me and I muddled through the next ten minutes asking her age (five), her favorite game (red rover), her favorite animal (hedgehog), and her favorite color (pink . . . or heliotrope). Just as I was about to ask what color heliotrope is, Sarah's door swung open and she saw my puzzled expression. With a slight groan she put her hands on Darcy's shoulders and steered her forward. "We are going now, dear. I'll see you later."

"Where are you going?" she demanded, her strange eyes pulled together with worry.

"Lots of places. Town. The ferry. The island. Maybe the lighthouse. Lunch, dinner. Who knows," Sarah said as she swept through the room, retrieving her keys from the coffee table and her purse from the floor. She stopped, looked me over to confirm I was ready to go, and said to Darcy, "So you need to run home. We'll be back tonight."

Darcy protested, but Sarah scooted her out the door and jumped into the car. "So sorry," Sarah said as we rounded the corner. "She should come with a bell so you know when she's about to sneak up on you."

"No, she didn't sneak. She stomped. That girl doesn't need a bell!" Sarah laughed and I assured her that Darcy didn't bother me. As tactfully as possible I asked about her unusual eyes.

"Her dad is half Japanese. He worked one of the boats for a year."

"I knew it!" I said. "I thought she looked Asian. But that hair!"

"Strangest mix I ever saw," Sarah agreed. "But beautiful. She is very striking."

"Very," I affirmed. I let the car grow silent before I gently asked, "So she and Nathan have different fathers?"

Sarah sighed and her jawline tightened. "Yes," she said simply.

I tried to show her that didn't mean anything to me with a shrug. I wasn't judging anyone. The silence returned. I rubbed my hands on my legs and said, "She told me that Nathan said I'm not pretty and I'm scared of crabs."

"What!" Sarah cried in horror. "Oh, Jasper."

"Who's Jasper?"

"No. Not who. It's just my expression. My word to use in utmost exasperation. My mother didn't believe in girls cursing. It stuck."

"Jasper?"

"I can't even remember how I came up with it. But back to Darcy—don't believe her. Of course you're beautiful, and I don't know about the crab thing. She's five and . . . she's Darcy." Her words were not convincing, but still comforting. "Nathan is really botching this, isn't he?" she said in frustration. "Just promise not to dislike him yet. At least let me make a formal introduction."

A little late for dislike, I thought, but I silently vowed not to despise him. Yet. After that the hours of the day flew by. Sarah took me to the docks to catch the ferry, which sounded very old-fashioned and romantic, but in reality felt a bit like an old city bus on water. Still, even a city bus seems exciting when it is chugging through the waves. The island, complete with storybook village and lighthouse, took me hours to explore. No trail along the high sea cliffs could go undiscovered, no quaint shop along Main Street could be passed without my happy exclamation of "Look!" While Smithport felt like the dress rehearsal of New England with the dirty, hurried dock work and faces full of concentration, Monteg Island felt like the performance. Even the fish in the windows of the seafood café sparkled silver in the sunlight. Here Maine put on her best show, the toil of the fishermen's lives and the battle with the elements hidden behind the exaggerated beauty of nature and the charming touch of man.

The conversation never meandered back to my mother except for the unscarred tales of childhood that Sarah shared enthusiastically. She spoke of my mother without a trace of resentment, and I stilled my questions, waited through the sunlit hours, the buzzing restaurants, the rolling ferry rides, and finally the peaceful, tired drive back to Shelter Cove. After night pulled her veil over the world, I would ask. Tonight Sarah would share the story I came two thousand miles to hear—the lost chapters of my mother's life.

CHAPTER 12

WE RETURNED HOME in the evening, slightly ill from eating so much good food all day, and thoroughly, deliciously, exhausted. The large cushions of the sofa caught me as I fell into them with a relieved sigh. I needed to call my Dad and Cleo, but I couldn't convince myself to move. Instead, I scratched Charlie's black ear and he stretched his head backward to give me a grateful lick. Sarah yawned, patted my leg, and said, "I guess we should pick our lines. Nathan usually comes over around eight-thirty, after he puts the girls to bed."

"He puts his sisters to bed? What about his mother?"

Sarah gave a deep sigh. "She has her hands full raising four children by herself. She relies on Nathan a lot. Too much. She had two children when she was still a teenager. That can be crippling." She modulated her message to sound more courteous. "But Judith has her good points. I don't mean to disparage her. She does her best." Sarah looked around the room, twisting her torso to see the bookshelves behind her. She changed the subject by asking me, "Do you want to search poems, essays, or novels for your line?"

She suggested I start with poems for our first reading because stumbling across something poignant in an entire novel can be difficult. "It's usually easier to find something in a book that you are already reading. That way you have the context," she explained. "Poetry is supposed to be on the top two shelves of that bookcase," she said, pointing. "But, I get careless and they get scattered. You can start there, though."

I took down an antique Tennyson with a damaged spine and perused the pages. The time passed steadily as we browsed for lines, piling discarded books in precarious stacks, loading our laps with potential favorites, and occasionally sharing some of our finds. Sarah chose one first but refused to let me see it. My dad called halfway through my search to ask about the day, and I had to cut him short to take a call from Cleo. I tried to skim the literature while talking to her, but I just ended up failing at both. I either lost my place in the poems or took too long to answer her simple questions. "Cleo," I finally told her, "let me call you back in the morning when I have time to tell you everything." I tried to stress the word *everything* to suggest her waiting would pay off. That finally appeased her, and I hung up the phone while Sarah smiled and shook her head.

"Oh, to be young," she murmured without further comment. When a light tap sounded on the front door, I quickly decided between two books and grabbed the Tennyson, my ferry ticket stuck between two pages to mark the poem I had picked.

"We'll be right out," Sarah said, not rushing as she set a few more books on the crowded coffee table. Charlie raced to the door, scratching it until Sarah yelled his name sharply. Sarah grabbed a bookmark, left the book behind, and led the way outside. I didn't ask questions, just followed, throat tight, stomach trembling, like I was stepping onto a stage instead of a small porch.

Nathan sat on the porch rail, his back against the slender post, with a battered paperback in his hand. He nodded at me with a clenched jaw. His face looked too young for the grim, thoughtful line of his mouth. Since he didn't say hello, neither did I. I seated myself on one of the two wooden chairs, leaving the other one for Sarah. She looked at both of us and said, "Nathan, my niece, Jennifer Newsom. Jennifer, my friend and student, Nathan Moore."

"Hi," I murmured. He only nodded again. The silence was not uncomfortable: It was agonizing. I broke it with a halting apology. "I'm sorry . . . about yesterday. I didn't know you lived here."

A muscle in his cheek flexed. "No problem. Sorry I scared you." He offered me a quick glance before returning his eyes to the ground.

"Okay, good," Sarah said matter-of-factly. Then she turned

just to Nathan and asked him about his day, and gave a quick sketch of our own activities.

At last he addressed me again. "Did you like the island?" There existed in his voice an intangible challenge.

"Of course," I answered, my own tone just as defensive and clipped as his. The scene of the island's tiny white village rose in my mind, the flowers laid in straight, blooming lines. "Not quite as much as Smithport, but all the same, it was beautiful."

His head jerked. "Why not as much?" This time he allowed his eyes to meet mine, and I stared a moment before answering. His face was a study in contradictions: the vulnerable, intelligent eyes, the slightly flaring nose, the ruddy cheeks, his firm jaw, the feathery, long eyelashes, and the crooked scar. He seemed pieced together by an indecisive creator who didn't know exactly what he was making. But for all that, the result was not unpleasant to look at.

"I don't know. It's a little picture-perfect for me. If it were real it would be like a Utopia, but it feels a bit contrived. . . ." Then, knowing it would tickle their fierce Maine pride, I added casually, "And too many tourists."

Nathan's lips pulled up at one corner, stretching his scar.

"I told you she'd be a Smither," Sarah said almost smugly. Nathan lifted one shoulder and smirked, but didn't argue. "So I'll go first tonight," Sarah said, and then turned and spoke only to me. "We tend to trade, but there's no real rule or schedule." She raised the laminated bookmark, its yarn tassel hanging limply against her fingers. " 'It takes a thousand voices to tell a single story.' A Native American saying," she finished.

I waited a moment before asking, "Is that all?"

"Yep," Sarah said with a smile.

It seemed too easy.

"Why did you pick that one tonight?" Nathan asked, rubbing one eyebrow.

"Because this bookmark was stuck in one of the books I picked up, and it seemed right for tonight. I think it fits. I've been thinking a lot lately about stories. My own, Claire's, and now Jennifer's." She gave me a meaningful look, and I knew she hadn't forgotten her promise. "So, do you two think it's true?"

"I can't find an argument," Nathan said. "Not without getting metaphysical."

"Makes sense to me," I agreed.

"A rare consensus," Sarah teased. "I guess we'll enjoy it while we can. Okay, then. Nathan, you're up. And thanks for sparing us the metaphysics."

He gave her a fleeting, reluctant look. "I have to read the entire poem tonight or the last lines won't make sense."

Something grabbed my attention that I hadn't noticed before in his short answers. "Is that your accent?" I asked in astonishment.

His eyes widened in annoyance as he waited for me to answer my own question.

Sarah laughed and pointed to Nathan. "She's not used to it. She doesn't know it, but she's made me feel very normal in the short time she has been here."

I asked her what she meant and she told me that it had been nice to have someone around who sounded like her for a change. "But you grew up here," I protested. "Why don't you sound the same?"

"I grew up here with my mother, who was the product of New York private schools. She always said that we could eat like Smithers, live like Smithers, fish like Smithers, even smell like Smithers, but no daughters of hers would talk like Smithers." Sarah grinned brilliantly. "She taught us to speak. And she untaught what we learned from the locals."

"Smell like Smithers?" Nathan scoffed.

"My father had the most incredible Maine accent, rich and musical and a symphony for the ears. I could listen to him forever . . ." Her wistful words faded as she spoke.

"So your mother let him talk like a Smither?" I asked.

Sarah huffed, "She loved his voice like I did. Men can get away with it. But she's right, it's not very elegant on a woman. It is a voice that belongs to the watermen."

Nathan asked if he could continue, his eyes sparking with amusement at our conversation. Sarah quieted and, instead of giving him her attention, she closed her eyes and leaned back in her chair, lifting the front two legs off the floorboards.

"You'll crack your head open," Nathan intoned dully.

Instead of cracking her head, she just cracked one eye. "You're off duty," she said. "Save it for the little girls."

Nathan sighed and opened his book. I looked between the two, feeling momentarily invisible. Their half sentences, cryptic references, meant nothing to me, but the relationship fascinated me. Not quite mother and son, but close. She seemed almost like an *aunt*. I stared at Nathan, resenting the decades he'd had her all to himself. I put aside my indignation when he began reading "Ozymandias" by Percy Shelly, his voice sounding normal until his accent snuck out, peeking unexpectedly behind syllables, surprising me, pleasing me. I understood how Sarah listened to her father for hours. Something about a rugged voice reciting an old British poem made a thrilling mix. Like his face. He came to the last lines and paused. "These lines are the ones I like best.

"Look on my works, ye Mighty, and despair!
Nothing beside remains. Round the decay
Of that colossal wreck, boundless and bare
The lone and level sands stretch far away.

"He wrote it about a monument built for a pharaoh. A millennium later, there is nothing left of the man but a broken statue half buried in the sand. I liked the image."

I imagined the sands blowing against the bleak scene of the lost Egyptian empire before my mind traveled to the vast, unfathomable waters of the ocean behind us. Both seemed wildly desolate to me.

"The lonely sands stretch away from all of us. From the wrecks of our lives," Sarah said delicately. Nathan asked her what she meant, but she smiled sadly and said she lost her train of thought. "I had it for a moment, I could see it. Funny how some things only make sense for a second," she said, covering her lips with her fingers. Charlie pulled his head up from the planks and looked at her, thumping his tail once in what seemed like sympathy.

"It's God," Nathan said, startling me.

"What's God?" I asked.

"Those flashes, those moments of truth. He is too much for us to see all at once. Maybe it's like looking into the sun. Just too much." The tension in Nathan's face ebbed as he spoke with disconcerting sincerity.

"Are you religious today, Nathan?" Sarah mused.

That made a true smile break across his face. "I usually am, Sarah. Have to keep an open mind." He tapped the side of his head.

"Too open . . ." Sarah interrupted.

". . . and your blessed brain will fall out. You would know." Nathan gave her a taunting smile. I peered in bewilderment at her face and then his, trying to interpret their conversation.

"He's mocking me because I'm always trying something,"

Sarah explained to me. "I used to be a good Methodist. Some days I truly think I still am. But there is a streak of Evangelical in me and some Southern Baptist, because sometimes I want to stand up and shout my Hallelujahs. Not demurely, not reverently, but pull it out of my diaphragm and really bellow!"

Nathan shook his head tolerantly, and in his softer countenance I could see some of the quiet boy that Sarah loved. "So she's a mess of faith. When you believe everything, you don't really believe anything, in my opinion," Nathan said, like a parent speaking of their child.

"I'm not a mess—I'm a work in progress," Sarah observed, then laughed.

Nathan snorted and pretended to hit his head against the porch post. At that we all laughed, and for the first time I noticed how the sound harmonized with the ocean song, adding light to the thunderous depths. "Okay, I've been ridiculed enough tonight. It's Jennifer's turn to read." Sarah tapped the book in my hand.

I swallowed once, my chin dipping down shyly. "It's Tennyson," I said, my voice cracking as I moved from laughter to reciting. I brushed my hair behind my shoulders and opened to my saved page. "Just the few lines, right?" I asked nervously.

"Whatever you want," Sarah assured me. Nathan relaxed his head against the post and turned away from me so I saw only the curving plane of his cheek, the corner of his eye, and the muscles in his neck as I began.

"Break, break, break,

 On thy cold gray stones, O Sea!

And I would that my tongue could utter

 The thoughts that arise in me."

My voice faded with each line, until the last came out in a hoarse, emotional whisper. At least Nathan had the decency not to look at me. He kept his gaze shifted up to the sky and I copied, noticing the black, spiky silhouettes of the pine trees against the canvas of night.

"You love her, don't you?" Sarah asked. I already knew when someone said *her* in that reverent tone, it meant the sea.

My throat croaked from a word I started and quitted. I paused, groping for the truth. "She is strange to me." I let my thoughts finish before the slow words rolled out. "Beautiful and intimidating and . . . strange."

"That proves she's a woman," Nathan said.

Sarah turned toward the house as if she could see through it to the midnight waves, and we lapsed into a comfortable quiet, each listening to the ocean's whispers. What the sea said to Nathan or Sarah, I cannot say, but to me she cooed something like: "Once upon a time . . ."

CHAPTER 13

ALMOST AS IMPERCEPTIBLY as the stars steal into the dark sky, Nathan slipped away with a simple, unassuming "good night." Once we were alone, I turned to Sarah to find her gaze fixed on me, which gave me a queer feeling of being stared at by my future self. If only I could end up so elegant!

Her lips parted, and I expected her to say something about the lines or Nathan or even the night. Instead she began without preamble and said very softly, very gently, "The story begins so beautifully." I blinked and dragged in a long breath while my limbs stiffened. I needed to know, but the thought of listening to a story that ended in the complete destruction of my family made me feel ill. I poised rigidly in my chair, a part of me, somewhere between my stomach and my spine, trembling timorously. "It was my senior year. My senior recital. Everything good at home. My father was having a tough time with his sardine catches and putting in some factory hours, but nothing out of the ordinary. I'd been accepted into the theater and art department at the University of Maine, and I was practicing my valedictorian speech. I was going to be a singer and a dancer—and save the world in my spare time. All the normal plans of a naïve idealist.

"Then a few weeks before my graduation, my father came down with the flu. We thought it was the flu. After two weeks of throwing up and stomachaches, he went to see the doctor." Sarah stopped and I watched her eyes fill with tears that grew heavy and fell before she could even blink them away. "Cancer. They thought pancreatic. They couldn't be sure because it spread everywhere. It was eating him alive. He died a month later, right after I graduated." My gut twisted, and I pushed my lips hard together, hating the words sliding into my ears. "He couldn't go. He was, well, he was mostly already gone." Her swimming eyes pulled me into their depths of dark sorrow. "It was so fast, Jennifer. From perfect and strong and laughing to . . . dead." The last word hit like an iron club, thudding against my soul in a terrible finality. "So fast.

"So I went off to college, dazed and in denial. I cannot tell you how many times I picked up the phone to call my dad . . ." Her voice faded into nothing, and I waited until she resumed. "We were always close. So I think I sort of detached. I didn't come home much, took summer classes, kept my vacations short. Always an excuse not to be here. Because he wasn't here. I couldn't stand it. I thought of my feelings a lot. I didn't really consider what it did to Claire to lose Dad and then me. I was a terrible sister in the meanest way. I never did anything outright she could point to and blame me for. There is nothing worse than indifference."

Chester clawed at the door and let out a deep cry, interrupting Sarah's hypnotic words. I quickly opened the door and scooped him up, grateful for something warm to hold as the icy words crystallized inside me. I sat cross-legged on the porch and said a quiet "I'm sorry" as I settled Chester into my lap.

Sarah watched the cat lean into my hand and let out a booming purr, but her expression remained empty, distant. "My junior year of college, I was starting to put life back together, falling in love, getting good parts in the productions. Healing. And then . . ." she stopped, indecision in her eyes, her posture hesitant. "I . . . I went on a research trip with a friend over the summer. I was gone for six weeks." She raised her head, a more businesslike tone to her voice. "You see, life is about timing. And my timing . . . it's like a curse out of Shakespeare. I manage to do everything at the wrong time. When I got back to school my roommates were frantic, saying they called the police, everything they could think of to get a hold of me. I asked them why—they knew where I was going—and they said I needed to call my sister right away. They barely looked at me, Jennifer. I knew it was bad.

"So I called. Claire answered the phone and started crying, just sobbing, and asked me where I had been and if I was okay. I told her I was fine, I'd been on a trip just like I'd told them, and asked her what was wrong. She said, 'Mother, Sarah. Mother had a stroke.' " Sarah's hands halted in midair. "If I ever go to hell, I will recognize it from that moment. My entire body full of a painful fire I couldn't escape. And then it got a thousand times worse. She said, 'She died, Sarah. I'm so sorry. We tried to find you. We did everything. We couldn't wait any longer to bury her.' "

Sarah paused again, probably in response to my expression of horror. I wanted to push my hand over her mouth, make the words stop. I shivered, my teeth chattering while I tried not to grip Chester too tightly. I could tell Sarah had told the story before, because she kept herself somewhat poised and factual, despite her fluctuating voice and wet eyes. I should have asked what happened next, but I couldn't control my knocking teeth long enough to make words come out.

Sarah sighed and skipped over some of the story by simply saying, "She was only forty-seven years old. Claire told me that they had buried my mother a week earlier. The town stepped in to help with paperwork and the will, but Claire was all alone. I got home to Smithport a few days later. When I opened the door, Claire came storming out of the house with a suitcase. I went to hug her but the look on her face . . . Medusa couldn't match it. I froze on the porch when I saw her and she started shouting. Hysterically shouting. When I finally got over the shock, I asked her what she was talking about. On the phone she sounded fine. I mean fine, between us. She sounded relieved to hear my voice, desperate to see me. I never understood what happened between my call home and that day." Sarah rested her gaze on me, hunting for some clue to put the savagely crumbled puzzle back together.

"Claire only said one logical thing to me that day. She said, 'You get the house. I'm taking the insurance money for school.' I watched her get into my mother's car, and I ran after her but she wouldn't even look at me. I thought she would calm down and call me later. I thought we would make up. I have not seen her since that day. I've tried, mind you, but she always kept me away. I finally decided that leaving her alone was the kindest thing . . ." Sarah let her hands, which had been gesticulating gracefully, grow still and fall into her lap. I hung my head, watching Chester's thick orange fur absorb my tears.

"Where were you, when they couldn't find you?" I asked nervously.

Sarah deflated, her shoulders falling heavily. "You would ask that. I suppose a story half told isn't a true story. I was in South Africa."

"South Africa?" I blurted. That answer was just one line above Outer Mongolia on the list of things I didn't expect her to say. "Why were you there?"

"I went as a research assistant. A PhD student was doing his thesis on dramatic therapy, helping to counsel people using role-play and drama. I took his class and he invited me to go as his assistant. We weren't exactly reachable. The school tried to contact us. We were at tiny clinics in the countryside and not following a formal schedule. We were on a plane home before they were able to get a message to us."

"You went to *South Africa*?" I tried to fit the label of "world traveler" into my image of her.

"It was a long time ago." She rubbed her neck, looking uncomfortable. Something about her eagerness to leave the topic alone made me more curious. Not quite willing to push my luck, I changed direction back to the original story.

"How long did it take you to get home after you talked to my mother?"

A nervous tremor shot up her body. "What do you mean?"

"You were only a couple hours away at the University of Maine when you called her. But you said you got home a few days later." I swallowed and took a steadying breath before asking, "Was it five days?" My mother's words marched like the condemned up and down the corridors of my mind—*five days, five days, five days.*

"I, I don't know," Sarah said, fear tightening her face. "I got there as fast as I could. I just, I went to tell John. I needed . . ." Her eyes flickered coldly and then refocused. "I had a . . . boyfriend. Let's just call him that. It doesn't really fit, but close enough. After our trip to Africa he went home to Boston to finish his research. Anyway, I went to tell him and then I went home." Sarah's voice changed abruptly, serious and dreadful: "What is five days, Jennifer?"

"He was the one you went with? John was the PhD student?"

"What is five days, Jennifer?" she asked, undeterred.

How could I tell her? I tried to look away, hide the terrible knowledge that hung heavy in my chest, but her eyes wouldn't release me. At last I answered reluctantly, "My mother didn't tell me anything. *Anything*. She just said that if she could ask you anything it would be how long you think five days is. That seemed to be what upset her the most."

"No." Sarah drew the word out, her voice dripping with distress. "Jasper! I was coming. I was half delirious and then . . ." She looked to me like I could absolve her, but I had nothing to offer. "I didn't mean to not come home. Truly, it was the worst timing . . ." Sarah gave up and sat still, looking as ill as I felt. I pushed my hand over Chester's fur, concentrating on the way his silky hair parted beneath my fingers. The world felt very big in that instant and I feared any movement, even a glance, would eject me from my place on the furiously spinning globe and throw me into the black abyss of space with only my aunt's pain as my last memory.

"I think I knew that was part of it, but I never realized that *was* it. That's what she's thought of all these years. Five days! And I did it. *I did it*," she repeated, revulsion distorting her voice. She decided "jasper" wouldn't suffice and swore under her breath. "I'm sorry," she said immediately, shaking her hand at me to erase the ugly word. "I'm so sorry!" She wasn't just talking about the swearing anymore. "Why won't she talk to me? Why?" she demanded, thumping her fist against the arm of her chair and looking at me, trying to find her sister's reasons somewhere in my face. But the answers didn't lie with me. Only more questions. And pity as deep as the sea.

CHAPTER 14

SARAH TRIED TO recompose herself, but ended up asking me to excuse her to go to bed, instead. I watched her wander to her bedroom, sorry for the hurt I caused by telling her about the five days, but certain, nonetheless, that she needed to know. I didn't want to stay outside alone in the hushed, humid air, so I slipped upstairs and sat on my bed replaying snatches of the conversation. I finally picked up my cell phone to call Cleo. She answered on the second ring and said, "I thought you were calling tomorrow."

"It couldn't wait. I know more about what happened—at least enough to start with." I repeated everything. As I told the story in my own words, I saw the picture so vividly—my mother lugging her heavy bag over to the brown Buick. Her refusal to look at her stunned sister. Barely older than me and utterly, voluntarily, alone.

After exhausting the topic of what happened between my

mother and Sarah, I gave Cleo a brief description of the lines and Nathan, which didn't interest her.

"So you all just read a line of something to each other?" she asked, unimpressed.

I sighed. "You don't have a romantic bone in your body, Cleo."

"Romantic?" she said too loud. "Do you like the boy? Are you reading love sonnets or something? You've only been there two days!" Her voice dripped with derision.

"Not what I meant," I said as tolerantly as I could manage. Truly, she is like talking to a calculator sometimes. Especially after getting used to Sarah. "I mean romantic as in the beauty of something. Appreciating the beauty of the words. The beauty of the night." I sat up straighter, stunned by my own revelation. "Cleo, you don't even recognize the beauty in yourself. I never thought . . . I never put it together before, but you never give anything credit for being beautiful."

Her irritated groan filled the phone. "Don't be stupid, Jennifer. I don't emote all over the place, but of course I think things are beautiful."

Undeterred, I asked, "What?"

"What *what*?"

"*What* do you think is beautiful?"

"I think you're tired or overwhelmed with poetry or something. Maybe we should talk tomorrow."

I laughed, glad to feel some of the heaviness of the night lift. "Just answer the question."

Her exasperated breath exploded in my ear and she answered in a monotone, "The wheat field. I think it's beautiful."

"Was that *so* hard?"

"Good night, Jennifer," she said, her aggravation only intensifying my enjoyment.

She hung up before she heard me say "good night," and it was a good thing, too, because I broke into laughter. One point for me for cracking her.

The next day dawned bright and breezy with less fog and an aqua blue tint on the horizon. Sarah met me peacefully at breakfast, but the puffy pink skin around her eyes testified to a long, sleepless night. Before I could ask how she was doing, she said, "I thought I'd invite Nathan's family over for dinner tonight. They are dying to be introduced." Sarah unceremoniously pushed Chester off the kitchen table, and he glared up at her with wounded dignity before stalking from the room.

I took great interest in buttering my toast while Sarah mentioned Nathan firing up the smoker that afternoon. "Would you do salmon, Jennifer? If I swear to make the meatiest, smokiest, least-salmony salmon you ever tasted, would you try it?"

I smiled and nodded doubtfully. "You can try. Maybe I'll be converted yet."

I accompanied Sarah into town after breakfast to grab fresh salmon from the men on the dock. Sarah picked out a "little one," roughly the size of a Maine coon cat. I averted my eyes and tried not to stare at the fixed, glassy eye of the slimy-looking fish while a man nimbly wrapped it in brown paper and tied it with a length of twine. I stepped back, making it plain that I would not carry the cold, limp corpse. I don't mind eating meat, but in Nebraska I don't have to go to the slaughterhouse and pick my carcass. It unsettled me, the piles of floppy fish packed into long, ice-filled freezers.

"Thanks, Harv," Sarah said to the man. He looked about Sarah's age, but his chapped, red face was carved with deep wrinkles around his eyes; the face of a man who lived on purpose.

His glance, which darted to me periodically as Sarah picked her fish, finally settled on my face. "That the girl? Claire's girl?" He spoke as if I couldn't understand him.

"This is Jennifer. Claire's daughter." Sarah said it cheerfully enough, but I sensed a deeper meaning to her words.

"Hmm," was all he said as he gave me a thoughtful evaluation. I squirmed, shifted my weight, and tried to guess what he saw when he looked at me so intently. It was a bit like being assessed by the Marlboro man. "Well, you look like a Maine girl," he said gruffly, and ended the conversation by turning back to his stack of fish.

Does one say thank you to that? I made a noncommittal sound and followed Sarah off the dock. We didn't speak again until we'd walked well out of the man's hearing range. "That is a high compliment, trust me," she said in a low voice. "In his own stubborn way, Harvey called you beautiful." And when she smiled at me I could see it: the fresh complexion rubbed clean by salt and wind, the muscular build from a life of battling the elements, and the strong independence in her footsteps.

Back at Shelter Cove I helped prepare the food, refusing contact with the fish, but happily snapping green beans and mashing potatoes while Sarah told me more about Nathan's family. "I call them the Beckers, because that is Judith's last name, and they'll all answer to it if someone says it, but they all have different last names. Nathan's name is Moore, his sixteen-year-old sister is Claudia Morgan, Hester is eight and her last name is St. Jean, and Darcy's name is Cass. Not that you have to remember all that. I just thought I'd warn you, because it can be confusing when it comes up."

I concentrated on her words and tried to ignore whatever she was doing with a tiny silver knife and the heavy, limp fish. "All different," I mused. "That makes for a complicated family."

"I guess all families can get complicated," Sarah said wryly.

"So Claudia is sixteen. How old is Nathan?"

"Seventeen. Almost eighteen. They're barely a year apart." She lowered her voice apologetically and said, "She is why Nathan's dad left."

"He didn't want another kid?"

"Not one that wasn't his," Sarah said slowly, pausing between her words.

It took me a moment before I very quietly said, "Oh."

"Is the eight-year-old anything like Darcy?" I asked, reaching for a less controversial topic.

"Hardly. She is so much like Nathan. Just as bright, possibly more so. And painfully shy. But when you get to know her, she is the most precious soul."

I smiled. "Then not much like Darcy at all." I realized my mistake and quickly corrected. "I don't mean Darcy isn't precious. I just meant the shy part."

Sarah flicked her hand dismissively and laughed. "They are all gifted. All four of them. I've never seen anything like it. Nathan is the most obvious, but Claudia has a mathematical mind that will blow you away, Hester's comprehension is light-years ahead of her age, and Darcy. Oh sweet, sweet, Darcy. She's too smart for her own good. She knows enough to be dangerous."

"You teach them all?"

"Not Nathan. He finished high school when he was fifteen. He's been taking long-distance classes from the University of Maine." Sarah grabbed an apron out of a drawer and looped it around her small waist. She caught me watching and said, "I don't know why I do this. I'm not really worried about flour on my jeans. Force of habit. My mother always did it." She made a face at herself and turned back to the counter.

"Why doesn't Nathan just go away to school, if he's been done with high school so long?"

Sarah stopped moving and raised her head. " 'Why' is a hard question. He never gives me the real answer. He says he needs to save more money, but colleges come begging for him. Lots of free rides. He got a perfect score on the SATs. Perfect. Then he says he doesn't want to leave the girls alone. His reasons are his. I don't know, exactly."

"Perfect? Can people do that? I've never heard of it."

"Just a special few. It's not common, that's for sure. And Nathan did it twice—just for good measure." She smacked her bottom to clean off her dusty hands and looked over my shoulder at the mashed potatoes. "Those look good. You make them at home?"

"My specialty."

"Well, there you go. Potatoes are something that Maine and Nebraska have in common." She ruffled my hair affectionately. While Sarah finished the more complicated parts of dinner, I chose a line to discuss for that night's reading and waited nervously for the Becker family. When I heard voices through the window, I hitched on a forced smile as Darcy's familiar clumps resounded on the steps.

"Sarah!" she called loudly. "Jennifer!" A small scuffle ensued followed by a "Shut up and knock on the door like a normal person." I replaced my fake smile with a genuine chuckle and opened the door to find too many heads trying to squeeze into the empty space surrounded by the door frame. Nathan hung back, but the girls jostled for position, trying to cross the threshold in a jumble of arms and legs and bodies, which thoroughly delighted Charlie as he raced into the room, black ear cocked and tongue waving.

I stepped back until they could sort themselves out, and a petite blonde girl detached herself by shaking Darcy's hand roughly from her arm. "Get off!" she mumbled. She looked at me for a long moment and then turned and smacked Nathan hard on the arm. I jumped more than he did. Then the girl smiled at me. I might like one of them, after all.

As she opened her mouth to say something, Darcy announced loudly, "This is Claudia Gale, my biggest sister."

Claudia bared her teeth at Darcy, rolled her eyes and then turned back to me, her hand raised in a wave. "Claude. Just Claude."

I waved back, thinking that she looked more like a ten-year-old than a girl my age. She could be only five feet, tops. Her curly blonde hair framed a delicate face with a sharp nose and not a trace of makeup. Her slight body was stick straight, flat-chested, and wiry. But she turned a warm smile on me that rivaled a Midwestern welcome. One of the few I'd gotten up here.

"Did she say Claudia Gale?"

"Yes, but like I said . . ."

"No, I won't call you that. But how do you spell Gale?" She told me and my mouth opened in surprise just as Sarah came into the room. I turned to my aunt and exclaimed, "My middle name is Gale, too! Spelled the same way!"

Sarah's surprise mirrored mine. "You're Jennifer Gale? You never told me that!" She studied me with grave eyes. "That's my middle name, too."

"Are you serious?" My mother named me after *Sarah*?

"But half the girls in this town have Gale for a middle name. Tradition. It's our way of naming them after her." Sarah tilted her head to the windows where the sea glinted.

I tried to digest it quickly so I could return to introductions, but I was speechless. Perhaps my mother didn't make as complete a break as I'd been led to believe. Some Smithport lingered in her yet.

"My middle name is Jean!" Darcy said loudly, not wanting to be left out any longer.

"Good for you, dear," Sarah said absently. She stretched out her hand to pat her on the head and ended up tapping her in the face instead. Sarah gave me a significant look, and we each filed away the subject for later scrutiny. We had guests to attend to.

"Hey, Jennifer. Good to meet you. I'm Judith." I turned my attention to Judith for the first time. I didn't like her. I know that sounds rash, but as Sarah says, a story half told isn't a true story. Her gruff voice, open posture, and straddled legs made her too rough to be appealing, despite a pretty face. And Sarah was right, the accent sounded wrong on a woman. *Why do so many men love her?* I wondered as I gave a polite smile and a two-finger wave. She walked up and threw her arm around my shoulder, squeezing too hard. "So ya like it he'e?" I nodded quickly and slipped out of her uncomfortable grasp.

"You already know Darcy," Sarah said in one breath, pulling me to the safety of her side, "and this is Hester." From the small mob emerged a willowy eight-year-old with light brown hair, freckles, and large, dark blue eyes the same deep color as Nathan's. She kept her lips locked together and only spared me a momentary glance.

Introductions complete, the Beckers stood in a disorganized line in front of me while Charlie jumped from one to the next, desperate, as always, to get his tongue on as much human skin as possible. They resembled a pack of strangers gathered randomly from the streets more than a family. Nothing matched: not their looks or their personalities or even their voices. I noticed Nathan's hand resting protectively on Hester's shoulder.

"Dinner's on!" Sarah announced to the motley crew, and we filed into the kitchen where Chester sat, staring at the stovetop with a fierce determination, his only movement a spasmodic flick of his tail. "Oh, go on," Sarah chided and scooted him with her foot. "I'll put some in your bowl."

"Salmon!" Darcy squealed in excitement.

Claude made an appreciative sound and said to me, "Sarah makes the best salmon I've ever tasted. Have you tried it yet?" I shook my head and picked a seat next to Sarah's as she finished bringing dishes of food to the table. Everyone settled into place, Claude taking the empty seat next to mine.

"Grace, tonight?" Sarah asked.

Darcy boomed quickly, "Me! I'll say it. Dear God, thank you for our salmon and we are very sorry they are dead now, but I hope you have a fish heaven with lots of seaweed. And I hope it's the same thing as normal heaven because we love fish very much, but Jennifer doesn't like crabs so try not to let them get too close to her and thank you for helping me find my orange sock today because Hester didn't think I would, and please help us leave some salmon for Chester because he doesn't like me unless I feed him . . ."

"Amen," Sarah cut in, extinguishing the rush of words. I lowered my head until I was sure I wouldn't laugh out loud and offend the little girl. Next time I'd tell Sarah to just let her go on. I could have listened to her all night.

The conversation began in earnest then. Claude apologized that Darcy mentioned the crab and I made a general announcement to the table at large, preceded by a piercing glance at Nathan, that I had no special aversion to crabs. Darcy wanted to know if I liked them, and I told her I didn't like or dislike them. They are, and always will be, just crabs.

"Are you scared of spiders?" Hester asked in a voice barely above a whisper. Everyone stopped talking and turned to her.

"Yes, I am," I said in surprise. "I hate spiders."

"Crabs are arachnids, too. They look scary sometimes." Her white cheeks colored, and she barely pronounced the last word.

"Crustacea," Nathan said gently. "Crabs and spiders are both arthropods, but crabs are crustaceans and spiders are arachnids."

Hester looked up at Nathan, her blush deepening. "It's okay," Nathan reassured. "There is only one tiny difference. Think of crab antennae . . ." He hinted.

Hester's chin shook for a second and Claude frowned. "Hess, don't worry about it. I thought they were arachnids, too. What do the stupid scientists know, anyway?"

Hester looked up to Nathan and hesitated before saying, "Two?"

"Exactly!" he said. "Spiders only have one. I think you were thinking of scorpions. But good connection." Despite the praise, her worried eyes fell back to the table.

"I think they look like spiders," I told her softly. "That's why I fell over. I saw it move from the corner of my eye, and I thought it was a nasty big spider."

"You fell over?" Darcy squealed with glee. I'd been certain Nathan already shared that part. He just smiled and shook his head minutely. "The crab made you fall down?" That piece of knowledge kept her entertained for ten minutes at my expense. She did an impromptu reenactment, squealing and falling to the floor with a resounding clatter of arms and legs on the wood floor.

Claude defended me by kicking her baby sister in the shins, and I took that as my cue to concentrate on my plate and, once again, curse that crab. To avoid any more attention I sampled the salmon. The meat fell to pieces when I tried to cut it with the side of my fork. I scraped up some broken scraps and tentatively put them in my mouth, knowing that Sarah was watching. At first all I tasted was smoke, followed by a cascade of spices running across my tongue and before I chewed twice, it was gone. Melted. Heaven. I stared at it, thankful I still had a plateful left and gave Sarah an awed smile. She grinned with deep satisfaction. I wasn't ready for mussels, probably never would be, but I could eat Sarah's salmon for breakfast, lunch, and dinner. I swallowed each bite in triumph, enjoying my seafood like a Smither.

The evening proceeded with a great deal of noise and laughter and jostling. Hester spoke to me two more times, something I perceived as a rare honor. Claude offered to show me around the town, but in the same breath, admitted there wasn't much to show. At nine o'clock Nathan reminded everyone that Darcy needed to go to bed so she could get up early for summer preschool the next day. The girls told us good night and waved good-bye to Nathan since he was staying for lines. Darcy raised up a wail that rivaled emergency vehicles and begged to stay and recite with us.

"You have to have a line, Darce," Claude pointed out.

"I do, I have one." Darcy insisted that she couldn't tell what it was, because lines were for outside and so we all traipsed out to the porch, which groaned under our weight as all seven of us, plus one tired dog, tried to find spots on a porch built for two, three at the most.

"Ahem!" Darcy announced. "Once upon a time . . . " My eyebrows shot up and I gave Sarah a this-should-be-good look. "Our forefathers brought forth a continent and gave us a star-spangled banner for the land of the free and liberty and justice to all." Darcy's dimpled hand covered her heart solemnly, and she stared at each of us to emphasize the profundity of her words.

Probably because she was the only one not in danger of laughing if she opened her mouth, Claude put her hand firmly on Darcy's head and herded her down the steps as she said "That was great, Darcy. Very insightful."

"Who said that quote, Darcy?" Sarah called out as Judith left with Hester.

"Donald Reagan," Darcy cried back from the darkness.

Sea song and laughter accompanied them all the way home.

CHAPTER 15

SARAH RAN INSIDE to get her line and left Nathan watching me as I bent my head back to follow the sway of the top branches. "All this heat is rare. It's blowing in front of a storm," he said. I turned to him, trying to figure out why he said it like a warning.

"A bad storm? Like a classic nor'easter?" I asked, making fun of myself.

He smiled. "You said it wrong. No, not a bad storm. Just a gale. Like your name. But then you'll really see Maine. This mild stuff is just a hustle. It makes the summer people think they can stand it here and then it smashes them like a prizefighter punch in the face."

"You think it will scare me off?" I couldn't help smiling. He obviously thought he had me pegged.

He shrugged. "Will it?"

"I'm from Nebraska, remember? I've been through a tornado." The door snapped open and Sarah appeared, carrying a bag of flour. "What . . ." is as far as I got.

"A tornado?" she asked.

"Well, a little one. It didn't hurt anybody. Why do you have flour?"

She searched my face before she smiled. "It's my line," she said.

She turned the bag until the glow of the porch light settled on the words on the back. "Just listen—*Harvested from the clean, open earth, beneath the endless, indigo sky, Sackman's wheat tastes of hard work, gentle hands, windy harvest days, and fresh summer rains.*" A playful smile toyed at the corners of her mouth. "Now what frustrated poet ended up writing product descriptions for wheat?"

"And what frustrated poet of a CEO approved that line instead of *whole grain goodness to improve energy, heart health, and mental function?*" Nathan asked.

I laughed and took the flour from Sarah's hand to read the entire paragraph. "It makes me miss home." I found myself telling them about my wheat field, trying to describe the graveyard, the openness, the sense of space. As I spoke, the pine trees seemed to scoot nearer to the house. Even the sky felt tighter, drawn in too close to the ground. I looked up at the low, vaporous clouds. When I finished talking, no one said anything so I mentioned Nathan's comment about a storm coming.

Sarah glanced up. "Probably. He's better at telling than I am. If not sooner, then later. The storms always come eventually."

"How do you say nor'easter?" I asked casually.

I give Sarah credit for not laughing. "I'm not sure anyone who isn't a New Englander should try, really. It would be a bit like me saying howdy."

"We do not say *howdy* in Nebraska!"

"Okay, but they do somewhere and if I said it, it would sound wrong. But if you really want to know, you say it more like noth-EE-stuh, but careful with the middle *r*. You replace it with a th, but don't pronounce it fully. And most importantly you say it like you're referring to an unworthy opponent, irritated and a little bored."

Nathan rolled his eyes at our impromptu lesson. He obviously didn't think an outsider could manage the blessed language of Maine. I was just regretting that I had to share a line with him when Sarah told me that I was next.

"I wrote mine down." I pulled a wrinkled slip of paper from my pocket and tried to ignore Nathan, except for quick glimpses to monitor for any more signs of disdain or ridicule. "It's a Longfellow poem. I just copied one stanza." I cleared my throat.

"Art is long, and Time is fleeting,
    And our hearts, though stout and brave,
Still, like muffled drums, are beating
    Funeral marches to the grave."

I looked up to Sarah and said, "It's the first line that got me. Art is long . . ."

"But the march to the grave?" she asked. "Does it bother you? Is it too morbid?"

In my mind's eye arose the Cowling family cemetery, reposing peacefully in the slanted rays of sun, engulfed in the golden hills. "No. It doesn't upset me—death. Not in the abstract, at least. But that first line seems to say that time is the only thing that really dies. Art is long. All the things we make, create, leave behind, all the works of our soul are long. Only time dies."

"I'll take you to the Smithport cemetery," Nathan said in a husky voice. "You'd like it." His sullen face fell away to something kinder and he spoke. "You have to concentrate on the rest of the poem. It's not about death. It's about living. I like to read it just so I can say 'bivouac of Life'! Now there's a line."

"Which, by the way—what is a bivouac?" I'm glad he pronounced it first so I could ask without slaughtering the word.

"A camp. Like a military camp where you stop and camp for the night but don't have any shelter," he said.

I tried to picture life as a sleeping bag in a field and then turned back to Nathan. "How do you know all that? How did you know the rest of the poem? And the meanings? And all the science things at dinner—about the crabs? How do you remember?"

Nathan shrugged grumpily, the same way Cleo does when someone compliments her appearance, and changed the subject. "I guess it's my turn." He tugged on his shoelace and never pulled out a piece of paper or a book. He just spoke. "Another Longfellow. Just a few words. 'Is it changed, or am I changed?' "

"I can't get the context," Sarah said.

"You know this one, Sarah. Think," he commanded.

She grew still, thoughts rolling through her eyes. "No, I can't remember. I can't do it like you can, Nathan."

He breathed out in frustration and continued:

"Is it changed, or am I changed?
    Ah! the oaks are fresh and green,
But the friends with whom I ranged
Through their thickets are estranged
    By the years that intervene."

"Are you asking me, or yourself?" Sarah asked him.

"I wasn't. It's just a line, Sarah." They glared slightly at each other in the quiet. I couldn't keep up with his fast mood changes. Placid to angry, defensive to tender. I just stared at his lips, pushed hard together, and the flare of his nostrils as he refused to move.

Sarah broke the uncomfortable silence. "I think you're asking me if Smithport feels different with my family gone."

"I'm not," he fired back with scorn in his voice.

"Then are you asking me what it will feel like when you come back?" Her words were coaxing and gentle, but his eyebrows furrowed.

"I'm not going anywhere," he insisted.

"Am I missing something?" I asked.

"No," Sarah answered in a grim tone, "I think I caught you up on everything you need to know."

Nathan's gaze broke as his head jerked to me, and then back to Sarah. "You told her?" he asked. "Everything?"

"Most of what I knew. She filled me in on the rest," Sarah answered. I balked at a tiny stress laid on the word "most." Nathan looked at me as my face went hot with confusion.

"So where has your mother been?" he asked me, not hiding the resentment in his voice.

"Nathan, don't." Sarah's words were calm but sharp.

I met his stare, not allowing the trembling in my body to make its way out to my skin. "She's been in Nebraska," I said icily.

"Is she coming back?" Nathan asked, but what his voice really said was *She'd better not come back.*

My eyes narrowed, but Sarah said, "Good night, Nathan," before I could reply. He met her stony expression and didn't speak another word except for a mumbled good night. He jumped the rail of the porch, and the rocks crunched under his heavy footsteps as he walked away. I looked to Sarah but she only sighed and said, "We're all protective of something."

"You?" I asked, while still looking into the darkness. "Is he protective of you?"

"He doesn't need to be. He's mad that Claire hurt me. He just forgets that I hurt her worse." The bald self-loathing in her voice pacified me.

"I don't know if I'd say worse."

"Then what would you say?" She turned to me like my response mattered very much to her.

The answer seemed to fall out of the still air. "I think you hurt her deeper . . . but she hurt you longer."

Sarah's lips parted as she softly repeated the words to herself. She looked up to me, something like hope resting on her face. "He doesn't mean to take it out on you. If Nathan didn't like you he wouldn't have come back for lines tonight. I know he sounds gruff sometimes, but he is just trying to decipher the world."

I frowned in doubt. "Shouldn't that be easy for someone as smart as he is?"

"On the contrary. I think that makes it much worse," she said without further explanation.

CHAPTER 16

UNBEKNOWNST TO ME, while I mulled over my strange new position between Sarah's happiness, my mother's resentment, and Nathan's shallowly concealed belligerence, the timeless forces of nature were sweeping a hot dry wind over the Saharan desert onto the cool waves of the Atlantic Ocean. Unconcerned with my adventures with Sarah and bike rides into town with Claude to meet her friends, and increasing fascination with nightly lines, a small cloud formed and funneled higher and wider, hitchhiking onto the warm currents of the jet stream. For four days it arched its back and spun up the Atlantic coast, giving me time to glean little treasures of knowledge about the new world I found myself immersed in. Like the fact that Nathan ran his own landscaping business, paying for online college courses and helping Judith tie up financial loose ends, since her salary as an elementary school receptionist only went so far. Like the fact that Claude captained her school's cheer squad of six girls and held Maine state records in the Math Bowl. Like the fact that Sarah pronounced "perhaps" and "stationary" just like my mother. Or, most surprisingly, the fact that no matter how often Nathan pierced me with a critical eye or froze me with his silence, it was the tense, quiet evenings on the porch that I looked forward to the most. Whenever he forgot to be defensive, whenever he dropped his sullen guard, a gentle intelligence infused everything he said. And when he recited the lines, a queer thing happened along my spine. I could feel, but not feel, fingertips stepping up my back. It was a ghostly sensation that left goose bumps pricking up my arm and made it hard to gather any volume when it was my turn to speak.

By my sixth day in Smithport, the tropical storm hit the cold water streaming down from the frozen lands of Canada and the growling, African winds shrieked and disbanded as the wet rain began its descent. One week after my arrival, Sarah closed and locked the black shutters of Shelter Cove (I didn't know that shutters actually functioned. In Nebraska they are only for decoration) and turned on the weather radio. Nathan's predicted storm straggled from the ocean, panting and gusting and, above all, crying a torrential rain. Just when I thought it was petering out after a long, bleak day, the reinforcements arrived and I tasted—in a small, bitter bite—the dark undercurrent of the sea.

The drone of the beating rain and the close, huddled feel of the shuttered house didn't remind me of cozy Nebraska storms where I curled up by the sliding glass doors and watched the electric lightning show. I felt imprisoned in Shelter Cove, the air wet and heavy and smelling particularly old after a day without open windows. I had already called my dad and Cleo. My mother listened on the line while I spoke with my dad. I could hear the tinny echo of two phones in one house, and the shuffle of her breathing while she held the phone against her shoulder, eavesdropping. Toward the end of our conversation she broke in with mundane questions about weather and the clothes I packed and, of course, when I would come home. I told her I would check flights. I just didn't tell her that I wasn't considering any flights in the very near future. She refused to contribute to any discussions that involved Sarah or Shelter Cove. But still, she was listening. It was a start.

Sarah's dinner of stew and homemade bread dispelled some of the day's dreariness, but by eight o'clock that night I was doing what I hadn't done since arriving—flipping from one mindless television show to the next. It bothered me how disappointed I was that lines were rained out. Without that to look forward to, I found myself getting ready to excuse myself for bed when a thunderclap slapped the house so hard that it shuddered. Before the walls stopped shaking, the lights popped off along with the television, followed by the eerie stillness as all electronics shut down. No hums, no buzzes, no fans—just the beating rain.

"Hold on, Jennifer. I'll grab lights." Sarah's voice came from behind me. I looked around, trying to find a break in the darkness. Some lighter gray shone around the edges of the windows, but that was all. I heard a drawer slide open and the sound of a hand groping blindly through the contents while Charlie's toenails clicked on the floor as he circled Sarah.

"I got it. Don't worry," Sarah called and a ring of light appeared, bobbing in front of her. "You okay?" she asked, aiming the light at my feet and not my face. The wind howled and pulled the rain sideways, making it sound like someone slopped a bucket of water against the window.

"Is it getting worse?" I asked.

"Sounds like it. And my generator broke last winter. I haven't had Nathan fix it yet, which is brilliant, I know. I think we are down to a few flashlights and candles tonight. We could have some fun with it, though. Do you know any ghost stories?"

"I hate ghost stories," I told her. "Unless they are sweet and romantic like a ghost leaving a note for his true love or something. But please do not mention chainsaws or bodies." I shivered, too scared by my own choice of images to continue.

"Deal. Sweet and fluffy. No bodies. I can do that." Sarah set the flashlight on the table, letting the circles of light shimmer on the walls. "Let me light some emergency candles in case these batteries give out and I'll think of something . . ." Sarah hopped off the couch and pulled out a lighter and some metal cans from a drawer.

I took a nervous breath before saying, "There is a story I've been wanting to hear." Sarah tipped her chin in curiosity and waited. My words wobbled coming out of my mouth. "I was actually wondering about your trip to South Africa."

"Really?" she asked in surprise.

"Yes. I just wondered, whatever happened to John? The one you went to tell when you found out Grandma died."

Sarah sat down on the sofa, pushing Chester to the side.

"Things didn't work out," she said with a shrug.

"Oh." Then mustering more courage, "You usually have more to say than that."

She studied me, the candlelight picking up green and blue waves in her eyes. "Usually I do. But that is a storybook that we shouldn't get off the shelf. Let's just say some of them don't end happily ever after."

"I know that, obviously, but . . ." I stopped abruptly when someone pounded on the door. Charlie jumped up from his spot under the armchair and raced across the room.

"Sarah?" Nathan's voice called from the downpour.

"Nathan?" she cried as she jumped up. "Come in, what are . . ."

The door opened, his saturated outline illuminated as a bright flare of lightning lit the sky. "Everything okay?" he asked as he scanned the dim room. His eyes stopped on me, and he gave me an unfathomable look as he blinked water off his eyelashes.

"We're fine," Sarah answered, a puzzled look mingling with

concern as she watched him dripping. "What are you doing out in this? Jennifer, get him a towel."

I rushed into her bathroom, listening intently while he explained how he had run over to a summer home to try to save some expensive bushes he'd planted the week before. Apparently someone had stopped him in town and told him that a boat had radioed in a report of a girl outside on the cove. I hurried back into the room, extinguishing one candle as the towel flapped behind me. I handed it to him, and he rubbed his face halfheartedly as he kept talking. "I called Judith, she said all the girls are accounted for at home, so I thought maybe. . . . I just wanted to check." His eyes flicked almost angrily to me.

"You thought Sarah would let me out in that?" I joked, trying to lighten his mood.

He shrugged in annoyance, but when he looked back up, his mouth raised minutely on one side.

"Maybe they saw wrong. Or had the wrong spot," Sarah guessed.

"Not Harvey," Nathan argued. "He knows this cove like his backyard."

"So do we have a genuine ghost?" I asked, smiling.

Nathan's face grew grave again. "I'd better go check. Just to be sure no one else is out there. Will you call Judith again and make sure they all stay inside?"

"Of course. But the phones are out. I hope she has her cell on." Sarah started walking to her purse as Nathan headed for the back door in the kitchen.

"I'll go with you," I cried, ignoring the way they both froze and stared at me in disbelief.

"No, I don't think so." Nathan's brisk words dismissed the idea.

"Jennifer, he can handle it. You stay here," Sarah said. I walked past both of them and grasped the door handle.

Nathan followed me and grabbed my hand off the knob, dropping it fast like it burned him. "I've got it. I'm sure there's no one out there."

In defiance I reached up and opened the door, which let in the battering rain, and gave him my best imitation of Cleo's glower before I dodged into the storm. I heard Sarah call after me again, so I sped up. For reasons unknown to me, I wanted to race to the cove with him, not in spite of the weather, but because of it. The driving rain hit so cold and fast that I felt as electrified as the flashing sky. Nathan caught up easily and ordered me to go back, but I shook my head stubbornly. I followed the shaking beam of his flashlight to the ridge where the lower beach comes into view.

He swept the light across the sand where it caught the shocking picture of a woman standing at the water's edge. For a moment my joke about a ghost didn't seem very funny anymore. She wore a white dress and her pale skin stood out in strange relief against the boiling, black ocean. And since I was evidently seeing ghosts, it makes sense that I nearly believed in Greek gods the moment I saw that water. Only divine beings could wage such a war. The waves stood up, their chests thrust out, roaring as they charged the shore, slamming the rocks and scraping the broken shells from the ground and dragging them back to the sea. Wind fought tide. Land fought ocean. As the waves crested, the gale shoved them backward, breaking the water, while lightning broke the sky. And in the middle of it all, the tiny woman stood, her arms raised toward the black clouds.

"Come on," Nathan yelled and gave my arm a nudge as he ran toward her. "Little!" he called, as if he were saying her name. "Little!" I pulled myself out of my reverie and forced myself to follow. In the flashlight's beam I saw that it wasn't a white dress she wore, but a nightgown, shamefully sheer in its wetness. And as the wind whipped her white hair, I realized that it wasn't a girl, but an old woman. She turned her wrinkled face on me, and her expression went from anger to interest.

Nathan handed me the slippery flashlight as he took her arm. "Follow me. We're taking her home. It isn't far." I wanted to ask what she was doing outside, but not in front of her. I trained the flashlight on the uneven ground and listened to Nathan's growling voice remonstrating her like a child. Her defensive body language and fierce scowl made it clear that only her need to grasp his arm kept her from smacking Nathan. When I blinked enough to clear the thick rain from my eyes I noticed her sneak a meaningful look at me, but I didn't try to speak above the noise of the storm. Nathan led us across the cove, down another path through the trees until a small, shingled house came into view.

Through the lit windows I could see a kitchen, gleaming yellow against the dark night. Nathan opened the back door, steered the woman inside first and then stepped aside for me. Once in the bright, cramped room we all looked at each other, half drowned and panting. "Jennifer," Nathan said quietly, "this is Little."

CHAPTER 17

I GAPED AT the sopping woman, struggling to make her name fit. She leered at me with a strange grin and I shook my head, trying to settle my thoughts.

Nathan was punching numbers into his phone and finally looked up in frustration. "No service. I need to go tell Sarah you're all right before she goes running out in this. And there are still lights here, so you might as well enjoy the electricity for a bit." He threw a speedy glance at Little and then turned away, blushing. "Besides, maybe you could help her clean up before I get back." I nodded, largely because I was too shocked to argue.

"I'll grab a towel." Nathan exited the room, but reappeared quickly and dropped a blue towel into her hands. He gave me a quick once-over, looked back at Little, and sighed as if he didn't trust God himself to keep us out of trouble. And then, reluctantly, he left.

Little draped the towel around her shoulders and stared at the tiny yellow kitchen as if to remember where she was. Her pale blue eyes grabbed mine—that is the only way to describe it—and held them hostage.

"There's a robe on the back of the bathroom door. No need to drip." Her voice broke the spell and I nodded awkwardly, realizing that I was shivering. I had no idea where the bathroom was, but the house was so tiny I knew it wouldn't take long to find. I left her as she lowered herself into a kitchen chair, slowly rubbing the water off her arms. I stepped from the kitchen to the living room and saw only two doors. The first one I opened was the bathroom covered in peach tiles and seashell wallpaper. On the door hung a thin, pink robe and I slipped it on, wondering how long Nathan wanted me to sit with her.

The lady's eyes tracked me as I shuffled back to the kitchen, made me hold my breath when she stared. "You Hazel's granddaughter?" she barked. I nodded again, scared stiff. "Claire's girl?"

"Yes." I almost said, "yes, ma'am," but I'd never used that term in my life and the *ma'am* stuck like a bone in my throat.

"You turned out pretty. You're all drowned right now, but I can still tell."

"Thank you," I murmured, lowering myself into the chair farthest from her.

"Not as pretty as me, but that's a rare curse, anyhow," she mumbled. "My name is Little. Little Fairborn."

"It's nice to meet you." The lights flickered and I jumped, looking up at the ceiling. The sunny colors of the walls and cabinets clashed strangely with the howling storm.

Little took the towel from her shoulders and started to mop her withered legs. I diverted my eyes so swiftly that it hurt my head. Her thin white housedress clung to her skin, her ancient underclothes comically apparent. I heard her laugh—another bark—and I forgot not to look.

"That ain't nothing you haven't seen!" she said with no trace of embarrassment. "Ain't nothing a lot o' people haven't seen." The color boiled up in my face and my throat constricted tightly. I could hear the water hitting the floor as it puddled around her chair.

"But I got something that not everyone has seen. I know you can keep a secret. There's no one in your family who wouldn't be born knowing how to keep a secret."

I hadn't begun to decipher what she meant when she undid the top buttons of her housedress. I skidded back in my chair, making a jarring, scraping sound as I stood. Whatever secret scar or wound or outrageous birthmark she had under her dress, I felt no need to see. Storm or not, there was only so much I could take.

Before I could form my excuse for good-bye, her deep voice boomed out in command. "Settle yourself! This ain't no circus sideshow."

I froze, my teeth chattering wildly. I could not disobey a direct order from an old woman.

She stood on tottering legs and turned her back to me, letting the dress dip just below her shoulders. "Eh?" she asked in a tone of pride. I pulled my eyes up at a snail's pace, trying not to focus my eyes until I knew what was in front of me. I looked at the pink skin of her back, surprised how soft it looked compared to the leathery wrinkles of her face. Just in the middle of her shoulder blades was a faded black tattoo that I couldn't make out. She tugged her shoulders forward under her chin, pulling her loose skin tighter.

I gasped. "Wings!"

"That's right." She crowed as she straightened her house-dress and took her seat again. "Wings. Well, used to be wings. Mostly just saggy feathers now. Been there for more than sixty years. Jus' in case I need a little extra lift gettin' to heaven. Now you have your own secret. Nathan don't know. Your aunt don't know. Your mother don't know. Jus' you and me know. Makes you a bit special, don't it? I guess I decided you're special so you must be." Her wispy white hair was drying slowly, making a fine cloud above her pink scalp, and hanging in a thin tail down her neck. She wrapped the towel around her shoulders and stared at me, waiting.

"If no one else knows, why me?" I asked.

Instead of answering, Little stood up. "I'm gettin' a dry dress," she announced. She left the room and raised her voice so I could still hear her. "One, you go outside in storms. I like that in a girl. Two, you looked so scared I couldn't help myself, and three . . ." Her head appeared in the doorway. "Why we always count things in threes?"

I finally smiled and shook my head to show I had no idea.

"Well, anyway, three is that I like the way you look. You got somethin' of your mama and Sarah mixed together. Like nature finally balanced those two." Little came back in, her clothes mercifully opaque once more.

"Why did you get a tattoo?" I asked as she sat down.

" 'Cause no one else did and I needed something drastic. Back then girls didn't get tattoos. I was different. I was different like your mama. But I didn't stay gone."

"How is my mother different?" I asked. Of anyone in the world, anyone at all, that I could have chosen to have an air of mystery about them, my mother would have been solidly, dead last. Other than not getting along with my aunt, there was not one thing about her that seemed out of the ordinary.

"She left. Nobody leaves. Well, everybody leaves, but she

stayed gone. Burned her bridges flat! She was one of the toughest little girls I ever saw. Took fate in her own scrawny hands. You'll figure that out, though." Little held me with her blue eyes, gripping tightly, but caressing some part of the inside of me as if she knew I would need the comfort. "But tougher don't mean better. It just means tougher. I didn't learn that soon enough."

"Is your name really Little?" My tongue slowly unglued, and that is the question that popped out.

"If it's what you let people call you, it's your name."

"But what is your real name?" I persisted.

Thunder cracked violently outside, and I moaned when the house shook and the lights wavered. Little's mouth opened into a half-crazed smile of glee and she clapped her hands together. "Now that's more like it!" she cried. "I hate a half-hearted storm. Show us what you've got!" she called up as if she could see through the roof to the churning sky. She caught sight of me in her pink robe and her thoughts came back inside the kitchen, which was fine with me because I, unlike she, did not want the house to blow down on top of us. "What are you doing here?" she asked me. "Your mama coming back?" At first I thought she had dementia and couldn't remember why I was in her kitchen. Then I realized she meant Smithport, not her house.

"I found out about Sarah last month. I came to meet her. My mother's not coming. Just me."

Little looked at me long and hard and then said, "My brother named me Little. My mother named me Lillian. She called me Lil. When Joe was three, he thought she was saying 'Little,' and that was that."

"Did that bother you? You never changed it back?"

"No. No." Recollections ran through her smoky blue-gray eyes. " 'Little' fit me fine. It seemed right somehow. Mostly because there is nothing little about me. So," she said loudly, changing the subject, "do you have a love story?"

"Me?" I wasn't sure what she was talking about, but I knew I was growing increasingly scared and intrigued by every word she said. "What do you mean?"

She gave me a pitying, disgusted look as if she were dealing with a very simple person. "A love story. No matter what anyone says the best loves belong to the young. By the time I was your age, I had the start of a love story that could rival anyone. But I tell no one. No one except those that can give me a love story first. It's a trade. But mine is always better."

"I . . . I . . . don't have one," I said, and for the first time I felt ashamed of my boring, routine life. I wished I could have gone toe-to-toe with that old woman, put her love story to shame, whatever it might be, but all I had was a lifelong determination not to get stuck in a sappy love story.

Little dismissed me with a glance, and I flinched. "Then come back when you have one, and I'll tell you mine." She nursed a cup of water in her hand, peering into it like it would show her the past in its depths. A shiver racked my shoulders and shot down my spine but it wasn't the temperature, it was the disappointment of having nothing to offer.

The front door opened, and every loose object in the kitchen rattled as the wind made a frantic dash through the room. Nathan shut it firmly behind him and wiped the water from his dripping hair as I stood up gratefully. "It's letting up. My house lost power, but that doesn't take much. It's still standing, at least. I'll take you home now." He turned to Little and said, "I hope you didn't scare her."

"Hah!" she barked. "She's tougher than she looks. She's a Dyer. How's your mama, Nathan? Are the girls all right?"

"Grumbling about the storm like all good New England women. Except Claude. She's ranting and raving. She lost her internet and her phone." Little waved her hand as if the mention of the internet offended her and wasn't worth a reply. I slipped off her robe, thankful that my T-shirt was thick and dark blue, and headed for the door.

"I'm all here, Jennifer." Little's low voice stopped me as I reached for the handle. I flinched and turned back to her at the sound of my name. "Some people think that all old people go soft in the head but I'm not old. Only my skin got old and I can't help that. Ugly, I know, but you should have seen . . . Boy, tell her that she should have seen me seventy years ago." She continued without pause so she didn't really expect him to say anything, which was fitting, considering. "I've got stories for you and when you're ready, I'll be here." She stroked the kitchen table, staring me down for a moment, and then turned back to her water. "Take her home, boy. I'll be fine."

"No more walks tonight. I mean it," Nathan ordered, and started to open an umbrella.

"What's the point," I asked, looking from the umbrella to my wet clothes. "Let's just go. Bye, Little."

She gave me a slow nod, her liquid blue eyes watering between folds of loose skin, but still lit with some unrelenting flame. The door opened and I sprinted out after Nathan, trying to navigate the slick, rocky ground with my eyes squinted against the rain. We jogged the long stretch to Sarah's house without speaking. Nathan beat me to the front porch and Sarah opened the door, looking relieved. "All accounted for?" she asked us as we stepped in.

"All's well," Nathan said. "Little was just taking a stroll."

Sarah handed us towels and smiled. "So you met Little?"

I rubbed my hair a moment longer before answering slowly, "Yes."

"Well," she said with high arched eyebrows, "I've been wondering how I should introduce you. I knew she'd want to meet you."

"She seemed to know me already," I answered under my breath.

"Everyone here knows everyone. And everyone certainly knows Little. She's a town legend. In fact . . ." she paused and looked to Nathan, "should we show her?"

"I'd better go help with Darcy and Hester. You go ahead." He handed her the towel and waved good-bye to me before stepping outside into the stormy night.

I looked back to Sarah to find her studying my dripping clothes. "Go clean up," she instructed. "I've got something to show you."

CHAPTER 18

I GRABBED THE flashlight and followed its wobbly glow up the creaking stairs and narrow hallway to my bathroom. With full authority I can declare that showering by flashlight is a unique experience. I set the light on the counter, the beam focused in a wide circle on the ceiling that barely lit my body as I shampooed the cold rain out of my hair. I watched the foamy white bubbles slide down my stomach, catching tiny pieces of light in their iridescent domes. Even the noise of the running water could not compete with the torrential rain hitting the roof above my head or the thunder that shook the walls. I finished in less than five minutes, threw on warm sweats, and hurried downstairs.

Sarah looked up from the couch, where she sat with her laptop cradled on her legs.

"I thought the internet was out," I said.

"I'm not on the the internet. I can't show you on the television because the power is still out, but I have some battery life in the laptop." I sat down next to her and she hit the play button.

A black-and-white movie came on to the screen. "Little comes in right here," Sarah said, pointing to a girl with elaborately curled hair.

"That's Little? The Little I met tonight?"

"Oh, trust me, dear, there is only one. Pretty, don't you think?" Sarah asked.

"Very, but . . . Little was a movie star?" I remembered the sagging tattoo.

"What else *could* she be with a name like Lillian Fairborn? This was her first movie. Nineteen forty-two. Just a few years after she ran away."

"She ran away from Smithport?"

"When she was only seventeen. Just like your mom. Left a Smither and came home an actress. After being gone for ten years she just reappeared in town one day and never went back to Hollywood. She's been at Pilgrim's Point ever since. That's the name of her house."

"So what has she been doing all that time?"

Sarah laughed. "Stomping around town and telling us all off is what. And we've loved every minute of it. We still get together every August and show one of her movies in the theater. We call it Little Day." We watched the movie until the battery died and then went to bed late.

By the time I pulled myself out of a fitful sleep the next day the rain had stopped, leaving a wet, gray sky filtering the weak rays of late morning sunlight. I hopped downstairs, grateful to find the dreaded black shutters open and the view of the washed world unobstructed once more. The only evidence of the storm was the branches scattered across the ground.

"Quite the night?" Sarah asked as she handed me a bagel. "It has a bit of a dreamlike quality for me today."

"Agreed," I said, trying to talk around my bite. "I dreamt about the movie, by the way. My entire dream was black and white."

Sarah stared at me too long, and a small smile crawled across her face. "You cannot possibly know how nice it is to wake up and have someone sit at this table and tell me about a dream. I haven't had morning company in . . . I don't know if I've ever had it." She paused while I gave her a shy grin. "I get my students at school and the Beckers visiting and Nathan in the evenings, but no one ever shares my mornings." To assuage my embarrassment, Sarah pointed to Charlie who was flopped by the back door. "Except that fool dog." He cocked his ear and rolled his eyes happily in her direction.

At that moment the doorbell rang and Charlie's limp body popped up like a marionette with its strings pulled tight and bolted for the door.

"You expecting anyone?" Sarah asked as I followed her out of the kitchen.

"Not a soul."

Sarah opened the door and there stood Little, enveloped in a housedress and wearing clunky walking shoes with white socks poking out the top.

"Little!" Sarah exclaimed in surprise.

Little curled her lip in displeasure and asked in a lifeless voice, "Can Jennifer play?"

My jaw dropped in open surprise, but Sarah laughed her best laugh, loud and light and contagious. "I don't know if she wants to play with an old grouch like you."

I threw Sarah a quick, panicked look, but she was too tickled to notice or care.

"Well?" Little demanded, looking at me.

"What do you want to do?" I choked out.

"Walk into town. Make fun of the fishermen." She gave Charlie the evil eye and he stopped mid-jump, rolled onto his back, and pulled his mouth into an ingratiating grin.

"Good grief, Little, I wouldn't miss that for anything," Sarah said. "You'd better let me tag along. Are you in, Jennifer?"

"Sure," I answered, surprised that Little could make a mile walk. I eyed her bony ankles with serious reservations.

"Well, we can't get there standing here," Little barked, and Sarah and I hustled to locate our shoes. Unfortunately, mine were still cold and damp, but I tried to ignore that.

"So you guys like being ordered around?" I whispered to Sarah as I tied my laces.

"Not many people can order around a Smither. It's nice to see someone try," Sarah answered under her breath.

"Just cause I can't hear ya don't mean my eyes are broken. I see your cussed lips moving. I'm not an idiot," Little growled.

Sarah looked up at me, her eyes twinkling. "Let's go."

Little turned and began a surprisingly brisk shuffle up the road, not looking like she cared if we followed or not. Charlie slinked behind her, his rear end constantly dipping close to the road as he tried to figure out how to walk and look submissive at the same time. Some kind of power emanated from the small woman that even the dog could sense. I kept my eyes on her thin, veined legs, sticking out from her housedress.

Sarah made several attempts at conversation (*"Look at the wild-flowers, Little. Aren't they pretty? . . . So you didn't lose your power last night? . . . Jennifer grew up in Nebraska. . . ."*), and to Sarah's great amusement, Little fended off every attack (*"Look like they always looked. . . . Didn't have power at all when I was little. . . . Never heard of it.*"). It was easy to see that it was a game they played. The more caustic the ancient woman got, the giddier her audience became.

Before we got to the town, a horn beeped behind us. We all turned to see Nathan's dented, white truck bumping down the road. He pulled up beside us and called through the passenger window. "Little, I always give a pretty girl a ride. How 'bout it?" I stared in amazement as he flashed her a charming smile untainted by his usual sullenness.

"You idiot, boy! Honk your horn at me like that and I could fall down dead. Would you wanna die in the middle of the street? You think that's fittin'?"

Nathan raised his hand in surrender. "Don't want to kill you. Just want to give you a ride." His laughing eyes slid to my face, but never met my gaze.

"Why? 'Cause I'm old?" Her blue eyes flamed dangerously.

"No. 'Cause you're pretty. Like I said." He leaned over and popped the passenger door open, making it swing on its squeaky hinges.

The corners of her mouth put up a valiant fight against a smile. "Idiot," she grumbled as she walked toward the truck. Sarah gave her a hand up into the cab.

"Jennifer and I will take the bed," Sarah called as she hurried to the tailgate. She dumped Charlie into the back with an unceremonious thud and then, in a fluid leap, swung herself up. I followed her, slower and clumsier.

"Is this legal?" I scanned the rickety vehicle.

"Jed won't care. It's just a mile and no traffic."

"Jed?"

"Our sheriff. Don't you love it—a sheriff named Jed? I try to work his name into casual conversation whenever possible because it does my heart good to say Sheriff Jed." I laughed as the truck gathered speed and rocked us in the fresh, windy air. Moments later Nathan parked on the main street close to the docks to let us out.

"Where are you headed?" I asked him.

"Not far. I'm power-washing a fence today. I'll stain it tomorrow."

"Oh. I'm apparently taking an old woman to make fun of fishermen."

Nathan nodded and grinned. "Have fun," he said.

"Oh, loads and loads, I'm sure." I paused and then asked, "Can I see what you're doing?"

I don't know where the idea came from. Furthermore, I don't know where I got the courage to ask. Maybe two people can't rescue an old woman from an ocean storm and not feel like some of the barriers are swept away.

"You mean come with me?" He said it like I'd suggested something insane.

Sarah overheard and jumped in. "I can take Little to breakfast at the Sturgeon. Jennifer should get away from us old folks for an hour."

"Dirty, boring work," Nathan said, peering at me like I was a subject under a microscope—mysterious and maybe a little dangerous. "Suit yourself. Whatever floats your boat." He grabbed a machine that resembled a canister vacuum cleaner and started down the street without another word. I threw one hesitant look at Sarah, trying to decide if I really wanted to go. Nathan was several yards ahead of me and gaining speed so I swallowed once and trotted after him, feeling like Charlie following Little. For a fleeting moment I thought of confronting him with a loud, "What's your problem," but the compulsion burned hot and brief, dying before it reached my lips.

Nathan surprised me when he broke the silence and said, "Did you get to see Little in a movie last night?"

I cleared my throat. "Yeah, part of one." Little's face in the storm flashed in my mind. "Nathan, when we found her in the storm . . . she wasn't trying to . . . you know . . . hurt herself?"

"Suicide?" he scoffed as he stopped in front of a small, yellow house.

"I don't know." The mocking in his voice made me timid.

His face softened. "Truth is no one knows why she does that stuff. We're all used to it by now. A little crazy, maybe."

"I don't think so. She seems clearheaded to me."

"Okay, not clinically crazy. Just conventionally crazy."

"I think that's a contradiction. I don't think you can be conventionally crazy."

"Well, what's your guess then?" He looked up from where he knelt with a garden hose with a smudge of dirt beneath one eye. I stared too long before answering.

"I'll just ask her."

That made him laugh as he stood up and turned the rusty spigot. "That's original." I opened my mouth to defend myself when he held up a hand and motioned me to stand back. "Don't let the water hit you. It will take skin off. Better back up a little more." He hit a button and the machine jumped to life. A sharp line of water hit the ground, making mud fly. Nathan pointed the sprayer at the rickety fence, and wherever the stream hit, the scaly lime and gray surface wood dissolved, revealing a richer brown.

"Can I try?" I asked, loud enough to hear over the power washer.

"Why would you want to?" he asked.

I shrugged. "For fun."

From the way he eyed me, he probably classified me as the same kind of crazy as Little. "If you must. Don't keep it on any one spot for too long. Keep it moving. Keep it even. Here's the off button if you panic."

"I'm not going to panic." I grabbed it from his hand and mimicked his slow movement. It was oddly soothing, the easy change of old to new, rotten to healthy. Neither of us spoke for several minutes while I worked.

"Not too bad. For a farm girl," he qualified.

Keeping my serene expression, I answered, "You can be a real jerk. Even for a lawn boy."

The hose shuddered in my hand before coming to a limp rest as he shut off the machine. "Do you always say everything that crosses your mind?"

"Not even close." *If I said everything you would know I think you're rude, reclusive, and scared to death of exposing your real feelings.* "Why? Do you think I talk too much?"

His poker face faltered. "Not too much as in *quantity*. You just don't, I don't know. You don't play the game." He leaned against the wet fence, his eyes trained on my face.

"What game? Another Smithport thing?"

His mouth lifted into a smile. "No, a human thing. Everyone else plays the game. Hides the bad stuff, the stupid stuff, the sad stuff. You are . . . you just radiate . . ."

"What?" I met his stare, fascinated that he saw anything other than utter ordinariness in me. "I radiate bad, stupid stuff?" I laughed in spite of myself.

"No." He grinned. "You just say it like it is, is all."

"Huh," I said, pursing my lips and assessing the comment. I made a special effort to hide the pleasure unfurling in my chest.

Nathan's smile grew. "That's all you're going to say?"

"Yup."

"I guess there is some Smither in you." He took the handle

from my grasp with gentle hands and turned the machine back on. I'm thankful he didn't turn around and catch the irrepressible smile spreading across my face when I touched the spot where our fingers met.

CHAPTER 19

ONLY MY CURIOSITY to see Little in full swing amongst the townspeople persuaded me to finally leave. I told Nathan good-bye and headed for the docks. I had gone several blocks when someone called my name from behind. I knew Nathan's voice instantly. I turned to see him jogging toward me.

"What's wrong?"

"Nothing." He slowed down as he drew level with me. "I just felt like coming. I'll finish up later."

"Whatever floats your boat." I managed to keep my voice casual. Maybe I am too vulnerable to suggestion, but for the first time in my life I felt like a girl who would say anything that crossed her mind. "Last night, did you really think it was me outside?" I asked him.

He ducked his head and looked away from me. "I hoped not."

"Why would I do that?"

He shrugged. "I thought you might not know how dangerous it is, not being used to the ocean. I thought you might be curious."

"I'm sure most people seem stupid compared to you, but I'm really not *that* stupid."

"I hate it when people think that." His eyes tightened, but didn't have the closed, untouchable glint that I'd grown accustomed to. "It's like saying everyone is fat to a skinny person. It doesn't work like that. I never thought you were stupid."

"Then what—naïve? No common sense?"

His disgusted face screamed at me to change the subject. "You have plenty of common sense. Maybe ignorance—of the ocean. Maybe naïve. Would that be so bad? Who said you should know everything? It's that whole 'sadder but wiser' theory."

"You think everyone who's wiser is sadder?" I looked at his bare arm, the way the tiny flecks of dirt stuck to the hairs and made him look like he was covered in freckles.

"Probably. That seems to be the consensus," he said. I chose the wrong moment to look up at his face, because our eyes met and there was something naked in his expression. I saw too much. I flushed and turned, trying to look nonchalant. "Just look at Little," he said in a much lighter voice to cover the tension. "She's been around for what? Almost ninety years? And she's about the saddest person I know."

"I do not concur," I said, raising my pointed finger. "She's not sad. She's not even mad. I think she's having more fun than all of us."

"Touché," he conceded.

I cocked my head. "By the way, I've always wondered what *touché* really means."

He retreated back into his sullenness, "*Touch*. Just French for *touch*. From fencing. If the sword touches somewhere vital, the fight is over."

I said "oh" quietly and tried not to stare. "You don't like answering questions do you?"

He huffed in frustration.

"Sorry. That's another question." I could barely contain my curiosity. Something happened in my stomach when the knowledge leaked effortlessly out of him. I could listen to his answers for hours. Before I managed to upset him again, we were back on the sidewalk by the docks.

Sarah stood up from a bench and waved to us. "We just finished breakfast. Little eats slow."

"I chew! You young dolts might want to try that some time," Little snapped. A deep laugh interrupted Sarah's answer. I looked up and saw three old men sitting one bench over. I approached Sarah and Little slowly, keeping an eye on the men who were watching our group. The heavy man wore a weathered hat, the skinniest sported a stringy, white ponytail, and the last clutched a black cane. The one with the ponytail winked at me and I started, but couldn't resist half-smiling back.

"See yuv got a new friend today, Little," the winker said. Little turned away with a *hurumph*. Undeterred, the man tried again. "Ain't ya gonna introduce us?"

"She don't wanna know you," Little shot back.

"Aw, shucks, Little, you can break a man's heart," said the man with the cane, looking like he had anything but a broken heart.

"How ya know? I don't see any men," she spat.

"I'll jus' have to introduce myself," the ponytail man threatened.

His threat worked because Little mumbled, "Jennifer, them's the Jacks."

"Excuse me?" I asked.

"The Jacks," Little repeated louder. Sarah snickered into her hand.

"All named Jack?" I asked.

"Yup. The Jacks," Little said.

"So should I call you all Jack, or do you go by your last names?" I asked. Nathan chuckled behind me.

"Oh, by all means, call them by their last name," Little said with a wicked grin.

"Okay," I looked at Sarah. She dipped her head back down, refusing to help me. No one offered any information so I knew they wanted me to ask. "So what're your last names?"

"Ass!" Little called out in joy. At that the entire party fell into abandoned laughter. Watching the men made me laugh harder than Little's words. Surely, they knew the punch line, but they stomped and shook like it was the first joke ever told.

Nathan spoke up from behind me while the rest kept laughing, "That's Russ with the long hair. Pete has the cane. And Glenn has the hat."

"So where are you from, sugar?" Russ asked me.

"Nebraska."

To my surprise, that made the Jacks laugh almost as hard as Little's comments.

"*Nebraska?* What do you wanna live in a place like that for?"

"No, Nebraska's nice," I squeaked.

They chuckled and the man with the cane scrunched up his face. "You boys ever seen Nebraska? What ya got there? Cows and . . . anything 'sides cows?"

"I've never been nowhere I couldn't sail the missus," the heavyset Jack answered.

"Who?" I asked.

"Glenn's married to his boat. Calls her *The Missus*," Russ answered.

"Don't mention it to the boat. It embarrasses the *hull* out of her," his friend added, pointing his cane down at the docks.

"You bloody fools. You wish your wives loved you like ma

boat loves me! At least I can still turn *The Missus* on," Glenn said with a triumphant flush.

"Sick old pirates!" Little squawked. "You talk like that in front of the girls?" She turned to me. "Just ignore the dirty old men. They spend all their time trying to figure out who's the best fisher, the best cusser, the worst husband, the stupidest, the smelliest, the—"

"You forgot one," Russ interrupted with a devilish grin. "Who's the best kisser? Pete there is the worst fisher, Glenn is by far the smelliest, but we don't know who's the best kisser. You wanna help us figguh it out, Little?"

"I suggest you grab a donkey's backside and give it a good try. You probably need to test it on your own species," Little growled.

The three Jacks let out a simultaneous hoot. "Someday, Little, you'll realize you are a mere mortal like the rest of us. Can't be young and beautiful forever." Pete smiled broadly, spreading his hands.

"I might be old and ugly now, but you started that way, Jack. I got my pride."

Russ let out another howl of approval and said, "He is ugly, ain't he?"

Glenn was the quietest of the three. He sat relishing his punch line about his boat, a smug smile on his heavy, jowled face. "Don't you go and make Hank's grandgirl all bitter, now," he cautioned with a grim set to his jaw.

"Well, I will if I let her see what boys turn into. Good riddance." Little stood and took my arm with surprising strength. I managed to wave before she tugged me away, the Jacks' jovial voices fading as we left.

Sarah followed, shaking her head. "You were in rare form today, Little."

"Keeps me young," she said in satisfaction. "I'd a died a long time ago if those stupid Jacks didn't irritate me so much." I turned around to see Nathan, but he was still standing with the Jacks, his back to me.

"They're not so bad, Little," I said with an amused smile.

"Hrmmp!" she grumped as she marched arm in arm with me. "Well, not as bad as what you got to work with. If I had to fall in love with one of the pansies running around today I'd join a convent. They're rotten from the start, most of them."

Nathan's scarred face and squinting eyes flashed through my mind. "They're not all hopeless."

"Hrmmp!"

"So were they better when you were young, Little?" Sarah asked.

"Whatever gave you a brainless idea like that? You think the world has changed any?"

"You just said . . ." Sarah began.

"I said nothing. There was one that was better. Only one."

CHAPTER 20

ON THE WALK home Charlie entertained me by retrieving small rocks that I kicked off the road until my cell phone rang. I flipped it open and saw my dad's number.

"Hello?"

"Jennifer, it's Dad. How are things going?"

"Things are great. Yesterday was crazy. Don't try to guess who I met last night, because you won't get it right. I met a movie star." Little snorted. "And I made it through my first Smithport storm. The power went out." I filled him in as I walked.

"Your dad?" Sarah mouthed. I nodded.

"Hey, Jennifer, I'm glad you're having fun." He didn't sound glad. His words came out thin and strained. I turned my head toward the trees and slowed down, letting Sarah and Little pull ahead of me. "I wanted to talk to you about your plans," he continued. He cleared his throat and his voice dropped. "I think you should pick a flight home now."

My feet hit a patch of quicksand. I knew from the sinking sensation and the way I couldn't take my next step. I glanced down, surprised to see the asphalt solid beneath my shoes. Charlie dropped a small rock at my foot and looked up eagerly. "Oh," I whispered, turning completely away from Sarah so she couldn't see my face.

"I know that you're having fun. I'm sure you could do it again sometime. But you have to consider your mother's feelings. I'm worried we are pushing her too far."

"Oh."

"Besides that, we miss you around here. Cleo stops by just to keep us company."

"Uh-huh."

"Jennifer?"

"Uh-huh?"

"Are you going to say anything?" A dry heat rushed up my throat and stung my eyes. If I spoke, my voice would crack. I made as casual a noise as I could manage without opening my mouth. The scent of the nearest pine tree filled my nose as I inhaled deeply.

"Look, Jennifer, this isn't a punishment. I'm not trying to upset you, honey. Maybe you can stay a few more days. I'd just like you to pick a flight and let Mom know when you'll be home. That's all."

"Has she said anything?" I asked, fighting the tightness in my chest. Sarah sidled closer to me. Even though I sensed her hovering, I refused to turn toward her.

"Sure she has. She talks about you nonstop. She's jumpy. She's worried. She needs to know you're safe. I just think she needs you home. Could you do that for me? For her?"

I treated him to another stubborn pause. If only Nathan knew how much I *didn't* say. "Dad, I'm out with some people right now and we're almost home. Can I call you right back in a few minutes?" My control slipped and the tears leaked out of my eyes and into my voice.

"Honey, don't cry. I'm not trying to make you cry."

"I'm fine. I'll call you back," I said in a hurried breath and hung up the phone. I dropped my head so Sarah couldn't see my expression as she inched around me.

"Jennifer? What's wrong?" She asked. I started walking again, my hanging head shaking back and forth.

"What happened?" Little demanded.

I took a deep breath and looked only at the trees, so thick that I couldn't see the water at all. "My mom wants me to come home." The tears dropped fat and fast.

"Sweetie, come here," Sarah said, her arm encircling my shoulders and pulling me into step with her. "I guess we knew it was coming, didn't we?" A few more steps and then, "So why does it feel so awful?"

"I don't know." I sniffed, wishing for a tissue. "It's not like I never want to go home. I'm not running away. I'm just not, I don't think, I don't know." I pushed hard against my eyes, like I could press the painful ideas out of my head.

"You're not ready yet," Little said.

I dropped my hand and nodded.

"Life is about timing," Sarah whispered. I glanced up and saw that she was trying to stay calm for me. That made it a thousand times worse.

"Why don't you leave the girl with me?" Little spoke to Sarah quietly, but her usual authority did not get lost with an absence of volume.

"Leave Jennifer?" Sarah asked.

"Yes. I need to talk to her for a bit. She'll walk me home and you can take that fool dog. He's getting on my nerves anyway." Charlie's tail lashed in excitement.

"I don't see why we can't all . . ." Sarah started to argue.

"Don't matter what you see. I need a private conversation with Jennifer."

Sarah squinted in doubt. I could tell she was going to fight this.

"It's okay, Sarah. I don't mind." My curiosity over what Little wanted to say to me in private was a welcome distraction from my disappointment.

"I'm outnumbered," she said with a sigh. "Come on, Charlie. I'll see you at home." She took off at a brisk pace and from the way her hand went up to her face, I wondered if her tears finally fell. Little watched Sarah's back until she was well ahead of us.

"Tell your mama, 'No.' "

"What?"

"You call your mama and you tell her no," Little commanded.

"Why?"

The old woman's eyes ran back and forth across my face. "Because—if Claire wants you to come home, she needs to come get you."

"What?" Straight to crazy.

"You heard me just fine." Little's piercing eyes were deadly serious.

"You want me to force my mother to come get me?"

"What I said." Little started walking again, leaving me behind.

"She won't come," I called after her. "She'll be so mad at me that she'll never let me come back. She'll send my dad." The scenarios flew through my mind, along with the image of my mother's horrified face. It wasn't hard to guess what she would do.

"Then you tell your daddy to stay put. That little girl needs to come get you."

"Little, it won't work. It would make everything worse."

"Says you," she answered, her anger growing.

"Yes, says me!" I drew up beside her, matching her brisk pace.

"And you're what—ten?" she glowered, spitting out my age like an insult.

"Sixteen." I glared back. "And I know my mother."

"Hah! Is that why she told you all about Sarah? Because you know her so well?"

Tears pricked at my eyes again—this time angry tears. Embarrassed tears. "She won't come," I whispered, my weakened voice barely making it out of my mouth.

Little's stare didn't stop at my face. I felt the blue fire racing past my eyes and into my chest. "She'll come. You make her come."

"Little, you haven't seen her since she was a kid. What makes you think you know what's best for her? You don't even know who she is anymore."

"I don't know what she's been doing all this time, but I know who she is." The burning conviction in her face made it impossible to doubt her.

I took a step closer to her. "Tell me what happened to my mother."

She looked back at me with calculating eyes. "No."

"No?" I barked in frustration and surprise.

"No. I told you I trade. So I won't tell you—I'll trade you."

"Trade *what*? What do you want, Little?" The question escaped in a sigh. Nathan was right. Most people played the game and I was tired of it.

"You tell your mama to come get you, and I'll tell you what happened. A trade."

"Jasper!" I whispered in defeat, but I felt a tiny thrill at the realization that I could say it just like Sarah. I turned a defiant face to Little. "And what if she says no?"

"She's gonna want you home sometime. She'll come get you." We paused at the end of her driveway. Equally stubborn. A stalemate. "I know you think I'm being mean, Jennifer, but I'm not. Claire needs this. I know better than anyone."

I closed my eyes and took a deep, painful breath. "And if you're wrong?"

"Don't be stupid, girl. I'm too old to be wrong."

CHAPTER 21

I FOLLOWED LITTLE into her tiny house, hoping to pry some more information out of her. The front door opened into a small, dim living room with velvet-flocked wallpaper. Little eased into an olive green chair with a grunt and started unlacing her walking shoes. "What is it you want to know?" she asked me as she yanked off her shoe.

"Anything you know. I want to know what happened after my grandmother died and my mother was alone." I made some tentative steps over to her sofa. Nothing in the house looked like it had been touched much in the last fifty years. The heavy drapes with an odd geometric design could only be from the sixties and the tufted, turquoise sofa looked like a museum piece. I sat on it gingerly. "Sarah told me she was in Africa when Grandma had a stroke. She was there with a man," I added, even though it made my stomach dip.

"Well, that ain't my story to tell. But I can tell you what happened here."

"Okay," I leaned forward in expectation.

"After you call your mama." She didn't blink.

I deflated with a hopeless sigh. "I told you I can't."

Little made a noise that sounded like "huh" and started untying her other shoe. "Did she want you to come visit Sarah?"

"No," I mumbled.

"She say no?"

"Yes." The reluctant answers slid between my closed teeth.

"She get upset?"

"Yes."

"You sitting on my mother's divan?"

I looked down at the rich, jacquard material, frayed at the edges of the cushions. "Yes," I whispered.

"Well there ya go. If you got here, you can get her here."

"But *why?*" I exclaimed, my aggravation finally injecting power into my voice.

"Because she's not free. She's not at peace."

"She seemed fine until my dad told me about Sarah."

"Don't tell me about acting," Little said in a low, menacing growl. "I know about acting. And I know about hiding." Her eyes went somewhere too distant and private for me to follow. I looked back down at the sofa, soaking in the deep green patterns.

"I didn't mean anything about acting. I meant that she really was happy."

"Then she woulda told you. She woulda told the whole story. When you're not runnin' from a story, you can tell it. She's still running. Never seen a body run like that."

I stepped over to a bookcase crammed with assorted treasures—teacups, a china lizard, ceramic birds, and a set of Russian nesting dolls. Lifting a silver thimble I pressed it onto my finger and kept pressing, calmed by the pressure of the smooth metal against my skin. "Why? Why is she still running? Why can't she just forgive Sarah and get over it?"

"She forgives Sarah," Little said. "She don't know it, but she does. She got it in her head that she can't come back. She ran away and left her pain here. She thinks it's still here waitin'. I'd like to see anybody 'just get over' what she went through."

"Then why should I tell her to come back to that?" I asked, sincerely needing to know.

"Because sometimes you gotta look under the bed to see that there's no monster." Little leaned back in her chair and folded her hands over her stomach. Every action and word resounded with finality. But even her tough demeanor couldn't disguise the fact that she lived here alone. No tacky school pictures in handmade frames, no greeting cards displayed on the mantle. Nothing that looked less than a decade old except for some prescription bottles on the side table beside some unopened bills.

I looked at her, tempted for a moment to reach out and touch her hand. Instead, I replaced the thimble on the shelf and asked, "Why did you run away?"

Little's blue eyes stabbed me before they closed. Her head rocked to one side like she was falling asleep. " 'Cause I needed to. I fell in love and I had to leave."

"Why?"

"None of your blasted business," she yawned.

"Little . . ."

"I tell you when you tell me. But I'm gonna need a nap soon, so why don't you just call your mama and get it over with. You're gonna do it 'ventually."

I blew out a long breath and waited to see if she would open her eyes again. She didn't. "I'll see you later, Little. I'm going out the back." I stepped through the yellow kitchen—funny how in the storm last night it seemed to glow cheerfully but against the bright noon sun it looked dated and dingy—and into her backyard.

She had even more tree limbs down than Sarah. They littered the ground like wounded bodies, twisted in the wind and left as casualties. I skirted between them, making my way to the beach so I could think alone before facing the phone call to my dad. I cannot say that Little's idea didn't intrigue me, but it didn't convince me.

My mother at Shelter Cove. I studied the stand of trees hiding

Sarah's house from my view and imagined my mother in front of them. I tried to picture her as a young girl, playing in her oceanic backyard and stepping where I now stepped, but I couldn't make it real. It was a flat picture in my head without movement or life.

When I turned to the beach, instead of my imaginary mother, I saw Nathan's little sister Hester hunched on the shore, piling pebbles on top of her feet. If it had been Darcy or Claude I would have shouted a greeting, but I couldn't raise my voice to shy Hester, even in salutation. When I ambled close enough for her to hear my conversational voice I said, "Hey, Hester. Whatcha doing?" Her head whipped around, pink seeping up her neck and into her cheeks.

"Just sitting." She stumbled on the words.

"Mind if I join you?" She graced her feet with a pleased smile so I took a seat. "I met Little today. Well, last night actually. In the storm."

"Nathan told me." It was hard to hear her words because she barely parted her lips.

"Are you two close, you and Nathan?" She nodded, this time turning her head completely away from me.

"Sarah tells me that you're even smarter than Nathan."

A small, short laugh before she answered, "No."

"In fact"—I studied her embarrassed face—"I think I believe her. I have a problem and I think you would know the answer better than Nathan." Hester blushed, but listened. "Little wants me to make my mother come home to Smithport even though it would really hurt her feelings and make her mad at me. Would you listen to Little?" Then as an aside, I said between clenched teeth, "They do say she's a little . . ." I tipped my flat hand back and forth and whistled softly.

Hester grinned and looked back at the water. "Do you think your mother wants to come back—subconsciously?" she asked. Her words wiped the smile from my face, and I looked at her darting eyes. Much smarter than I thought, and much older than any eight-year-old I'd ever known. Even Cleo couldn't compete with this mind.

"I don't know. It doesn't seem like it." I lifted a handful of sharp sand and let it sift between my fingers.

"I think I'd tell her to come," she said.

"Why?"

When Hester turned to me, the wind stirred some untidy hair off her shoulders and her upturned nose flared slightly as she took a deep breath. "Because I think people belong at home." I read pain in the tiny spaces between her words. She wasn't talking about my mother.

"Where's your dad, Hester?" I asked in my kindest voice.

She shrugged and looped her arms around her knees. "Connecticut."

"Do you ever see him?"

"No," she sighed. Her head fell onto one of her arms and she looked up at me, her eyes blinking slowly. Only when I saw her sitting there could I imagine my mother, a little girl with her toes in the tide.

"Would you do it—give an ultimatum? Make her come back?" My tone changed. Now I spoke to her as an adult instead of a child half my age.

Hester pushed her lips to one side. "I think so."

"So I should?"

"I don't know. I think so."

The truth gripped my stomach and gnawed on it like a predator that starts eating its prey while it's still alive. I flinched with physical pain. "I think you're probably right," I finally admitted. "It just scares me."

"Yeah." She nodded in sympathy and we both turned our faces to the rushing water, my thoughts jumping from heartache to heartache—Hester's, my mother's, Sarah's, Little's. As the cold water draped a foamy lace over the hard sand at my feet, I realized that I could not include myself in the ranks of the heartbroken. Life had left my heart solidly intact. It made no sense, not even to me, but I shivered as the loneliness passed over me. I felt inferior. Untested. Ignored by God himself. I thought Hester sighed, but when she looked up I realized it was me.

CHAPTER 22

WHATEVER I DID the rest of the day it was to the accompaniment of Little's voice in my head, "Tell your mama no." Through dinner and phone calls, through reading and conversations, those four words punctuated every thought. Only Hester's words could cut through Little's gruff voice: "People belong at home."

We did lines in the backyard as we gathered the branches broken in the storm into a burn pile. Sarah recited Frost's "Stopping by Woods on a Snowy Evening" from memory because the drifting pieces of ashes reminded her of snow. I watched Nathan as he recited over the open fire, the flames that curled and devoured the leaves lighting his face as he spoke. I always faltered over mine after listening to him. Mary Oliver's "The Journey" never sounded so meaningful as when he spoke of the prying fingers of the wind and "fallen branches" while the fire consumed our pine boughs.

He could tailor another person's words so effortlessly to his own tongue, while they always felt loose and ill-fitting on my own.

When lines were done and Sarah's yard was clear again, she turned her head to the far side of the cove. "Kudos to you, Nathan, for finding a verse so fitting. Perhaps we should help your mother with her 'fallen branches' too."

A tight, unwelcome expression crossed Nathan's face. "I can handle it," he replied tersely.

Sarah either ignored his mood or didn't notice and waved us toward the trail in the woods that led to his house. "That's what you always say," she called. "Many hands make light work."

I looked to him for permission, but he was scowling at the fire, the strange shadows accentuating his displeasure. He relented without a word and walked ahead. When we got to the trees, he held back a low branch and motioned me forward as if he were holding open a door. Farther along the trail I heard Sarah scuffling through the brush, but she had walked too far ahead to see.

"Have you been over yet?" Nathan asked.

"To your house? No, not yet. Sarah and I have been keeping busy."

He nodded, his worry visible despite the falling dusk. "Well, it's inevitable, right?" he mumbled cryptically. "Welcome to my neck of the woods." I followed him as he led the way, bending any trailing vines or branches out of my way. The woods in the gathering night were "dark and deep" just as Sarah's lines had said, but there was a foreboding in the shadows that made it hard to feel the "lovely" part. He stopped and held out his hand to signal me to pause. I was imagining a snake, but he turned and looked at me, his face obscured by the black branches.

"Hester told me you talked today."

I tried to read his voice, listened for disapproval, any hint for what his next words would be. "Does that bother you?" I probed.

"No. I just . . . If you had asked me . . ." The slight accusation in his voice made me chew the inside of my lip. "I would have asked you what your mother is like. Will she be mean to Sarah if she comes? It might just make it worse."

"But Sarah wants to make up," I argued as I pushed my hands into my back pockets. "How can they make up if they never see each other again?"

"You are the only one who knows both of them. Sarah's forgiven the past. Your mom hasn't. It doesn't sound like a good mix."

I resented his tone when he spoke of my mother like she was the moral inferior of the sisters. "I'm not the only one who knows them both. Little knows them both, and it was her idea. My mother isn't meaner, Nathan. Little said she was just tougher. She had to be. She buried her mother alone."

"She almost destroyed her sister, too," he shot back.

"Sarah almost destroyed her! Neither of them meant to. You're right. I'm the one who knows my mother. She is as stubborn as . . . well, as *you!* She gets mad when she's scared. I hate that about her the most. She used to yell at me when I fell off my bike. Like actually got mad at me for bleeding! But she was so scared when I got hurt. If she is this mad, she has to be scared to death, like Little said. And Little said that she has to come here to see there's nothing to be scared of anymore."

Nathan rubbed a knuckle against his mouth and exhaled as he thought. "That's a lot of 'Little said's. That's putting all your fruit in one crazy basket." A smile climbed into his voice and I fought returning it, but failed.

"Nothing else has worked. Maybe crazy is our last option." I pulled my hair over one shoulder and the cold air crawled down my neck. "I don't like these woods at night," I admitted.

"Sorry," he answered. "Just consider that it might be best to leave it alone."

"You sound like my mother," I told him, taking the lead and crunching back down the path.

"Point taken," he said and fell in step behind me.

I was grateful when the path ended abruptly and I stepped into the open backyard of a weathered, shake-shingle home that was in no way remarkable or worthy of the shame that it seemed to elicit in Nathan. Sarah was already picking up sticks. She waved and came to join us.

"I like it," I tried to reassure him as I studied the small gray home. "I feel like homes need introductions here," I said. "Are you going to tell me her name? Or is this one a he?"

I could see Nathan's smile in the glow of the lights, but it was a joyless, bitter thing. "The house is called Boulder Bend"—his words crawled out of his clamped jaw and his hands flexed—"but everyone around here just calls it Bastardo Bend."

"Nathan," Sarah scolded him. "You don't have to—"

"What? Tell the truth? Or be angry at the idiots who say that about my family?" He leveled his gaze at Sarah but flinched when I answered.

"You don't have to be mad at the people who *don't* say it," I suggested.

Whatever fierce reply he wanted to give was silenced when Hester opened the back door and waved in delight when she saw Sarah and me. I finished hastily, before he could sneak in anything cynical. "People are stupid. You just have to have a modicum of perspective." Hester approached and gave me a shy hug and I turned my smile to her in greeting. "Now that I've said that, I've always wondered what 'modicum' means."

"It's Latin," she answered. "Modicus. Moderate. A little bit."

I turned my surprised face to Sarah just as I did every time something in the town surprised me, as if she were a tour guide who could give an explanation. "They teach Latin in Maine?"

"Nathan taught her," she said.

When Hester registered my shock she qualified. "Just a little bit. I can't *speak* it. I can just read a little. Come inside," she invited.

"Latin?" I whispered in my most incredulous voice. Nathan only rolled his eyes.

"Nathan's home!" came a cry from the second story when the screen door creaked open loudly. Darcy hurled herself downstairs in a whirl of red hair and flailing limbs. She changed her trajectory when she saw her brother had brought guests. "Jennifer!" She launched herself into my arms, causing me to stagger.

"Hey Strawberry Shortstuff," I said breathlessly. "Good to see you, too."

Sarah extricated her from my neck and gave her a smacking kiss. "Why aren't you in bed?" she asked.

"Nathan didn't read to us yet." Darcy adjusted her nightgown, which was falling off because it was one of Nathan's T-shirts.

"What about your mom?" Sarah said.

"She already read us three. Darcy's just looking for excuses to stay up," Hester chimed in.

"I'll come back down when I'm done," Nathan said as he started to shepherd the girls toward the stairs. "But it's getting darker. You two might want to head home, and we can clean up the branches tomorrow. There's no hurry."

"How about I read to them tonight instead?" Sarah offered. While Darcy squealed her approval, I studied the spotless kitchen, cookbooks arranged by size on the counter, even the magnets in a straight line across the top of the refrigerator.

"Where's Claude?" Nathan asked the girls.

"Not here." Judith's voice came from another room. "She went out for a late dinner."

"Hess, did Claude tell you who she was going out with?" Nathan asked. "Did you see who picked her up?"

"It was Will," she said, her face strained.

"Hess, did you tell Mom it was Will?" he asked.

"I did! But they were already gone by then."

"Leave it alone, Nathan," Sarah warned.

"What am I missing? What's wrong with Will?" I interrupted. My memory conjured up the face of a tall boy who worked on one of the ships. Claude had introduced us and he had seemed completely harmless to me.

Nathan answered by swearing under his breath before he looked at Darcy and told her to get in bed.

"No, you said a bad word and I want to play with Jennifer," Darcy pouted.

"I'm about to say another one and Jennifer is leaving." He nudged Darcy toward the stairs, but she retreated to Sarah for support.

"Let's go, girls," Sarah agreed. She leveled one final stern look at Nathan. "Take Jennifer home and leave it alone. I'll see you at the house after I read to them," she told me. Hester gave me a shy wave and they all retreated up the tiny staircase hidden beside the refrigerator.

"It's darker now," Nathan pointed out, "and you didn't like

the woods. Let's take the road instead." He led the way into the living room, where Judith sat knitting in front of the television. She raised her head and said hello, without slowing her hands.

"Hi, Judith," I said. "No one told me you knit. What are you making?"

"A blanket square. I make baby blankets and give them to the hospital because we don't have space for any more in this house."

"Really?" I asked, unable to conceal my disbelief. I never took her for a philanthropist. Just like the kitchen, the living room felt old, but immaculate. The carpet was worn and stained, but vacuumed. Little girl shoes lined up in a tidy row beside the front door, and toys were neatly collected in wicker baskets.

"Sarah's reading to the girls. And if Claude isn't home by ten she's in trouble," Nathan said as he opened the door.

"I know," Judith said, her silver knitting needles flashing as she worked. I stepped outside, taking a last glance at Judith, her makeup-free features softened in the glow of the TV as she bent over the shapeless heap of green yarn. It was the first time I thought she looked pretty.

"So do you do the housekeeping, too?" I asked Nathan after he shut the door.

"Huh?"

"Sarah said you take care of a lot of stuff around here. The house is spotless."

His eyes swept to the dark ground. "That's all Judith. She's a neat freak."

"Really?" I realized how unflattering my voice sounded only after I said it.

"It's something easy. You can put a house together with just a little work. A couple hours to perfection. It's about the only thing in life that she thinks she does well." I stole a glance at his face, trying to see if he agreed with her or not. It was impossible to tell. "If the house happens to be messy when she gets stressed out . . ." He sucked in a breath and let it out in a loud, dejected puff. "I came home once when she was having a bad day. She was throwing all the dirty dishes in the garbage. She couldn't clean them fast enough. She probably would have burned the laundry next if I hadn't calmed her down. I got her to organize the spice rack, and that gave me time to finish cleaning the rest of the house. Crisis averted."

I didn't notice until he stopped talking that I had drawn closer while he spoke, his words pulling me to his side. "You do so much," I whispered.

"It's not like she's helpless," he insisted. "She's just . . . textbook. Her dad was a total jerk, and she keeps picking up every jerk, convinced that one of them has to be the perfect man in disguise. Impossible. Predictable. When she gives herself a little credit, she'll be fine."

"Do you give her credit?" It was so audacious of me to ask that I regretted it immediately.

He just shrugged and picked up his pace. The road was wide and easy to follow, even without streetlights.

"Sorry I asked," I apologized.

"I don't mind that," he replied. "I'm just ticked off about Claude. That girl! She is doing her best to be everything I hate."

"What do you mean?"

"Running around with kids who have no bigger aspirations than putting a new engine in their daddy's boat. She isn't like that. She doesn't belong here. She certainly doesn't belong with one of those . . ." Nathan couldn't find an adequate word to describe Claude's friends, so he just smacked his fist into his hand. "I swear I could take him out in one punch. One false move and I'll do it."

"I didn't take you for the violent type," I said. "Sullen, moody, sure, but violent?" Then he turned his scowling face to me and I saw it, the pent-up power and frustration. I wouldn't bet against him in a fight. I must have looked alarmed, because his shoulders suddenly slumped.

"I'm not violent," he said. "Not if I can help it. Not unless it's really necessary. Didn't Sarah tell you why I left school?"

"No. I thought it was because you're smart."

A short, callous laugh. "That sounds better. I finished the work, but Sarah pulled me out early because of the fights."

"You fought in school? Like *fist*fights?"

He finally smiled. "Most seventh-grade boys don't really respond to philosophy and debates."

Shelter Cove came into view, glowing white at the top of the sloping street. "What did they do?" I asked, wishing we had much farther to walk. "Did they make fun of you for being smarter than everyone?"

"Like I'd care if they said something about me!" His voice dropped, halted. "They started talking about Judith. Then they started on Claude. Trust me, it was necessary."

"What did they say?"

"Can't you make an educated guess? Pretty girl with a mom who isn't exactly monogamous. Just put it all together."

"Oh." How I wished I always knew the right things to say.

"And now after all that, after I thought I scared them off, what does she do? Goes running into their filthy arms! Maybe you should take her back to Nebraska with you."

"People are the same everywhere, Nathan. I'm sure she's not doing anything stupid."

"Are you?" He looked down at me, a speculative frown on his face. "Do you know people like that? What they're like?" Nathan stopped in the driveway, and I paused beside him. I had a feeling that he was actually asking me, *"Are you like that?"*

"I don't know what you mean by 'like that' but probably not. I mostly hang out with my best friend, Cleo, and I'm pretty sure you've never met anyone like her."

"I'm listening," he said.

My stomach dropped unexpectedly. "Oh, she's . . . she's really smart. Gifted."

"I've met a few people like that." He smiled, the gloom lifting from his eyes.

"And she's very blunt. She's tough. She doesn't like boys."

Nathan's face turned a surprising white. "You mean she's . . . are you . . . ?"

"Oh no! Not that! I meant she doesn't like boys *yet*." My face burned red. "She thinks teenage boys are idiots. She doesn't talk to them."

Nathan's shoulders relaxed. "Really? Sounds entertaining." Now I'd piqued his interest. Unfortunately.

"Do you have a picture of her?" he asked. I hid my face by looking toward the black forest. It was the last question I wanted him to ask. I couldn't compare with Cleo.

"I'll show you later. You should probably get home in case Claude gets back."

He looked reluctant to leave, but his glance twitched to the road. "Probably."

I cast around my brain for something to say. "Do you want any help staining the fence tomorrow?" I asked him.

He turned to me with amusement in his face. "Talk about dirty. You'd be orange for days. It stains your skin."

"I don't mind."

I watched as his eyes roamed the front yard, only occasionally crossing my face. "Whatever you want," he said. "You can keep me company. From a distance. But no staining." He let out a breath that trembled. When I looked up he averted his face and mumbled, "I like you the color you are."

By the time his words registered and the surprised, happy flush brightened my upturned face, he was long gone.

CHAPTER 23

NATHAN'S TINY COMPLIMENT rushed through my consciousness like a river crushes through a broken levy. I felt a flood of giddy energy, but when I went inside I forced my smile into a demure grin, holding the memory away from my thoughts and saving it for bedtime, when I could analyze it thoroughly. Those brief words, the embarrassed turn of his head, made Little's scheme seem downright plausible. Of course I could get my mother to come home and reconcile with Sarah. I could possibly talk China out of communism or calm the warring tribes of Africa. Nothing felt impossible for a girl who just earned a grudging compliment from Nathan Moore. I cleaned up for bed, plotting exactly how I could implement Little's plan. I knew one thing: I needed my father on my side. I could fight one of them, but not both parents.

The possible scenarios distracted me as I brushed my teeth

and washed my face, but when I crawled into bed, my mind was not in Nebraska or with my parents. It was completely my own, filled with pictures from the day, of the crackling fire, of Nathan. I closed my eyes, not to sleep but to remember. I could barely stand to touch my skin because even my own fingers sent jolts of hot electricity through my nerves. I lingered on every image of the night: Nathan's stare over the jumping, crimson flames, the black water spilling onto the sand as we passed the beach, the unconscious kindness of his hands as he held the branches away from my face. Sometimes the memories seemed too much and I couldn't understand how I'd stayed so calm when those things actually happened, but lost my breath in the shadowy remembrances. I grabbed my extra pillow and squeezed it tight against my stomach as I tried to fall asleep. If I held it there long enough, maybe it would smother the butterflies bursting out of their cocoons and taking their first frantic flights in the middle of my body.

Even waking in the cool morning had an added charm. Before I finished opening my eyes and stirring from my stiff, curled position, I felt feathers of happiness unfolding under my skin. It seemed that through the unconsciousness of sleep my body remembered what my mind did not—I would see him today. That was enough to rouse me from my soft blankets and send me hustling through my morning routine. I took special care with my hair, brushing and drying until it looked like my wheat field. I couldn't bring myself to put on any makeup other than lip gloss and a tiny bit of mascara. Anything else would look absurd for staining a fence. I tried on every T-shirt, but then settled on my oldest because I didn't want to ruin my best ones. Sadly, when I was done, I looked exactly like I did on any other day. But even that couldn't weigh me down for long. It was hard to fret over myself when using the bulk of my concentration to review every conversation we'd had, each comment he'd made at lines, and all the expressions that crossed his face.

Apparently the hectic activity going on inside me did not reveal itself in my face, because Sarah didn't notice anything at breakfast. The moment I adopted Little's scheme, I made a conscious choice not to tell Sarah. If my mother threw a tantrum, I wanted Sarah's hands to be clean. She didn't need any more strikes against her.

When Nathan rapped on the door at eight-thirty I restrained my feet, making them take easy, measured steps. "Hi, Nathan," I said, proud of how friendly and nonchalant it sounded. "You want a bagel before we go?"

His expression, though polite, was stiff. "Sure. Morning, Sarah."

"Hey, Ace," she said, throwing a bagel through the air. He caught it on his finger.

"Ace?" I asked him. He just shrugged and waved good-bye to Sarah.

He didn't look at me as he got into the truck. I pulled open the squeaky door and climbed inside, carefully pushing a few tools aside. He riveted his eyes to the dashboard, avoiding my face as he backed onto the road. Curiosity made me wonder how long he would go without speaking. Though the quiet oppressed me, I clenched my hands in my lap and waited. And waited. We had one short mile to drive, but the road stretched out interminably, seemed to expand with the silence. His mouth twitched once, but his lips pressed back into a thin line and he tapped the steering wheel softly.

"Did you talk to your mom last night?" he finally asked.

"No. I haven't figured out how to say it yet." I directed my smile out the window. At least he spoke first.

"Are you nervous about it?"

"A little." Not as nervous as I felt waiting for his next word, his next expression.

"Wouldn't you rather go home and talk to her? Spraying a fence is noisy and messy and I won't have time to entertain you." He squirmed farther away from me, the wiggle working up from his legs to his shoulders. My face trembled as I tried to ignore the flat, burning disappointment running down the back of my lungs.

"When have I ever asked you to *entertain* me? You know, you sort of have a Dr. Jekyll, Mr. Hyde thing going on."

"I what? How?" He swung his face toward me just as Main Street came into view.

"You get mad at me. Then nice. Then mad. It makes no sense, really."

"I'm not mad at you. Why would I ever be mad at you?"

I was surprised by how defensive he sounded. "Naturally grumpy?"

"Naturally nosy?" he retorted, with a smirk.

"I'm really not usually," I said. "You are just harder to figure out, I think. Why . . ."

"Try?" He parked the car beside the small, yellow house with the stripped fence and stared through the chipped windshield. He didn't take his hands off the wheel. He didn't unbuckle his seat belt.

"Why not?" I asked softly.

"Where do I begin?" he replied as he finally freed himself from the seat belt and hopped out of the truck.

"How about at the first reason?" I said to Nathan's back as he knelt over the paint sprayer, adjusting nozzles and knobs.

He didn't look up. I didn't know if he would even acknowledge me until he muttered, "It's a lot of trouble for someone who's just visiting. This is your vacation. Maybe you should dig for clams and stop prying into psyches."

"I don't like clams. Second reason."

At last his head came up, his nose and brow wrinkled, but his mouth just shy of a grin. He looked like I puzzled him. And pleased him.

"Even if you came back, I probably wouldn't be here. So it's a waste of time."

"Where would you be?"

"School. Work. I'll be eighteen next month. Sarah says I have to leave sometime." He pried open a can of stain with a screwdriver and signaled me to back up. "It spatters," he said under his breath.

I walked to a soft patch of grass and lowered myself beneath a large tree. Taking advantage of his concentration on the messy work, I asked, "Where do you want to go to school? What do you want to do?"

"Dunno," he said. One hand caught a large spill running down the can. He pushed as much as he could back onto the rim and wiped the wet remainder on his T-shirt, leaving a brown streak across his stomach that resembled dried blood.

"You have no idea?" I challenged.

"No," he snapped. "It's noisy when I turn it on." He closed the subject by hitting a switch that released a cloud of wood stain out of the spray wand. The vibrations and noise made conversation almost impossible, and I didn't feel like shouting back and forth. I could take a hint. I leaned against the tree and watched the slow progress of the stain as it advanced across the fence. I think he forgot that I was there, because when I finally stood, he startled and turned the sprayer off.

"Do you mind if I walk down to the docks?" I asked him.

"By yourself?" He looked torn between his job and trying to babysit me.

"It's two blocks. I can manage. I wanted to say hi to the Jacks. If they're there."

"They'll be there, all right. Come get me when you're ready for a ride home. But just a word of advice—don't mention politics. Or anything related to politics. At all."

"Why no politics? I don't mind a good discussion."

"I'm not talking about a spirited debate. I'm talking blood in the streets."

"Oh, come on . . ." I searched his face for a sign of jest without finding one. "The old men are going to beat up a teenage girl?"

"No," he said in exasperation. "They won't touch you. They'll kill each other." He used his shoulder to wipe the sweat off his upper lip.

"They're friends."

"With rules. Just trust me. Last year Russ broke Pete's jaw during midterm primaries."

"Are you serious? Why?"

"Because they are complete and total idiots with access to alcohol." He studied the fence.

"They're still friends after that?"

"Never better," he insisted as he tugged on a loose slat. And then gave an agitated sigh, "Idiots. So just don't bring it up, okay?"

"I promise. No politics." I gave him a lighthearted salute and walked away, feeling free as I stepped down the street. Only nine days in Smithport and already the crooked sidewalks and weathered houses were starting to feel familiar. I walked behind the restaurants and small store to the slanted ramp that leads to the boats. The largest Jack, once again wearing his cap, sat alone on the wooden bench that commanded the best view of the docks. He looked wrong by himself, with no one to heckle him.

"Morning," I said as I approached.

He looked up with a faint scowl until he recognized me. "Oh, Nebraska. It's you. You here with the womenfolk again?"

"Nope, just me." I eyed the bench, curious if it was reserved for only the Jacks or if I could sit with him. Too timid to try, I stuffed my hands in my pockets and rocked onto the balls of my feet.

"How's your trip going? Having fun?" he asked

"Definitely." Fun didn't truly convey the depth of my experience but it would do for casual conversation. "Where are the other . . . Jacks?" I stumbled on Little's label, but I couldn't remember their real names.

"Not here yet. We come and go. I stay the longest. Don't like to be too far from *The Missus*." He nodded down to the docks. "I guess I'm just a family man," he said, his eye twinkling.

"Are you Russ?"

"God forbid it! If I were Russ, I wouldn't know the North

Star from the North Pole. Pitiful sailor." His words faded out and then he looked up at me. "I'm Glenn," he barked. "But Jack is fine. A rose by any other name, right?"

"You like Shakespeare?" I looked over the portly man in doubt.

"He the one who said it? Huh. Don't matter. I don't know yuh name, neither. Can't remember. Just know you're Hank's grandbaby."

"You knew my grandfather?"

"Knew 'im? Course I knew 'im! But it's been a long time. We all know Sarah, though. She's the daughter of the town. We sorta all adopted her after Hazel went like that. Saddest thing I've seen, for sure."

I sidled toward the bench, watching for signs of disapproval if I took a seat. "Do you remember my mother—Claire?" I asked him as I gingerly sat down.

"Sure. Sure. Last saw her at the funeral. Not a good memory for an old man."

"Why?" I tried not to stare too intently, forcing my eyes away from his drooping jowls every few seconds.

"Just sad. No, worse than sad. Scary. Her standing by the coffin by herself. I thought she'd pass out right in the funeral parlor. Wouldn't a blamed her if she did. She just stood there about half-dead herself. And jus' a little kid. When I shook her hand, she wouldn't let go. She looked into my eyes and asked me if I would . . . Ah don't like to think on it."

I felt the blood drain from my face, hearing my mother described like that. "What did she ask you?"

He hesitated, his thick lips fumbling. "She asked me to look after Harvey."

"Harvey?" I cried. "The Harvey who sells fish? Why?"

"Sure! Didn't you know they were sweethearts? Harvey was crazy about her. She scared me when she talked like that because I worried she was going to try to join her parents. It never occurred to me that she was planning to run. Darndest thing. So she went to Nebraska, eh? That beats all," he mumbled. When he spoke again, it was in a much louder and brighter voice. "My girl would never run away. You wanna meet *The Missus*?"

"Your boat?" I asked, but I couldn't turn off the image of my mother clinging to Glenn's hand, pleading for his help. Harvey the fisherman seemed much more intriguing all of a sudden. My mother's first love.

"*The* boat," he stressed. "Best steaming vessel in the ocean."

"I'd love to."

Glenn rose with a huff, and I followed his slow progress down the concrete ramp onto the solid lumber of the docks. He led me to a small boat, squatting low in the water and hung with colorful tarps. White letters spelled out *The Missus* against the black bow and a small white room stood in the middle of the deck looking like little more than a glorified Porta Potty with a steering wheel.

Glenn swept her bow to stern with a worshipful gaze. "Ain't nothing she wouldn't do for me. Not a wave she wouldn't mount. Not a storm she wouldn't bring me through. Best boat in the waters. She's got a living soul in her."

"Why is everything here a girl? The ocean. The boats. The storms. All girls."

Glenn chuckled and grabbed his thick jaw in his hand, pulling it thoughtfully. "Guess 'cause those are the things that give us the most trouble." He laughed and turned back to his vessel. "But *The Missus*, she's a good lass. Some boats are nags, always complaining, always falling to pieces, never wantin' to do what ya tell 'em. Those boats are the shrews. But not my *Missus*. She's a lady, and a lady needs a little love. Needs someone to pet her, feed her ego. A lady needs to be complimented, seduced. Then she's putty in your hands."

"All that knowledge about women, and you never got married?" I grinned.

"Ah'm an Eagle Scout. Loyalty. One woman for me," he said, tapping his hand on *The Missus*. "But you're a Maine girl through and through. If you get yourself out of Nebraska, some young sailor will set his compass by you. Can't ask for more'n that."

I blushed, oddly flattered. "Not sure I'd want a fisherman, Jack. Too much competition. They just love their boats."

"Mebbe so, mebbe so. Many a man sleeps in his boat when his

lady kicks him out. But I don't see how you'd avoid it. What else do men do?"

I grinned at his joke, before I realized he wasn't kidding. His world began and ended where the water rippled against the long wooden posts of the docks, blackened by years and slime. When I found my voice, it came out gentle and slow.

"Jack, they do other things."

"Huh. Suppose they do. Somewhere. Poor saps."

CHAPTER 24

"THE JACKS THERE?" Nathan asked when I returned. He put down his sprayer and started the futile process of scratching some of the brown stain off of his skin.

"Yeah. I swore allegiance to the Libertarian Party, and they went at each other with fish hooks. Carnage."

"You said *I* wasn't funny."

"You're not. I am. Only Glenn was there. He let me meet his boat."

"That's an honor."

"So I gather. You got farther than I thought you would. How much longer do you think you'll be here?" The stain now covered a good two-thirds of the fence.

"Still need to finish this coat. Then a second coat. I'll be here a few more hours, at least." He squinted as the sun pierced through a cloud and spread over his face. Beads of sweat shimmered on his skin. "Do you want me to take you home so you can call your mom?"

"Why do you keep asking that? I need to talk to my dad first. Then I'll tell her."

He gave me a doubtful frown and mumbled "uh-huh" before turning his back to me.

"What? You think I won't do it?" I asked half amused, half offended.

He shrugged without looking at me. "If you say you will, you will."

I glared as I processed the skepticism in his voice. "Nathan, I will. I just have to figure out the perfect way to say it. So it works." It made me angry how much it sounded like an excuse coming out of my mouth. He slowly faced me, his expression blank but his eyes calling the bluff. His skepticism ignited my pride like a flash fire. I pulled my cell phone out of my pocket. "So you just want me to dial and say the first stupid thing that comes to my mind? Just stand in some stranger's yard while you stain a fence and tell my dad I'm going to blackmail my mother? That'd go over well."

"You can do it however you want." He turned and stepped back toward the fence.

"Then don't turn on your stupid sprayer, because then I won't be able to hear my dad scream at me. You really are a jerk."

By the time he spun around to respond, the phone was ringing. His eyes rose to mine, a stunned light in the dark blue centers. "No, I didn't mean . . ."

"Oh, what do you care?" I mumbled almost too low to hear and stepped into the shade of the tree.

"Jennifer, stop," his voice croaked weakly. It felt surprisingly satisfying—this sudden reversal of roles, watching him squirm while I lost my temper. *Had he ever said my name before? It sounded good.*

"Don't, Jennifer." *He said it again.* "You're right. Not here."

The phone rang as Nathan walked toward me, his hands signaling me to stop. "I'm sorry," he said. I held up my hand and pointed to the phone to shut off his words. My irritation held off my fear until my father said hello. The first thing I said was "Dad, I hope you trust me."

"There's some famous last words," he grumbled. "What's going on?"

"I know you won't like this idea at first, but please try to keep an open mind."

"Jennifer . . ." The edge in his voice sharpened.

"I know. Just give me a minute. I'm willing to come home . . ." I inhaled, but the air didn't seem to make it all the way to my lungs. ". . . if Mom comes to get me."

"What?"

"I want Mom to come get me."

"You mean there? You want Mom to fly out there?"

"Yes."

"Well, I want to win the lottery," he rebutted.

I felt Nathan move closer but I ignored him. "Dad, I'm being serious. I've thought about it a lot, and I think she needs to come home and fix things with Sarah. Sarah loves her. Lots of people here care about her. I care about her," I reminded him. "This might be her chance to put it behind her."

"Jennifer, I appreciate your thinking. I do. It's just not realistic."

"But you agree with me? You think she should come?"

"I wish she *wanted* to come," he clarified. "She doesn't. Trust me."

"But Dad, if I asked her . . ."

"Do you think I never tried that? Jennifer, it's not that simple. I tried to get them back together years ago. It didn't work."

"You did? What did you do?"

"I called Sarah when you were born."

I finally turned my face, found Nathan's concerned eyes. "When I was born?"

Nathan squirmed in curiosity, guessing at the other half of the conversation.

"Your mom wouldn't. I thought Sarah should know that she had a niece." His voice smiled. I remembered the way Sarah said my name the first time I called her. I was right that she knew about me.

"I bet she loved that," I said.

"Sarah did. Your mother—not so much. I wanted to put your

aunt down as your guardian in the will, just in case, since I don't have any brothers or sisters."

"What did Mom do?"

"Just about killed me. Which makes the will more useful, I guess."

I kicked my toe into the grass and laughed. But when the sound died, my dad and I both sighed, groping for the next word, the next step. "I think she needs to come, Dad. I think it's been long enough. Sarah never meant to hurt her and the movie star Little says that she won't stop being afraid of her past until she comes home to it. Everyone's been worried about her for twenty years."

"So what do you propose?" His wary voice bled with distrust.

I looked back into Nathan's face, his lips parted just where the ragged line of his scar touched them. I turned toward the sound of the harbor where the clank of boats and machinery carried over the quiet streets and remembered Hester's wounded words, *I think people belong at home.* "I'll tell her I'm coming home, no arguments, no sulking, when she comes to get me. All she has to do is show up. She doesn't even have to come inside."

"And when she says no?"

"She'll want me to come home sometime," I said. It sounded much better coming from Little. Nathan's hand moved forward like he wanted to touch me, but he fingered a low branch of the tree instead.

"And when she sends me to ground you for the rest of your natural life?"

"You tell her no."

He huffed in frustration. "So you're taking us both down?"

"No. I'm bringing her home." I bit down on my thumb, rubbing my bottom teeth against the smooth nail, while I waited. I sensed that everything depended on what he said next.

"If she doesn't come, are you going to live in Maine?" he challenged.

I felt a weakening behind his questions. "No. If summer comes to an end and she hasn't come to get me, then I'll give up and come home. If she really can't do it, if she really can't face it, then all she loses is a few weeks with me." The tortuous silence filled the air around me, amplified my thumping heart.

"I'll think about it."

I had to replay the sentence twice before I understood him. "Are you saying . . . ?"

"I'm saying I'll think about it. Don't you do anything until we talk again."

"I promise. I swear on my life." My voice rose in excitement and then lowered with gratitude. "Dad, I love you. I really think this is the right thing."

"Maybe," he mumbled. "*If* we do this and I end up crippled and alone, you'd better take care of me."

"I don't think it will be that bad. I just have a feeling."

"I don't like feelings," he complained.

"I love you, Dad." But I said it more like *Thank you, Dad.*

I blinked as I closed my phone and turned my head to see Nathan. His worried eyes were riveted to my face, awaiting the verdict.

"So?" he asked.

"So, I think he'll let me try. Are you finally happy?" It came out brusker than I meant, but I didn't amend it.

"No," he said. "Not happy." He took a tentative step toward me and reached out his hand. "But impressed." He gently touched a spot under my eye and held up his finger to show me the smudge of dirt he'd removed. His stained, muddy finger felt cold against my raging blush.

When I looked from his finger to his face, he was too close. The same distance most people normally stand, but for Nathan, far too close. I tried to swallow, but there was no air. No throat. I unfastened my stare from his eyes, letting my gaze stumble over his scar and down to his brown hands which he returned to his pockets. "I'll take you home," he said. All I had to do was walk ten feet to the truck. And keep breathing.

Sometimes life asks too much of us.

CHAPTER 25

"YOU CAN'T TELL Sarah," is the first thing I managed to verbalize when I settled onto the torn, vinyl seat. As soon as I said it, I felt the grip of Smithport tightening its noose around my mouth. Secrets. I was just another Smithport girl with a secret.

"You think she'll get mad?" Nathan asked as the engine thundered under the hood.

"She wouldn't let me do it. And I've finally convinced myself that I have to do it." I looked at Nathan, my resolve brittle. "I'd better be right."

"I think you handled it really well," Nathan said.

I laid my head against the cold glass of the window, feeling it vibrate as the car accelerated. "He still hasn't totally agreed. He knows my mother won't appreciate it very much."

"What do you think she'll do?"

"Oh, this and that," I mumbled, inwardly flinching at the conversation I had ahead of me if Dad agreed. I barely noticed as the town dissolved into a dense line of trees along the road. "I have to call Cleo," I said.

"Your friend. Are you going to show me a picture of her today?" Nathan asked.

I sighed. I suppose I was defeated from the moment he first asked. "Why not?" I muttered.

He shot me a puzzled look, but didn't ask about her again until we made it to Shelter Cove and were standing on the porch with the photo album I had brought to show Sarah. She'd studied it in detail from my kindergarten picture where I had a black eye due to a brutal run-in with a doorknob to my shots of Mother at the top of Pike's Peak last year. I purposely turned past all of my embarrassing adolescent pictures to the end of the book.

"And why doesn't she like people?" Nathan asked as I searched for the right page.

"She does *like* people. She doesn't *trust* people. They've always reacted too much to the way she looks. She thinks they're shallow." I paused to point out a few pictures. "That's my dad and my mother." My finger lingered on my mother's smiling face.

"I see your mom in you, but you really do look more like Sarah," Nathan commented, as he studied me.

"I know." We skimmed through a few more pictures until we got to my sixteenth birthday party. "That's Cleo," I said, watching him carefully as I touched her picture. In the photo her head was turned, her long hair swinging and her pink lips parted as she said something. It couldn't convey her full beauty, but it got the idea across.

I waited in dread for his response, but Nathan's eyes didn't widen. He just studied the photo and turned back to me. "She looks nice."

Did he mean "nice" as in *kindhearted* or as in *supermodel*? I fumbled for an answer and just said, "She is."

"She's not the prettiest girl I've ever seen," he said as he tapped his knuckles on the colorful floats hanging off the rail.

"Then you must have some mutant girls around here."

He chuckled. "Something like that."

I started to ask him what he meant when I caught his eyes sweeping across my face. I felt the weight of the air compound into something solid, pinning me in my chair.

"I've got to get back. I'm sorry about earlier. I didn't mean to be a jerk. I'll see you tonight." He hesitated and then, "I'll try not to go Mr. Hyde on you." He flashed a fast smile and left me seated, speechless, my heart thumping a high, tight rhythm in my chest.

By eight-thirty that night my nerves were stretched thin and taut, waiting for Nathan's knock at the door. When I couldn't stand it any longer, I asked Sarah if she would like to join me on the porch.

She agreed and grabbed a book. "I haven't actually found mine yet, but it never takes long to find one good line. The worst writers can manage one good line, even if it's by accident."

"That sounds like something you should write down."

"See!" she said. "Even I can sound brilliant!" I laughed and then sat quietly, watching her skim the pages. The sun had already sunk below the horizon, but its blazing arms had not dropped from the sky yet. Pink fingers scraped through the clouds, leaving purple bruises under the tired eyes of day. I thought I heard a footstep and I turned from the heavens to the dark shadows of the trees. When he came into view I inhaled, feeling my lungs swell with the brisk air. His gait was awkward, but I didn't mind. It seemed right that way. I wouldn't change it if I could. As he stepped onto the porch he shot me a self-conscious glance and nodded.

"Finish the fence?" Sarah asked. After Nathan answered *yes,* she said, "I'm going last because I'm still looking for a line. You can go first, Nathan."

Let it be a love poem, I silently wished.

He pulled out a piece of paper, even though I knew he didn't need it. He appeared relieved to focus on it instead of Sarah and me. His tongue briefly wet his top lip. "It's from a poem called 'Vocation,' by Tagore." One of his dirty shoes rose up and scratched the back of his leg nervously.

"He does what he likes with his spade, he soils his clothes with dust, nobody takes him to task if he gets baked in the sun or gets wet.

I wish I were a gardener digging away at the garden . . ."

The disappointment fell heavy. What could be further from a love poem than a poem about dirt?

"Oh, come on, Nathan," Sarah said in exasperation.

"What?" he asked.

"An obvious bit of justification, I'd say," she scolded. "Do you want my blessing for weeding flowers the rest of your life because someone wrote a poem about it?"

I saw his reaction before he voiced it. A tight ripple slid up his neck, stiffening his jaw. " 'Time is never lost that is devoted to work.' Emerson."

"I didn't say that the work is a waste. I'm glad you've discovered the good of manual labor. It's cleansing. It's important. But you can't hide behind lawn clippings. You almost have your bachelor's. It's time to focus."

"I'm not your project, Sarah. Not your protégé. I can be just as valuable trimming trees as building spaceships. Don't be a snob."

Sarah's eyes blazed. She gripped the wooden arms of her chair and half rose before sitting down sharply. "Below the belt,

Nathan! I don't think education makes you a *better* person. I think you would be a *happier* person. Your brain gets cramped all closed up in that *hard, thick, stubborn* head of yours." Her tongue lashed out the words. "It wants exercise and movement and freedom. It wants to learn in some way other than textbooks."

To my utter shock, and despite his scowling face, he shrugged and grumbled, "Maybe." It reminded me of Glenn. *Mebbe so, mebbe so.* "But speaking of why I *can't* leave," he said pointedly, "you need to talk to Claude. It's getting worse. She won't listen to me anymore."

"What's wrong with Claude?" I interrupted, grateful that the tense moment had not erupted into a fight. I'd had enough anxiety for one day.

Nathan only looked at Sarah when he answered me. "Will. She's getting more serious about him. If he doesn't watch it, Sarah . . ."

"Don't threaten. You need to stay calm and stay out of it. Let Judith handle it."

Nathan gave her a rather rude "hah."

"The bigger deal you make of it, the bigger deal it will be," she insisted.

Nathan shook his head. "That's childish logic—like telling a kid to ignore a bully."

"It's sound logic," Sarah insisted. "Like not giving a tantrum too much attention. Don't make Claude your excuse. You know how unfair that is."

"Responsibility, not excuse!" Nathan said between clenched teeth.

"I didn't get to comment on the poem," I interrupted too loudly. In the quiet instant that followed, a cricket trilled twice. Both of them turned to me looking mildly surprised that I was still there. I met Nathan's gaze with narrow eyes. "I didn't like it."

"What?" he asked.

"It was boring." My jilted feelings roared approval.

"Boring to you?" he suggested.

"Boring to everybody. It sounds like a child wrote it, since you are talking about 'childish logic.' "

"It's from the viewpoint of a child." His face was doing strange things as his expression fought for an emotion to settle on.

"Well, it sounds like it," I grumped.

Sarah examined me in confusion. "Are you all right, Jennifer?"

Nathan's face brightened with genuine amusement. "Are you pouting? You never seemed the type."

I glowered at him. "I'm fine. I'll go next." I pulled out my paper and felt my stomach tighten. " 'I know I am but Summer to your heart, and not the full four seasons of the year.' Edna St. Vincent Millay." My voice started strong and sullen, but it dropped when I got to "heart." The lower it dipped, the more my control slipped on the syllables, trembling. The air felt cold on my moist eyes. "Why do words always do that to me?" I burst out.

Sarah laughed. "Words in the soul. The only people who cry

at a concerto are people with music in the soul. You must have words in the soul."

Nathan didn't comment. He just asked his usual question, "Why that one tonight?"

"Why *yours* tonight?" I demanded. "Why dirt?"

"Why not?" he asked, clearly baffled by my outburst.

Of course, why not. I put my heart down, defeated. Every heedless, weightless feeling I'd experienced, every panting, eager moment waiting for his voice belonged to me alone. He had no reason to discuss love or youth. Only dirt.

"I picked it because it sounded pretty," I answered in a dull monotone.

"It reminds me of John," Sarah said. Her words swept aside my anger. I forgot Nathan for a moment as I turned to her. "I was just a summer to him," she admitted. Her thick hair, the same color as wet, harvest wheat, framed a fatalistic sadness in her features. How a person could see her as "just a summer" bewildered me.

"Why?" I asked, desperate for an explanation. Something to make sense of the ageless suffering of unrequited love. And still, for all my faith in my aunt, for all my infatuation with lines on her front porch, I knew the answer wasn't there. Wasn't anywhere. Simply wasn't.

"His reasons are his. Maybe we don't even know our own reasons. But the point is that I made him all four seasons of my year. Of my life. And I forgot to ask what I meant to him. There is that narcissistic, headlong rush into the arms of destruction. Nothing like first love." Sarah raised her hand as if toasting us. Did she know? Did she know the feelings waking and stirring in the depths of my body?

"He's an idiot," Nathan mumbled.

"I wish it were that simple," Sarah replied. "But thank you, anyway."

"Was Harvey my mother's first love?"

Sarah pinned her surprised gaze on me. "How in the world . . ."

"Glenn told me today." I think I might have looked a bit triumphant. It was nice to hold a few cards, know a few things I wasn't supposed to.

"Figures," Sarah sighed. "They dated. Harvey went crazy when she left. He tried to track her down. He only stopped when she sent the letter telling him that she was fine and she didn't want to be found. It was sent from Ohio. She sent the same letter to Jed—proof that she was fine and a request to be left alone. Those were the only two things we ever heard from her. Harvey wasn't himself for months after that."

"But he recovered?" I asked.

"He did what all watermen do," Nathan crept back into the conversation. "He worked hard. He got back to life. There's something to be said for it," he hinted.

"Nice try." Sarah rolled her eyes.

"Little said that the best loves belong to the young," I added, wondering why I never asked my mother about her first love.

"How'd she come to that conclusion?" Sarah asked. "Because her young love worked out so well?" I didn't like the sarcasm. It sounded wrong on her.

"I don't know. I don't know her story," I answered. "But whatever happened, she's convinced that young love is best."

"Are you?" Nathan asked.

The trees stopped their restless shuffling, and silence clapped its hand over the night. I dared one brief glimpse into his penetrating stare. My eyes dropped. "I wouldn't know," I whispered. I felt a physical stab under my ribs that I later recognized as sadness.

"I'm sorry, Jennifer," Sarah said softly. "I didn't mean to argue with you."

"Don't apologize!" I responded quickly. "You argue with Nathan. You can argue with me. I can hold my own."

"Fair enough. You're right. You're not a child. You can probably handle a healthy dose of skepticism."

"No coward soul is mine," Nathan muttered.

"A quote?" said Sarah.

"Who said that—No coward soul is mine?" Nathan's eyes squinted in thought.

"I don't know. I don't recognize it. Just give it a second. It will come to you," Sarah assured him as he squeezed his hands into fists. "I have one I can read while you figure it out. This one might cheer us up. I can skip the middle stanza." She flattened the spine of her book and read.

"An awful tempest mashed the air,
The clouds were gaunt and few;
A black, as of a spectre's cloak,
Hid heaven and earth from view. . . .

"The morning lit, the birds arose;
The monster's faded eyes
Turned slowly to his native coast,
And peace was Paradise!"

"Emily Dickinson. And it's fitting. We just had a storm. But all is well. All cleaned up. And look how beautiful this night is." I tossed my eyes to the horizon, which had faded to a murky green dripping into the dark blue twilight. I couldn't feel the beauty. Couldn't feel anything but the numb disappointment of—of nothing. To think he saw me as nothing. He was thinking of sweaty gardeners and my line, my words, my thoughts all meandered back to him!

" 'No coward soul is mine, No trembler in the world's storm-troubled sphere,' " Nathan declared triumphantly. "It was a Brontë."

His voice sparked with excitement, and I turned reluctantly, my heavy mind unable to untangle one word from the next. My gaze rested on his stained T-shirt. It still looked like blood. But it should have been my shirt. My bleeding heart. His eyes found mine over the garish glare of the porch light and his secretive smile puzzled me. "Is that better than dirt?"

I had no idea what he was talking about.

CHAPTER 26

BEFORE NATHAN SAID his good-byes, my cell phone detonated with a keening ring. I grabbed it and looked in dread at my dad's cell phone number on the screen. "It's my dad. I'll take it inside." I hurried through my words, shut the door behind me, and flipped the phone open to say a breathless hello.

"I've thought about it all day" is the first thing he said.

"And . . ." I tripped on the stairs as I tried to hop over Chester as he sprawled across the second step.

"I think it's a horrible plan."

I stopped breathing while my stomach dropped inside me.

"But," he continued, "it's the only plan we've got. Beggars can't be choosers."

"Are you serious?" I lowered myself on the top step with a view of the hundreds of faces along the wall. "You're okay with it?"

"Not okay, but not . . . is 'freaking out' what you still say? Or does that make me sound like a dweeb?"

I laughed. " 'Freaking out' is fine, but 'dweeb' made you sound like a loser." I suddenly wished I could elbow Cleo and watch her roll her green eyes.

"Anyway, I'm supposed to be taking out the trash and I can't talk for long. I just wanted to let you know that I'll try to help you. I'll try to make sure she doesn't take it too hard."

"You mean fly out here and kill me?" I teased.

"I will definitely try to curtail that. Try to break it to her as nice as you can," he requested.

"I will."

"I know you will. That's why I trust you to try," he said.

I put my hand over my heart where his words swelled against my ribs like warm air. He didn't wait for me to blubber a thank-you, but told me he loved me and hung up.

Dazed by my sudden turn in fortune, I let my eyes travel through the maze of photographs stretching below me and didn't stop until they came to the one of my grandfather beside his boat. Sitting in his house, looking at his face, remembering the story of my mother's iron bed, made me feel very close to him. I tried to imagine what he would say to me if I brought his youngest daughter back home, but all I could imagine were his hands throwing fish into the ice chests on the dock.

And when I pictured the dock, I remembered Glenn's face as he stroked *The Missus. I've never been loved as much as that boat.* It was too unjust that a homely little fishing boat had a better love story than I. I wouldn't have cared a year ago, a month ago, a week ago. But that was before Nathan touched my face. Surely I could say something, do something, to soften his voice again. If he complimented me once, if he touched me once, he could do it again. I gave the picture of the fishing boat on the wall a defiant glare. I would not be out-loved by floating scrap metal. I jumped up and thumped down the stairs, hopping over Chester who, not trusting me to spare his precious person, twisted and rose with a hiss. "Oh, stuff it," I mumbled.

Sarah and Nathan were discussing Claude when I returned, their voices low and fervent. Sarah finished saying that she would talk to Will's father, but after that they both killed their private conversation and turned to me. "Everything okay?" she asked me.

"Actually . . . it really is, believe it or not. My dad just wanted to tell me that my mother is doing okay. I can stay for now."

Nathan gave me a significant glance while Sarah said how happy she was. "I wanted to get one of the boys to take us out in a boat before you go—get you on the water."

Just then, the house telephone gave a shrill yell. "I guess we're destined to be interrupted tonight," Sarah said. "I'll get it." The screen clattered shut behind her and the night grew closer, more aware, as Nathan and I sat in silence, listening to Sarah answer. "Yes, Judith, I called earlier," Sarah said. She turned back to us, giving us a nod and sat on the couch.

"My mom," Nathan said. "Sarah's going to talk to her about Claude. She'll probably be on for a while." Sarah's mumbled voice filled in the spaces between his words. "So you convinced him? Like I said, I'm impressed."

"Looks like it. Now I just have to figure out how to tell her."

"Good luck with that." I could hear the sympathy and doubt behind his humor.

"Do you still think it might end badly? Do you still think I shouldn't try?"

Instead of answering, Nathan stood and rolled his shoulders. "I think we both know it could end badly. Calculated risk, I guess." He looked up at the dim sky. "I'd better get going."

I stood as well, wondering what I could say to make him stay longer. When he got to the side of the yard, I hopped down the steps and called his name. "Nathan, I forgot to tell you. I remembered something about my mother today. Something I haven't thought of in years."

He stopped and waited for me to catch up, his expression interested and curious.

"When I was ten, I wanted to be a ballerina. It was a disaster, but for a year I really tried." I moved toward the beach and he fell in step beside me. "I had a recital and we all got a little ballet solo at the end. When we took our bows, the house lights came up and I saw my mother in the back, by the exit. She was crying. And I wasn't *that* bad of a dancer."

He returned my smile. "You think she remembered Sarah?" he asked.

"I think that's exactly what happened. I think she saw Sarah when she looked at me up there. I had no idea then . . ."

A grasshopper jumped onto Nathan's chest as he grazed his hands through the tall sea grass. I stopped talking as he cupped his weathered hand over it and with infinite care set it back on the sand. We both stared at the insect in silence until I found my voice. "I've decided I have to try to bring her back, even if you think I'm wrong."

"I don't know if I think you're wrong. That's what makes it hard." He looked away and pushed his hands into his pockets. "Pythagoras says choices are the hinges of destiny."

"I hope I'm opening the right door then." I looked to the water where the tips of the waves blazed with light.

The moon had come out of her dressing room arrayed in a streaming, white gown. A dark circle surrounded her in the sky where no stars dared to stand too close. "That's the prettiest I've seen the moon since I've been here," I said. I doubted even Nathan could resist the pull of that wild, fractured shore.

"How long have you been here? A week? Two?" His eyes swept quickly across my face, darting as they went from side to side.

"I think tomorrow will be ten days." How could ten days, ten tiny days, see the birth of these new feelings? Surely whatever gripped me now had to have a longer gestation than ten days?

"It seems like a lot longer," he said. I scanned his face, certain for a moment that he was thinking something similar. Feeling the same. "It's been fun," he admitted with a minuscule lift of his lips.

"I know."

He stood still long enough for me to lose my breath. Just as I wondered if I should inch closer he retreated a step. "But you'll be leaving," he said, a trace of anger souring the words that were already so bitter for me.

I wanted to argue. "I know. But I'll be back." It was the best I could do.

A sullen curtain closed over his face and after rippling over his expression, it came to a stop, smooth and blank and terrible. "Well, you've had a nice adventure." He blew his breath out to the sky and before I could respond he said, "I *really* have to go. I have other girls to worry about." The cold defiance of his tone was like falling into a snowdrift on a warm day. I shivered and leaned back. *Just another girl. Another person to trouble him. Another problem.*

"Nathan?"

"Good night," he grumbled miserably and turned with fast, stiff steps. I waited until the trees hid his black silhouette to fold myself onto the cold ground, too numb to cry. Too wretched to want to.

CHAPTER 27

THE NEXT TWO days tumbled past me like a slippery ball that I couldn't quite grasp. I spent more time alone by the water where I discovered the calming effect of putting my face against the shard-like sand and watching the surf leap toward me and recede while the sharp grains bit into my cheek.

No matter how often I gave myself a rousing pep talk, none of my platitudes helped in more than the most transitory ways. *You just need to give him time* loaned me a bit of comfort until I remembered that time was the one thing I didn't have. I tried to tell myself to put it all in God's hands, but that rang the emptiest of all. When I thought of hands I thought of Nathan's calloused fingers, scraped knuckles, and thick fingernails. And then I remembered his touch on my face, and I didn't get around to God again until much later.

I thought my worst fear was facing him again. That is, until

Nathan told Sarah that he was too tired after his irrigation job and needed to skip lines. Only then did I realize that his anger, his resentment, his distance, was nothing—nothing—compared with his absence. "Does he do that often? Skip?" I asked her.

"Oh, sure. We both do." She said it with such ease. Like it didn't mean the death of the best part of the day. "You and I can still do it," she assured me with questioning eyes.

"No, that's okay. We can take a break." I rose and started washing the dishes so she couldn't see my face.

CHAPTER 28

SARAH AND I did lines alone the next night, after Nathan cancelled due to a "headache." Our conversation quickly left the realm of literature. After we read our lines Sarah asked me if I knew when I was leaving. The subject always threw my emotions into a frenzy. "Are you getting sick of me?" I teased, stalling for time.

"Quite the opposite," Sarah answered. "I'm worried I'm getting too attached." When I looked up at her I saw my own face mirrored in hers, my pain, my doubt, my impending loss, all sketched lightly in her features. When I hesitated too long, she continued. "I really didn't think I was lonely. And now I feel like a fool."

"Why?" I asked, trying to convey sympathy and disagreement in one tight syllable.

"Because I was so deluded. I thought I was fine putting out fires for Judith, helping Nathan, teaching my students, having dinners out with the teachers. I told myself it was enough. But it's different having someone in the house, having a family again. I'm a little scared to face the quiet when you leave."

My stomach seized and I rubbed a hand over my face, burying my eyes. "Would it have been better if I never came?" I asked myself more than I was asking Sarah. My mother's face, Nathan's grim frown, the picture of my wet cheek pressed into the sand all surged through my thoughts.

"Are you kidding?" Sarah cried. "I never thought you'd come to that conclusion! I just meant that I'm a feeling a little raw tonight. And thinking of you going—I'm wondering if it will be like watching Claire leave again. I wish I knew how much time I have. To prepare myself."

I tapped my sandal against the railing, remembering the thumping sound of my foot on the table leg when I told my parents I was leaving. Such a full circle to be sitting in Maine, telling my aunt I was leaving. I always seemed to be upsetting someone. "I don't really know. I'll stay as long as I can."

After a few quiet moments of looking over the tops of the trees to the shadowy clouds sailing across the sky, I asked, "Do you miss the theater?"

"The theater? Do you mean the acting, or the singing, or the dancing?" Sarah asked in open surprise.

"Yes." I smiled. "All of it."

"Well, I don't ever think about it much. I don't think so. What brought this on?"

I deflected her question with one of my own. "Why did you stop?"

"Really?" Sarah laughed, clearly in doubt that the topic deserved any attention. "I, well, in all honesty, I stopped because of John."

Again, a voluntary mention. My heartbeats hastened. "What did he do?"

"Nothing. I just met him while I was performing, and I wanted to make a clean break when he left. I also had to make a real living when I lost my parents. No one was there to catch me if my Broadway career didn't pan out." She laughed at herself, mocking the idea of her success.

I ignored her self-effacing remarks and asked, "Will you sing me something?"

"What?" she cried. "No!" Again the disbelief widened her smile.

"I'm being serious."

Her eyes narrowed. "Did Nathan tell you—"

I didn't expect his name to stab so sharp. "No," I cut her off. "He doesn't talk to me anymore."

"He doesn't talk to you?" Sarah asked, all jesting abandoned.

"No, not *doesn't*," I stammered. "He *hasn't* talked to me. Lately.

With his work and everything. We haven't seen him." Despite my embarrassed blush, I think I buried my mistake. A shallow grave, perhaps, but still . . .

"Well, I'd never just sing for no reason," Sarah said. "Too scary."

"You used to do it for an entire audience. Why not sing for me?"

"Because you're sitting too close. I can see you. And I've grown some pride since then." She threw her head back and groaned. "Seriously?" she asked helplessly.

I shrugged, chagrined.

"What do you want me to sing?" she asked.

"Just anything. Anything you like."

"I'll feel like a fool," she said, covering her face in her hands like a schoolgirl.

"You shouldn't. I won't look at you." I turned away, the air thick with her self-consciousness. I heard her rustle in her chair and sigh. After several long beats of silence, I stopped listening for Sarah and started listening to the night. The wind and waves made one unified song, a sweeping of the air, like heavenly brooms brushing across the world and clearing away the daylight.

Quiet and shy, Sarah's voice entered the night. I knew if I looked at her face it would be scarlet and agonized, so I kept my promise and watched Chester stalk across the yard. The first words were so weak she half spoke them. One of her notes faltered and her voice shook. But slowly, slowly, some instinct took over and her throat relaxed, letting the music come. She sang an Irish-sounding melody about a handsome boy named Johnny. After the last, short verse, her song closed, handing the solo back to the night.

"Sarah?" I asked softly. "Do you still love him?" I was still turned away, but now I did it for my own privacy and not hers.

"I think you always do, somewhere, in some way."

It's what I feared. "Couldn't you just find someone else who is better for you? Wouldn't that be better than crying over him?"

"Ideal, actually." Sarah grinned when I turned back to her. "It's a great plan. The only problem is putting it into practice."

"Why? Why can't you love anyone else?"

Sarah let the smile slip from her face as her eyes seemed to fall back into a dark well, sinking farther and deeper by the second. "I haven't found anyone who made me forget yet. And maybe I don't deserve to."

I wanted to answer, wanted to reassure her, but the doubt and sadness bound me, tied my tongue.

"I didn't mean that to sound martyr-ish. I just seem to have a unique gift for hurting people. Probably best to keep it to myself."

I shook my head in disapproval. "That reminds me of my mother's excuses for not coming home. I don't think it's a very good reason."

"There are no good reasons, are there? They all sound like excuses when we say them out loud. I think I'll just figure it all out someday. I really do." Sarah's voice lightened, her eyes relaxed. "Plus, you have to admit my pickings are a little slim here. Jed's already taken . . ." She let the punch line dangle into the air until I gave in and laughed with her. "Why all this tonight?" she asked. "The singing, the questions about John?"

"I don't know. Maybe because we're alone. Girl talk."

That satisfied her and she leaned back in her chair. "I've missed girl talk. Even my pets are boys!" She laughed.

"You sing beautifully. Really. I could have listened for hours," I told her.

She avoided looking at me by pulling Charlie's front legs onto her lap. His tongue flicked out and he dropped his jaw in an adoring dog smile. "See, Charlie," she cooed. "We can howl at the moon together." I snickered and let the compliment lie. She could pick it up later, when no one was looking.

❧

After Sarah went inside I wandered to the woods at the edge of the yard, the ghost of her song still hanging in the silent air. I pictured my mother beside me and knew that it was time. With my new heartache added to the world, it seemed time to retire an old one. I found a spot under a withered pine tree and pulled out my phone, shifting it between my hands as my courage built.

"Hi," I said to her when she answered. "I was just thinking of you. How are you?"

"How are you?" she quickly countered.

"Safe and sound," I promised. If I let her hear my smile, would she follow suit? I picked up a dead pine needle and swirled its sharp point across my lips, prodding myself into finding the right words. She saved me the trouble and spoke first.

"I have a confession. I went to your graveyard."

I couldn't fit that simple statement into something as ominous as a confession. "You mean the Cowling Cemetery? Why is that a confession?"

"Because I never went there before. It was yours. I think a girl needs a place where her mother doesn't go that is only hers. Don't you?"

I thought of the headstones. Maeve. Ann. William. Maybe they could tell her something, give her something that I couldn't. Surely they knew something about regrets. "I never realized you wanted to go. I never knew you were stopping yourself. You shouldn't do that. You should go." The pine needle was pressing into my tender top lip, the tiny piece of pain sharpening my thoughts.

"It is so beautiful there. I hate graveyards. But not that one," she said.

"I love graveyards. They're proof that we survive everything, even death."

"That doesn't make sense," she said, her tone less melancholy.

"It does to me. I think it does to Maeve. I'm glad you went. You should go back. Cleo won't make up stories about them, but

I think Maeve is my favorite. I always sit by her. I think she was funny."

"Maeve? I didn't pay enough attention to the names. I was reading the dates."

"Don't. It doesn't work that way. It doesn't matter how much time they had. It's who they were. Try talking to Maeve."

My mother almost laughed but it turned into a sigh. "I don't want to bother her."

"That's the thing. It's impossible. She loves to talk." I could sense her smile across the space between us. I wished it wasn't so sad. "Mom?" I asked, knowing that the time was now or never. I pulled in a breath and braced my hands against he tree. "I just wanted to let you know that I'll come home now, if that's what you want."

I heard a rush of air over the phone as she breathed out in relief. "Jennifer, I'm so glad. What flight are you taking? What day?"

"I don't know. Exactly. It depends."

She sounded so blissfully ignorant when she asked, "On what?"

"Umm—you," I pushed the word out.

"Me?"

I choked. How to put the next line? All of my reasons rushed out my head in a stampede, leaving my brain in a dust cloud. "Could you come get me?" I asked, my voice high and helpless. It reminded me of my first sleepover when I was six and the reality of dozing off in a strange basement finally hit me at ten o'clock at night. I think I'd said the exact same thing—*Can you come get me?*

"Come get you?" Her voice faltered.

Darn it. I didn't mean to ask. I meant to demand. With confidence. "I want you to come get me," I said, forcing some power back into my words.

"Why? Is something—did something go wrong?" Her alarmed words rose in pitch.

"No. Not at all. I just miss you."

"You know I can't go *there*. What is going on? Do you need me to call the airline?" The agitation in her voice made my shoulder curl against my ear to rub away the sound. "Do you want me to send Dad?" she asked.

"No. Just you." My breath shuddered. "When you come get me, I'll come home." Silence as she processed the way my voice leaned, curving the sentence into an ultimatum. I had hoped it wouldn't come to that.

"Is that . . . a *threat*?" she asked, her voice tainted with shock. "Did Sarah . . ."

"No! It's Little, actually. Little wants you to come get me. Sarah doesn't even know." *Just throw the old woman under the bus!*

"Little? You know Little?"

"Yeah, and Little really thinks you should come get me."

"Are you kidding me? She hasn't seen me in twenty years."

"I think that's the point."

"Jennifer, this is all wearing thin. It's the last straw. Get on a plane and get home."

"I can't."

"What do you mean you can't?"

"I can't. Until you come get me. I think Little's right." I clutched the trunk, digging my fingers into the deep ruts of the bark.

"I don't care what anyone thinks. I've gone along with this for long enough. If you don't come home, I will send your father."

"I'm not going home with Dad. I'm only going home with you."

"You'll go home with—"

"No! I won't. I need to talk to you about all this. All you have to do is knock on the door. You don't have to talk to Sarah. You don't have to come inside Shelter Cove. Just show up. Just knock. I'll pack my bags and go. I'll even pay for your ticket."

"Jennifer, you have no idea what you're asking. It's not possible. It is *not* possible!"

"Mom, I know you're scared. I know that. Sarah's scared, too. But it's time. Just think about it."

"Jennifer, don't . . ." she warned. I could tell that more words would only make things worse. She was just getting warmed up.

"Please think about it. You know I'm just asking because I love you. I don't want to fight with you. I have to go now but I'm not hanging up on you. I'm not. Bye."

"Jennifer!" is the last thing I heard before I hit the end button. My head buzzed with a heavy dizziness, like a spin cycle inside my skull. I realized that I had leaned all the way into the tree, my forehead at rest against the sticky trunk. My eyes burned. My throat constricted. I blinked and turned my head toward the sound of the water I couldn't see before I pushed my palms against my eyes, trying to hold back the tears. When my mother's angry cry echoed in my mind, the waves replied with a gentle *hush, hush, hush.*

CHAPTER 29

I WAITED UNTIL my face was clear and calm again before I went inside to clean up for bed. I escaped to the quiet of my bedroom, hoping to sort through my thoughts. The clear night gave me a view of the moon scraping the tops of the pine trees, and I opened the rickety, metal window to smell the clean air. As much as I loved Nebraska I would miss that—the wind surging in with no invitation. It never relented, even when it dwindled to the softest breeze. I pulled the desk chair under the window and carefully folded my grandmother's quilt around my shoulders before I lowered myself into the seat.

I tried not to look at the trees that hid Nathan's house. It made his absence much crueler when my mind flattened a few scraggly pines and viewed him within shouting distance. Maybe too far for shouting. But certainly a good scream would carry. *If*

I screamed now, would he hear me? I wondered as I dared a quick glance to gauge distance. It was in that glance that I saw someone move beside the large boulder where Sarah liked to sit. My first thought went to Little taking another late walk. If the half-moon lent enough light, I might be able to see what she did when she went to the water alone.

The person moved again, a shadow on shadows. As he or she walked away from the boulders, the beam of the moon reflected like tiny candles on the water and in the faint glow I recognized Nathan as he peeled off his shirt, leaving a sheen of light on his naked back. He took a few slow steps to the water and just as I was wondering what he would do next he plunged himself into the black, icy waves.

I yelled a wordless cry and smacked my hand against my mouth. I'd felt that water in the heat of the summer day and even then it threatened to curl the skin off my bones. He'd kill himself. I stood, trying to decide whether to panic, when his head bobbed back above the water and his arm flew out in a clean, powerful stroke. The light on the water broke and bobbed around him, glinting off his wet head as he cut through the lapping waves. My grandmother's quilt dropped in a colorful heap as I fled the room, taking the stairs as quickly and quietly as possible. Sarah's bedroom door was closed, so I snatched up my sandals and tiptoed on flying feet to the kitchen and turned the doorknob slow enough to avoid creaking. Charlie hopped up from his cushion in the corner of the kitchen and clicked over the hard floor to me. I opened the door wide, letting him race out so he wouldn't bark when I left.

And then I was running. Outrunning Charlie. Not stopping until I crested the ridge where I halted long enough to pull on my shoes. Charlie barked joyously at my hopping, running game, but I clamped my fist around his muzzle and gave him a threatening, "Hush!" When I looked at the water again I saw Nathan striking back for shore. I watched his strong arms propel him through the blackness. He stepped back onto land just as I made it to the boulders.

"Is sea salt therapeutic?" I called out.

Nathan jumped and whipped around to me, his body dripping. "Excuse me?" he said, visibly shaken. He pushed Charlie back to stop his frantic licking.

"The sea salt. Because you said you couldn't come tonight because you had a headache. And last night you weren't feeling well enough. The night before that you were just tired. So I'm wondering if a sea bath is good for headaches? Fatigue?"

"How did you know I was here?" he asked as he grabbed a towel and draped it over his shoulders.

"I saw you from my window. Talk about someone who looks like they're committing suicide!"

"Sorry to disappoint you, but I'm not." He leaned his head over and shook it vigorously, clearing water from his ear. His eyes were so belligerent, I almost missed the soft arch of worry that crossed his brow.

"Good to know. But if you feel well enough to join the Polar Bear Club, why didn't you come to lines?" I shuddered in the cool of the night as the wind hit my bare shoulders. I could only imagine how icy Nathan felt.

His lips shook from the cold as he answered, "I don't know."

"Neither of us is stupid enough to believe that," I objected.

"Sometimes I just don't feel like doing it. It's not a requirement, you know." He stretched his T-shirt back over his head, wet splotches appearing as the water on his skin soaked through.

"You're doing the Mr. Hyde thing," I said. "I don't know why you're mad at me. I don't know why you won't even talk to me for three days. I thought we were friends and I'll be leaving anytime now . . ."

"Exactly!" Nathan interrupted. "You're leaving. You don't live here. You don't belong here. Why do you care?" On each syllable of *why do you care* he pounded his towel into a smaller ball until it was a wet lump in his hand.

"You'll wake somebody," I hissed, stepping forward and pushing a warning hand on his cold arm. I knew the houses were too far for anyone to overhear, but the night felt so quiet. In the air I sensed watching eyes. After that touch I looked up into his unreadable face. Whatever I imagined I would feel standing in the moonlight, holding his wet arm, I was wrong. There was no lust trailing its fiery, forked tail through my body—only anger tinged with a determination to stand toe to toe with his temper. I would not be dismissed. I released his arm, but refused to step away. Pointing to the sand beneath my feet, I said, "I might not live here, but I belong here. Right here." My arm flew out toward Shelter Cove. "My grandparents are buried in this town. This is as much mine as it is yours." My voice calmed. "I just didn't know it until now."

"Really?" His defiant word was tempered with an unexpected softness.

"Yes, really," I said.

"And when you leave?"

My heart paused before resuming its fluid beats. "I can't help that, Nathan. But wasting our time worrying about time doesn't make any sense."

"There are a lot of ways to waste time." He ran his fingers through his sandy hair, dropping water on his shoulders.

"Like being mad at your friends?"

"Do you want to be friends, Jennifer?" He forgot to be flippant halfway through his sentence.

No. Not friends. Not just friends. My brain beat the words against my eyes like Morse code, hoping he could see the flashing message as he studied me intently.

"Yes," I answered weakly.

"Really?"

No. "Yes."

His cold, calloused hands closed around my upper arms and he leaned closer. For a breathless moment I knew he would kiss me, but I couldn't close my eyes. Couldn't even remember that I had eyes to close.

He let go and took a step back. "Well I don't have a lot of practice with friends." He studied my expression, questions running across his face. I can only guess that he saw it—some remnant of how I truly felt. "So I hope your expectations are low. I'll come back to lines tomorrow. I've just had a lot on my mind."

I fingered the damp spots where his hands encircled my arms and tried to understand what just happened. Was I supposed to say I didn't want to be his friend? Would he have kissed me then? I fought for some way to amend my words, but my brain was slugging through the shock of his touch. Like being submerged in fast, black water. Even I didn't know where I would finally surface.

He gathered his shoes to leave and I groped for anything neutral, anything easy, to say. "How often do you enjoy a nice evening swim like this?"

"Once in a while. When I'm stressed. You can't worry about anything else after you jump in." His arms rippled in one big shiver. Beads of water still clung to the hair on his legs.

"Yeah, well, trying not to die of hypothermia can kind of bring things into perspective. But you should go with a partner. It's not safe."

Nathan smirked and rolled his eyes. "Are you volunteering?"

My laugh came out too loud in the quiet night. "Not on your life!"

"There you go. And a partner would negate the being-alone-when-you're-stressed objective." We both looked back at the dark water. I was about to tell him about my conversation with my mother, but something held the words back. For this small moment I didn't want her here, didn't want the ghosts of the past here. I just wanted Nathan and his thoughts.

Instead I asked, "What are you so stressed about lately? Claude?"

"Oh, I don't know. A little of everything." He yanked the towel tighter around his shoulders. "Doesn't matter." A fast pause before he said, "Sorry I yelled at you. You surprised me."

"Ambushed you."

"Kind of."

"At least you didn't slip and fall in! If you ever come to Nebraska, I hope you're scared of cows and fall in a mud puddle. Then we'll be even." Only after I said that did I realize that he had no reason to come.

"You found my secret. Terrified of bovines." His lips pulled up on one side into an amused grin.

"Ah, so that's your Kryptonite, huh?" As I stood there, I realized that my stomach was not sinking or soaring. My skin didn't crawl or tingle or flame. I smiled at him happily, grateful for the easiness of the moment.

Before I could blink or think or move he leaned over and rested his lips lightly against mine. I've tried so many times to remember exactly what I thought in that moment, but I can't recall a single organized concept in my mind. A light, victorious feeling sprung up at my lips and washed over the rest of me. In the fastest instant it was over and I looked up with a surprised smile.

The calm grin on Nathan's mouth melted into a straight line, and his eyes narrowed in a mixture of confusion and regret. "I'm freezing. I'd better get inside." I couldn't move yet. The warm, triumphant feeling was still swooping up to my chest and meeting the icy fear that Nathan's face triggered in my mind. Like a storm front under my ribs. "I'll see you tomorrow. Sorry." His eyebrows inched up in a silent plea and he slipped away, fast and quiet.

His "sorry" had been so gentle, so soft that I couldn't tell if he meant *sorry for leaving so fast* or *sorry for kissing you*. My churning emotions collided and a cold, dousing drizzle in my chest extinguished the light of his kiss. I found myself, once again, abandoned to the moon's indifference.

But this time I knew that Nathan felt something for me. And despite the clammy, sinking sensation in the pit of my stomach, my mind skirted around the dark hole that his exit left. Tonight, when I got back to my bed, I had a kiss to remember. And a promise that he would come back tomorrow. It was enough. For now.

CHAPTER 30

IT TOOK HOURS to convince myself to go to sleep. I lay in bed, picturing him across the cove, his head sunken into a lumpy pillow, his eyes staring up at the dark ceiling just like mine. I hoped he had the same secret smile that tugged at my lips. I'd never considered sneaking out in my life, but now it crossed and recrossed my mind. If I could just lean up against his house I would sit there, my back to the wall where he slept, only wood and plaster between us. Something about touching the rough shingles of his home seemed very important, almost as important as touching him. Instead of stealing back into the night, I revisited the beach in my mind, watching my first kiss. I tried to see it from different angles. I tried putting my arms around his neck. I tried closing my eyes. I tried to make up words for him to say, but I always scratched those out. My words didn't work on him. I tried putting his hand in my hair.

That was the best one. A finger trailing right behind my ear. Then I made him lean back and smile. And I fell asleep.

The next day dawned warm and, to my relief, busy. Sarah arranged to take me out on the boat owned by Will's father, Jake, and we spent the morning packing food and sunscreen and bottled water. Anything that sped up the daylight hours was a blessing to me.

"So is Claude coming?" I asked Sarah.

"Hah! Not in this lifetime!" she said as she shoved granola bars into our beach bag. "Claude hates boats. Won't set foot on one."

"Why?" I asked. That was like someone in Nebraska being repulsed by tractors.

"No clue. She has no clue. She can't remember anything bad ever happening on a boat. They still terrify her."

"You made me sound weird for not liking seafood. And I've never lived here!"

"True. There is someone weirder than you. That's got to feel good." Sarah winked over the bulging canvas bag. "Let's go."

In town we found the Jacks on their usual bench. "They sort of look like gatekeepers," I whispered to Sarah and nodded toward their position right at the top of the ramp that led to the docks.

"Hah! 'Abandon hope all ye who enter here!' We should inscribe *that* on their bench!"

"How do, girls?" Pete asked with a broad smile. "Looking fresh and lovely today."

"Playing the polite card today, Pete? I like that one. You almost pull it off."

"Now, Sarah, I'm hurt. Nothing stings like an insult from a pretty girl." His eyes twinkled over his frown.

"I forgot how very tender you boys are," Sarah jeered. "Like little old lambs."

"Nowt but the lambs of God," Russ said with an angelic face.

"Oh, please," Sarah laughed. "More like the lost sheep. But we can't chat today. Jake's taking us out on his boat. Jennifer's maiden voyage."

Glenn spat on the ground in contempt. "That warehouse on water? You're taking her out on *that*? That amounts to sin, is what! Sin!"

"Just got to show her the rest, Glenn. Then one of these days you can show her the best. She'll appreciate *The Missus* more if she has something to compare her to." Sarah's soothing voice unruffled his furrowed brow. "And," Sarah continued in a tempter's tone, "if she's still here for Independence Day, you can give her a show. Jake never has anything much better than bottle rockets."

"They got nothin' on us, do they boys?" Glenn perked up right away.

"I ordered some rockets straight from Thailand this year. Not even approved for use in America. Smuggled them in from eBay," Pete bragged.

"That's . . . disturbing," Sarah answered and sighed a "live and let live" kind of sound. "We'll see you when we get back."

"*If* that cheap heap gets you back," Glenn mumbled. Sarah rolled her eyes and hustled me past.

"What's all the talk about rockets?" I asked as we stepped onto the docks.

"Fourth of July is a big deal here. All the fishermen push off from shore and shoot fireworks off their boats. It makes for a great show. If you're still here, you'll love it. Your mom used to lose her head over the fireworks. She would have eaten spaghetti and lentils all year just to save money for my dad's rockets. His show was usually pretty good."

She smiled at the memory of her father, and I remembered the feeling of being close to him on the living room stairs. Sarah raised her hand and let out a piercing whistle that probably carried for a mile.

"How did you do that?" I asked.

"Talented tongue" was all she said as the fishermen went back to their work.

"We're ready for you, Sarah," a man shouted.

"Thanks, Jake. This is my niece, Jennifer." Jake was average height, average girth, and handsome in a very ordinary way. I stole a quick glance where Harvey's boat sat at the dock, wondering how to convince him to tell me about my mother, but he was nowhere in sight.

"Come on up, Jennifer," Jake said, extending his hand and pulling me aboard. "You've met Will before, right?" he asked, and I affirmed by giving Will a smile and wave as he unwound a net on the deck of the boat. "I knew your mom. Went to school together. She used to make me paper airplanes to fly at recess. Had a little crush on her. But there were only twenty girls in the school, so we all had little crushes on everybody." I liked Jake instantly. It felt good to hear someone talk about Mother so graciously. He directed me to the bow of the boat where I could enjoy the wind and speed (it felt so much faster than I imagined a fishing boat would) and I stayed there, next to Sarah, for most of the next four hours while we watched Will and his father at work. I studied Will throughout the trip, trying to see him both as Claude and as Nathan did. I failed both times. He was too ordinary to love or hate. But after watching him pull in the nets for hours with a good natured smile I realized I sided closer to Claude. I liked him.

By the time we returned to the dock my invigorated brain was bursting with the new smells and sensations and sounds, but my body was exhausted. "How do the watermen do it?" I asked Sarah as we drove home. "It's depleting."

"They're tough. You can't live in Maine and not have a tough streak in you. It's a hard place to make a living."

"But worth it?"

"Undeniably worth it," she affirmed.

After a dinner of leftovers it was already seven o'clock. The distractions of the day were over, and my every thought wandered back to seeing Nathan. Wondered if he would kiss me again. My fingertips trembled as I looked over the books, wondering how much to reveal in the passage I picked. I obviously couldn't read "How do I love thee, let me count the ways . . ." but I didn't want to recite about dirt either. Something subtle. Something that hinted. In book after book, it eluded me. It took nearly an hour to decide on a line. Sarah walked through the living room and absently pulled a book off the shelf. After a fast perusal she marked the page and was done.

I huffed and tapped Charlie on the top of his head with my pencil. The waiting was the hardest. At eight-thirty I heard his steps on the porch and shot up from the couch. No room for pretense. I know the delight showed plain on my face when I opened the screen door and stepped out. I could feel it throbbing against my cheeks like a sunburn.

Nathan's tanned face never betrayed a blush, but a deep red blazed around the collar of his T-shirt. He swallowed, his Adam's apple bobbing, and sat down nervously. He opened his mouth to say hello, but decided on a nod instead.

"Hi, stranger." Sarah joined us on the porch and threw Nathan a jolly greeting. "We've missed you." I dipped my head. She had no idea.

Nathan nodded again and his voice cracked a little when he answered, "Hi, Sarah."

"Who is first tonight?" she asked with a clap of her hands.

"You," Nathan hastened to reply. I nodded in agreement.

"All righty. I picked Hermann Hesse. A favorite of mine."

"They're all favorites," Nathan said in a comic aside. Sarah smiled and ignored him. I was just grateful to see him joke. When he joked I knew he was there. The real Nathan. The open Nathan. Sarah read with gusto, read convincingly,

"Leave me alone, you unendurably old human grief!
Let it all be pain.
Let it all be suffering, let it be wretched—
But not this one sweet hour in the summer,
And not the fragrance of the red clover . . ."

"It's from 'Lying in Grass,' " she finished, but I didn't say a word. My lips made a small O where they parted in the middle.

"Can I see it?" I asked, taking the book from her hand. " 'Not this one sweet hour in the summer,' " I read quietly, tracing the words with my finger. "I like this one," I whispered.

"Good! I like it, too. It gives me hope. No matter how terrible life gets —and doesn't he put it well, 'unendurably old human grief'?— there is always a reprieve. A moment of grace."

"A sweet hour in the summer," I said.

"Precisely," Sarah agreed.

I looked to Nathan, only to find him staring at me. We both diverted our eyes.

"So don't waste time?" he said in his low, shy voice.

"Exactly. Not the good time. Put the misery away and enjoy yourself," Sarah answered. Nathan glanced up again, a troubled look in his eyes.

"Do you think it makes the grief worse—contrasting it with the good?" he asked.

"That's an age-old question," Sarah said. "But no, I don't. I think it makes the grief more bearable. We need a pattern of hope in life. We need to think we will keep returning to better days."

"And what happens when you've had your last 'better' day?" Nathan asked, a desperate edge to his voice. "What if the best is not 'yet to be'?"

"Nathan, you're eighteen," I scolded. "You can't think the best of life is over."

"No. Not me. I'm talking philosophically. What if someone wakes up and realizes that they have already lived the best part of their life? What do you do with that?" He leaned forward, waiting for an answer, looking to Sarah and me.

"Then you have time to savor it, I suppose," Sarah offered.

"Is that good enough?" Nathan asked.

"Not really. But we make do," Sarah said.

"You say it like it's fate, Nathan," I interrupted. "Like God deals the cards and if you already played the ace, then too bad for you." They both looked at me thoughtfully, the intelligent spark in Nathan's eyes almost blinding me.

"So how do you see it then, if that's wrong?" he asked.

"I don't know. You just . . . you . . ."

"You pull a new card," Sarah finished for me. I looked at her with a grateful, knowing smile.

"Exactly. Just deal again," I said.

"So what did you bring tonight, deep thinker?" Sarah asked Nathan.

He leaned back and rubbed his lower back, wincing. "Okay, well, you know it," he said to Sarah. "You'll be sick of it. But I'm saying it anyway." He turned to me. "Every New England child has to recite this one in school at some point. It won Frost the Pulitzer, and it's called 'Nothing Gold Can Stay.' " He kept his eyes steadily averted until he came to the last line and his serious gaze fell on me. He said it like he meant me to understand something.

" 'Nothing gold can stay.' "

I met his stare, frozen by the new intensity in his voice, and tried to find the meaning in the slope of his searching eyes.

"So we've gone from 'enjoy the moment' to 'accept that the moment can't last,' " Sarah stated.

"That's the problem with great truths," Nathan said in frustration as he turned away from me. "There's always a contradictory great truth. How can that be?"

"I don't think they contradict at all," I offered. "One says that nothing good lasts forever. The other one says to put our grief away and appreciate our happiness. They go together. Maybe we appreciate joy . . ."

"*Because* it is finite," Nathan finished.

"Exactly." My soul expanded and settled into a quiet smile on my lips. He finished my sentence. He finished my thought. I took it for a sign. I can't say a sign of what, precisely, but a good sign, nonetheless.

He groaned. "That kind of sucks."

"Beautifully and artfully put," Sarah admonished with a twist of her eyebrow.

"Sorry. I find that to be an unsatisfying concept." He didn't mask his sarcasm, but Sarah ignored it.

"Better," she approved.

"Lots of things last," I said. "They're not all finite. Some things really are enduring." Sarah looked at me with encouragement in her bright eyes.

Nathan's frown turned from surly to thoughtful. "But the poem," he said, "did you notice in the poem that nothing *gold* can stay. Nothing of real value. It's the good things that leave you. Doesn't that upset you?"

"A frog can't complain he's green, Nathan," Sarah interjected. "We're mortal. Life passes. Things go. Happy people make peace with that."

"I never claimed to be a happy person," he muttered. He looked at me, and I remembered his mouth on mine. He had been happy in that instant. I tasted it on his lips. I breathed it in the air. Whatever emotions followed, I knew he acted effortlessly when he kissed me. Seeing that moment in my head and then looking back to his serious face overwhelmed me with embarrassment.

"What did you bring tonight?" he asked me.

My heart on my sleeve. A million questions. The need to touch you. "A poem by Thomas Moore," I said. I found my page and read.

"Oh! think not my spirits are always as light,
        And as free from a pang as they seem to you now;
Nor expect that the heart-beaming smile of to-night
        Will return with to-morrow to brighten my brow."

Nathan opened his mouth, and I held up my hand, beating him to it. "I chose that one tonight because I was thinking of things that don't last." All three of us laughed together.

"Must be something in the water," Sarah said.

"One-track minds," I agreed.

"So *I* was thinking of saying good-bye to Jennifer. What

brought it on for you two?" Sarah looked at us, her wide hazel eyes innocent of the position she put us in.

"Saying good-bye," I repeated softly.

Nathan shook his head. "Don't know," he mumbled.

"Come on, Nathan. 'Nothing Gold Can Stay'? That's elementary stuff for you. Something made you read it tonight," Sarah pushed.

"Sometimes there's no reason," I interjected. As nice as it would be to hear his true feelings, I couldn't bear the trapped look on his face.

Nathan nodded in deference to me as if saying "See, there!" to Sarah.

"If you say so," she relented.

"Saying good-bye and something else." I returned to my first answer, mustering my courage. "The way people change. The way everything seems fine one day and entirely different the next."

Nathan cleared his throat. When we looked at him he stood hastily and cut off my words. "I'm gonna get going now."

"What? Already?" Sarah asked. "We were just getting started."

I looked at him, baffled. He turned away from both of us. "Yeah, sore back. I filled in rock beds today. I'm beat."

"Well, take it easy, then, I guess. Good night," Sarah said reluctantly.

"Yeah, no problem. 'Night." He smiled at me, but the grin didn't reach his eyes.

I watched him turn, a panic rising to my throat. I'd collected nothing. Nothing comforting to remember as I fell asleep. Nothing to add to my memories of him. He stepped down the stairs and walked away. I don't recall deciding to stand. My legs rose of their own accord. And then I was following him, catching him at the side of the house. "I'll walk you home," I told him as he halted.

"No. Don't worry about it." His eyes shied away from me.

"Why?" I whispered, so Sarah wouldn't hear. I looked toward the porch and he did the same thing. He took my arm and pulled me firmly but gently into the backyard.

"I'm really sorry about last night," he said in a voice I had to strain to hear.

"Sorry?"

"I don't know what I was thinking. It was crazy. Stupid."

"That's . . . insulting. A person has to be crazy and stupid to kiss me?" There was no anger in the words—just confusion.

"No," he said, directing me even farther from the house. "Did you tell Sarah?" he asked in a fervent whisper.

"Of course not! Why?"

"Her line. It seemed like she knew something." He looked behind us like he expected her to materialize from thin air.

I dodged into his line of vision, forcing him to look at me. "What is there to know, Nathan?"

"Nothing. There's nothing to know, except that I was rude. I don't usually run around kissing younger girls. It was late and I was cold and you were being nice and I might have been experiencing mild hypothermia . . ." he babbled on with dogged determination.

"Younger girls? You're only a year and a half older than me." The words came out crooked and strange.

His head tilted, his mouth paused, open. "Well, biologically," he conceded and ignored my sputtering. "Not that kissing you isn't nice," he confessed, a mortified expression crossing his face, "but I imagine you only want that from someone interested in . . ." His bumbling words started tripping, falling in strange places. "Well, in *you*."

The blow of his last word sent my mind reeling. I nearly reached out to him to steady myself and caught my mistake just in time, pulling my hand back to my side. "So you're . . . not?" I didn't recognize my voice.

"I'm sure it's mutual," he offered. "We live so far apart. We're practically cousins, since Sarah's like family to me and . . . I just didn't want to offend you by being so stupid. It's one of the dumbest things I've done." He lifted one side of his mouth in a guilty grin. If he meant it to reassure me, he failed miserably. I looked down at my shirt, nonplussed to see how solid the fabric looked. I'd been sure he could see my wrenched heart through an open window in my chest. I cannot imagine what my face looked like. I cannot even say what I felt like. Every nerve froze. Waited. Swallowed the poisonous words. "I guess I should get home now," he finished. "I'm sorry. I'm sorry."

I felt my feet on the sandy earth, rocked back on my heels. *Do I smile? Do I agree?* I was so far beyond dignity, so far beyond salvaging the moment that I just turned and walked. I don't remember getting back inside my bedroom. Don't remember what I said to Sarah. I just remember the cool, brass knob under my hand as I shut my bedroom door.

"I'm not a little girl," I choked to the empty room. And then came the tears. Hot tears that washed the numb away. The numb I would give anything to get back.

CHAPTER 31

I LOST THE next day. When I took too long coming down to breakfast, Sarah tapped on my door and asked if I was feeling ill. I didn't have the mental strength to conjure up an explanation so I seized on her excuse. I told her I felt sick and fell immediately back into a dreamless sleep. By lunchtime I was still wretched and I looked repulsive but I was also starving and bored. I made my way downstairs, keeping the quilt wrapped around me. Something about it comforted me. I liked studying the tiny squares, imagining my grandmother's sharp needle stabbing in and out of the fabric, undaunted by the mountainous task. I would have ended up with a potholder.

Sarah jumped up from the couch, her face full of concern. "You're awake? Are you cold? Are you getting a fever?" She put her hand on my forehead. "You feel cool," she searched me over, looking for a visible symptom. "You don't look well, Jennifer. I thought you might be coming down with something last night. Does anything hurt?"

More than I ever knew I *could* hurt. I kept my symptoms vague, saying I felt tired and achy. Sarah said that she would call Claude and cancel our lunch plans and let Nathan know we weren't doing lines. When she looked back to me, her panic rose again. "You are so pale. And your eyes are watering! What can I do?"

"I'm hungry," I told her weakly, swiping my tears before they could fall. That excited her. I think she knew it couldn't be anything too terrible if I still had my appetite. She asked if she should make some Jell-O or start a crock of soup. I shook my head and told her I would warm up some leftovers. Only after I finished a plate of Hawaiian chicken and sweet potato casserole and chocolate cake did my hunger subside.

"You weren't kidding!" she said after she watched me finish my second large glass of apple juice. "You must be trying to get your strength back."

"I suppose. I'm getting tired again."

"I should call my doctor," she said, her fingers flitting nervously, looking for something to do. "So help me, Jennifer, if anything happens to you here. Claire . . ." The scenario was too dreadful to elaborate.

"Don't worry. Just a bug. It's not that bad. Maybe I got seasick yesterday."

"*After* the boat?" Sarah tilted her head in doubt.

I shrugged and told her I would camp on the couch and watch television. It was a mindless day. When night came I felt nothing but relief. I laid in the darkness and thought of flights home. I could leave immediately. Surprise my mother. Get far away. And as tempting as it was to run, to put a thousand country miles between myself and this pain, I knew the truth—I couldn't outrun my own chest. The hurt would pace me, stalk me. And when I got back to Nebraska I would lie down in my bed and be a thousand miles from him. I turned onto my stomach and groaned into my pillow. *If I scream, could he hear me?* Now the question distorted in my mind, sneered caustically, *If he heard you, would he care?* I fell into a troubled sleep.

The next day I made myself shower and dress. In the early morning hours Little's face crossed my fitful dreams. I longed for a dose of her gruffness, her toughness. Maybe it would rub off on me. I managed to escape Sarah's scrupulous care by saying I wanted to take a walk to get some fresh air. I made a rush for Pilgrim's Point as soon as I was out of the backyard. The closer I came to her tiny house, the more my hands started to shake. What would I say? What excuse could I give for being there in the first place? How could I explain the sudden tears that welled up for no reason, with no warning?

I stopped in her backyard, bent over the stitch in my side, and tried to breathe deep to deter the sob that wanted to break free. I probably looked like I'd just run a marathon instead of jogging across the cove.

Several ragged breaths later, Little yelled out from her back door, "What happened to you?"

I brought my head up, looked at her, and then dropped it again. "Nothing" was the brilliant reply I finally gave.

"You want some baklava?" she asked.

"What?"

"I got some baklava, if you want some. My nephew sent it. He gets my birthday wrong every year, poor idiot!"

I shook my head, feeling half asleep. Seeing her in her blue housedress, waving a butter knife, made me feel like I was wandering around in one of those dreams where any character could say anything and it would still make sense. Somehow.

"Bakla-what?" I asked as I straightened.

"Baklava. Cake from . . . who knows? Who cares? Somewhere."

The next thing I knew, I was seated at the kitchen table, stabbing my fork into a stiff, sticky slice of something. After one timid bite I started putting it away in earnest. It was perhaps the best thing I'd ever tasted. But then, I was starting to realize that food is exceptionally improved by depression. Little sloshed a glass of milk in front of me, causing several drops to jump onto the dark, wooden table. She stared hard at my ducked head as I shoveled in another bite. "I used to eat like that," she said as she looked at my disappearing slice. "After I slept with somebody."

I choked, the milk flying in a high arch and splattering onto my plate. "Little!"

"You still too young to hear 'bout that, I reckon, and I'm too old to want to remember it," she mumbled. "What'd you come over here for anyway?"

I dodged her stare and let my eyes glide across the yellow lino-leum. "I was taking a walk."

She frowned and looked at my empty plate. "Let's walk then." I finished my milk, and waited while Little meticulously straight-ened her laces and tied her shoes. She led the way out her front door to the road.

"I've only known a girl to go out walking for one reason."

"That so?" I said in a flat voice that sounded more like *I don't care*.

She puckered her lips and changed tactics. "You tell your mama to come?"

"Yeah, I told her," I sighed.

"Well, I owe you somethin' then, don't I? Whatta you wanna know?"

I stopped on the rough shoulder of the road and turned toward the old woman, feeling infinitely more ancient. "Little, I don't want to play anymore. I don't think I even care anymore. I just want to go home. I want to get away from here."

I don't know if some of the grief from Nathan's rejection leaked into my words, but Little's eyes narrowed into slits as I spoke. "What happened?" she demanded.

"Nothing" came my dejected answer. That word sounded hideous to me. Desolate. Plaintive. *Nothing*. My heart had pulled out of my chest on its first solo flight and . . . nothing. A stain on the sidewalk.

"That Becker boy?" she asked.

"No! I swear. Nothing." I felt the wet film in my eyes and blinked hard. How had she guessed so fast? Had everyone guessed? My legs shook and I wanted to melt to the ground and hide my face in the dirt. Instead, I contained myself to a small groan and turned back to Little's house, my feet impossibly heavy. "May God strike me down, nothing happened!"

I heard her shuffling behind me. "Sometimes nothing is the worst thing," she said, her voice as soft and gentle as I imagine her voice could go. Still gruff, but comforting—like Chester's gravelly purr. I raked my hands through my hair, trying to disguise how I covered my ears. To my relief she didn't say anything else until I got to her driveway. I stopped, but she bypassed me and walked behind her house without a word, heading straight to the beach. After a long hesitation, I trudged after her and drew up beside her as she neared the sand.

"So I guess I'll tell you about Newell," she said in a matter-of-fact voice that could have said, *I guess I'll wear green socks today.*

"Who?" I asked as I gave her my arm to steady her as we made our way down the steepest slope of sand.

"The only man on Earth I ever knew worth loving," she answered.

I turned my shocked face to her. She met my questioning eyes, and her grip hardened at my elbow, pinning me to the slippery spot of earth.

"You said you'd only trade your love story for another love story," I stammered.

"That's true," she said, holding tight as she lowered herself to the ground with a series of uncomfortable grunts.

Her body looked even more fragile in front of the ageless immensity of the sea. I took a place beside her, curling my legs tight into my chest. "Well, don't tell me then, because I don't have one. No trade. Nothing." I turned my head, the bleak, vacant truth burning as it made its way up my throat.

I felt her watching me even though I hid my face from her. After a moment she said, "Even so," in a smooth, small voice. The only time I ever heard her sound small. That finally made me turn, just in time to see a mysterious smile fading from her lips. "Even so," she said more loudly. "You did call your mama and I'm in a talking mood." She jerked her thumb at her house like a hitchhiker and continued, "I was born in that house. Two months early. Not even four pounds. Nineteen twenty-two. My mother gave birth to me all alone while my father was fishing. He came home and found me, wrapped in blankets from the oven. I was three hours old and my mother was nearly unconscious. He ran for the neighbors, and they ran for the doctor and everyone prayed over my mother and me that night. Doctor said I wouldn't live long." She gave me a conspiratorial grin, and the deep wrinkles around her eyes pushed together.

I couldn't resist a laugh. "Guess you proved him wrong," I said.

"Not half! And I ain't done yet. Got nineteen years to go!"

"Nineteen?" I tried to imagine almost twenty more years of wrinkles on her face. Where would they go?

"My daddy grabbed me from the doctor and said I'd live to be a hundred and ten if he had anything to do with it. I loved my father. Can't make a liar of 'im." Little's eyes traveled over the water. The same water that lapped these shores the day her father defied the doctor. The same water that would lap these shores on the day of her funeral. I bit my lip and waited.

"So Newell Carson was my father's fishing partner. Couldn't neither of them afford a boat so they bought one together. Worked together ever since I was a baby girl. Newell was a few years younger than my father, but he could have passed as his son. He had one of those boyish faces. He was married, but I don't remember his wife. I just remember going to her funeral when I was eleven. Don't even know what she died of." Little recounted the tale briskly. No emotion. No pity.

"That's sad," I said, more because I felt pressured to say something.

"It's not," she snapped. "I've visited her grave. Elizabeth Carson. She has his name on her tombstone. He loved her." I thought her voice actually broke, but she cleared her throat with some terrible old person sounds and continued.

"I didn't know I loved him then. But I remember wanting to hug him at the funeral. He was standing by the casket and I wanted him to feel better. *I* wanted to be the one to make it better."

A gull let out a brazen cry and swooped toward the water. I watched the sun reflect off of its white breast as it twisted in the air. "You fell in love with someone as old as your father?"

"Nearly. I was fifteen before I knew I loved him. Got my first proposal that year. Those little boys followed me around, sent flowers, showed up on the front porch, packed themselves in like sardines on my family's pew at church. A handsome one, well-to-do to boot, asked me to marry him when I was sixteen. We'd never talked for more than ten minutes at a time."

"But you loved Newell?"

"I loved Newell," she said. Her calm voice shook me with its honesty. "A stupid, old widower . . ." she looked at me and held her tongue. "That man didn't pay a moment's attention. He patted my head like I was still a child. I was sixteen. He was thirty-three. A young thirty-three. It wouldn't have made much difference." She shrugged like the years were nothing to her. Now that she was ninety, they probably were. I wished Nathan were listening so he could hear how stupid he sounded lamenting a year and half age difference.

"He ate dinner with us every night after Elizabeth died. And after I found out I loved him, I thought my heart would up and fall out of my chest just from looking at him. I was sure one day the ache would overwhelm me and I'd die right there at the table, my head in my chowder." She grinned at the thought, but even her smile couldn't mask the pain. I knew exactly what she meant.

"Did you ever tell him?" I asked.

"Well, who's tellin' this story?" she croaked. "You kids can't wait for water outta a faucet!"

"Sorry!" I held up my hands in surrender. "I'll be quiet."

"Good!" she said. "But where the Sam hill was I?"

"Dinner with . . ."

"So we ate dinner with him every night and one night he brings a girl. No, not a girl. A woman older than him. With two children! An old, wrinkled widow! And he's pulling out her chair and talking to her brats, and I know the woman from church and I thought I'd leap across the table and scratch her face off. Never felt so violent. So I decided that if he was out looking for love, and resorting to widowed mothers to get it, I'd let him know how I felt."

"Did you?" I asked breathlessly. She turned a livid face to me and I squeaked, "Sorry!" before leaning back.

"I tried. It was a bad job from the go. I was a child to him. His best friend's child. I'm sure the thought never crossed his mind. I was turning seventeen and decided that I would find a way to get him alone. If I could just explain that I was a woman—that I loved him far more than that widow ever could—I thought I could make him listen. But I waited too long. He came back one week-end good and married. She'd wanted a quiet affair, and they didn't have much family or money. The preacher married them Sunday afternoon at her mother's house. We didn't even know they were that serious."

"Oh, Little . . ."

"Never had a chance to fight for him. I loved him like . . . I've never really found a comparison for that." She patted my arm and I looked down at her soft, withered fingers.

"So he never knew?"

"Never. I saw him kiss her one day. Kiss her like a brother, all prim and polite, and something exploded in me. I knew if I got to kiss him . . . well, you'll know someday."

I squeezed my legs tighter against my chest and wished I didn't know.

"I left that night. Packed one bag and what money I had and I left. Just hoped I could use my pretty face to get a few rides, a few meals, until I figured out what to do. I didn't care what happened to me. I was dying by inches watching him. Anything'd be better than that.

"Hitchhiked to Coney Island. First thing that came to my mind. I walked into the first restaurant I found and asked if I could get a job. Still in the Depression, mind you. Wasn't no one just giving out work. But the owner liked how I looked and I got lucky. Hired on the spot. I told him I didn't have a place to stay and he told me about a boardinghouse for the showgirls. I got a room that night. It was like Providence was just waitin' for me to ask. Need a job? Take one. Need a room? Take one. Sometimes the only thing holding us back is not askin'."

"Weren't you scared?" I tried to imagine plunging alone into the world like that. Like my mother.

"I was so mad at him. So mad that he never even considered me. I held onto the anger because it kept the sad away. That's how I know what your mama's feeling. When someone stays that mad for that long, they're just sad. Sad lasts so much longer than mad. Hurts more, too." She looked down at her hands and started rubbing a bulging blue vein. She pushed it down with her finger and then let it go as if surprised that purple tracks and age spots belonged to her skin. "Well, I can't tell most of the next decade. Not decent for little girls."

I bristled and tried to protest, but she gave me a shrewd stare. "It's no good, anyhow. I ran into every pair of arms I could find, just to pretend for a minute that they were Newell's. Used men. Got used. Didn't care. It got me from Coney Island to Los Angeles, and I landed some little parts in shows there. Then bigger. Got work in Hollywood. Paramount Pictures. Then I got my first contract and I was in the business. I worked in film for nine years. I visited Smithport, but I never stayed long. It was too hard to see Newell. I would have traded everything for him—the parties, the dresses, the money. There wasn't much money in it anyhow. Not after the big stars took their share."

"I was twenty-seven and talking to my mother one day on the phone when she told me that Newell was in a car accident. Went off the road on some ice and straight into a tree. No airbags back then. No seat belts. His head went through the windshield."

I cringed.

"He died?"

"No. Don't jump ahead," she snapped. "He lived. Barely. They took a piece of his skull off because his brain was so swollen. Infection set in after that. It was the gift of my life that I was skiing in Vail with my friends when it happened. If I'd been in California I wouldn't have made it home in time. I packed a bag smaller than the one I took to Coney Island and left on the next train. Got to the hospital two days later. I was sure he'd be gone by then. I could barely walk into the hospital. My daddy was there. Sure surprised him! No one knew I was coming. No one had any reason to think I'd care much. Newell's wife was taking the kids to her mama's, so I sent my daddy to get some breakfast. Told him that I loved Newell like a father and I'd sit with him. It was a sick lie, but if an actress can't lie, who can? I closed the door and sat down by his bed, finally all alone with him." Little looked up at me, her eyes sharp and alert. "This is where I tell you the greatest moment of my life, so don't interrupt this one."

I swallowed and gave her one wide-eyed nod.

"I sat there for two hours until his wife got back. Sent everyone away and they went, too, because they thought I was a movie star. I wasn't, but that's neither here nor there. After a good long time just looking at him—He was handsome, mind you. Not like the boys in the movies, but better. Not so pretty. Stronger—I started telling him everything. Told him he was a stupid fool. Told him what a stupid fool I'd been. Told him I'd loved him from the time my body knew what love was. Told him all I ever wanted was a life with him.

"And then, after an hour of telling him that I loved him and hated him for not loving me back, his eyelids moved. Not opened, but moved. Like he was looking for me, but couldn't open his eyes. I grabbed his hand. The only time I ever touched him since I was a child and I begged him to wake up. I told him I'd live to be an old lady and wait until he was an old man and someday we could love each other. And then I lifted his hand. The one that didn't have all the tubes in it. I've never seen such a hand. I'll never forget his hand. And I kissed it. I kissed it like I've never kissed anything. All my life on my lips. One touch and it meant more than all the other touches of all the other people put together." She looked back at me. I should say, came back to me. I knew she had been far away, in that hospital room, his motionless fingers under her burning lips. "Made you cry, huh?" she said with satisfaction. "That's fitting. It should make a body cry."

"What happened?" I asked, not bothering to mop my face.

"Well, do you see him?" she asked. "He died. He died that day. His plain, little wife came back and sat by him while he died. And I stood outside the room and wished to die myself."

I remembered the night of the storm, Little's feet in the water. "Little, you wouldn't ever . . . do anything drastic?" I raised my eyebrows, hinting delicately.

"What, do myself in? Don't be stupid."

"But that night of the storm when I met you. You were out here . . ."

"Out here yelling, is what! I wait till God starts throwin' a tantrum and then I go and scream back. We've had some good fights. He tried to knock my house down a few times." She smiled a wicked grin. "But it's still standin', ain't it?"

"How does a person fight God?" I asked her, looking at the endless blue of the water reflected in the endless blue of the heavens. Too big to conquer.

"Oh, you just let it out. He don't mind much. I think he likes a good row now and then. All these pious fools saying *it's all for the best*. Well, it ain't! It ain't all for the best. We make the best of it, is all. And I still got a couple decades' penance before I get my way."

"Penance?"

"I got some making up to do. Lotta other men I . . . well, I never kissed a man after the day Newell died. Didn't wanna taint it. And after I'm done with this long, lonely life, I'm calling it sentence served and flying up on these black wings of mine. There are some things you can fix in this life and a precious few that will have to wait till the next. And when I'm resurrected and young and beautiful, I am marching straight up to that man and kissing him proper. My first item of business. Hope heaven don't mind kissin' too much, 'cause I've got a kiss comin'." Her voice slowly faded and she retracted back into her thoughts. That's why I jumped when she suddenly barked, "Now are you gonna help me up or just watch my arthritis kick in while you pine?" She grabbed my hands and after an awkward moment, we managed to get her back on her feet. "So there." Her head bobbed in finality. "You gonna tell me your love story yet?" she asked with defiant eyes.

"Little, I told you, I don't have one."

"Well, when you're ready to tell it, you owe me a story," she said like she didn't believe me.

"Has anyone ever given you a really good one?" I asked her as we grappled up the inclined beach to her home.

"Not as good as mine. But Sarah came close." Little's eyes flashed, knowing she was holding up a ball of string to a kitten.

"Oh no," she said before I asked. "That one is hers to tell. You never take a love story away from a body when the story's all that's left."

CHAPTER 32

LITTLE'S STORY GAVE me just enough strength to bear lines that night. If she could look across the dinner table every night at the man she loved when she was my age, then I could face Nathan for half an hour. And despite my worst fears, it went better than I expected. Though I almost choked on the tension in the air, Sarah never seemed to notice. Nathan tried on nonchalance, tugging its ill-fitting shape over his uncomfortable shoulders. It did not suit him. No matter how many times he put on a careless smile, I missed his thoughtful, straight mouth. I missed the way his eyes sparked when a real smile fought its way to his face. I noticed every twitch of his arms, tap of his fingers.

It made me wonder what he saw when he looked at me in the faded light. Did I reveal my feelings in a turn of the eyes, a movement, a word? I held my hands firmly in my lap and tried not to move or speak more than necessary. Only once, when I mentioned that I'd been looking at flights home, did his face twitch with unspoken emotion.

When Sarah read a funny quote from Oscar Wilde, my thoughts traveled back to Little. Had Newell ever seen a shadow of pain cross her sapphire eyes as he sat across the table? If she had stood up and told him just how she felt . . . I looked at Nathan, knowing the answer. If she had told him he would have run. Like Sarah's John. Like Nathan on the beach. They all run.

Sarah asked me about my line and I raised my head, trying to remember what I was supposed to say. I read a short, unoffending line from *A Tale of Two Cities* while avoiding Nathan's face. And all the while, despite his painful admission that he had no interest in me, I kept wishing for Sarah to retreat. I could not entirely relinquish hope that another talk alone with him would revive whatever feelings made him kiss me. And I would take it. Anything. Even knowing he would run again, I would put all pride aside and scrape up whatever crumb he dropped.

I called my dad after lines and told him that I was second-guessing my plan. "I think I've changed my mind. Maybe it's time for me to come home."

"But it's only been three days. I've got things under control here." Did I imagine disappointment in his voice? "I even thought about taking your mother away for the Fourth. Get her mind off things." He tried to put it diplomatically, but I heard the hint. Their plans didn't include me.

I wasn't going to spoil a romantic weekend for them just because I was too cowardly to face Nathan. We settled on a compromise. If my mother didn't come before their weekend trip, then I would catch a flight home right after. It meant looking at Nathan's face for the next week, but that was both pro and con. The only thing worse than being with him was being without him.

"Just don't tell your mother," my dad made me promise. "She is starting to talk about Smithport for the first time in years. I think she's getting closer. I don't want her to lose all motivation now."

I promised to keep my plan to myself and hung up, feeling that it had become a game to him, as well. A point for everyone if Claire shows up. Never mind that Jennifer was stuck on the fifty yard line with no pads and no helmet and staring down at a brutal heartache waiting to sack her. Never mind that I was already battered from the last several plays. Never mind that I didn't think I would survive another tackle. Never mind.

I tried to distract myself from the entire situation. Sarah helped coordinate the town's Independence Day celebrations every year, so I spent several days helping her hang red, white, and blue buntings from the light poles and wrapping the trees on Main Street in red, white, and blue lights. To my chagrin, Nathan also helped every year, so when he wasn't landscaping, he was with us, climbing the ladder and handling the highest branches. But I must admit that when he worked he seemed like a different person. He was so relaxed that I started to believe our kiss was truly just an impulsive accident. As I tossed him clips to hold the lights, the fishermen on the docks tossed their catches, and the sounds of work and the light of day chased the awkwardness away. There were moments I almost didn't care that he had no interest in me—that he saw me at worst as a nuisance, and at best as a cousin. Almost.

Then I would see the worried curve to his lips when something went wrong, and I would forget to act like I didn't care. He was hard at work on Wednesday untangling some light strands when a broken light bulb sliced through his finger. I grabbed his hand instinctively, looking at the narrow cut covered in blood. "It's nothing," he said, tugging back his arm, but I didn't let go.

"It's bleeding." With my spare arm I yanked a napkin from my pocket where I'd stashed it after eating a cinnamon roll from the bakery and pressed it to his finger. Again, he pulled away. "Just wait," I insisted, engaging in a strange tug of war with his hand in the middle. "You'll get it all dirty."

At last he relented and I finished wiping it, rotating his hand as I studied the cut. Just as I noticed a raw hangnail, I remembered Little taking Newell's hand and kissing it, defying ten years of absence, a score of lovers, and two wives, living and dead. The impulse burned a hot fire through me. A few inches is all it would take. A few inches and I could put my lips to his skin. That made me hastily drop Nathan's hand, pronounce it "all better," and turn before he noticed my flushed face.

I never saw such a hand. Little's words echoed in my mind. I'd seen bigger hands, stronger hands, but never such an *intelligent* hand. Is that what Little saw in Newell's hand? And then I felt like a blasphemer, comparing my two-week infatuation to the love of her torrid, adventurous life. *But it started like this,* I justified as I watched him scale the ladder. When she had described her sixteen-year-old self, I felt like she had broken into my private thoughts and stolen several intimate pages from my heart's history. *Just like this.*

Some unspoken, mutual agreement to stick to unromantic topics made lines more bearable, though far less interesting. Sometimes when he was reading a philosophical and stoic passage, I remembered him kneeling down across the burning pile of branches, his words low over the crackle of consuming pine needles and billowing smoke, and I ached for another chance to talk to Nathan. That Nathan.

And the week passed. I can give no accurate accounting of the hours. Claude helped to fill in the days, and one afternoon Will showed up at Claude's house with his friend Michael. After some persuasion, they convinced me to join them and we ended up at a dollar theater watching a bad movie I'd seen with Cleo three months earlier. But two hours of forgetting was better than two hours of remembering.

After the movie we sat outside on the patio of the Sturgeon, sharing a plate of French fries and sipping milkshakes while the boats came and went. The more time I spent with Will, the less I minded his pinched face and clumsy, elongated body. He was far from brilliant, often missing the simplest innuendos, but his affection for Claude was obvious. If she didn't mind that he could barely grasp long division, and he didn't mind that she couldn't stand on the boat where he made his living, then God bless them both.

Will's friend Michael threw a few admiring glimpses my way, but I barely registered his interest. Next to Nathan every boy seemed to be cut from cardboard, not entirely real. While Claude described Darcy's attempt to attract a stray cat that actually attracted a stray opossum instead, Harvey's fishing boat pulled into the harbor and docked next to *The Missus*.

"Excuse me," I said to my friends, who were beginning to fling French fries at each other. "I have to talk to someone. I'll be right back."

Michael stood to follow me, and Claude protested and asked for details, but I held up a hand and jogged away. "I promise. Right back."

I pushed my shoulders back, hoping I could catch Harvey alone. What I needed to ask was difficult enough without an audience. My sandals thumped against the dock as I drew nearer, my presence obvious and conspicuous. One of Harvey's fishermen glanced at me, but returned to his work. Only when I approached the helm did he stop and raise his eyebrows.

"Is Harvey here?" I sounded like a second-grader, my voice high and uncertain.

He studied me suspiciously, but hollered, "Harvey. Kid wants you."

"Who?" came a deep bark from inside the boat. I flinched, almost ran, but he emerged from the cabin, squinting in the light. Or maybe he just always squinted, a habit of years of water reflecting the sun into his face. He looked at me and his eyes narrowed even farther. I waited for him to approach because my voice was too frightened to carry. "Yeah?" he asked.

"I could come back," I stuttered. "I was just going . . ." If only he would stop searching me with his hard face. In Nebraska a man would smile. Help you along a bit when he saw you were nervous. The rules were different here.

"Jennifer, right?" he asked.

I nodded.

"Sarah need something?" he asked.

"No. I just . . . Glenn told me that you dated my mom."

He crossed his arms over his chest, the light blue of his eyes disarming. "He did, huh?"

I nodded.

"Old men talk too much," he said, loud enough to earn a chuckle from the other fisherman.

"I was wondering if I could ask you something?" I asked in confusion.

"Reckon you just did." I could not read his smile. It felt too much like mockery.

"About my mom," I clarified.

He stepped off the boat with a cooler in his hand. "Okay," he said as he led me to a vacant slip and emptied the half-melted ice into the harbor.

"I know about Sarah not coming home for five days. She can't tell me what happened here . . ."

The lid of the cooler tumbled out of his hand and splashed into the bobbing water. It took him a moment to retrieve it, but after he did he sat down, his feet hanging over the waves. I joined him.

"I don't like telling other people's business. If she wanted you to know, she had a whole lifetime to tell you," he pointed out. "But . . ."

I sighed in relief.

"If you already know, I guess I can tell you that she thought Sarah died."

"Sarah?"

"When she didn't show up, she figured something happened. Anything. A dinosaur might have stepped on her. Claire figured she was cursed."

"Like actually cursed? Like witchcraft?" That sounded nothing like my sensible mother.

"Like God hated her. Like every bad feeling she ever had for her family killed them. Like she deserved it."

"What bad feelings?"

Harvey took a deep breath like he'd exhausted his quota of words for the day and the conversation was costing him dearly. "Sarah got a lot of attention. She could dance like one of those real ballerinas, and she got every part in every play. Your grandparents gave her a lot of attention. Sometimes Claire felt a little . . . forgotten. Jealous."

"So when Sarah didn't show up, my mother thought she had died, too?"

"Yup." Harvey stood up.

"But then why was she mad when Sarah showed up just fine?"

Harvey laughed once. " 'Cuz she wasn't dead." He walked back to his boat. "We're a sorry lot, aren't we?" he asked with a smile and a shake of his head.

Someone called Harvey's name. A voice I knew too well. We both looked down the dock where Nathan startled when he saw me. He approached like an animal sniffing a trap.

"Hi," he said suspiciously. "What are you doing?"

"Talking to me. I got all kinds of company today," Harvey said. "What brings you?"

"Your new lamp bulb came." Nathan held out a cardboard box with a mailing label. "I told Meg I'd bring it to you since I was passing by."

"I was just leaving," I mumbled. "Thanks, Harvey." I ignored Nathan's stare as I walked away. Even though I tried to imagine

Sarah insensitive, selfish, belittling, it was impossible. It would only take two minutes with her for my mother to understand how much she had changed.

"What took you so long? What were you doing by the boats?" Claude demanded when I returned.

"Nothing." I looked back down to watch Nathan making his way up the dock.

❦ ❧

The way the terrace kissed the sidewalk, I didn't see how Nathan could avoid passing our group, and I knew that he wasn't happy with three out of four of us. As he made his way past the Jacks, his gaze rose to our table and his eyes found mine watching him. Claude, fortunately, had her back to him, and no one noticed my diverted attention. Just as Nathan assessed the scene with a tense frown, Michael tugged a piece of my hair playfully, leaned in close, and presented me with a small plastic card that he had managed to wrestle away from Will. I jerked in surprise and looked down at the driver's license, complete with the obligatory terrible photo. The camera had captured Will with his eyes half closed, a ferrety look to his face. I smiled in spite of myself.

"Isn't that the worst?" Claude asked.

"Sorry, Will, that's pretty bad," I said with a chuckle. Will pretended to plunge a knife into his heart and by the time I looked up Nathan's back was to me. I swallowed against the panic, wondering if he confused our spontaneous outing for a date. Then I bit the inside of my lip, remembering that it didn't matter what he thought. I already knew how he felt.

I turned to Will and Claude. Whenever she smacked him playfully, he would take her offending hand in a gentle grip and return the slap with a squeeze. I wanted to ask them how they had tamed love so that it did not break them, trample them, defeat them. I doubted they would have understood the question. Love seemed docile and easy in their hands.

Little visited the house several times that week, but I steered clear of her probing eyes. I don't know how, but she knew too much. What Sarah's eyes missed, what even Nathan's eyes missed, she seemed to glean in a glance. Maybe she knew the look too intimately—the shy, tortured flick of the eyes when he crossed the room. I don't know why she cared so much, but I theorized that it was odd for her to see it from that angle; to watch from the outside as a love-struck girl held her tongue around the boy who would never acknowledge her beyond a child.

I sympathized with her star-crossed love story. She had seventeen years to overcome with Newell. I had only two. Two years, two thousand miles, and about two hundred IQ points. And when I listed the obstacles like that, I realized that the odds were more stacked against me than I cared to admit.

CHAPTER 33

WE HAD TO delay lines on Thursday. We were up to our elbows in construction paper and not paying attention to the clock because we were making paper flags with Hester and Darcy when Nathan walked into the living room.

"Have we switched to a nightly art project?" he asked as he looked at the room buried in paper scraps. My head jerked up at the sound of his voice.

"Just another way to express ourselves," Sarah joked as she waved a pair of scissors in the air. "In fact, Nathan, I think I'll start having you draw a picture every day instead of finding a line. I like that idea."

"I hope you like stick figures," he warned.

"Nathan, look!" Darcy squealed as she held up a large piece of paper oozing with glue that held a hodgepodge of cut paper shapes.

"Wow, Darce. Wow. So you guys are making . . ." He paused, searching for clues until Hester held up her neat American flag, complete with fifty small stars, and Nathan winked gratefully at her. "Flags! Nice flag, Darcy!"

"It's the flag of Darcyland. All of the colors are symbotic." Darcy didn't notice when Sarah laughed. She was paying too much attention to her own voice. "Pink is for everything beautiful," she said pointing out a skinny, pink heart. "Blue is for the water because Darcyland is an island. Yellow is for happiness . . ." Her large, yellow oval flopped off the page when she touched it. "Darn it."

"I'll fix it," Sarah said, reaching for it.

"Heliotrope is for flowers," Darcy continued, pushing her finger at a crudely cut purple flower.

"So that's heliotrope," I said.

"What's the orange symbolize?" Nathan asked her as he sat down on the couch and rumpled Hester's hair.

"Tigers."

Hester giggled, a young sound from her wise face. I liked it. "Of course. Beauty, water, happiness, and . . . tigers." Nathan grinned.

"I don't have a line yet," Sarah piped up. "I'm not even sure I can find my books. Is it that late already? We need to get the girls home."

"I don't have preschool tomorrow. It's Friday," Darcy said as she tore a white sheet of paper down the middle. "Is it time for the fireworks yet?"

"Saturday. You get to see them on Saturday," Nathan answered. "Two more days." Darcy dropped her paper and padded in her socks to Nathan, scrambling into his lap. She looked like little more than a baby in his muscled arms.

"Will you take me to the rock to see the fireworks this year?" she asked.

"No!" Hester cried with a joking look of horror. "Not the rock with Darcy again!"

"What's the rock?" I asked. The name conjured visions of Alcatraz.

"There's a tiny island inside the bay. Nathan rowed us out there last year to see the fireworks, and Darcy drove us crazy!" Hester answered, ignoring Darcy's pink tongue that whipped out between her plump lips.

"I didn't!" Darcy called.

"You said you saw a yeti!" Hester retorted hotly.

"A what?" I interrupted.

"I did," Darcy said with her hand clutched to her heart. "I did see a yeti, up on the cliff."

"And a giant squid, and a submarine, and what else, Hess?" Nathan asked.

"Everything. Every shadow in the water was a shark or a whale or a sea monster," Hester added.

"I saw a yeti!" Darcy squealed.

"It was a white cat," Hester replied in a patient, albeit annoyed, tone.

"It was the *ghost* of a cat. That's why it was white," Darcy said in a low, mysterious voice.

Nathan groaned. "Thanks, Hess, I almost forgot. No rock for Darcy this year." He put his face an inch from Darcy's and imitated her scowl. "You attract too many monsters."

That erased her frown. "I do?" she asked, deeply honored.

"Jennifer can come with us," Hester suggested. Silence fell like a heavy, wet blanket. Maybe I was the only one who felt it, because Sarah threw it off easily.

"Yes, take Jennifer! Claude won't go out there with you, and I'll stay with Darcy and Judith. She would love it."

Nathan met my eyes. I expected his panicked expression, but he looked surprisingly calm, especially considering the implications: A night row to an island. Stranded with Nathan beneath the fireworks. Even with Hester there, it would be too close. I waited for his excuse. "Don't you already have plans with Claude?" he asked.

"No," I answered. "She's watching from the dock with some of her friends. Will is helping his dad with the fireworks."

Nathan rubbed his face in thought. "It's the best place to watch them. When the boats start shooting, you feel like you have a front row seat to the Spanish armada."

Still no invitation, but I dared to hope.

"Remember that year the Jacks borrowed that real cannon?" he asked Sarah.

"Hah!" she laughed. "I'll never forget. I thought they'd sink themselves. I could hear Russ's wife bawling him out from three blocks away!"

I only half heard them, waiting for Nathan's answer. He seemed to remember I was there and looked up at me. "I don't mind taking you, if you want to see it from there." His words were so cool that I couldn't even imagine romance in them. But his eyes were not cold. They glistened with something warmer.

"That might work," I answered quietly, keeping my head tucked over the piece of paper I was cutting. He didn't reply.

Sarah stood and kicked the scraps aside to make a walking path. "Girls, you need to run home. There's still some light left, so hurry quick. No stopping to play." We told the girls good night and watched them from the porch until they disappeared around the curve of the road.

"I gave her the ultimatum," I told him when Sarah went inside to grab her Billy Collins book.

"You did?" He took the chair next to mine and bent close so we could speak low. "When?"

I almost told him the night he kissed me, just to see him suffer, but I wasn't brave enough. "The night you took your little swim."

His cheek reddened as if the words hit his face instead of his ear. "What did she do?"

"Nothing yet. It's been a week now. But I'm starting to think—"

The door snapped open and Sarah took a seat next to us, silencing me.

"Ready?" she asked.

Nathan hid it well, but I could see his disappointment at not hearing the rest of my sentence. We finished lines, but just when I thought he would say good night and leave, he cleared his throat and faced me.

"Do you want to come get some ice cream in town?" His message made it clear that the invitation was for me alone, and not Sarah.

"Me?" I stammered, unable to hide the shock.

"Yep," he said like it was something he asked me every day. "Do you mind, Sarah?"

"Not at all," she answered, her voice slow and her eyes, for the first time ever, glinting with suspicion.

"We'll be back in a few," Nathan promised and paused at the bottom of the steps, waiting for me. For one malicious moment I considered refusing just to pay him back for his indifference, but curiosity and the promise of an hour alone with him overrode that instinct.

"See you soon," I told Sarah, giving her a small shrug to show her I had no idea what he wanted. I gave him a wide berth and rushed to open my own door to make it obvious this was not any sort of a date. I turned to him as he pulled out of the driveway, and this time he didn't make me wait for his words.

"Can we skip the ice cream?" he asked. "I was looking for an excuse."

"Excuse for what?" My voice marched out almost as firm as Harvey's. Maybe I was learning a few new tricks.

"To talk. Can I take you somewhere?"

"That's specific," I said, folding my arms.

"Hard to explain. I'll show you." He went north where the road stretches toward the richer, newer homes. In a few minutes he pulled down a long driveway that ended in the skeleton of a massive house. The walls were only wooden sticks, the concrete floors pooled with rainwater, the night sky spilling into the roofless rooms. Nathan left the headlights pointing at the structure and led me toward the backyard, walking slowly, since bricks and mis-shapen clumps of cement littered the entire site.

"It went down in a storm and then, halfway through the rebuild, they foreclosed on it. It's been sitting here for a year. I come here sometimes." He made his way to the back porch that over-looked the white-tipped waves. We sat down next to each other, dangling our feet over the unfinished edge of the deck. The soli-tude made every word and movement strange and important.

"What did you want to talk about?" I asked, with the hope

that it would be less disastrous than our last private conversation.

"I wanted you to finish telling me what happened. What did your mom say? Is she coming?"

"I'm not betting on it. I haven't talked to her all week. She won't answer my voice mails. She thinks I've turned against her, I think."

"Have you?" he asked.

"Of course not! Everything I did—leaving, coming here, giving her the ultimatum—I did it all because I want her to take her own life and . . ." My fingers grappled with the air, making a shaping, twisting motion. "I want her grab her life and shape it, not just run away and hide. She always taught me that, but she won't do it herself. I don't want a hypocrite for a mother. And it's selfish! All her running and being afraid cost me Sarah, cost me . . ." I so very nearly said "you." ". . . cost me too much."

Nathan put a gentle hand on mine, stopped my fingers from their attempt to mangle the night. " 'All men should strive to learn before they die what they are running from, and to, and why.' " He took his hand away. "James Thurber."

"You don't have to do that anymore," I whispered.

"What?"

"Borrow the words. You can say everything you need to."

"They say it better," he argued.

"No they don't. I've always liked your words more." The wind rustled the plastic sheets on the house, making them billow like white sheets on a clothesline. Nathan looked down at his hands and I did, too, watching him rub his thumbs together.

"So if she doesn't come . . . ?" he asked.

"I'm leaving next week regardless."

"What do you mean?" His volume startled me. "I thought you said you'd wait . . ."

"I think I'm ready to go. I think I'm homesick." The quiet words slipped off my lips like they'd been looking for an escape for days.

"Why?" he demanded, his voice more urgent than usual.

"No specific reason. I just miss it. I miss my friends. I miss my house. I'm ready to go." My heart paced across my chest, all my anxiety building to impossible levels as I tried not to let him see anything of the turmoil I'd felt over the last week.

"Jennifer . . . " His voice saying my name made my eyes gloss with tears. I blinked several times and managed to command them back to the heartache from which they came. "Won't you miss . . ." He cast his eyes around zealously and pointed to the high tide. "The ocean?"

"The ocean?"

"Yes, won't you miss it?"

I shook my head. "I get a little claustrophobic here, actually."

"Here?" he asked incredulously, looking out to the endless plain of water.

"Yes, here. I know it's big, but it's not like Nebraska. It's not like the fields." He turned his curious eyes to me and waited. "Here—this." I gestured to the waves. "A person feels small. You feel like you live in the shadow of something bigger and stronger than yourself. You feel like the world just ends and you could just drop off, drown. Here, the ocean feels endless."

I pictured the winter wheat. It would be harvested by now, the muddy field, stubbled and brown. "But in Nebraska, a *person* feels endless. You look out over the fields and you turn in every direction and there's nothing to stop you. You feel like the world is just waiting for you to strike out in any direction. When I sit beside my wheat field, it encourages me. When I sit beside the water, she intimidates me, reminds me that she's bigger and tougher."

"You're plenty tough," Nathan muttered. "Are you sure you won't stay? Wait for your mother? Just a little longer?" His words were so soft that I think if I had turned to him, given him my face, he would have kissed it again in the shadow of that desolate home. Maybe just as an experiment to see if he could view me as a woman and not a little girl. I shuddered and watched the sea drop her arms full of foam on the waiting beach. I don't know if it was pride that stopped me, but something kept my eyes trained forward.

"I'm pretty sure, Nathan." My stomach was diving, but I sat still, waiting for the dizzying sensation to pass.

"But you'll still come to the rock, right? You'll stay for the

Fourth, right?" He was more open than I'd ever seen. I knew he wanted me to say yes.

I exhaled a breath I didn't know I'd been holding. "Nathan, why do we do this? This back and forth? This pretending?" His eyes widened in baffled innocence, but there was guilt in the small movements of his mouth. He swept his eyes over the beach, calculations running through his head. As curious as I was for his answer, I knew it wouldn't be real. He was weighing every word. Every reaction. Lying to both of us, slowly and wisely. I sighed my defeat. "I'll come see the fireworks." Before he could convince himself to leave me once again sitting in the night, I rose up. "I told Sarah I'd get right back."

"Wait. I'm trying . . . " The words struggled to his lips, but he refused to free them.

"I know. But I don't think either one of us wants to hear your answer." My stomach sank and my heart dropped in complaint. My body wanted me to stay, regardless of pride, in spite of reason.

He nodded, something like regret in the set of his chin. We rode home in the thickest silence I ever knew.

CHAPTER 34

TEN O'CLOCK FRIDAY morning found me shifting my weight outside the Sturgeon while Nathan stood on the roof, obeying Sarah's shouts from the ground on how high to hang the banner. The words on the sign rippled, making a red, white, and blue wave on the air that spanned from the brick roof of the Sturgeon to the top of a light pole across the street. I was following their progress, trying not to look as useless as I felt, when a car horn beeped sharply. I turned to see Claude leaning over Will to call out of his open window.

"Jennifer, we're going to get some more fireworks. Come with us!" She motioned to the car as Will pulled over to the curb across from me.

"Have to go to the next county. Can't buy 'em here," he said.

Michael cranked down the back window manually—the old car didn't have automatics—and waved at me.

"I'm sort of helping here," I said lamely, as I stood empty-handed in the middle of the street.

"No, it's fine. It's already up. Come with us," Claude insisted. I looked down the street where Sarah was still calling directions.

"Pull the top one more—it's still a little crooked," she instructed.

"I didn't ask Sarah," I stalled. They were fun to be with, but I preferred to stay closer to home, closer to Nathan.

Claude checked the street for traffic and hopped out of her door, jogging to Sarah. A minute later she yelled, "It's fine. Sarah says okay."

"Excellent," Will said. "You can talk to Claude about the smart stuff." He winked at me. Claude's shouting got Nathan's attention and he looked over the side of the building, first seeing her sprinting down the street, and then my upturned face. As soon as he took in the old, khaki-colored car, his eyes narrowed.

"Come on," Claude commanded and pulled on my ponytail, leading me to the Oldsmobile. The door creaked as Michael shoved it open and I dropped in beside him, out of excuses. I dared a last look up at the roof and glimpsed Nathan's angry expression.

Just as we got to Haven Lane I said, "I need to stop at the house." Will glanced in the rearview mirror and made a smooth turn onto the road. I made my excuse nervously, hoping it wasn't too transparent. "I forgot, but I promised to call home this morning. You'll have to go without me."

There was polite arguing as they told me to call in the car or call later, but when Will parked in Sarah's driveway I apologized again and told them I couldn't call later. From the porch, Charlie stirred and let out a volley of excited barks before running to me.

Claude's lip pushed out in a small pout, but Will smiled at her as I stepped out. "That's okay. Jennifer'll be more surprised if she doesn't know what we're shooting off."

"Yes, but then I have to hang out with you *boys*," Claude complained as I pushed Charlie's head down so he couldn't jump on me anymore.

"Oh, the horror," Michael teased her as he pretended to shake with fear. "See you later, Jennifer. You're going to watch them with us, right?"

"Uh, no. I don't think so. I'm watching from somewhere else." I didn't think Claude knew Nathan was taking me, and since they were not in each other's good graces at the moment, I didn't want to bring up his name. "But I'm sure I'll see you around this weekend. Bye guys." I made a hasty retreat, glad that Sarah had given me my own key. Charlie followed me into the house and I sat on the sofa, relieved by my escape. Not that I didn't like Claude's friends. I liked them much better than Nathan did. I just didn't feel like the jokes today, didn't want to be three towns away if Nathan decided to talk. I could tell he was thawing again, slowly melting out of his icy solitude.

I picked up Sarah's Billy Collins book and searched for the poem she had quoted the night before. Several poems later I gave Chester's back a stroke and lumbered into the kitchen looking for a snack. I was cutting a slice of pumpkin bread from a small loaf when the sound of an engine rumbled through the open window along with the crunch of gravel of the driveway. I knew it was Nathan and Sarah when I heard her voice over the slam of heavy doors.

"Do you want to come in? You look tired," she said to Nathan. I paused by the kitchen door, well out of sight.

"I'm not tired," he answered grumpily.

"Nathan, is it Will *again*?" Sarah sounded exasperated. "They are just buying some fireworks. They'll be back soon."

"He's always with her, Sarah. Always! I know you don't think it's serious, but it is. And I know that Claude thinks he's a nice guy. Even Jennifer believes that!" His voice rose, spitting out my name in disgust.

"He *is* a nice guy, Nathan. You really don't know him." Sarah's weary voice came from the porch where they stopped to talk.

"Even you! He's got a foul mouth. He's got one thing on his mind."

"He's a teenager. And he's not like he was when you went to school with him. He's growing up. He's changing. People change."

I couldn't see Nathan's face but there was a long silence. For a second I worried they would walk in to get a drink and catch me eavesdropping in the kitchen. I edged closer to the back door, ensuring a quick getaway.

"Is that really the problem, Nathan? You think Claude and Jennifer are going to be seduced at a firework stand? I know you're protective, but . . ."

Nathan's words burst out of him, cutting her off. "Women are tar pits!"

A pause before Sarah asked in a puzzled, almost clinical voice, "Are you quoting?"

Nathan swore and I could imagine the angry set of his face. "No, Sarah. I'm not *quoting*," he said it like another swear word. "But you can write it down if you want, because truer words were never spoken!"

"How are we like tar pits, Nathan?" she asked softly, psychiatrist to patient.

"I can't get free of any of you! My mother can't take care of herself, let alone four kids. My sisters need me to be their dad. Even you!" he hissed. I imagined Sarah leaning back under the assault of his words. I know I would have.

"What about me?" Her professional voice quivered.

"I worry about you! You're too smart and good to be alone. So I hear your niece is coming, and she loves you and I think I will at least be free of one worry . . ."

"But what?" Sarah asked, her voice tight with anxiety.

"But I take one step too close and she's just another tar pit! Another reason to stay where I can't stay. Another reason to go where I can't go. Just a tar pit!" he roared.

I slunk against the wall, down to the floor, my heart jackhammering inside my chest, making my pulse throb in my hands and thunder in my ears. A tar pit. A reason. He was stuck with me. I closed my eyes and filled my lungs with a scratchy breath before squeezing my hands into fists.

"You like her," Sarah said so quietly I almost couldn't hear.

Nathan didn't say anything, but I would have given anything to see his face, read his answer. I heard Sarah's murmurs but I could not distinguish any words because the dishwasher burst to life, beginning its timed cycle. Scared by the sudden noise, and terrified of being discovered, I jerked out of my stupor and opened the back door, escaping noiselessly. All the way to the beach I threw paranoid glances over my shoulder, praying they stayed on the porch where they couldn't see me.

Even the ocean could not still my frantic pulse. My heart beat in jagged contrast to the sea's slow hiss. A tar pit. Is it strange that I found those words the most beautiful I'd ever heard? Harsh and wild and beautiful. Like the cove itself. I don't know how long it took before my body settled into more natural rhythms and my thoughts started to organize. As soon as I felt calm enough I considered walking in the back door and announcing myself, but I wasn't sure I could face him yet. If I caught him that emotional, he'd likely avoid me for a week. And since I had only a few days left, I couldn't risk it. I decided to stay put, let him go home before telling Sarah I'd decided to stay and spend some time on the beach. I was trying to decide how much time was enough when Nathan appeared suddenly over the ridge. I stood and we both froze, carved statues dropped on a deserted beach.

"What are—" he started, but I jumped to the offensive.

"Aren't you working today?"

"No. Not much. Did you guys decide not to go?" He came closer until we stood ten feet apart, assessing each other. Did he see a tar pit?

"They went. I just didn't feel like it. I decided to come read on the beach."

Nathan's eyes swept the ground. "No book."

My face blanched. "I left it at home so I've just been thinking."

"You were here all the time?" he asked, a worried note in his voice.

"All what time?" I asked innocently. It was equally satisfying and disturbing to find out what a good liar I was.

"Since they left."

"Yeah, mostly since they left. I hung out at Shelter Cove for a while. Are you just walking? If you wanted to be alone I can go . . ."

He continued to walk toward me. "No, I'm just . . . hanging out." The casual term sounded ridiculous from him.

"Oh, okay." I sat back down, interested to see how much space he'd leave between us. He surprised me by lowering himself only a foot away from me.

"Still determined to leave?" he asked.

"I think so," I told him. I'd been asking myself that same question. Could I bear to leave right when I knew he felt something for me? Could I bear the angry look in his eyes every time he realized it? "I found a cheap flight for Tuesday morning."

He nodded. "They'll be glad to see you."

"I guess." What mattered more was whether he'd be sad to see me go. "Nathan, about leaving—can I ask you something? Something personal?"

He turned guarded eyes to me. "Sure." He made it a slow, two-syllable word.

"Why haven't you ever left? Really?"

"It's not because I'm scared," he answered.

I looked at his sullen face, trying to see past the bitter frown. "I'd never think you were. I just wondered why you just do college classes online, especially since you're so smart."

He grimaced at my compliment like it hurt him. "I'm nearly done with my bachelor's. I'm not even eighteen until next month. Isn't that good enough for you?"

"It has nothing to do with me. It would be good enough for anybody. It's really impressive. But . . . now what?"

"What do you mean?" He entwined his fingers tightly, the tips of his knuckles whitening under the pressure.

"Well, you have a bachelor's in what?"

"Liberal arts."

"So now what? What are you going to do with it?"

"You like the million-dollar questions, don't you?"

"Why waste time on the cheap ones?"

He looked up at the sky like he thought someone would have written his lines for him overhead. "I don't know. I can't leave."

"Bull," I said as softly as I dared, without losing the power of the word.

"Excuse me?"

"You can't leave the same way my mother can't come back and Sarah can't fall in love. You're making up your own rules."

His eyes sparked with indignation. "You have no idea what it's like looking out for my family. Being the only man. Four girls! Have you ever tried to comfort four girls, provide for four girls, at one time? They would spontaneously combust if I wasn't here."

"You're right," I said, putting my hands up in surrender, "I don't know what it's like. I'm sure it's really hard. But don't you think you might give them some more credit? Somehow I think they'd muddle through." An offended shadow crossed his face and I looked down, ashamed that he thought I was belittling his sacrifices. His love.

"Maybe I want more for them than that—just muddling through," he replied, clamping down on his words to keep them from sounding too harsh.

"But everyone has to muddle a little bit. It's how we figure things out. I just don't think you need to do everything for them."

"What do I do for them?" It came out so spiteful that the blood rushed to my chest, making me feel very hot under the afternoon sun.

"Everything!" I fought back. "You tell them what to do, when to do it, how to do it, when not to do it! Especially Claude. And she adores you. Wants to be like you. You could give her the benefit of the doubt sometimes."

"I don't want to *control* them! I didn't want the job in the first place. Do you think I wouldn't give anything to have a dad take over? To have someone else earn the extra money and scare off the boyfriends and talk Judith out of her depression when she wails that she'll die alone? I didn't want it. I never wanted it!"

It was so difficult to restrain my hands from reaching out to him. I wanted him to know that he didn't need to take care of me, didn't need to babysit me, didn't need to worry about me. I just wanted him to let me sit next to him. To stay still and take my hand when he wanted to take my hand. To resist the urge to run away when his heart drew up close to mine.

I marshaled my strength and gave him the honest answer, the one that broke my heart to give. "But you've done it. All that and more. Now it's time to get out of the way, Nathan! Judith isn't as bad as I thought at first. She's got her weaknesses. She hasn't got love figured out. I think my entire trip is proof that none of us do.

But she can take care of the girls. Maybe not like you would, but still. And Sarah's here. She can help. Little's here. She can . . . well, Little's here." We both lowered our defenses long enough to give one wry laugh.

"And if I go, if I just up and leave, what happens when Judith comes home pregnant again? Or Claude?"

I recoiled from the ugliness of his words. "Is that what you think about your sister? You think that the boys you fought were *right*? Is that why it made you so mad? You thought it was *true*?"

A mixture of shame and defiance burned through his cheeks. "I think it's easy for people to make mistakes. The heart is deceitful."

"Yeah, well, I don't love Will, my heart isn't deceived, and I know he's not like that. I've seen them together enough to know . . ."

"You don't think he'd jump at the first chance . . ." he left it unsaid. Thankfully.

"No. I think he loves her. Sure he's attracted to her. He's not a monk. But he's not . . . he's not what you think he is."

Nathan huffed in dissent.

"There isn't always an ulterior motive. It's okay to love people, Nathan," I uttered.

"Sometimes," he countered. "When everything's in place. When it's the right time."

My eyes moved from his lips, bisected with the thin white scar, to his nose, finally settling on his dark, churning eyes. I felt like Little. Alone. Looking at Newell. "Sometimes you wait for the right time and you run out of time altogether."

He studied my face, seeing, I'm certain, a new intensity there. We weren't talking about Claude anymore. "So, you're of the 'carpe diem' variety? Just dive in headfirst and if you break your face it's 'better to have loved and lost than never to have loved at all'?"

"I prefer the 'happily ever afters', myself."

Nathan smirked mirthlessly. "So you're more a mythology fan."

"It's not just fairy tales. My mother found a love that worked. But she had to leave first. Go find what life had in store." In that moment I said out loud what I didn't realize I knew. My mother left. Little left. I left Nebraska. Sarah went to Africa. Nathan had to leave. Step from the nest. The tree. The entire forest. It was a migration. Away from all you know. It was a tide. Rolling back. I couldn't capture it with words, couldn't own the thought, but it sidled up to me, swept through me. I held it for a fleeting moment. "You have to have a little faith and go and try."

"So I abandon my family, and life magically all works out?" he challenged.

"No. Maybe it never works out. But people leave and learn and come back better." It sounded so wise that it made me sad, like a good-bye to the days when such things made no sense.

Nathan closed his eyes and lay back, his head resting against the sand. "I want Claude to leave and come back better," he said.

"Leaving doesn't count when someone pushes you out. You have to let her choose to go." I let my voice grow playful and added,

"If Claude makes the wrong choice for twenty years, like my mother, *then* you can push her."

"So there's a twenty-year rule?" He cracked one eye and raised his head, squinting at me as the sun hit him in the face. After an exasperated smile, he lay back down and closed his eyes again.

I studied his face, traced every feature that I would miss like air when I left, lingered on his closed, slightly purplish eyelids. "What would you do if you didn't have to stay?" I whispered.

One cheek pulled up. "Here's where I say nuclear physicist or neurosurgeon or astronaut, right? Everyone wants to know what the genius will do. How long till he gets the Nobel or is teaching at Oxford? Do you know how impossible it is to choose when everyone is watching?"

"I asked what you want to do. Not what anyone else wants you to do."

He grabbed his forehead like it hurt. "It's not that simple. It's the responsibility. When you get a brain—this brain that most people don't have—you're obligated to be exceptional. So can I go and be a garbage man? Can I waste it?"

"You want to be a garbage man?"

Nathan's eyes grew so still that I could see the pupil vibrate against the dark blue. "It might be nice to have the option," he said. "What if, just what if, Jennifer, I wanted to get married and buy a boat and take my winters off eating chowder and watching football?"

"That's what you want?" My eyebrows arched in disbelief.

"No! I want to do so much . . . But why is it okay for anyone else to want that and not me? Why do I have to do more?"

"Because you are more."

Nathan's long lashes blinked several times and his lips moved like he would argue, but at the last minute he conceded with one reluctant nod. "I might want to teach. Like Sarah. Teach the best of the best. Teach the little, uppity twerps who go to Harvard. Put a new idea in their heads. Or maybe teach the little kids like Hester, the ones who are just on the verge of greatness. Be there when they figure it all out."

"So?" I asked, looking at his tormented face. "Why not?"

"So, when I say it, I mean it. But then I think of the field researchers for museums, debunking myths thousands of years old. And I want to be one of them. I know I could." I opened my mouth, but he held up his hand and sped up, cutting me off. "And then think of mission control at NASA. Think of looking at that black screen and everyone's looking at you, because you're in charge, and the first picture flickers and through the static you see a brand-new universe. In color. I could do that, too." A slightly manic gleam came over his face as he spoke, but when he looked back at me, he was just Nathan. On the beach. "So what do you choose when you have too many options? Whatever you choose, you lose. You throw away a hundred possibilities that would have been equally rewarding. And forget it all, because they all mean leaving, and the girls are here and I have to stay."

"Says who?"

He rolled his eyes up to the sky and swept them back across the wild landscape. "Says life. Says God. Says everything."

"Not says Sarah. Not says me." His chest swelled as he took a breath, and I lowered my voice. "If we count for anything." I imagined him a crouched eagle, throwing open his strong wings and diving into the world like a thunderbolt, just like Tennyson says. But his wings were as fragile as mine. As locked in place as the ink trapped on Little's back.

He didn't answer, just shook his head despondently. But he didn't move away, either. I looked down to the coarse sand where his fingers rested inches from mine. And we stayed, the waves beating the shore as our thoughts beat the insides of heads, a silent, ripping undercurrent pulling us out to the uncharted sea of our future.

CHAPTER 35

THE NEXT DAY Sarah's backyard transformed into the quintessential scene of a holiday by the sea. Nathan made an impromptu table large enough for all of us by laying a long board across two sawhorses, and Sarah draped it with red plastic tablecloths. Around it flocked a mismatched collection of lawn chairs and camp chairs posed like strange, exotic birds stopping on their flights to warmer climates. Colorful sand buckets sprinkled the grass haphazardly, resting where the last person dropped them. The meat smoker ran all day, puffing out a steady stream of white vapor as it cooked pork ribs and salmon fillets. The usual smell of salty air was nearly obscured by the roasting meat. Little griped at us for moving too fast, laughing too loud, breathing too hard, and in between her complaints she kept her sharp eyes trained on Nathan and me. I tried to ignore her as I helped Sarah and Judith carry the food outside. Even Darcy managed to convey a bottle of soda, which no one dared open after its being dropped so many times.

"Save it for the fireworks," Sarah suggested. "It'll make a good explosion."

For only eight people, the noise was fantastic. Maybe I was comparing it to life as an only child, or three long weeks of quiet days with Sarah, but the commotion of the milling bodies, arms reaching for spoons, paper plates with their full burdens of food, and the savory smells crowding the air made it seem like there were far more than eight people in the backyard.

The sea, which I always considered strong and somber, joined the festivities and frolicked with the younger girls. The waves darted up to the rocks, batting them playfully and jumping back from shore. When I saw Hester scream in delight and leap to avoid the rushing tide, I knew that the holiday had put its carefree spell on everyone.

At seven o'clock, Sarah called for final clean-up and Nathan, the sole male in the crowd, made a general announcement. "No bathrooms on the rock. No bathrooms on the pier. So wherever you are going, go here first!" There was a flurry of shoving dishes that didn't fit into the refrigerator and packing last-minute provisions before our party divided.

Claude left first, when Will's familiar car pulled up with a friendly honk. While the rest of us wished him luck at the show and pressed food samples into his hands, Nathan melted into the background, scowling. He was still sulking when Hester climbed into the middle seat of the truck, her skinny body settled between Nathan and me. Judith and Sarah tried to convince Darcy that fireworks on the dock were much more exciting than the fireworks at the rock. Unconvinced, she let out a shrill wail until Judith reminded her that they could get ice cream from the general store in town, but no one sells ice cream on the rock. After that, she gave us a smug wave as we pulled away.

"So, how exactly do we get to this rock?" I asked as we neared town. I'd never seen the road so busy. Cars lined Main Street, and bodies spilled out of the stores and restaurants, crowding the sidewalk.

"We row," Nathan said, passing Main Street altogether and pulling onto a road closer to Shanty Street. "The Lawsons have a dinghy they let me use whenever I want." Nathan parked at a small house and helped Hester out of his door before pulling a backpack from the bed. The motion lights on the house sprang to life as we followed him through a yard that backed up closer to the water than any of the houses on the cove. I glanced back at the unremarkable structure. It looked like one good wave . . .

"Okay, Hess, grab the oars," Nathan directed, pointing to a shed with weathered, white oars leaning against it. "And get some life vests."

While Hester obeyed, I followed Nathan to a tiny wooden boat, overturned in a patch of weeds. "Is that big enough for all three of us?" I asked.

"Easily. Grab that side and push toward me." We leaned down and gave it a shove, but two seconds and one scream later I was standing ten feet back.

"Spider. It touched me," I said, too upset by the black memory of its spindly leg to care if he laughed at me. He did.

"It wasn't anything poisonous," he assured me.

"You don't know that and I don't care," I answered, keeping my distance. "I'm not getting in unless any spiders get out first. Seriously, if one of those crawls on me when we're on the water, I will go overboard." Nathan laughed again and began a lackluster search of the boat.

"They're gone. There were only two. Probably interrupted their date." I was about to say something when his foot slammed against the side of the boat. "Okay, three. But not anymore!" he called.

I gasped and took another step back, nearly knocking into Hester. "I'll go check it for you," she offered. "Nathan doesn't understand about girls and bugs. He doesn't even care if a bee lands on him!"

"Thanks, Hess." It wasn't right to let a little girl half my age do the dirty work, but I couldn't bring myself to touch the boat again until I knew. She ducked her head gingerly into the dinghy, checking the floorboards under the seats.

"It's okay now, Jennifer," she promised.

I shuffled forward, watching my feet carefully. Two of them got away, after all. "Put it in the water first," I insisted. "Just wash it off a bit. Then I'll get in."

Nathan shook his head, chuckling as he pushed the boat toward the water. It clattered and grated its way to the waves where it sank gratefully into the water. "You never disappoint, Jennifer! You know that?" he said as he stood shin deep, holding the boat steady, waiting for us. "I never know what is going to come out of your mouth."

"Glad I amuse someone," I muttered dryly as I followed Hester. She stepped into the water, shoes and all, and waded out to Nathan who picked her up and deposited her in the boat. When I got to him I paused awkwardly, knowing the obvious thing was to give him my hand, but worried what the touch would do to his face. Before I could overthink it, he took my elbow in one hand and my hand in the other and steadied me as I made a high step into the boat. It rocked under my feet and I put my hands out like a tightrope walker as I took a seat.

Nathan pushed the boat and then followed, his tennis shoes and the bottom of his shorts sopping wet. "Sorry," he said as some drips hit me. He didn't mention the torn, floppy lifejackets at our feet so I assumed they were there for emergencies and not necessary to wear at the moment.

"Is it far?" I asked as Nathan pulled against the waves.

"Over there," he said, pointing with his jaw at a tiny island far to my right. "But the water is shallow the entire way."

"If anybody sees a yeti, I want to know. That'd be something to tell them in Nebraska." Hester laughed and I relaxed in my seat, turning sideways to hang my hand over the edge, letting my fingers skim through the tips of the waves. We rowed in relative quiet, interrupted by only the sound of the oars breaking the surface and the calls of a few curious gulls who followed us. I asked Nathan if he wanted any help rowing. That only made him laugh again and roll his eyes. "Just enjoy the ride, Jennifer."

The sky was not dark yet, but it was adorned with vibrant silk ribbons. The dark pinks reflected in the distant water, and I forgot to make polite conversation as I watched the ripples of light weave patterns of dark and bright atop the sea. As Nathan neared the rock, I saw that it was bigger than I realized. A huge boulder stood up at one end like a hunchback giant rising from the ocean, but it tapered into a narrow, flat band of pebbly land before plunging back into the water. At the flattest edge of the island, shrubs grew large enough for Nathan to secure the dinghy to the bottom of their trunks.

"It's slippery here. And the ground isn't even," he warned us as he dismounted from the boat and clutched the rocking side to balance himself. "Hess, you might get wet, but let me carry you." He lifted her from the boat and she threw her legs around him, trying to shimmy as high on his chest as she could manage. Nathan slipped a little as he set her down, and a slapping wave caught her at its peak, covering her red shorts in water. She yelped and scurried to dry land.

"Sorry. It'll dry quick, I bet," Nathan told her.

I stood as he came back for me. My heart could handle him taking my hand, but my pride wouldn't let him carry me. "I'm okay," I told him. "I don't mind getting wet."

I stepped down into the cold water and his hands seized my ribs from behind as I slipped on the slimy rocks. "Easy," he said. "It's really slick." Only after I made it to the more stable ground did he let go, my heart pounding under his touch.

"Thanks," I murmured, keeping my face from his view.

It only took a few minutes for Nathan to start a small fire with a lighter and some branches of the tangled bushes. "Just let that dry you off, Hess," Nathan said as he propped his wet shoes up beside the flames.

I was grateful for Hester's presence. She helped me keep my wits about me, which was difficult with Nathan so close, and the sky so achingly beautiful from a sunset that seemed to want to upstage the fireworks before they started. The boats appeared in the water, positioning themselves like chess pieces across the horizon. Ten boats. Twenty. I lost count.

"Who starts it?" I asked.

"The sun," Nathan answered. "When she finally gives up and the sky is completely dark, one of the fishermen will dare to be the first. And then they go. We'll put out the fire before they start, to see better."

The shadows were already deepening. We split a bag of potato chips and watched the silhouettes of men on the boats, until even those faded into the blackness. At last a lonely whistle filled the air and my eyes scanned the sky, searching for the right spot to focus when a small pop produced a shower of red lights. They drifted toward the Earth and were extinguished in the silence. And with that, the disorganized skirmish began. Over the sides of boats came the screaming whines and bursts of light. Nathan emptied several handfuls of sand onto the fire until the flames smothered into nothingness. In the sudden darkness and hissing smoke the lights in the sky were more thrilling.

"Where's *The Missus*?" I asked, trying to find something to distinguish the Jacks from the other boats.

"Just look for the boat all the other boats are launching smoke bombs at," Hester said. "They used to shoot bottle rockets at each other, but one year Bart Jenkins lost his eye. It hit him right in the face. Now the mayor fines them if they throw anything but smoke bombs."

Sure enough, the air around the boats grew thick with colored smoke and it seemed to concentrate on an area toward the back of the cluster.

"It's a guy thing," Nathan said when he saw me looking worried as the outlines of the boats fluctuated in the thick cloud. "Male bonding. Just throw flaming smoke at the guys you like the most."

"They said they had illegal rockets from China or something," I said.

"Lord help us! Good thing there's a lot of boats out there to save them if they sink *The Missus*," Nathan said, squinting into the darkness.

"Would Glenn survive? If she really sank, I think he'd go down with her," I said.

"True." Nathan's eyes flicked to me. "A man's no good without the girl, right?"

"That's what I hear," I answered as casually as my baffled mind allowed.

Hester looked up at both of us, but didn't seem particularly interested in the conversation. "I'm getting cold, Nathan," she said. "My clothes didn't get all dry."

Nathan rummaged in his bag and pulled out a thin felt blanket. He reached behind me to put it around her shoulder, and then pulled it around mine as well.

"You're wetter than I am," I protested.

"I'm not cold."

Hester's warm head leaned against my arm and I studied her brown hair. Pulling her closer I adjusted the blanket and closed it around us. As the colorful fire rained down and the fishermen called out like little boys playing pirates, I felt a fraction of Nathan's responsibility. Hester's tiny pieces—her thin wrist wrapped around her ankles, her small face against my arm, her little noises of delight—made me feel very protective. I cradled her in the night and wanted what Nathan wanted—to be able to give her a father to tuck her in, to row her to the rock, to take her out on his boat. I gazed at the crooked part in her hair, not sure that I could leave her, either.

When my eyes wandered back to Nathan he wasn't watching the show at all. He was watching me watch Hester. And he didn't take his eyes away when I caught him. Instead, his expression seemed to ask, *See what I mean?*

A thunderous crack broke through the night above all the other explosions, and we all jumped, our hands flying to our ears. "What in the—?" I asked, and a commotion of shouts filled the air. Following the sound, my eyes locked on yellow flames leaping from the top of one of the boats.

"Oh, no!" I cried, as we all rose in unison. We leaned forward on our toes, searching through the dark to make out what was happening. Hester grabbed my hand in a frightened clasp. The yellow flames climbed higher until a jet of water from another boat knocked them down. Laughter drifted through the air from the boats, but we weren't close enough to hear the joke.

"I don't think it did any real damage," Nathan said, still trying to decipher what happened. "I think they lit their ropes on fire." Over the water, volleyed from boat to boat, came the cry, "Jacks. It was the Jacks."

We joined in the laughter, hearing the echoes of every spectator lining the water. "Russ's wife will really kill him this time. She's been threatening for years, but I think she'll have blood on her hands tomorrow," Nathan said.

"The show isn't over. Maybe he'll finish the job for her," I replied. Hester giggled and sat back down. I put the blanket around her shoulders and sat a short distance away. At one point, two rockets collided in midair and the crowds screamed out their wild approval. From our lonely spot on the rock, it sounded like barely more than a happy whisper in the night.

"You were right," I told Nathan. "This is the best spot to watch. I don't think the Fourth of July will ever be quite as exciting to me again."

"Unless you come back," he said. "It's this good every year." His cool fingers suddenly enveloped my hand resting at my side. I turned to him, but he fixed his face toward the water, refusing to meet my eyes. He never moved his fingers, never stroked mine, never gave any indication that he was aware we were touching. He just maintained his firm clutch on my loose fist, leaving our nested hands on the ground out of Hester's sight. In those long minutes, I could not feel anything but his grip on my curled fingers. The wind stirred through the air, swept my cheeks, but it was the tapping finger of a child unable to get his mother's attention. The lights spun and dipped and burst into the air, but I only acknowledged them out of courtesy. Not even the Jacks' giant flares distracted me from Nathan's touch.

With a final enthusiastic display of firepower, the show ended, and the cheers from the audience resounded like ghostly voices from the night. Nathan let go and turned to me for a moment, with a look that I cannot categorize. The closest I can come is to say I saw a certain resignation in his eyes. A truce. An admission.

And as I tried to tell myself to keep moving, keep speaking, keep thinking, it didn't seem that anything in the world really mattered anymore. If we rowed off the edge of the Earth I'm not sure I would have noticed. If a yeti stuck its brutish head over the high sea cliffs, I might have mistaken it for a white cat.

THE LIGHTS INSIDE Shelter Cove were blazing by the time the old truck rolled into the driveway. Hester lifted her head from my shoulder and yawned. "Good night, Jennifer."

"Good night, Hess. Thanks for sharing that with me. It was amazing." I waved to her and gave Nathan a soft smile, trying to convey everything I felt in the shy curve of my lip. "I'll see you tomorrow," I said quietly over her head and shut the door. I'm certain my steps swayed as I tried to walk to the front door, tipsy with the memories.

Sarah greeted me when I got inside and gave me a quick synopsis of her adventures with Darcy, who managed to catch her hair on fire with a sparkler. "Don't worry," Sarah assured me. "Judith was fast. It only got a few strands." She gave me a shrewd look and asked how our night had gone.

"It was beautiful. Really nice." Outside a loud boom thundered through the air. I cringed. "Are they still going?"

"Sorry. The Jacks do that. They bring their boat over to the cove and set fireworks over Little's house just to get her riled up. Those four might be worse than schoolkids."

Sure enough, another explosion sounded and white sparks fell over the trees. "How long do they do that?"

"Until their beer runs out. Last year it was about three in the morning. I'm afraid you won't get your best sleep tonight." I chuckled all the way up the stairs, and once in bed I didn't mind the glittering lights outside my window. I wasn't counting on sleeping anyway. It was about two in the morning when the celebration dwindled to silence, and I closed my eyes, still feeling his fingers on the back of my hand.

As a result of the late night I didn't finish showering and dressing until well after ten o'clock the next morning.

"We're both behind today," Sarah said with chagrin, looking up from her toast. "I was thinking of going to church, but I missed the morning service being lazy." I sat down with a glass of orange juice and watched her tapping the tabletop. "Would you like to see your grandparents' graves today? Does that seem morbid? It's just that tomorrow is your last day . . ." Her voice faded.

"I would love that," I assured her. "It's not morbid at all. I want to see." I shifted in my chair. "I . . . I haven't even started packing yet. I can't make it seem real to myself."

Sarah nodded and sighed. "I know."

Tuesday night I would be at home, watching television or shopping with Cleo, and Sarah and Nathan would be sitting outside in the cool wind without me. It felt so terrible that my entire body gave a great shiver, trying to shake off the sadness.

After we finished eating, I wandered upstairs to organize my clothes, but when I pulled out my suitcase it reminded me of an animal carcass waiting to be stuffed. I couldn't bear to touch it. I left it lying lifeless on the floor next to the bed and trudged down the stairs to find something to distract me from the looming good-bye. I gently took down the Tennyson I had recited from on our first night of lines. *I'll have to leave you here,* I thought to the battered book. *The quilt. My grandfather's picture. You all belong here.* And every tiny good-bye seemed doubly cruel when I thought that Nathan would see it every day. Come back and back and everything would be what it had always been without me.

Sarah found me sitting on the couch, the unopened book pressed loosely to my chest. "Are you ready to go?" she asked.

Even getting up to find my sandals had a weary tedium to it, my legs protesting with each step. "How often do you go?" I asked her as I put my phone in my pocket.

"Depends on my mood. The weather. Often," her subdued answer was overlapped by the sound of a car in the driveway. It rumbled too loud, cut off too suddenly. Sarah and I both turned to the noise as a car door slammed. Before I'd taken two steps, the door shook with a single pound that was more battering ram than knock.

Sarah whispered "What the—?" as she hurried forward. In the next instant the door flew open so hard that it knocked into the wall behind it. I yelped and cringed.

"Nathan?" Sarah and I both cried in unison. His face was an inscrutable mask and his eyes ripped over the room, obviously searching for something.

"Did Claude sleep here?" he asked urgently.

"Claude?" My face must have been a complete blank because he groaned and grabbed a clump of his hair.

"Nathan, what's going on?" Sarah demanded.

"She never went to Amanda's last night."

"Nathan," Sarah interrupted in a voice fighting to keep order. "Where is Claude?"

"Somewhere with him!" he yelled. He spun around and threw the door closed with all his might, rattling the house.

Sarah flinched, but didn't admonish him. "Are you sure? Absolutely sure?"

The enraged look he threw at her quelled her words and she closed her mouth, convinced. "Did you go to his house yet?" Sarah's voice trembled even though she tried to appear composed.

"I just got back. They said he stayed with a friend after the firework show. I thought maybe she . . . she would have come here. I went home to double-check and sent Hester to go ask Little if she'd seen her. I'm running out of ideas. Judith is calling people." He grabbed his head and fell onto the couch looking like a man defeated.

"Nathan, we'll . . ." I started to say, "We'll find her," but he looked up in a rage.

"I told all of you! I told you this would happen. She's run off with that stupid . . ." no word in his vocabulary matched the loathsome expression that crossed his face. "I swear I will kill him if he laid one hand on her."

"Did you check his boat?" Sarah asked, her green eyes intense with worry.

A dangerous glint passed through Nathan's eyes, and I knew he was imagining what pull an empty boat might have for two young lovers. Sarah saw it, too, and hastily added, "I think you should let me handle it. I don't think you're calm enough."

"She wouldn't go on the boat," I pointed out. "It's Claude. She would never touch a boat."

Sarah jerked her head in a nod. "So then?" She looked around the room as if she thought one of her books held the answer.

"Let's check the boat," Nathan said with a clenched jaw.

"But, Nathan . . ." is as far as I got.

"Do any of us really know what she would do? She lied to us. She spent the night with him. She made her best friend cover for her. I don't pretend to know what she'd do!"

"Nathan, I don't think you should come with us. I think you need to wait here," Sarah repeated. His vehement glance made her sigh in defeat. He would not be deterred.

"Let me get my purse," she said, pointing a firm finger at his chest. "Don't move. Wait for me. I'm driving." She left to grab her things from the kitchen.

I thought I heard Nathan swear, but he was so distraught that I didn't dare look directly at him. It wasn't that I thought he would turn his wrath on me. It was more that I didn't want him to associate me with the horrendous feelings ripping through him at the moment. Sarah hadn't returned yet when two slow, small knocks sounded on the door. I was closest, so I gave Nathan the briefest look of relief and hurried to open it, sure it would be Claude. I was so expecting her small frame that I opened the door with my eyes trained down where Claude's face should have been and found myself staring at a gray jacket over a woman's chest. I jerked my head up and looked into my mother's pale, quaking face.

I don't know if I had been taking a breath in or out, but whichever one it was, suddenly reversed and I choked on thin air. "Mother!" I sputtered. I sensed people moving behind me, heard a strange, tight cry, but I could only process her stiff face.

"I came to take you home," she said, the effort of the words making her face go even whiter. I reached out and clutched her shaking arm. She leaned on me, but her pale face betrayed no emotion.

"Claire!" Sarah gasped behind me. She drew up behind me, but my mother recoiled. I could tell that Sarah didn't know how to help. She couldn't touch my mother—that much was obvious. Somehow Mother let me guide her inside to the couch. I'm not sure she knew what was happening. She was just responding to my touch. Obeying.

"Mother, what are you doing here? I thought you went to Kansas City this weekend."

"We did," she answered robotically. "And we were right there by the big airport and I thought, I thought, if I came to get you . . ." Her answer ran out of steam. She looked around the room like a person trapped in a bad dream. "You said I didn't have to come in."

"You don't. You just need to sit down. Let me get you some water," I told her. Sarah leapt at the chance to do something and disappeared into the kitchen. I was kneeling, holding my mother's hand, when I heard a faint cry came from outside. I cocked my head, listening. "Did you hear that?" I asked Nathan. He shook his head, his wide, disbelieving eyes trained on my mother.

"Nathan!" This time Hester's voice was loud enough for us all to hear. Even my mother lifted her head. I suddenly remembered that we were in the middle of Claude's crisis.

Nathan mumbled, "Maybe she found her at Little's," and rushed outside, trying not to disturb us. I watched him until he disappeared through the screen door, wanting to know what was happening, but unable to leave my mother.

Hester shouted again, her gentle voice sharp with panic. "Nathan! Sarah!"

"Was that Hester?" Sarah asked as she came back in the room with the water.

"I think so."

She handed me the cup hastily, spilling cold water across the side of my hand, and hurried outside. I knew nothing else could have convinced her to leave my mother, but when Hester made a sound like that, it could not be ignored. And then my mother and I were alone. Our eyes met as I handed her the glass. A general commotion of voices reached us through the screen door. Something was wrong. I had a million questions I didn't have time to ask. "I'm so sorry," I told her in a slur of fast words. "I am going to be right back. I promise." I gave her one anguished look and pulled my hand away from her to join Nathan and Sarah outside. With a dread I cannot explain I jumped both steps and landed beside Nathan thinking "Not Claude, not Claude."

Nathan was clutching Hester's shoulders, giving her too firm a shake. "What?" he growled, his voice low and menacing. I knew he was bracing for the worst news. I wasn't even sure what the worst news could be.

Hester tried to take a breath to answer. "Little. I went to ask Little and I think, I think she's . . ." It didn't matter that she couldn't finish the sentence. Her huge, dark eyes spoke terrible volumes. Nathan and I looked at each other in horror. *Like a curse out of Shakespeare. Life is about timing.*

"She's what?" Nathan demanded, his fear making him angry, just like my mother.

"Hester, honey, what did you see?" Sarah asked, prying Nathan's hands from Hester's quaking shoulders.

"I knocked and she never answered. So I looked in the window and she is in her chair, but when I knocked on her window, she never moved. I couldn't see her breathing! She didn't look . . . normal." Hester's voice rose in panic. She clutched her own face like she was trying to pull the memory out of her head. For a short moment I forgot my mother. Forgot Claude.

"Should we call the police?" I asked.

Sarah paused and then gave a slow, "No. I think I should go check first. Maybe she's all right. If she's . . . we'll call Jed if she's . . ." No one could say it.

I felt closer to fainting than I ever felt in my life. I wasn't sure I could walk into a room with a dead body. I'd had nightmares after my grandmother died four years earlier, and in every one I had walked into her home and been the one to find her. The midnight fear of those dreams gripped my stomach despite the midday tranquility. The sun was high and warm, reflecting white on the water. The leaves fluttered effortlessly on the trees. Nothing fit with death. Or tragedy. Or losing Claude. Or finding my mother on the front porch. I meant to say, "I can't," but inexplicably, it came out "I'll go." Nathan's eyes darted in concern to my face. I told him that he could keep looking for Claude; we could take care of Little.

"No. It can wait. I wouldn't . . . I'm going." And then we all looked at each other, not sure how to take the first step.

"I'll go," came my mother's weak voice behind us. We all spun around, silenced, and saw her walking toward us, her grave face colorless, but determined. She didn't look at us. She cut straight through our group and made her way to the road, turning toward Little's house.

Even Hester pulled out of her terrified stupor long enough to stare up my mother. "Who is that?" she whispered, but no one answered.

"Mother, wait, don't," I said as I edged in front of her, blocking her way. "You don't have to do this. We'll get Jed."

Sarah came as close as she dared. "She's right, Claire. Don't let this be your homecoming."

My mother turned a haughty, superior stare on her sister. "I know what to do. I've been through it before," she said and continued around us. Sarah and I looked at each other in shock, not sure how to reply. And so our ragtag group followed as my mother led the way to Pilgrim's Point. She didn't hesitate until she got to the house and then she turned to Hester.

"Which window?" she asked.

"In the back," Hester whispered, pointing.

As we started toward the back of the house I turned to the little girl. "Hess, I think you should wait over there. Let us take care of it." I pointed to a large tree and looked her straight in the eye to show her I meant it. Without argument she nodded and went to stand in the shelter of the distant branches. Nathan's hand brushed my arm in a silent thank-you. Even with death looming, and Claude missing, I couldn't deny the jolt of happiness.

My mother peered inside the small living room window, cupping her hand around her eyes and tilting her head as she squinted into the dark room. "I see her. I don't know," she said slowly.

Sarah and Nathan took their turns at the glass panes while I pulled up to my mother. "Let's just call Jed. I don't want to do this." Even more than that, I didn't want my mother to do it. Not death again. Not this morning. I silently cursed the timing. Against my better judgment, I crept to the window and looked into the shadowy room. I saw Little's legs propped up on her olive green ottoman, her skin peeking out from between the end of her housedress and her short, white socks. Reluctantly I moved my eyes up to the chair. Her body rested in the shadows thrown over her by the curving wingback, but I could make out her lolling head, dropped to her shoulders, and turned away from us. My stomach heaved with nausea.

"She might need help, if she's still . . ." Nathan said quietly. It was Sarah who steeled herself and walked up to the window and gave two sharp raps. Little didn't move, though the rest of us jumped. "Crap," Nathan muttered.

"Try the back door," my mother said as she walked toward it. The handle turned in her fist. She pushed the door and it swung into the yellow kitchen. We all stared at the open doorway in silence. "I'll go," she repeated as she looked at our frozen faces.

"Turn on the light," I said as I grabbed the switch, and the room brightened. To be honest, it made me feel a little better. Before I could follow the others into the living room, Hester's small hand found mine and grasped it.

"Hess, you're supposed to be outside."

"I'm coming," she said, her determination a mirror of her brother's, my mother's.

"Stay with me," I said needlessly—her vicelike grip proved she had no intentions of leaving my side. Nathan flicked on the living room light, flooding the room in a sickly, yellow glow. Every object seemed to stare at me, the ceramic lizard on the china hutch glaring with his beady eyes, the divan reaching out its wooden arms in supplication. In the middle of the silent room Little rested peacefully in her chair, her motionless face still so lifelike.

"Little?" Sarah was the first to speak. She said it like someone apologizing for waking a person from a nap. She tried again, this time louder. "Little?"

Nothing.

Hester took a shaky breath and I held her back with my hand as I leaned forward to see better. But already I knew there was nothing to see. Just her body, so meek and silent in death. We all drew nearer, our faces somber and appalled. It was my mother who reached down and gently touched Little on the shoulder. I shuddered when her shoulder shook and grew still again.

"Little?" she asked.

I felt a rush of bile in my throat and swallowed hard against the burning sensation.

"Let me check her pulse, in case she's unconscious," Nathan said in a soft voice, pulling in front of my mother and Sarah.

We all watched as he stretched out his hand and took her wrist with infinite care. "Still warm." He placed his fingers against her thin skin, walking them lightly as he searched for the right place to press down. We waited for his conclusion in profound silence.

"What the *hell* are you doing in my house?" Little's head rose like a sleeping monster roused, and her gravelly voice exploded over our bent heads.

Hester and I both screamed. Nathan dropped her arm and stumbled.

"Little!" Sarah yelled. "You're all right?"

Little's narrowed eyes swung across our astonished party, boring us with her angry glance, but she didn't answer. She shuffled in her chair and reached for a small object on the side table next to her. Her hand went to her ear and she fidgeted, tossing her head over.

"I ain't got my hearing aid in," she grumbled. "I can't hear you."

I heard a shaky laugh and realized it came from me.

"Her hearing aid," Nathan repeated humorlessly.

"This better be good. Have you all arrested for trespassing." Little's eyes stopped on my mother whose white lips trembled, and her indignation transformed to surprise. "You come back, did ya? How long you been here?"

"She's only been here for ten minutes," Sarah snapped. "So all she's gotten to do is come see if you're dead!"

"Dead? Who said I'm dead?" Little's eyes impugned us, looking for her accuser.

Hester's hand shook in mine. I spoke before she felt the need to explain herself. "We knocked on your door and your window and we didn't . . . we didn't see you move."

"A body can't sleep anymore? Those Jackasses set off fireworks all night long. I finally had to take my hearin' aid out. I'm tired!"

"Then we'll go," Sarah retorted sharply, her fear giving way to irritation.

" 'Sides, I wouldn't die now. Not when things are getting good," Little looked from my mother to me to Nathan and smacked her hands together, hungry for someone to say something. When we all glared at her, she addressed my mother again. "You gonna fight it out? Or have a nice talk? I've seen it work both ways."

Sarah rolled her eyes. "Jasper!" she spat in genuine anger.

"I'm taking Jennifer home," my mother whispered in confusion, her lips barely moving.

"First you got things to say. You got things to do. You pick up after yourself and then you can get home," Little said.

"It's not funny!" Sarah yelled. I'd never heard her raise her voice and we all cringed. Except for Little. "Don't say it like it's funny. You leave her alone." Her voice broke on the *her*, and when I looked at her angry, teary eyes I saw an older sister. I saw the same pain that filled Nathan's face when he told us he couldn't find Claude.

Claude.

"We can't go yet," I said quietly, over whatever retort Little tried to give. Everyone turned to me, but I looked at my mother. "I know I promised—I swore—that I would go with you right away, but I can't leave yet. My friend is missing. We just started looking for her when you showed up and when Little . . . didn't die." My eyes shot to the old woman, daring her to speak. "I just need to know that she's okay before we leave."

I couldn't tell what my mother was thinking. Her blank face never altered.

"Jennifer, I'll find her. You and Sarah should stay here," Nathan said in his low voice.

"No," I answered without equivocation. "Mother? Can you stay with Little? For just a while? I will be right back." I sounded like a parent reassuring her child on the first day of preschool, a calm voice mixed with pleading.

"Who's missing?" she asked, like she thought I had told her and she forgot.

"Judith's daughter," Sarah answered. "She didn't come home after the fireworks last night."

"Judith has a daughter?"

"Three," Sarah said. "And this is her son, Nathan." My mother looked into his face, and I wondered if he could hide his antagonism for the sister who abandoned Sarah. To my surprise, he nodded respectfully.

"Your sister didn't come home? How old is she?" she asked him. Some mothering instinct to gather information was kicking in. "Have you called the police?"

"She's Jennifer's age. And we think we know who she's with," Sarah said, watching Nathan. "It's Jake Garner's son. We think they're together."

"Mom, I'm just going down to the docks to see if Jake's boat is there. It won't take long." I begged with my eyes. I couldn't drive away now. Not like this.

"She'll be fine here," Little said, looking to my mother. "Go find the girl."

"No," my mother declared. "I'll go with you."

Her eyes met mine and I didn't try to argue. She studied me a moment and looked down to Hester, lurking behind me, and Nathan, fighting his urge to resume his search, and Sarah (perhaps the most staggered of our party), wiping her eyes. "Has it been this crazy the whole time?" she asked me as if the others couldn't hear her.

A smile wobbled on my face. "Only since you got here."

CHAPTER 37

"IF EVERYBODY'S GOIN', then I'm goin'," Little insisted. " 'Sides, the girl'll need someone on her side."

"Her side?" Nathan challenged in disgust.

"Tough gal. It's hard to go after what you want," she said as she pushed herself up using the arms of her chair.

"She's a little girl!" Nathan shouted at her. Little's eyebrows rose in scorn.

I whipped around to Nathan. "She's my age!"

"Never mind," Sarah said above us. "We can't afford to fight right now. Let's just go." Nathan and I broke our glaring contest. "I'll get my car. Hester, girl, you run home and tell your mom that we're checking the dock. Tell her to call us if she hears anything." Hester nodded, a gleam of regret that she had to miss whatever came next.

"That's your sister, too?" my mother asked Nathan as Hester disappeared.

He nodded quickly, flicking the question like a fly. "I'm not waiting. I'm leaving now," Nathan said. With Little safe from the grip of the Angel of Death, his urgency resurged.

"No," Sarah demanded. "No. You let one of us get there first. I know you, Nathan."

He started to argue, but I put a hand on his arm and spoke to Sarah. "I'm going with him now. I'll make sure he doesn't do anything stupid." I looked to my mother's stunned face. "Are you going to ride with Little?"

Her hazel eyes flickered in confusion. "I'm going with you."

Nathan wouldn't tolerate another word. Seconds later, we were at his truck, climbing onto the torn vinyl bench. I was so close to Nathan that I could smell him. Every time he changed gears, his shoulder knocked into mine, and despite my worry for Claude, despite my mother squished beside me, I couldn't make my body ignore his touch.

"Do you think they eloped?" my mother asked as the engine roared and Nathan slammed it into fourth gear, knocking my knee with his knuckles.

"I have no idea what the age laws are. But she's sixteen. I doubt it's legal," Nathan responded with a curl of his lip.

"What if they aren't there? At the boat?" I asked him.

"If Harvey's there, we'll ask if he's seen them."

"Harvey?" my mother asked, a new worry appearing in her voice.

"Yes, your Harvey. I'm sorry, Claire, but we have to go see him," Nathan answered.

"*My* Harvey? He isn't . . . how do you know me, again?" she asked Nathan, her face bewildered.

"I don't have time for delicacy," Nathan muttered, watching the road as he hit Main Street too fast. "I know you because I know Sarah. Everyone knows you." My mother opened her mouth to protest a strange teenage boy telling her life story, but Nathan kept going. "And don't worry. Harvey's fine. He married a girl from Portland. Three kids." The truck engine cut off abruptly and Nathan leaped out. "You can come or stay. Doesn't matter," he told us through his open window as he paused with his door half open.

"I'm coming," I said and slid out behind him.

My mother shoved her door open. "Did you know about Harvey?" she asked me.

Nathan ignored her and grabbed my hand. "Come on," he urged me. His grip was warm and tight.

"Didja see . . ." I heard one of the Jacks ask as we hurtled past them. I would have to apologize later. I scanned the dock. The water lapped smoothly where Jake's boat usually sat.

"Harvey!" Nathan yelled, rushing past the empty square of ocean toward Harvey's boat with the dull red hull. The wrinkles around Harvey's eyes crowded together as he poked his head out of his cabin and squinted into the sun to see who was calling for him.

"Harvey, have you seen Jake's boat?" Nathan asked.

Harvey slowly mounted his small staircase. "Yup. He took it out a couple hours ago." He scratched his stubbled chin.

"Was Will with him?" Nathan enunciated each word clear and slow, his hands poised in an open position, like he meant to capture Harvey's answer with his fingers.

"Nah. Don't believe so. He took it out hisself. Just checking the pumps. Something wrong?" His words drawled out, the answers unfurling at an agonizing pace.

"We can't find Claude," Nathan answered. "Or Will." His lip curled with dislike when he added the last two words.

"Well, I reckon . . ." Harvey's eyes, which had been roaming vaguely, focused on something over my shoulder. He dropped his words, letting them slur into silence. "Claire?" he murmured.

I turned to see my mother walking slowly behind us, her hand raised to chest height in a stiff wave. The pink of her face deepened as we tracked her approach. She stopped several feet away from us. "Hi, Harvey," she said, like she expected him to attack her.

Harvey chewed on something in his mouth, but I think it was his own cheek. He never took his eyes from my mother's face as he reached into his holey jeans and pulled out a toothpick that he shoved between his back teeth. I couldn't see any similarities to my proper, shy father. I studied my mother, looking for any sign of regret. *Could this have been the man she spent her life with?* Even Nathan bridled his impatience long enough to observe the unfolding scene.

"So yuh home, huh?" Harvey asked, his face betraying no emotion, but his teeth gnawing vigorously.

"I'm *here*," my mother corrected gently. She looked at me. "You met Jennifer?"

He nodded once and said "huh" in an agreeable tone.

"And you've got three of your own?" she said too brightly.

"Huh." The toothpick bobbed on his lip as he chewed.

In the uncomfortable quiet my mother shoved her hands into the pocket of her light jacket and sucked in a breath like a diver about to go under. "Harvey, this isn't the time or place, but I'm only here today, so I'd better just tell you that I'm sorry. It doesn't count for much twenty years late. . . ."

"Huh." This time his mouth flicked up in the briefest smile and the flexible syllable stretched into something that seemed to say, it's water under the bridge.

My mother shifted her weight, relief and shame leaving her face a mottled red. "So you haven't seen the girl they're looking for?" she asked.

"Nuh." Harvey managed to shove the toothpick with his tongue to the other side of his mouth. "She's not around here. I thought that was the one scared a' boats," he said to Nathan.

"She is. But we're running out of places to check." Nathan scanned the horizon and I knew he was deciding where to go next.

"We could ask the Jacks," I suggested.

"They were too drunk last night to remember anything." Nathan glanced up to their bench.

"Jake said something about a proposal last night," Harvey said off-handedly.

"Decided to mention that, did you?" Nathan's hand flew up in frustration.

"Didn't suppose he meant Will. Just thought he was talking about one of his deckhands," Harvey shifted his weight to his other leg.

"What exactly did he say?" my mother asked nervously, as if afraid to interrupt.

"Jus' said it was a romantic night for a proposal. I was getting' my fireworks ready. Didn't hear no mo'."

"But Will was on the boat for the show, right? So they had to go somewhere after . . ." I thought out loud.

"Yuh, he was on the boat. Call the hotels yet?" Harvey's bored voice made his question a hundred times worse.

I diverted my embarrassed eyes, trying not to see the flush of fury washing over Nathan's face. "We can try Michael's house," I suggested.

"That'd be real classy," Nathan muttered in disgust.

His cell phone let out a jarring jangle, and Nathan thrust his hand into his pocket like he was grabbing a drowning man from water. Before the second ring sounded, the black phone was at his ear.

"Yeah," he said, his teeth not opening to let the word out. His tight jaw flexed and he gave another clipped, "Yeah. Bye." A flat, black fire burned at the center of his eyes when he turned to us. "They're home."

I breathed a sigh of relief in unison with my mother. Harvey just pulled the corner of his lips down thoughtfully. "Well, then." He gave my mother one nod. "It's good you came back," he said before he turned back to his boat.

She lingered uncertainly, watching his back before she gave a timid "Thanks."

Nathan stalked up the dock in silence, anger building visibly under his skin, stiffening his limbs. "What's the matter?" Glenn asked gruffly when we passed them. Nathan didn't slow or turn his head. I'm not sure he knew Glenn was there. I'm not sure he knew *he* was there. I shrugged a fast apology and tried to keep up with Nathan.

"I'll drive," my mother said when we got to the car. Nathan turned his dead face on her and she ignored his expression, holding out her hands for the keys. "Trust me, it's hard to drive when you want to kill someone," she said calmly, her eyes not moving from his. I watched in disbelief as he dropped the cluster of keys into her hand. I took my seat in between them and felt the car jerk to life. "Roll down your window. Try to calm down," my mother instructed him like a flight attendant.

"I didn't know you could drive a stick," I told her.

A grim smile crossed her face. "Judith still live at Boulder Bend?" Mother asked.

I nodded.

"I don't think we should take him yet," she said, tilting her head at Nathan.

"Try and stop me," he growled.

"Nathan, we don't know anything. Let them explain first," I begged.

He didn't acknowledge me, just kept his face trained out the open window. The wind blew his sandy hair and whipped strands of mine onto his shoulder until I reached up and pulled it into one hand. The truck bounced onto Haven Lane, past Shelter Cove, and down to Boulder Bend. A small congregation waited on the front yard; Sarah and Little stood beside Judith and across from them Will slouched awkwardly beside Claude, guilt and worry wrinkling his forehead. Claude stood tall, but her defiant stance didn't make her tiny body look any older. My mother rolled to a slow stop and killed the engine.

The door whipped open and Nathan jumped down, midstride, plunging toward Claude. "Where have you been?" He kept his voice just below a shout.

"Nathan," she said, half angry, half placating. "Wait."

"Where have you been?" he yelled. Sarah and Judith moved toward him. I left the door swinging on its hinges and followed behind him. My mother said my name but I ignored her. Nathan was a torrential wave, not stopping for anyone, headed straight for Claude and Will. "Were you with him all night?"

"Not like you think," Claude said, her hands up in surrender.

Will slid in front of Claude right as Nathan reached them. As fluid as his undaunted stride across the yard, Nathan's fist swung over his head and then down in a grand arch, collecting Will's face as it plunged toward the ground. I heard other screams over my own and watched Will collapse almost to the grass before staggering back up, his fists clenched.

I'd never seen someone make another person bleed, but bloody spit trailed from Will's mouth. I heard Sarah shouting angrily at Nathan. She was running, but Will put his long arm up, telling her to step back.

Claude, over her first abrupt shock, sprung on Nathan with a vicious wrath. Her small fists pummeled his arm as she screamed. I could tell she didn't even know what she was saying. Just letting the anger spew out like Will's blood.

"Feel better?" Will asked, quieting everyone. His small eyes glinted with hate for Nathan, but he took a step back to show he wasn't going to retaliate. Nathan was strong, but I'd seen Will working on the docks. He could do damage if he wanted.

Nathan took a threatening stomp closer to him, but Claude was in the middle now, her hands up to her brother. "What did you do?" Nathan yelled. "What did you do to her?"

"Nothing!" Will shouted and spit some blood from his mouth. "We . . . I, I asked her to marry me."

"She's sixteen!" Nathan screamed.

"Not now. Later. In a few years. I just wanted to ask!" Will retorted, holding up a defensive hand as Nathan leaned closer.

"Over my dead body. Over yours!" Nathan yelled as he pointed a deadly finger at Will's face.

Claude wrenched his hand away from Will. I noticed a glint of gold flash in the hot sun. "What do you think you're doing? You can't tell people what to ask me! You're not in charge of the world." But even she, as tough as she was, stepped back under the tidal wave of Nathan's rage. It crushed her into silence.

Will spared a fast glance for the circle of appalled women around him before addressing Nathan again. "Don't you see what happens if we do this? It's like Romeo and Juliet and that cousin of hers. Claude gets hurt no matter who wins. I'm not doing it."

Nathan's voice snaked down to a hiss. "You read *Shakespeare*? Is that to impress her? Is that to make her think you could actually stimulate her mind and not just . . ."

"We watched the movie," Will explained, stepping to his left as Nathan stepped right.

"Trying to educate the village idiot?" Nathan asked Claude. "You think it will make it okay to waste your life on him if he's seen an old black-and-white movie?"

Even I wanted to slap him for that one. If he wasn't so coiled to fight, so ready to swing his fist blindly, I might have.

"It wasn't old," Will said. "It was the new one. With the guns. She's not trying to make me anything I'm not."

Nathan paused like an actor when the director yells cut. His face smoothed for a short instant in disbelief as he spoke to Claude, "The DiCaprio movie?"

"I like that one best!" Her shrill cry pained my chest. "Better than the old ones. Better than the book. We're different, Nathan. I'm not like you. I've never been good at the things you're good at." Her red, embarrassed face was beseeching. "That's okay. That we're different. Like it's okay that Will and I are different."

Nathan shook his head, throwing away her words and turning back to Will. "Did you tell her what you said about her? Tell her why you started paying attention to her. Did you tell Judith?" His voice punched Will with each word, making him crouch.

"What? When? What are you talking about?"

"Don't play dumb with me!" Nathan shouted. "Tell her that you hoped she'd take after her mom. *Like mother, like daughter!*"

Nathan's voice cracked and the red leaked from his face to his eyes. A tear trembled on his bottom lashes.

Claude stumbled, taking a step away from Will, her face white with betrayal.

Will froze. "I never . . ."

Nathan lunged forward, seizing the small clearing Claude made by stepping back. Claude reached his arms just in time to deter him and helplessly she screamed, "Jennifer, do something!" I don't know why she thought of me before her own mother, before Sarah, but it was my face she held with her terrified eyes. Her words woke me from the stupor of a spectator and I rushed forward, grabbing Nathan's shoulder. It shook with power beneath my palm.

"He doesn't remember, Nathan. That was years ago."

"I beat the brains out of his head—I think he remembers why!" Nathan said as he struggled to control his arms that wanted desperately to flail, but couldn't with two girls so close.

"I don't!" Will said, a frantic plea in his voice. "I don't. I'd forgotten all about that. I would never. I didn't start liking her . . . She isn't like that!" His mouth fought for traction on his slick thoughts, looking for the words to make Nathan understand. His eyes pleaded for Claude to believe him.

"What did you do with her last night?" Nathan demanded once more. I blushed as deeply as Claude. I didn't want to hear.

"Nothing! I took her to Bredford to see the lighthouse. I asked her if she'd want to get married in a few years."

"And then?" Nathan snarled.

"And then I told him I don't know!" Claude shrieked. "We talked. I called Amanda and told her that I couldn't come over because Will and I had to talk."

"Talk?" Nathan shredded the word with doubt.

"Yes, talk! And we fell asleep. In the car. We didn't. We've never . . ." Livid tears fell down across her red face. "Thanks for thinking so highly of me, Nathan."

For the first time the savage tremors racing through Nathan slowed. I was surprised to see my hand still clamped on his shoulder. I slid it down to his arm, holding onto his elbow.

"And you're thinking of it? Marrying this waste of space?"

"He's not!" Claude yelled. "You stupid, impossible jerk! He's smart. He's good. You never give anyone credit. I've been trying to be good enough for you my whole life. Make up for the fact that I'm the reason your dad left. But I can't! I'll never live up to what you want me to be."

Will's hand went up to Claude's face, and he put his fingers to her mouth and looked at Nathan with a dark, accusing flash in his eyes. I'd never seen Nathan look so confused or shocked, but his expression mirrored mine, Sarah's, Judith's. "Make it up to me? Be good enough for me? That is the stupidest thing I've ever heard. You're good enough for anyone. He's not good enough for you!"

Will answered quietly. "I get it, Nathan. I know she's smarter. I know she's too pretty. I get it." Will flinched at his own words, embarrassed. "But she likes me anyway." His eyebrows drew up in surprise, like he couldn't believe it either.

"Yeah, well, there's no accounting for taste," Nathan mumbled, the heat of his temper fading.

Claude took Will's hand. Her head didn't quite reach the top of his chest and I looked at the mismatched pair, her proud eyes gazing up at his sunburned face like he was a rare prize to be won.

"Nathan." Sarah came forward slowly. "My dad"—her eyes went to my mother—"our dad was just a waterman. My mother's family hated him. She didn't. Sometimes it works." I released his arm, suddenly too aware of his warm skin under mine. Too aware of the eyes around us. I drew back a pace to my mother and took her hand instead, needing something to hold. She clutched my fingers tightly, and I couldn't tell which of us was the scared child. Both, most likely.

"Your mom wasn't sixteen," Nathan started.

"May work. May not," Judith interrupted. "That's to be seen. But you're still grounded for . . . ever. Get inside." And her finger cut a path from Claude to the front door. She then raised it to Will, who looked like he would be grateful if an assassin took him out before she spoke again. "And *you*! I always liked you. But if you ever pull a stunt like that again . . . If you ever . . . I will sic Nathan on you so fast, so help me!" she vowed.

Nathan's mouth raised in a smirk until her finger made its

way to him. "You shut up! You don't fight with your fists. Not with a mind like yours. Get inside. Now!"

We all stood back in shock as Nathan made his way to the front door, turning his head just long enough to see his mother following behind him.

CHAPTER 38

THE DOOR SHUT behind Judith, enveloping the yard in an eerie stillness. My mother flashed her eyes to Sarah and Little, and all the questions that waited behind the unfolding dramas of the day rushed the gates of our minds. I felt mine building. Saw the confounded look in Sarah's eyes as she looked at her sister. Whatever my mother was thinking she hid well. She gave my hand a small tug and said, "Let's get your stuff and go."

I felt the blow of her words across my back, lashing me home, away from Sarah, away from Nathan. I couldn't argue. A promise is a promise. I looked up to Little with my stricken expression, something that said, *this is it*, and let my mother guide me forward. I was certain one of the women would save me from this abrupt departure, say something to slow my mother's exit, but they watched us cross the yard to the road.

"Mom," I said when I recovered my speech, drawing my hand out of hers as we reached Shelter Cove. "The thing is that I thought you would call first. Give me a warning. So I could say good-bye. I haven't said good-bye to anyone."

"You can say it on your way out. We need to leave now." She wasn't angry, but there wasn't an inch of compromise in her voice. "Just throw your stuff in your bag."

I struggled against the tears, out of ideas. Obediently, I left her standing in the driveway while I walked inside, trying to understand that I wouldn't walk in again. Not for months. Maybe a year. Even Chester sensed something amiss, because he graced me with a rare caress across my legs after I entered. Everything was slow, each step, each turn. I mounted the stairs and gathered my clothes, neatly folding even my underwear. Stalling. Computing. Waiting for someone else to think of something. I had finished packing one drawer when I heard footsteps outside my room and braced myself to look at Sarah, to tell her bravely that I would be back soon. It was a different face that peeked in—my mother's.

"Are you done yet?" she asked impatiently, as if she didn't want the house to hear her. Even though she spoke to me she was looking at the room, her eyes drinking in the details like I had the first time I saw it.

"Almost," I said, looking at the drawers of clothes I hadn't emptied yet. I let my gaze wander, trying to see the room as she saw it, after twenty years. "Do you remember when you wanted to move in here with Sarah and you got stuck between the beds?"

She pierced me with a frown but didn't answer; looked like she never intended to answer again. "Sarah told me about that the first night I got here. She laughed so hard she cried. Do you remember?" I looked down at the quilt beneath my suitcase, waiting for a response she refused to give. "Was this quilt on the bed when you were here? I've been using it since I got here." She recoiled when I said that, turned toward the desk and ran her hand over wood, disregarding me. My pride prickled and the heat of it rose up inside of me. It didn't really matter what I said anymore. I just wanted her to answer. "Do you remember her making it? Do you remember anything? Do you remember Sarah's senior recital, when she had all the solos? Do you remember when your dad took you with him on his boat?" I wasn't pausing to let her answer—I was reciting any stray story I could remember Sarah telling me. "Do you remember . . ."

"Stop it, Jennifer! You don't know what you're talking about," she snapped. "I remember everything. You don't need to ask."

Not good enough. "So you remember when you begged your dad to buy extra fireworks because you wanted the best show, and how your mother wouldn't let you talk like the other kids . . ."

She turned from the room and disappeared. I jumped up, leaving my clothes in a heap on the bed and stalked her down the hall, down the stairs, unrelenting. "And Harvey? Remember him? And the storms? And your cat that you buried with fish bones because you'd just learned about the Egyptians feeding their dead?"

At the bottom of the stairs my mother spun blindly, pacing the living room. "Do you remember your father working at the factory and your mother wearing her aprons? Do you remember?" I didn't know what was happening to me. Maybe Little's unexpected resurrection and Nathan's violent fight were too much for one morning, but my voice was growing, a hot balloon inflating in my chest, ready to break. Explode. "Do you remember Sarah trying to talk to you, trying to find you, trying to be your sister? Do you remember lying to me for sixteen years?!" There was an ugly scream ripping from my mouth, a noise I'd never made before. And all along, as hateful as it sounded, I never once hated my mother. Resented, certainly, disapproved, but never hated. I was trying to reach her across an ocean of pain—bring her back home.

At last she flung herself to face me, her neck scarlet. "Do you really think I was lying to you, Jennifer? Protecting you? I was lying for her. Protecting her!" My mother threw her hand out to the wall of pictures, stabbed her finger at her own senior portrait. "I was trying to keep her, me, away from here so I wouldn't have to remember the call from the hospital! Or burying my father. Or remember being the only one here to bury my mother! I remember picking out the clothes to put on her dead body! So don't play this game with me. Don't play *do you remember*, because I will win every time. I remember *everything*! I *can't* forget anything. I can't!"

The front door slammed and we both looked up to see Sarah pressed against the golden wood, blocking it with her body, her hand guarding the handle. "I remember, too," she said softly. "And this time I'm not letting you run out on me. There are things to say."

"Don't push me," my mother threatened, looking like a cornered animal. I wouldn't have put it past her to claw her way out. She looked nearly as mad as Nathan when he confronted Will. She turned toward the kitchen, looking for her escape, but I anticipated the move and stepped in front of her. She stopped midstride. Trapped. She wouldn't fight me.

Sarah's voice was level. "You do what you have to do. You can scream and hit me and bite and I don't care what else. I don't care what it takes. You can leave, but not like this. I won't survive if you run out of here again."

"You won't survive? *You* won't! Is it always about you?" My mother looked to the tall picture windows, wild to get out of the tiny space. I felt the walls of the room shrinking, pulling the three of us closer. Dangerously close.

Pain crossed Sarah's face but she didn't interrupt. Didn't move. Just kept her back pressed to the heavy door. When she saw my mother was done speaking, she quietly asked, "What did you bury her in?"

"What?"

"I've always wondered what you buried her in. Little couldn't remember when I asked her. Harvey said he didn't see her clothes because there was a blanket around her."

My mother's lips moved, her head shook, fighting the impulse to answer. "I wouldn't have had to pick anything! If you came home. If you were here."

"What did you bury her in?" Sarah was cracking her, the lines in my mother's forehead deepening.

"You should have picked it! She asked for you! And I told her you were coming. She woke up and she could barely talk but she asked for Dad and she asked for you and I told her you were coming! I lied to her. The last thing I ever said to her was a *lie*."

I wanted to throw my arms around both of them. Their similar faces mirrored decades of anguish. My mother was breaking from telling the truth for the first time; Sarah was breaking from hearing it.

"At least you were there, Claire," Sarah said.

"She didn't want *me*. She never asked for me. Not once." Mother choked on the last word.

"She never had to," Sarah whispered. "You were already there. You were the one she could always count on, without asking."

My mother continued like she didn't hear Sarah. "She remembered that Dad was dead and she gave up. I wasn't enough. She wouldn't stay for me. But if you had been there, maybe if there had been two of us . . ." My mother wiped her tears away so roughly that it looked like she slapped herself in the face.

Sarah waited, watched, before she spoke again. "That wasn't it. You were enough. She didn't give up on you. She loved you. It's my fault that thought ever crossed your mind. I never let you have the limelight. I was always the center of attention, even in our own family. No wonder you wanted out." Her voice fell even softer, and as it dipped lower, a certain calm emanated from Sarah. "I'm so sorry I wasn't there. I'm sorry for you, and yes, I'm sorry for me. I would give anything to go back and be by her side like you were."

"That wasn't your fault," my mother said. "I forgave you that because you didn't know. But you didn't come! I told you and I thought you'd be here that night. And I *waited*!" A torment I couldn't comprehend filled her last word and I closed my eyes, willing the pain to pass.

"I know. I'm so sorry. I'm sorrier than you'll ever know." I don't know how Sarah kept her composure. Maybe the shock of my mother's sudden appearance helped numb her to the stabbing words.

My mother ignored her apology. "Where were you?" she cried, a sob tearing the words, a child breaking out of her adult face.

"I meant to come right away. Can I tell you? Really tell you? Will you give me two minutes?"

"Two minutes? Why not five days? Take all the blasted time you need!"

"Claire, I—"

"One day!" my mother screamed, slamming her finger against her palm. "Two days!" Another finger fell.

"Claire!"

"You listen to me! Three days! Four days!" Could the gavel hitting the bar on judgment day sound any more dreadful than her slapping fingers? "Five days!" She held up her hand, fingers outstretched, and I thought of Lady Macbeth, dripping with blood.

Sarah took a hesitant step from her post at the door, eyes glued to my mother's face. "Claire, I know. I know. Can I tell you?"

"You're not even listening to me," my mother cried. "You just want your turn to talk. You shut up! My turn today!" Nature itself seemed to clap its mouth shut at her command. The slap of the words resounded across Sarah's face. "I sat by the door and thought you'd be home. I waited all night. By morning I thought you were dead. Just like them. I thought I was cursed, that I did it—killed all of you. I was too scared to call anyone and tell them you were missing because once they found your body that would be it. All over. And I couldn't bury someone else by myself. Especially not you." My mother's fierce voice faltered, and the memory broke painfully over her face. Neither Sarah nor I dared moved. I'm not sure we breathed.

My mother inhaled and continued. "When I finally told him, Jed put out an alert for your car. We got in touch with one of your roommates and she said that you left upset and called the next day from Massachusetts. Massachusetts!" My mother threw up her hands and defied the universe to come up for an excuse for Massachusetts. "What in hell were you doing in Massachusetts? Why did you call a *roommate* and not me?"

Sarah opened her trembling lips but my mother plowed over her. "Who cares? I was done. You might as well have died. I didn't care anymore. I packed my bags. I never wanted to see this place again. I don't even want to be here now!" The long fettered words careened around the room, the only things that dared to stir.

After a dreadful stillness Sarah finally spoke. "But you are here," she whispered. "I don't want my turn for *me*. I want it for *you*. You deserve to know what happened. Can I tell you?"

Mother crossed her arms tight over her chest, but she stayed. Sarah cautiously took it as permission. "I drove to Boston. I thought I could get there and still be back sometime in the middle of the night. That's what I meant to do. I went to pick up a man named John."

My mother turned just enough for me to see the perplexed slope of her eyebrows. "What man?"

"My professor. I was in love with him. He didn't usually teach at UMaine. He was an assistant PhD at Northeastern. He filled in teaching a summer class in Maine and I met him."

"What in the world does this have to do with our mother?" my mother demanded.

"It has to do with us. Why I was late coming home. Why you thought I didn't care about you. He's the one I went to Africa with.

Just the two of us. In Africa." And when she said it like that, pausing between the slow sentences I knew just what she was telling my mother. I imagined the sunsets blazing over the plains, streaming through the wide, green leaves of the twisted trees. I imagined dirt floors, and brown faces singing, and cooking fires, and Sarah. And a man. And I knew what she was saying.

"A man?" My mother's voice was so perplexed it sounded like she was trying a new language. "You didn't come because of a man?" There was in her low, whispered voice something more menacing than any shout.

"I hate me, too." Sarah lowered her head and somehow continued. "I couldn't tell Mother. I told both of you it was a research trip, but I never told her that I loved John. I never told her it was just us. I never told her that I thought he felt something for me, too." Sarah gave me a self-conscious look, but continued.

"We . . . he . . . he was the only man I ever . . ." Again she looked to me, her face a shy apology. "In Africa I found out he cared for me, too," she finished neatly. "So I was on top of the world. I only had one year of school left and I'd found someone to spend my life with, so I thought, and then I called home. And I, I don't know how to explain it. I thought I couldn't face it alone. I thought if I went and told him he would help me. I thought I could just run into his arms and he would fix it. I was a fool." Sarah's voice dropped flat.

Confusion was pushing the pain from my mother's eyes, and pushing the breath from my lungs.

Regina Sirois

"I got in the car, thinking of Mother the whole way to Boston. I can't tell you how relieved I felt when I pulled up outside that little brick townhouse. I ran up to the door, thinking everything was about to get better." Sarah pressed her fingers to the side of her head. I wasn't sure she could continue.

"What happened, Sarah?" I whispered.

She slid her eyes to me and gave me a somber, fleeting smile. "His wife answered the door." She shrugged like it didn't crush her to say it. Like it didn't hit me in the head like an anvil.

"His wife?" My mother broke her silence.

"Yes. He came to the door right behind her, and I don't know which one of us looked more mortified. I must have looked like a person who just took a bullet. I think I said something about having a message for John and garbled something about research notes and said I would tell him later. I slept in my car that night. Shredded the passenger seat with my nail file. I called his office from a pay phone the next day to curse him to oblivion, but when he answered the phone he was so relieved to hear from me. He'd called my roommates. He knew about Mother. He asked me where I was and he rushed to meet me, and he sounded like he cared so much and that was maybe worse."

"Maybe Jennifer should leave," my mother said, too riveted to stop the story, and too much a mother to let me hear the details.

"Maybe. I never told her any of this. But the worst is over.

He told me that he really had fallen in love with me. Too late in his life. I think I believed him. I think he believed himself. But what did it matter? It was too late. The timing . . . so I left. I just drove. I don't know how long. I don't know what roads. I just know that I stayed in a hotel in New Hampshire the next night. Claire, I thought it was one night. I swear I did! I don't remember calling my roommate. I think I had a nervous breakdown. Time didn't mean anything. All I knew was Mother was gone, John was gone, Dad was gone. I forgot . . . I forgot about you." A tear tracked down her ashamed face.

"That's why I deserved everything. I forgot all about you when you were the only family I had left. Who does that?" Sarah's question hung in the air, unanswerable. "I was in my car one day, going over a bridge and the road was empty and I stopped. I just stopped and got out and looked down at the river below me. I'd broken every rule Mother ever gave us. I'd made a mess of myself. And I was alone. I thought I was going to . . . I thought about just ending it. I imagined how sorry he would be."

Sarah looked up to my mother and I didn't understand how she could smile at a moment like that, but she tenderly raised her lips and stared into her sister's eyes. "That's when I remembered you, Claire. I remembered that you were the one who called me. You were at home. I remembered that I had a home and some- one was waiting for me there and it didn't fix anything, but it was enough to start with. I drove home to get you." Her smile faltered and fell, memories battering her face. "While I was killing you, you were saving me. I'm so sorry."

I tried to read my mother's reaction. She sat down heavily on the arm of the chair halfway through the story, her unfocused eyes lingering on the floor. Her subdued face showed little emotion other than a deep weariness.

I was the one who spoke, not wanting to leave Sarah alone with her painful story. "So you got here and then mother left? And then . . . how did you . . . ?" I didn't even try to fit words around the enormous question. I knew my limitations.

"It's funny what freedom you gain when you lose everything," she said wryly. "It's like David in the Bible when his child got sick. He ripped his clothes and shaved his head and wouldn't eat and prayed all day and begged and cried, and everyone was scared to tell him that the boy was dead. But when he found out he washed his face and ate breakfast. When there's still a chance to salvage something you torture yourself. When it's gone, you wash your face. You wake up. You start picking up the pieces, no matter how tiny and scattered they are. And then suddenly, the life that you had that was whole is suddenly a mosaic made of the old pieces. And something entirely new. I don't know how. I just know it happens."

She gazed at my mother's hanging head, a thoughtful frown on her mouth. Her mouth opened. And closed. And finally opened again. "Claire, I deserved everything you did. I think I know why you had to do it. I think you needed to be free of this place, and that meant being free of me. But please, please don't leave like that again. I want the fight to end now."

"It wasn't just you I was running from." I had to strain to catch my mother's words. "I was trying not to be the last one. They left me. You left me. If I ran first then I wouldn't always be the one that everyone left. I wouldn't be that girl that isn't worth staying for."

I looked at my mother, the woman my dad had worshipped my entire life, and wondered how she could think that about herself. She continued, "If I didn't hate this place—if I didn't hate this house and you and Harvey and God for putting me here—I never would have been able to leave. Hate was the only weapon I had to save myself. If I let go of hating this place, I might stay. And when I stay, everything goes wrong. Besides, it's too late. I don't know how to fix it."

"I know how!" a sharp voice barked from the kitchen. We all jumped and Sarah gasped "Little!" in shock. She hobbled in from the kitchen muttering a short apology for scaring us. "I came in the back when Claire came in. Didn't want her to go running off before I talked to her," Little said as she stumped into the room, looking unconcerned at our stunned faces. "I was jus' sittin' there for Hazel," she said, staring down Sarah's glare.

"For my mother?" Sarah asked.

"She'd a killed me if I let Claire go before you two talked. And I'm not quite ready to die yet, despite what my neighbors think." Little looked at us narrowly in remembrance of our gaffe that morning. "I've been sitting at the table, to see if you need me. And you said you don't know how to stop up a big, twenty-year hole and I know. The way you plug up a hole that big is with that one," she said, pointing her brittle finger at me. "You both love her and she's bigger to both of you than the past."

My mother's slowly mellowing face hardened again. "I'm here to get my daughter. That's it. I told you I hate it here."

"Since when?" Little bit back.

"Since terrible things started happening. My father, my mother. Do you want me to wait for something like that to happen to Jennifer? I've been here for one hour, and you nearly died and a girl went missing and the boys had a fight and now I'm finding out about affairs and suicide attempts and I'm done. I'm done! This place is cursed," my mother said loudly.

Like a curse out of Shakespeare. I felt the doom of it spreading like black, tattooed wings over the entire town.

Her tirade didn't ruffle Little. "Sit down," she ordered, though my mother was already sitting. "I'll tell you the only curse you got—the human one. You're human and people die. Don't tell me about people dying. You know and I know. And don't you tell me about people lovin' the wrong people," she said, turning from my mother to Sarah. "You know and I know. And don't you get that girl all full of ideas that it all ends foul. Most of the time it does, but she got a right to figure that out herself." She jerked her head to me, but her finger flew to my mother. "You came home and found me taking a pleasant nap. I can't help that you all acted like idiots. And then a boy got hisself the girl he wanted, and a bloody lip ain't such a bad thing. The girl's worth it. So stop sobbing about your curses. Ain't nothing bad happened here today."

And when she finished I wanted to laugh at myself. Laugh at all of us. Laugh at Nathan for agonizing over the future. Laugh at myself for agonizing over Nathan. I knew it wouldn't last, that the reality would come snaking back in, but for a moment I saw it, the futility of trying to mold love into an expected shape. The foolishness of whining when it didn't fit.

Little caught the strange change in my expression and flashed me a momentary, gruff smile. "When's your flight?" she asked my mother.

"It's, it's tomorrow morning. Early. Eight-fifteen."

I ground my teeth together. The clock was ticking. The sands had nearly finished funneling through the hourglass into a soft, misshapen mound.

"Then you got today, don't ya?" Little said encouragingly. "You stay. You finish saying what you need to say and you get up early and go."

"I can't stay here," my mother answered reflexively.

"You can do anything. You forget I was here. I helped ya.

And I never met a girl so tough." Little's eyes roamed to Sarah and rested there. "Except for your sister." I jerked my eyes back to Sarah, whose eyebrows raised in a question.

"Tough is tough, but gentle is tougher. I lost it when Newell married that woman. I got so tough I didn't know how to be gentle anymore. Sarah lost everything and she kep' something soft. She found a way to love and hate at the same time. Now that's a trick. She didn't grow a shell like us." My mother stood rigidly, ignoring the words, but Sarah's eyes glossed over. "I never told ya that, did I?" Little said, nodding her head to Sarah. "But I kep' meaning to."

In the awkward quiet that followed Little's words, I found my voice. "Can we please stay this last night?" I asked my mother, the hope in my question beating its wings against my throat. My mother shook her head, refused to look at me.

"If you came all this way, you should pay your respects to your mama. You ain't ever even seen her headstone." Little swung the tempting words in front of my mother whose head finally rose. The old woman walked up to her and rested her wrinkled hand on her wrist. "Go see her with Sarah. Tell your sister what your mama's wearing. Put this sad story to bed. It's time to end it now. For your mama. For your girl. For you."

The air in the room stilled, the atoms seemed to stop their frenzied spinning, waiting for the future to unfold. "I can't end it, Little. When I'm here, it just keeps going. Tragedy after tragedy. It will follow me. Something else will happen," my mother said like she needed someone to refute her. I opened my mouth to try, but Little beat me to it.

"Somethin' bad'll happen anywhere. To anyone. To everyone. Don't think you're so special. But I think this cup is empty. I think you drank the last bitter dregs, you and your sister. You've been running like the devil's at your tail because you probably figgered he was! But the ole Screw has to move on to other people. I ain't seen him muckin' around here much lately."

And then the silence came back, and no one would lift its smothering weight from the air. Just when I thought I would suffocate in the thick quiet, my mother said, "I'll go to the graveyard." My mother opened the unguarded door and we followed her to her rental car. For a tense moment I wondered if she would let Sarah sit next to her in the front, but Mother didn't react when Sarah opened the passenger door. Little grunted her way into the backseat beside me and we rode in thoughtful silence to the cemetery, the car swinging through the quiet Sunday streets.

The graveyard was well inland, half at the bottom of a wide hill, and half atop it. We came to the black iron gate that threw long, straight shadows across the green grass and white headstones. It was beautiful. Like a museum with rows of sculptures, the art of lives lined up for all to see. Some tall, brave spires rose from the ground, pointing eternally to the desired destination of the people below them. Others were too old to read. My mother stopped at a grave that was deep in the shadows at the base of the towering hill. I peered closer, seeing my grandmother's name, Hazel Dorothy Dyer. Beside her rested another stone inscribed Henry Samuel Dyer. I tried to think of my grandparents, but I couldn't picture them in my mind. All I could see were their two daughters standing together for the first time in twenty years. My mother whispered, "Mama," so softly I barely caught the word. I took a small step forward, leaving my mother and Sarah behind me. Alone. Together.

"She's wearing her purple blouse," my mother said quietly. Sarah drew in a breath and her eyes filled with grateful tears, but my mother wasn't finished. "She wore it to your recital and she liked it. It was the last thing dad ever bought her, as far as I know." Her words continued, small and weak, but unyielding. They were making their escape, running for daylight before she could seize them again. "But it's a silk blouse. And it gets so cold when the snow comes and I kept worrying that she would be cold." Her voice cracked. The little girl I had seen huddled at the back of her visage when she yelled at Sarah came creeping back into view. "I buried her with her wedding ring quilt. The one she made for me. And then when I married Tom I didn't have it and I thought about it all day—that quilt. Because she made it for me, and it seemed like I should have one of her blankets. But I didn't want her to be cold." Her tears fell thick, one behind the other, impatient for their liberation.

At that moment I knew nothing my mother could say or do

would deter Sarah. She threw her arms around her baby sister, and though my mother didn't hug her back, she didn't fight the embrace. Just crumbled beneath it. They both sunk to the ground, weeping, cradled on the warm grass of their mother's grave.

"You can have a blanket. She's not cold. You can have it," Sarah repeated over and over, stroking my mother's head. It is no use pretending I wasn't crying with them. I didn't want to interrupt one second of their reunion, so I cupped my hands over my mouth and cried with myself.

When I looked up at Little, the sole human standing in that field of death with me, she met me with a stare that had seen far more than I, and bowed her head in approval.

CHAPTER 39

IT DIDN'T TAKE long for my mother to exhaust her supply of tears. When Sarah finally released her, my mother put her forehead to the spiky grass, like a child hiding in her mother's lap. She stayed there, motionless, except for a gentle caressing of her fingers against the grass until she finally emerged, face mottled, eyes red, hair disheveled.

Leaving the graveyard and driving through the town felt strange. There seemed both too much and too little left to say. No one really tried. Little asked to be dropped off at her house. "I suppose you two can hash the rest out yuhselves, and I never finished my nap."

When we pulled up to Pilgrim's Point, she gently tugged a chunk of my hair. "You owe me a story. When you get back." I smiled into her wizened face, and threw a troubled glance to the front seats, wondering if the peace would last without her mediation. She just patted my cheek and said, "They'll be fine. Eventually. Our wings may be small, but then again, so are we." And with that final word on the subject she grumbled as she pulled herself out of the car and slammed the door, like she blamed the automobile for her stiff joints.

Sarah took us back to Shelter Cove, where Nathan was standing anxiously on the porch when we pulled up. "Nathan!" I said with mingled surprise and delight as I opened my door.

"You're still here," is all he said, his hands deep in his pockets, his shoulders falling in something that looked like relief. "I saw the car gone and I thought maybe you'd left. I thought Sarah might need . . ." He watched the two sisters emerge from the car. In the sunlight I saw the similarities, the small noses, the arching eyebrows, the finely shaped lips. Both certainly looked a little the worse for wear with their flushed faces and pink-rimmed eyes, and Sarah's khaki pants sported a dark grass stain on one knee.

"We're leaving early in the morning. Eight o' clock flight. Little convinced her to stay." I tried not to mind that he'd only come back because he was worried about Sarah. I tried to focus on the fact that he was here. Two feet away. A gift tomorrow and the days after wouldn't bring me. "That means we can stay for lines."

Sarah and Mother drew up behind us. "I don't know," Sarah said. "Maybe we should postpone. I need the time with Claire."

Both of them looked eternally tired—shoulders heavy and

faces drawn—like they would never be fully restored again. But I couldn't mistake this surrender from my mother for reconciliation. She held herself away from Sarah, avoiding her touch, avoiding eye contact. She might be signing the treaties, but wars leave scars. I could see years of awkward, halting attempts slowly filling in the craters left by absence and anger. Eventually, the new growth of the future would cover the decimated past and blooms of new memories would burst open like the poppies at Flanders field. Today, the barren landscape of the past was still muddy, brutal, strewn with victims. But quiet. Quiet. Peaceful.

"She can do them with us," I insisted. "I need them tonight."

"What are you talking about?" Mother asked.

"A non-game we play." My chin dimple caved in as I smiled secretly at Sarah. She looked at me in wonder like she wasn't used to it, like she hadn't been doing it all day, every day, for almost a month.

"Jennifer, I think you and Nathan should do them tonight. I think I need to talk to my sister." Sarah's eyes rushed up to my mother's worn face and she amended her words. "Or listen. Both." Nathan watched them, unaware of what the last hour had brought.

"Is everyone all right?" he asked, his concerned glance roaming among the three of us. Sarah put a hand on his shoulder and told him that we were all fine. "Will you meet me in the cove at seven?" he asked me, his eyes neither anxious nor wary. Only determined. I reminded him that he needed to put the girls to bed first and he assured me that Judith could handle it for a night.

When he left, Mother asked about him, and that kept the conversation going for almost an hour. There was a mountain of talk to climb. I don't know if I was hungrier to speak or listen, but we kept tripping over each other, rushing ahead, jumping back, interrupting, being interrupted. For the next three hours we did nothing but talk. Even when we all unanimously agreed that we were in an advanced state of starvation, we took the conversation to the kitchen, talking over the sandwiches, talking around the bites in our mouths. Not a merry discussion. Not three girlfriends joking. It was something deeper than that, word after word, like shovelful after shovelful, filling trenches so we couldn't jump back in. We left ourselves nowhere to hide, nowhere to retreat.

Mother talked about my dad; Sarah talked about the town. I shared my Smithport stories, watching my mother's face as I spoke about the ferry, the boats, the Jacks, Darcy. Nathan I kept to myself. That story was mine. Was Little's. I owed it to her first. But also, that story wasn't a story yet. It was a paragraph a writer studies and stews over and waits to see if a story comes. I still didn't know. I stowed it away carefully, wondering what our last meeting on the beach would bring.

When the clock made its journey all the way to seven, I left them still talking on the front porch, and made my way to the beach for the last time. The sun was low, but bright, and the water reflected its yellow glow, throwing everything into the still, waiting, golden light of late afternoon. It reminded me of the wheat field. I was sorry that I missed them cutting it. I wished it would still be waving at me when I got home. Nathan wasn't there yet, so I sat close to the water and watched it slide across the sand and retreat. I understood Claude's need to talk with Will all night. I felt the brevity of the evening. Felt too close to my last good-bye. The one that hurt the most, because it felt the most final. Sarah would be my aunt forever, always the same love, always the same relationship. But Nathan—Nathan could change. I might be nothing to him in months, maybe in days. I closed my eyes and tried to push the thought away.

He came quietly. He didn't wear shoes. I'd tried that before but the sand was too sharp even for my tough feet. He lowered himself much closer than usual, his shoulder grazing mine. It reminded me of the jolting ride in the car that morning.

"Is everything better with Claude?" I asked.

"It's . . . okay. She's grounded, like you heard. Can't see Will for a couple weeks. I'm sorry I got that mad in front of you."

I shrugged. "I don't think you could help it. You were scared for her." The tattered strings that hung from the frayed hems of his jeans draped onto the sand. I looked at his feet next to mine, trying to forget how far apart we would be tomorrow.

"Is Sarah all right? And your mom? I can't believe you got her to come."

I explained that my dad probably had more to do with it than I did. I doubted that their proximity to an international airport had been a mere coincidence. I then gave him a quick sketch of the fight at Shelter Cove. He let out a ringing, light laugh in the middle and exclaimed, "She was hiding in the kitchen the entire time?"

"Would you expect any less from Little? I think she was getting back at us for this morning." I looked at him, taking advantage of the break in the story. "Nathan, did you know about John? Being married?"

"Yeah, I knew," he breathed out. "Only the Jacks could come up with a name he deserved. Only a real sailor can say something like that."

"But Sarah never met anyone else?" It was the detail that didn't make sense to me. Her intelligence, her beauty, her talents, her kindness—surely she deserved a legitimate love.

Nathan sighed. "She tried. A few times. She loved him. She couldn't let go. Or hold on. He got divorced a few years later and came to find her."

"What?" I cried in shock. "But then, why didn't . . ."

"She didn't want to be a home wrecker. Didn't want to win love at someone else's expense. She blames herself for wrecking her own family and she didn't want to ruin anyone else's. John told her he had a daughter." He stopped to let me process that. "Sarah told him to go home, make up with his wife, and take care of his girl. She saw no other option."

I dropped my head in disgust. "Sarah didn't wreck anything. She didn't. She shouldn't have taken the blame."

"They say the heart has its own reasons."

"You would know what they say."

"Speaking of quotes, what did you bring?" He looked down at my pockets, expecting me to pull something out.

I held out my empty hands to show him I had no notes, no papers, no book. "I only remember a few words. I don't even know if I'll get them right. You read it my first week here. And I don't know who said it. It was something like, 'Is it changed, or am I changed?' "

"That's Longfellow. And you said it perfectly." His eyes stroked my face, a touch more personal than any he'd given me with his hands.

"Which one is it, Nathan? Did the entire universe change since I got here or is it just me?"

"Explain," he said softly.

"I don't think I can. It's all upside down. The things that mattered before, don't. I have a family that didn't exist two months ago. I have all these . . . " I blushed and looked away from him. "I feel like the same person, but everything around me and inside of me is different. I can't figure out if life changed or I did."

"It's not just you. Things are changing," he said, looping his arms around his bent legs and looking above the water to the space between Earth and sky. I watched his fingers moving restlessly against each other and I felt a wave of cold fear wash over me. He was too preoccupied. Too nervous.

"You're going, aren't you?" I asked.

His shoulders rose in surprise like the same icy wave had reached him. "I'm going," he admitted. "I can't afford Harvard, but Northeastern gave me a full ride with living expenses. They don't even do that. One of the board members called me personally and offered to fund me. I'll finish my bachelor's this year."

"That's amazing. They must think you're really special." Why did my stomach drop at those words?

"You saw Judith today. She did . . . she did a good job. I'll be four hours away, but I can come home pretty often, make sure they're doing all right."

"They're lucky to have you," I told him. "When I told you to leave them alone, I didn't mean . . ."

"You were just saying whatever came to your mind. I know. And you were right."

I smiled, but it held more sadness than joy. "I don't say everything," I insisted.

"I know," is all he answered.

"Nathan? What are you going to major in? How did you decide?"

He reached into his back pocket and pulled out a piece of

paper. "I'm going to get my Masters in special education. First. Who knows what comes after that. I figure I can give a good twenty years to at least three different things, don't you think?"

"Sixty years, and you're nearly eighteen now. So yeah, seventy-eight. You'll be a spring chicken, like Little. She's still got nineteen years left."

"Nineteen?" he asked, baffled.

"I'll tell you next time." And then my sentence dropped like a fishing line sliced, the captive creature just a ripple in the water. There was no next time. Only the smoke trail from a plane across the sky. And if he left for school, he might not be here when I returned. I looked at the cove and shuddered at the thought of sitting here without him. Lines without him. Life without him.

He unfolded his piece of paper. "This is a first," he said. "I've never quoted myself before."

"Yourself?"

"I wrote this. For you." He swallowed and looked at it, before handing it to me.

"Are you going to read it?" I asked, taking it from him. He shook his head and signaled me to read it on my own. With unsteady fingers that made the edges of the crisp paper tremble, I settled it into my lap and read to myself.

On summer days I've walked amidst
A fire on the hill,

Like India's faithful dirges sung
Atop the burning coal—

I've lain among the golden flames
That flicked and swayed above
And while the light enclosed my face,
I barely even moved—

It danced before my hazy eyes,
Entwined with fogs of Calm
A blaze that hid the world away—
While I slept slow and warm.

I stared at the words long after I finished; at his handwriting on the paper, messy and slanted, and beautiful.

"I know it's stupid," he finally said, but I shushed him before he got any further.

"Don't. It's perfect. It's my wheat field, right?"

He nodded and cleared his throat. "I'm going to imagine you there. When I think of you." It didn't much matter what he said next. He would think of me.

"I'll be there," I said. "But I don't know where to picture you. I guess I'll just imagine big brick buildings, ivy, trees. That probably covers most colleges, right?"

He grinned and I looked up at his scar, traced it down to his lips as he spoke. "Imagine me here. At home. I'll be back a lot."

My breaths quickened to keep pace with my heart. "I want to come back for the holidays," I said softly, trying to conceal the feelings rushing up inside me.

"I'll be here," he said with a smile. "But there'll be snow by then. You might realize that you're a tourist after all. Not sure a farm girl can handle Maine in the winter."

"I'm tougher than you think." I tried to say it like a joke, but the lead weight of good-bye wouldn't release my words. They sank to the ground.

"No coward soul is mine," he muttered.

"Tomorrow you'll be at lines with Sarah," I said, unable to keep the complaint in my mouth any longer. "I'll be gone." I knew he couldn't change it, so I can't say why I wanted him to argue with me.

"I know." He gently reached for my hand and turned it palm side up. His rough finger stroked the white skin, slowly, thoughtfully.

"Nathan?" He met my eyes, and I could see the ocean waves in his dark blue orbs. "Did you know that Cleo and I are graduating early? Like Claude. Just one more year and I'll be away at school . . ."

"Decided to mention that, did you?" he said with a grim smirk. He squeezed his hand around mine. "Go Huskers?" he asked quietly.

"Maybe. I'm starting to like the East Coast. If you ignore the people, of course."

"Of course." He took a steadying breath. "So tomorrow morning, huh? This is it?"

No. No. This isn't it. This can't be it. Why couldn't he ever hear what my mind was shouting? "I suppose so." I tilted my head back at the sky and inhaled. Long, quiet minutes passed as we watched the sky grow dim, his hand still clutching mine.

I finally asked him, "Are you ready to go home? Are we through?"

His eyebrows tilted down like the question perplexed him. "No," he answered, as he watched a gull cut a slim, white line over our heads, "we're not through. But I'll walk you home." He rose first and gave me his hand, pulling me up in his firm grip until I was so close that our bodies almost touched. He looked down, his face bending over mine, and what thoughts raced through his mind, I'll never know. I don't remember thoughts. Just sensations. Something like drowning. In the best possible way.

I felt the kiss in his eyes, so instinctual and pervasive that the ghost of it tingled on my lips, but Nathan refused to move any closer. That stubborn glint burned in his eyes.

He might have had the strength to resist, but I did not. I raised my face, watching his eyes tighten. With uncommon understanding, Nathan gently turned to the water and looked at her while he spoke to me. "I'd be a hypocrite, after what I said to Will."

Something hot ran down my shoulders into my ribs. Disappointment flavored with relief. It wasn't that he didn't see me, he'd just convinced himself he shouldn't. Same outcome, but the subtle difference meant everything. "If you let him hit you, you'd be even." I'm not sure I knew I'd said it out loud or that it was funny until his laugh, buoyant and free, broke loudly over my head.

"Nice logic, Jennifer." He sighed the word "tempting" in a way that made it impossible to tell if he was tempted by the punch or the kiss. Before I could respond, he grabbed my hand in a decidedly friendly way and tugged me forward. I nearly dug my heels into the sand trying to retrieve the stunning tension of hope, but he had made up his mind. I couldn't beg. When he walked, I obeyed, allowing him to lead my weak, reluctant feet over the sand and dirt and grass to the back door. I prayed he would stop, break his rules, see me how Newell never let himself see Little, but he opened the door and held it with his outstretched arm, waiting as I passed under. My hair grazed his hand as he closed the door behind me. The faint touch shivered on the back of my neck and I stopped to catch my breath. He stopped too, still and silent. We paused there, not more than a handful of seconds, unable to do anything more but look at the floor together, before he walked into the living room.

Mother and Sarah looked up from a photo album as we entered. The quilt from my bed was wrapped around my mother's shoulders. It looked very right, piled around her neck, protecting her. At great sacrifice I left Nathan's side and sat beside her. She pulled me under one arm, the blanket engulfing me and I smelled her familiar scent mingled with the clean, powdery smell that clung to everything in Sarah's house.

"Are you bringing this home?" I asked, fingering the tiny, familiar squares. I loved the idea of her keeping it, but it didn't seem right to take it from its home where Hazel had made it.

"I think so," Mother answered, rubbing my arm.

Nathan stopped in the doorway, leaning against the thick wooden frame. He looked tenderly at Sarah as she sat across from her sister. The same way I looked at Hester on the rock. "Good night, Sarah," Nathan said with a knowing smile that said, *I know it is a good night for you.* He looked to my mother and me. "It was nice to meet you, Claire. I hope you come back soon. We'll miss you, Jennifer." I tried to understand the strange set of his face, tried to hear his mind over the sound of his words. "I'm glad you came. I'll see you again." I felt my mother's stare, Sarah's eyes fastened to my pink cheeks, but I ignored both of them, not able to acknowledge anyone but him.

"I'll miss you, too," I said, my throat swelling around the wounding words. "I hope you're right."

He gave me a small wave and turned. When the door clicked closed behind him, something splintered and fell inside my chest. I took a quick breath, surprised by the physical pang. I avoided Sarah's concerned gaze—avoided her pity.

My mother turned the page of the album. "He seems like a

nice boy," she murmured. I couldn't even find the power to nod. An odd, concurring "hm" came out of my throat. She pointed out a photo of her mother, saying, "That was her first year here, before she met my dad." I looked at the blurry face and blonde hair of the girl who fell in love with a Smithport fisher. She was short, like Claude, slight like Sarah, defiant like my mother. I wondered what trait we shared, other than the thick, light hair. Maybe just our love for the two women looking at her photo.

I tried to concentrate on that accomplishment—the fact that they sat in the same room—and forced myself to ignore the instincts that called me back outside, urged me to run across the cove and talk to him. The compulsion to speak to Nathan throbbed inside of me, but I stayed and looked at the pictures, my head on my mother's shoulder until I grew too heavy with the sadness to sit upright. I took myself upstairs and slid into bed, opening the window wide to catch the sighs of the ocean. Tonight she sounded like my heart felt. One breath after another. And nothing else.

When the last of the light seeped out of the dark sky, I pulled myself back up, crept downstairs and found Sarah alone in the living room. She looked up when the stairs creaked. "Where's my mom?" I asked, looking toward the kitchen.

"She went for a walk down to the water. We thought you went to bed," Sarah said, closing her eyes.

"I tried. Are you all right?" I asked.

One eye popped open and scanned me critically. "You told

her you wouldn't come home unless she came to get you?"

"I didn't really mean it," I sighed.

"That was playing with fire, Jennifer."

"I know. But it worked, didn't it? Aren't you glad?"

A tired smile lit her face, and Charlie whined happily, as if he felt her pleasure. "Indescribably."

"Me, too," I said. "You two look good together." My feet padded against the thick wooden planks of the floor and I walked behind the couch, gently touching her head. "I think I'll go join her."

"Jennifer." Sarah's voice caught me at the doorway to the kitchen. "I'd bet good money that he's here in the morning."

I only met her eyes for a moment. I was too fragile to avoid the way the hope pulled into my chest like a deep breath. It was just enough to dull the shards of disappointment.

"Thanks, Sarah."

I slipped outside into the still night. The wind was the only thing stirring as I crossed the shadowed yard. Unlike the night with Nathan when the moon was a bright circle, tonight it hung lopsided in the sky, looking punch-drunk and weary—the morning after.

My mother stood far from the water, taking in the black shapes of the land and trees against the sky. "Mama?"

She turned slowly to me and then back to the water. "You were so quiet I thought you were asleep already," she said.

"Hardly. I was just thinking. About leaving. It's going to be hard for me. I fell in love . . . with this place." There was a certain power in saying it so plain—in almost admitting out loud to another human being that I loved him.

"I know," she said bracingly. "But it will still be here. We can come back."

"Is that what you told yourself all these years? That it would still be here when you were ready to come back?"

She gave a laugh and shook her head. "No. I told myself it fell into the ocean. Then I didn't even have to think about it. It didn't exist. I think I believed my own lie."

I sat down at her feet, feeling the cold sand through my clothes. "I'm glad you came."

Her doubtful eyes pressed me. "Even if it means leaving?"

"I was coming anyway," I admitted. "Tuesday."

Before she could vocalize the stunned question on her face, I told her that I never really decided if Little was right. "I kept worrying it was wrong, to blackmail you that way."

"No, this time the crazy woman was right. I'm glad you did it." She sank to the ground next to me, pulling the hair from her eyes. "It was brave." The next time she spoke it was with a different voice, something more personal. "I feel like I'm seventeen again tonight," she said, and I knew she wasn't telling me as a daughter. She was telling me as a woman. "I feel like the night after her funeral when I sat out here and tried to understand what it all meant. I tried to decide what to do. I thought Sarah would

know . . . I don't think I realized that she was just a kid, too."
Her voice trailed until it was just a sigh mingled with the breeze.
"I think that is a special gift—knowing how to blame the right
people. I wonder what my life would have been if I stayed when
Sarah came home."

"Do you regret it?" Only after I asked did I realize I feared
either answer.

"You? Your dad? Never," she proclaimed. "I found love. I got
a girl who looks like a golden wheat field. What regret is there
in that?" And when she said the word "golden," I remembered
Nathan's line: *Nothing gold can stay.* It sounds conceited to say, but I
understood for the first time that he meant me. I was the gold. He
was warning me. He was warning himself. I don't know what happened to my face when I realized, but I never heard my mother's
next words. She caught my expression and stopped speaking altogether. For a moment she studied me and when I met her eyes she
said very gently, "And there was Harvey. It's hard to leave the first
boy you love when you're seventeen." My eyes felt hot as the tears
collected. "But you know what Emerson says, right? 'When half-
gods go, the gods arrive.' I always loved that one."

That's when the tears dropped and she pulled me under her
arm. I didn't agree with her—the implication that there was something or someone better than Nathan. But she gave me a line. In
the quiet moonlight, on her beach, she played the "non-game." I
didn't need to confess the turmoil inside. She didn't need to say she

knew. It settled around us as surely as if we spoke the words aloud. I smelled her neck as I leaned into her, thinking of how she didn't have a mother when the heartache hit her.

"Will you promise me something?" I asked.

She nodded her head and squeezed my arm. A light from a single boat flashed far out at sea and we watched the tiny dot make its way over the vast waters.

"Please don't tell Cleo. She'll never forgive me."

My mother chuckled and shook me lovingly. "She'll figure it out eventually."

"That's what I'm afraid of." I pulled up my head to see her. Her face looked like the ash-covered ground after a forest fire. Decimated. Destroyed. Peaceful. Just about to burst into new life. She deserved a new secret to plant. A good one.

"Did you know that Little has a tattoo?"

"Really? I guess I'm not shocked. What is it? Or dare I ask, *where* is it?"

"Two black wings right in the middle of her back. To get her up to heaven. Because the only man she ever loved is there. She is going to tell him off and then kiss him like no one's ever been kissed."

Mother leaned her head up to the sky and laughed. "That would be something to see."

I thought of those small wings, growing limp and saggy on

Little's wrinkled back as the decades passed. "Do you mind if I go say one last good-bye?"

There was a grimace in her eyes as her smile retreated. "I guess that's okay. But it's late. Don't stay long."

I watched her puzzled expression as I stood and turned left, away from Boulder Bend and Nathan. "I'll be home as soon as I'm done." If Sarah was right—*let Sarah be right!*—I'd see him in the morning. Morning was a deep, warm longing in my stomach.

The moon's confused gaze followed me to Pilgrim's Point, laying a broken path of light across the uneven ground. Before I made it to the back door, I called out without restraint, like Darcy. "Little!" The night shook with the sudden sound, and high overhead a bird burst from a tree in a wild flap of feathers. The sound felt good in my throat, filled it with words instead of waiting tears. "Little!" I shouted again and rapped her back door sharp enough to wake her, living or dead. The curtain over the window shook as she pulled the door open and stood in front of me.

She didn't look surprised to see me. She didn't ask. Didn't admonish. Didn't joke. She waited, her face set in a sober frown. Before I could speak one word, the brewing storm shattered inside of me and water, saltier than the sea, washed down my face. She pursed her lips in sympathy, the wrinkles falling into each other across her puckered face, but she didn't interrupt the loss washing over me. Didn't try to save me from it. "I came because . . ."

The wind gave a mighty push across my body and wrapped me in the fresh spray of the ocean. Like a quilt. Like words curling around me.

I looked at her eyes, swirling with the same stormy waves, the same hidden currents, as the fathomless ocean. And in that moment I knew that Newell had seen. Whatever excuses he invented or reasons he gave himself, he must have noticed the blue flames lapping through the icy whites of her eyes.

"I have a story," I whispered.

QUOTATION SOURCES

Bronte, Emily. "Last Lines." *American Poetry, the Nineteenth Century Volume One, Freneau to Whitman*. New York: The Library of America, 1993.

Dickinson, Emily. "An Awful Tempest Mashed the Air." *The Complete Poems*. Boston: Back Bay Books, 1960.

Emerson, Ralph Waldo. "Give All to Love." *Collected Poems and Translations*. New York: The Library of America, 1994.

Frost, Robert. "Nothing Gold Can Stay." *Collected Poems, Prose, and Plays*. New York: The Library of America, 1995

Hesse, Hermann. "Lying in Grass." *Poems*, translated by James Wright. New York: Farrar, Straus and Giroux, 1970.

Longfellow, Henry Wadsworth. "Changed." *Poems of Places: An Anthology in 31 Volumes.* Boston: James R. Osgood and Company, 1876–79.

Millay, Edna St. Vincent. "Eight Sonnets." *American Poetry: A Miscellany.* New York: Harcourt, Brace and Co., 1922.

Moore, Thomas. "Oh think not my spirits are always as light." *The Poetical Works of Thomas Moore, including Melodies, Ballads, etc.* Philadelphia: J. Crissy, 1835.

Shelley, Percy. "Ozymandias." *The Norton Anthology of Poetry, 5th Edition.* New York: Norton and Company, 2005.

Tagore, Rabindranath. "Vocation." *The Crescent Moon.* London and New York: MacMillan and Company, 1913.

Tennyson, Alfred. "Break, Break, Break." *The Norton Anthology of Poetry, 5th Edition.* New York: Norton and Company, 2005.

Tennyson, Alfred. "The Eagle: A Fragment." *The Norton Anthology of Poetry, 5th Edition.* New York: Norton and Company, 2005.

Thurber, James. *Further Fables for Our Time.* New York: Simon and Schuster, 1956.

Acknowledgments

It is my husband who deserves the lion's share of my gratitude. He is the beginning, middle, and end of my great love story. Thank you for proving to me that young love never grows old.

It is my daughters who teach me, mend me, inspire me, love me, and stretch me. Thank you for keeping our home crowded with muses and full of love.

It is my sister who first believed. Thank you for giving me a reason to write on.

It is my parents who never spoke to me like a child and expected great and creative things from me. Thank you for your examples of intelligence and faith.

It is my agent, Wendy Sherman, my writers' group, and test

readers who helped me refine and fight for my voice. Thank you for your encouragement.

It is Penguin/Viking, Amazon, Create Space, and *Publishers Weekly* who saved me from drowning in the slush piles by giving me the honor of being the winner of the 2012 Amazon Breakthrough Novel Award. Thank you for a dream come true.

It is my editor, Joanna Cardenas, who polished my story until I could see my heart in it. Thank you for your friendship, advocacy, passion, and amazing talent. My work is safe in your capable hands.

It is every reader who took this journey with Jennifer who kept me working late into the night, day after day. I write, always, for each of you. Thank you.